CHEESECAKE
AND
TEARDROPS

CHEESECAKE AND TEARDROPS

FAYE THOMPSON

www.urbanbooks.net

Urban Books, LLC
1199 Straight Path
West Babylon, NY 11704

ISBN-13: 978-1-60162-174-0
ISBN-10: 1-60162-174-4

First Printing August 2009
Printed in the United States of America

10 9 8 7 6 5 4 3 2 1

This is a work of fiction. Any references or similarities to actual events, real people, living, or dead, or to real locales are intended to give the novel a sense of reality. Any similarity in other names, characters, places, and incidents is entirely coincidental.

Distributed by Kensington Publishing Corp.
Submit Wholesale Orders to:
Kensington Publishing Corp.
C/O Penguin Group (USA) Inc.
Attention: Order Processing
405 Murray Hill Parkway
East Rutherford, NJ 07073-2316
Phone: 1-800-526-0275
Fax: 1-800-227-9604

Lorraine, Barbara, Adrienne, and Alvina,
with friends like you who needs chocolate?
And, Boobie, with Evie, Velma, and Dennis,
who needs dessert?

www.fayethompson.com

Behind every successful woman is herself.
—Unknown

Joy Cometh in the Mourning

I close my eyes and your face appears
Forever etched in my heart
Along with your laughter
Blended with my own
Making beautiful music.
Was it a lifetime ago or am I
Reliving a lifetime of yesterdays
With each breath I take?
Somewhere, our souls are dancing
The dance of eternity.
Of endless sunrises and sunsets.
And yet, we are both still
Embracing time as our own.
But we both realize we can't have forever.
This is not our time.
So we replay our dance in our hearts.
Along with our memories and teardrops.
And as we release, I discover a joy
A new joy
A different joy.
I discover you.

1

Charisma

Charisma Dearborn had just enough time to shower, apply makeup, and finger-comb her short, glossy locks before grabbing the keys to her silver Honda off the kitchen counter and heading to work. She was already ten minutes behind schedule. She despised being late today of all days when her new boss started. Damn, the Sunrise Highway was bumper-to-bumper. She'd make better time on the service road. The hooptie in front of her made an abrupt stop, forcing her to slam on her brakes. Where'd you get your license, lady, Target? she almost asked as she drove past the Green Acres Mall.

Charisma knew she shouldn't have let Dex stay over last night, but she had a weakness for well-groomed corporate types with strong backs, and Dex Spencer had all three. So she gave him a good workout last night and again early this morning. He left shortly thereafter, promising to call her later that night. She and Dex had a great relationship. Dex wanted more. She wasn't ready for a commitment, but she did have her needs. . . . Charisma smiled at the recollection, but she was paying for it this morning.

Okay, she could just about make it if she could find a parking space close to the building. Parking was always at a premium. What else was new? She circled a couple of times before spotting a Nissan a few feet ahead pulling out. She went for it, but so did a black Camry. His loss. As she stepped out into the early October air and gathered her jacket and briefcase, she could see Mr. Camry shake his head and grin before driving off. She had six minutes to spare. Thank God for small miracles.

Charisma took the elevator up to the eighth floor. She could tell that the new boss hadn't yet arrived. She was safe, proceeding to get her coffee and heading for her office. She needed to complete a marketing report by noon, and the morning staff meeting would only delay progress.

She'd been working on the report for about twenty minutes when Amanda Smith, the assistant manager, stuck her head in the doorway of Charisma's office. "Nate Arquette's here. The staff meeting will start in ten minutes in the conference room," she told her.

"Thanks, Amanda. I'll be right there." Charisma logged off her computer and stopped at Lauren's desk. The two fell into step as they headed to the conference room.

"I hear he's a real ballbuster," Lauren admitted. She had earned the reputation of being the office gossip, but she was also a sweetheart.

"Lucky for us we don't have balls," Charisma answered. In her eleven years as a marketing analyst with Freeman LTD, she had seen executives come and go. Most of them only lasted a year or two. This one probably wouldn't be any different. The turnover was incredible. Charisma had been turned down for every promotion she applied for in the past three years, and to whites at that. It was like they belonged to a secret club. No matter how hard she worked, her efforts went unrecognized. When Chase Martini, the office slut, was promoted over her this last go-round, she realized that the old *saying it's not what you do but who you do* was more than just that.

They were all seated and waiting for Nate's arrival. Finally, Amanda walked in with a tall, honey-brown man in a navy double-breasted suit. When he got to the center of the room, Charisma realized who he was. Shit, it's Mr. Camry! So much for making a good first impression. Amanda introduced Nate Arquette to the staff of forty.

"Thank you, Amanda. First, let me take this opportunity to tell you how pleased I am to be here and how excited I am to be working with you all at Freeman. Just to give you some background, I started out at Sandrell Incorporated fresh out of USC in an entry-level position and worked my way up the ranks. So, I believe in hard work and dedication. I stayed with Sandrell for eight years before becoming an assistant manager at Elliott Brothers. I worked at EB for the past seven years, and I hope no one is doing the math." Nate paused, smiling.

They all laughed politely.

"Now, I would like to meet with the department managers this afternoon at three. And I certainly do want to apologize for being late this morning. I didn't realize parking was at such a premium," he admitted.

"Sorry, Nate, we'll get your permit registered right away. Welcome aboard," Amanda replied.

"Thanks. That's all for now," he said, dismissing them.

As they broke up, Chase Martini, the resident rich bitch, whispered to Charisma, "That's just the way I like 'em—tall, dark, and handsome. And not a wedding band in sight!"

Just what every office needs, Charisma thought, a slut with morals. Luckily for Chase, she kept it moving. She had beat Charisma out of the last two promotions simply because she spread easier than butter and threatened to file a sexual harassment lawsuit against the former boss. Ultimately, he couldn't stand the heat and fled. So, Charisma didn't have much to say to Chase.

Charisma returned to her office totally prepared to focus on the report, but the phone wouldn't let her. First her mother called.

"Charisma, your brother wants you to come by for dinner Friday evening so we can all meet his latest," Jena Dearborn said.

"Knowing Eric, she's his latest and his greatest."

"Well, at least he's moving in the right direction. If you're not careful, your little brother will settle down and make me a grandbaby before you do," she warned.

"I'm in no hurry, Mother."

"I know. That's the problem. You're too busy being independent. Don't you know men like to feel needed? You're probably scaring them all away."

"Mother, I don't have time for this now. I have tons of work in front of me. I'll see you and Daddy Friday night."

No sooner had Charisma replaced the receiver when she received another call. This time it was an inside call.

"Charisma Dearborn," she said.

"Miss Dearborn, this is Nate Arquette."

Silence.

"I understand you're working on the biweekly report. How's it coming along?"

"We've had several new clients last month. I'm still gathering data, but I should have the figures on your desk by noon."

"Fine. I'll let you get back to work, and I'll expect that report shortly."

"Yes," she said simply before hanging up. Determined to have the assignment completed ahead of schedule, Charisma absorbed herself completely in the task at hand. In fact, she allowed her voice mail to answer all other calls rather than being further distracted. As a result, by eleven-thirty she had the report proofed and printed. No sense getting off to a bad start with the new boss. She dropped the report off in his office, noticing a single framed photo of him playing tennis with what must have been his son. They were both wearing tennis whites and from his son's smile, he must have won. The photo was right next to his *Go Get 'Em!* coffee mug.

Just as she was about to leave, Nate walked in.

"Is that the report?" He was easily six feet one.

"Yes, hot off the presses."

"And early at that," he added.

"Timing is everything."

"Yes, especially when you're driving, what, a silver Honda, Miss Dearborn?"

Charisma rubbed the hair on the back of her neck and laughed. Nate laughed too.

"You know, it just happened so fast . . ." she admitted.

"Hey, I admire a woman who goes after what she wants. If this report is as impressive as your parking skills, this company is in for a smooth ride."

"Let's hope so."

Later that evening after a long, hot bubble bath Charisma felt revived. Tempted to phone Dex for another steamy session, she opted instead to call her best friend, Tangie. That way she was certain to get her much-needed seven and a half hours of sleep. Few things were more vital to her well-being than her beauty sleep, plenty of water, and consistent exercise. People didn't realize their impact, but she knew the role they played in keeping her balanced and focused. Not to mention giving her caramel skin a glow most women envied but refused to take the energy and effort to maintain. Sure, the right cosmetics did wonders for *all* women—natural beauties and plain Janes alike, but some things couldn't be bought at the makeup counter. The superficial pampering of manicures, pedicures, and weekly salon visits weren't enough. Some things had to be done the old-fashioned way, and Charisma was her own best investment.

She ended up leaving a message on Tangie's machine and whipping up dinner. Chicken breast and a salad were a breeze to prepare, but the best part was the room left for red velvet cake. In fact, she was curled up on her sofa with dessert, listening to the stereo, when Tangie returned her call.

"Are we still on for dinner Saturday night?" Charisma asked.

"Yeah, Heather called me today at work. She said she'll meet us at eight. Her car's back in the shop, but she's picking it up Saturday afternoon." The three friends had a girls' night out at least twice a month. They looked forward to playing catch-up and exhaling. They'd been friends forever.

"Great. Tangie, remind me to bring your Jill Scott CD."

"Okay. I'll talk to you later."

Charisma prepared to leave work Friday evening and head over to her parents' for dinner. Her new boss had just popped his head in her doorway as she was about to leave.

"Charisma, I have a proposition for you," he said.

"And what might that be?'

"You seem like a woman who knows how to have a good time. I was wondering if you could show me some of the city's nightlife one evening."

"I guess I know a few of the hot spots. I would love to show you around. Just say when."

"You're sure your boyfriend won't mind?" Nate asked.

"Not at all," she said simply.

"Good. Let me know when you're available."

"I'm free next week."

"Sounds like a plan. Oh, and Charisma?"

She looked up from packing her briefcase.

"Thanks."

"Don't mention it."

Less than an hour later Charisma was in her mother's kitchen preparing a salad. Charisma was the spitting image of Jena, from her long, sexy lashes and fine, glossy black curls to her slender build. Her father, Ellis, a hardworking loan officer, was due home any minute, and her brother Eric was bringing his latest girlfriend over to meet the folks. Five years her junior, Eric often brought his girlfriends home for inspection. Why, in the last year alone, he had brought home three girls. Charisma was beginning to lose track of all his women.

"I'm home," Ellis Dearborn said as he entered the house through the side door.

"We're in here, honey," Jena said from the kitchen.

"Hi, Daddy." Charisma kissed her father on the cheek.

"Hi, princess," he said, kissing her back. "Is Eric here yet?"

"No, he just called. He'll be here in about twenty minutes," Jena said.

"Good. I'll have time to shower and change," he said, heading upstairs to the bathroom. Ellis Dearborn was a salt-and-pepper–haired man of average height. He had a slight potbelly and the warmest brown eyes to match his gentle smile.

Jena and Charisma finished making dinner—London broil, macaroni and cheese, salad, and dinner rolls. Jena had even left work early so she'd have enough time to make Eric's favorite German chocolate cake.

"You know, Charisma, having a career is fine, but there's more to life than just work. When are you going to settle down, get married, and have some babies?"

"Mother, please, not tonight. You act like I'm ancient. I'm

only thirty-four. What's the rush? Just because *you* married at nineteen, doesn't mean that's the law of the land. And besides, I haven't met the right man yet. I know you don't want me to marry any ole thing that comes along just for the sake of having a husband. Or do you?"

"Don't be silly, Charisma. I just don't want you to end up like your cousin Candace. She gave away all her candy until there was none left. Now, *nobody* wants her. No man wants a woman who's been too picked over. You're too intelligent to be foolish. I just want what's best for you."

Charisma sighed.

Jena continued. "I may not always be right, Charisma, but I'm never wrong."

Charisma shook her head. "Okay, Mother. Now can we please change the subject?" Charisma glanced out the kitchen window. "Eric and his latest are pulling up."

"What's her name again?" Jena asked.

"Sophia," Charisma reminded her.

"It would be a shame if your little brother beat you to the altar. I keep telling you, Charisma, you're not as young as you think you are."

Charisma drove the short distance down the Sunrise Highway to Red Lobster in the Green Acres Mall for dinner with her two best friends, Tangie and Heather. She found a parking spot close to Best Buy just as another car was pulling out. It was Saturday night, and the restaurant was packed. Tangie had already arrived. They waited about half an hour before being seated at a booth. The waitress came shortly to take their order, but they decided to wait for Heather.

"Before I forget, here's your CD." Charisma reached inside her purse for Jill Scott's latest.

"Thanks," Tangie said.

Charisma and Tangie had been best friends since kindergarten. From the very beginning, people often mistook them for sisters. Known affectionately as Tangie, Tangela Winter-hope was a force to be reckoned with. Her shoulder-length layered hair and copper highlights only emphasized her golden skin tone. If a man didn't notice her bedroom eyes first, it was because they were too busy checking out her DD cups. Naturally friendly, Tangie had been boy-crazy ever since Charisma could remember. Like Charisma, she loved shopping and often spent hours at the mall looking for the perfect shoe, the perfect dress, the perfect lipstick . . .

Finally, Heather arrived. She was a full-figured biracial woman with warm green eyes and a naturally curly honey-brown mane that fell way down her back. "Sorry I'm late. My car wasn't ready until half an hour ago. Would you believe it? It was supposed to be ready this afternoon. Those damn mechanics get on my nerves, and they charge an arm and a leg. Have you guys been waiting long?" she asked as she squeezed into the booth next to Tangie.

"No, we just got here," Charisma said.

Heather signaled for the waitress and they placed their order. As the youngest of the trio, she had met Charisma and Tangie during an orientation weekend at Howard University. They were amazed to discover that Heather was from New York as well. Despite the three-year age difference, they clicked and promised to keep in touch. When Heather entered Howard on a full scholarship that September, Charisma and Tangie immediately took her under their wing, giving her the inside track on everything from which professors to avoid to where the best on- and off-campus dorms were located. Heather affectionately referred to them as Howard's Angels, and held them partially responsible for her summa cum laude degree.

The waitress returned with piping hot biscuits and their drinks—Tangie's Sex on the Beach, Charisma's Long Island iced tea, and Heather's seltzer water. When she left, they raised their glasses in their customary toast. In unison they said, "Behind every successful woman is herself."

"I know that's right," Heather agreed. "So what's new?"

"Blade and I celebrate our two-year anniversary next week." Tangie smiled.

"I'm not sure if I should congratulate you or offer my condolences. The minute he gave you that recycled Valentine's Day teddy bear with some other chick's name on it, you should have kicked him to the curb. It's October, and you're *still* seeing him?" Heather shook her head.

"Cut him loose," Charisma agreed, biting into a biscuit.

"I will. Eventually," Tangie promised.

"Who is she kidding?" Heather looked at Charisma. "Tangie, he's not the only man out there."

"I know, but he's got some sweet meat," Tangie admitted.

"Then suffer the consequences. You know how he is." Heather stirred her seltzer with a straw.

Tangie shook her head. "All I wanna know is, who let the dogs out?"

"Doesn't matter. Why do you keep letting them in?" Charisma asked.

Finally, their appetizers came—mozzarella sticks and stuffed mushrooms. They dived right in, all except for Heather.

"Heather, you're not eating. What's up?" Charisma asked.

"I'm skipping the appetizers. I'm on a new diet. I'm supposed to lose ten pounds in two weeks," Heather admitted.

"Eating what?" Charisma asked.

"Mostly broiled seafood, baked chicken, salad, and I take a supplement before every meal. I gotta get this weight off. The holidays are coming." Heather took another sip of seltzer.

Tangie quickly said grace and bit into a cheese stick. "How much are you trying to lose?"

"I'm about two-twenty now, but I would love to get down to one-sixty," Heather said.

"One-sixty on a five-foot-seven-inch frame? You'd be hot. You should come to the gym and work out. You'd lose the weight in no time," Tangie suggested.

"As huge as *I* am? Imagine me waddling around the gym. It's not a pretty sight," Heather admitted.

"Heather, the average woman is a size fourteen," Charisma reminded her.

"Please," Tangie told her. "Look at you. You're gorgeous. You have flawless, creamy skin, beautiful almond-shaped eyes, and a head of hair most women would die for. Count your blessings. So you're a little overweight. You can lose it. Lots of women have lost more. And what's in those pills you're taking, anyway? Are they safe?"

"I bought them from the health food store. They're fine," Heather said. "Where's our dinner? I'm starving."

"Have a mushroom. One can't hurt," Charisma said.

"No, I'll pass," Heather decided.

"If you change your mind and wanna hit the gym, let me know. I can get you a really good deal. Just say the word." Tangie, who worked at Canyon's Club, told her.

"Okay, enough about me. Did you get that promotion, Charisma?" Heather asked.

"No, I didn't get this one, either," Charisma said. "Guess who did?"

"Who?" Tangie and Heather both asked.

"Chase Martini. Miss Crappuccino strikes again." Charisma shook her head.

"What excuse did they give *this* time?" Tangie asked.

"My boss claimed that she was better qualified and that she had completed more extensive special assignments than me. Who's he kidding? She's a part-timer who spends half of her day on her cell." Charisma grabbed another mozzarella stick. "The only special assignments she's been on lately have been in somebody's bed, probably his. Thank goodness he's history. Come to think of it, the last three promotions were filled by whites. I'm sick of it. It's almost like they belong to a sect. Who do they think they are, the privileged sect? I'm ready to file a discrimination complaint."

"Sometimes that can hurt your career," Heather said.

"I just want some answers," Charisma admitted. "Oh, they just hired a new manager in my department."

"White?" Tangie asked.

"No, a brother, actually," Charisma said.

"Interesting. What's he like?" Tangie asked.

Charisma smiled, recalling how she had beat him out of a parking space that first day. "I was so embarrassed."

"Well, at least he knows you can maneuver your way into a tight spot," Tangie said. "Men like that kind of information."

"A few days later he asked me to show him some of the city's hot spots." Charisma grinned.

"See, I told you," Tangie said. "But we all know which hot spot he was *really* talking about. What's he like?"

"He's tall, nice build, pretty brown skin," Charisma said.

"Just your type." Heather smiled.

"Does he have tight sugar buns?" Tangie asked

"I wasn't looking there," Charisma exclaimed.

"Well, you should have been, 'cause you know he was scoping yours. As much as you're packing back there? Please, you could run the Big Apple from your back pocket," Tangie told her.

"And you could light the city with your DD headlights, honey. No need for Con Ed," Charisma said, referring to the utility giant.

"You two are so bad." Heather laughed.

The waitress returned with their entrées: Charisma's shrimp scampi, Tangie's creamy crabmeat Alfredo, and Heather's broiled salmon. Charisma and Tangie dug right in. Heather downed a diet pill first.

"I bet your boss'll ask you out," Tangie said.

"I bet he will too," Heather agreed. "It's just a matter of time." She cut into her salmon and chewed slowly, savoring every bite.

"And you know what they say. The woman decides when a relationship will begin," Tangie said.

"I know. And the man usually decides when it'll end. But in this case there'll be no end cause there'll be no beginning," Charisma insisted.

"But Charisma, you could have so much fun," Tangie said, swirling her pasta.

"How do you know? You haven't even met the man," Charisma said.

"Don't have to. Imagine dating your boss. It's the forbidden fruit thing," Tangie told her.

"Forbidden fruit? I'm not trying to get in a jam. You know, I make my phone call first thing every payday morning to make sure my direct deposit is there," Charisma said, referring to what they called their single-girl call. "I need my job. And besides, you know I'm seeing Dex."

"See them both," Tangie insisted.

"And divide the pie?" Charisma asked, enjoying her shrimp scampi. "Uh-uh."

"Well, it's not like they don't do it to us," Tangie said, rolling her eyes.

"You wanna know something?" Heather asked without waiting for an answer. "Dex is nice and all, and I know he suits your needs, but you're settling."

"And you think I should give my boss a shot?" Charisma asked.

"Why not? What have you got to lose?" Heather shrugged.

"You're both crazy." Charisma shook her head.

"We just want to see you get swept off your feet," Tangie said. "One of us deserves it."

"You're all business," Heather told Charisma. "So what

could be better than meeting the man of your dreams at work?"

"Haven't you heard that working girls should keep their legs shut and their eyes and ears open? Anyway, who says he's even available? A man like him probably has them lined up around the block," Charisma said as she sipped her drink.

"Maybe. But if he were available, would you be interested?" Tangie asked.

Charisma thought for a moment before speaking. "Nope."

2

Heather

Heather Grey drove down Merrick Boulevard to her fa-vorite cosmetics and skin-care shop, When We Were Queens. Her atrocious eyebrows looked like two bushy caterpillars plastered to her forehead in need of waxing. She was more than overdue.

Thank God Cinderella was in, and they were delighted to see one another. As usual, Cinderella greeted her with a warm embrace, kissing both cheeks. "Now queens," she said to her other clients. "Say hello to Queen Heather."

"Hi," they all said in unison.

"You look fantastic, my darling," Cinderella told her.

"I lost five pounds," Heather whispered.

"That's wonderful. Call the cops!" Cinderella smiled. "Let me guess." She laughed. "You need your eyebrows done."

Heather nodded. "Uh-huh."

"Let me finish Anita's, start Queen Ethel's, and then put wax on yours," she told Heather, keeping track of everyone. It was well-known that Cinderella did the best makeup and eyebrows in Queens, and she was the premier choice for many a bride. By this time, four more customers had walked in and all for their brows. Cinderella's assistant helped out. Heather was glad she came when she did. Cinderella worked her magic and handed Heather a hand mirror to review her work. Heather glanced at her reflection, pleased with what she saw until her eyes landed smack-dab on her nose. How could she miss it? She hated the sight of it, from its hideous bump to its flaring nostrils. It was probably the only thing standing in the way of her lifelong dream of becoming a model. That, and the extra pounds that enveloped her girth prevented her from even being a plus-size model. She quickly looked away and returned the mirror to Cinderella. She was stuck with that curse until she hit the lottery or at least until she saved up enough money for a nose job. All her extra funds were being saved for her plastic surgery. In the meantime, she'd just have to deal with what she called her bowlegged nose.

She spent another hour with Cinderella and left with a bagful of much-needed cosmetics.

"Without God and you we truly could not survive," Cinderella told her as she headed out the door.

Heather rented the basement apartment of her mother's Laurelton home. She headed home, anxious to get out of her tight clothes. She always slipped into something more comfortable after she came in from work as a librarian at the main branch of the Queens Library off of Jamaica Avenue. It was funny. Heather Grey loved heather gray. She had a drawer full of heather gray T-shirts, leggings, and sweats. She practically lived in them during her downtime. It also amused her that she was a little black, a little white, and a Grey. Could she be any more colorful?

Heather surveyed herself in the full-length bedroom. There goes that nose again. No amount of makeup could camouflage it. Lord knows she had tried. If she ever hit the lottery, look out, world. Between a nose job and liposuction, she'd reinvent herself. Why diet and exercise for months when a skilled surgeon could whittle her down in a matter of hours? She'd save herself a lot of stomach growling. That's for sure. Yet, she still got hit on by the fellas. Some men just liked 'em extra thick. Or maybe they were just greedy. They wanted their share and someone else's too.

Heather headed for the kitchen. It was Thursday evening, and she didn't feel like cooking. She popped a frozen dinner into the microwave and poured herself a glass of diet 7UP. It was starting to drizzle outside, and her warm, toasty home was the perfect place to be on a damp, chilly night. She popped a diet pill, ate dinner, and cleaned up her kitchen. It was seven-fifteen. Good. She had finished eating before seven-thirty. She wouldn't be sleeping on a full stomach.

Heather plopped down on her living room couch and reached for the remote. There was nothing interesting on TV, just a bunch of half-naked skinny girls shaking their behinds on some music videos. She switched to another station. Two-bone thin heifers walking down the street stopping traffic. Why couldn't she be one of them? How long did she have to be miserable? Life wasn't fair. It wasn't right. She tried so hard, and she was still a whopper.

There was a pint of butter pecan ice cream in her freezer calling her name. She tried to ignore it, concentrating instead on some DVD's Charisma had dropped off the other day. The ice cream called her louder. She was doing so well on her diet that a little reward shouldn't hurt. She debated for a few moments and then headed for the kitchen, knowing fully well that each step toward the Häagen-Dazs was a step in the wrong direction. If she turned back now, her dignity would remain intact.

Too late, she had passed over the threshold. There might as well be a sign saying *Abandon all hope, all ye who enter here.* Heather took a deep breath and reached for the refrigerator door handle. The ice cream was right where she usually hid it behind the vegetables. If she got out now, she could still save herself. If she didn't, she was a goner. She took another deep breath, reached for the pint of ice cream, and quickly closed the door to the fridge. She removed the lid and liner, and microwaved the pint for twenty seconds. She had it down to a science. Perfect. She grabbed a spoon and let the sweet concoction slide down her throat, enjoying its creaminess. It was sinfully delicious, her guilty pleasure. She had entered the twilight zone, sucking down one spoonful after another until it was gone.

Moments later, the guilt began to seep in. No wonder she had a body by Häagen-Dazs. If only she had stopped herself after a spoonful or two, but no, she had allowed herself to get caught up in the moment. It had been so easy, too easy. When would she learn?

Feeling defeated, Heather inspected her full face closely in the bathroom window. She was still five pounds lighter. "Right?" she said weakly. But she knew that if she stepped on the scales the next morning, it would register a different tune. The pride she had felt an hour earlier had now been replaced by shame. She had been doing so well. *Please, God, don't let me blow it. I'm so sick and tired of being fat,* she silently prayed. As a tear ran down the side of her hooked nose and cheek, she wiped it away with the back of her hand. The damage was done. She'd get back on point tomorrow.

The next morning, Heather gulped down a cup of coffee and half a slice of whole wheat toast after popping two of her diet pills. The hunger pangs in her stomach were not satisfied, but she told herself that it was a small price to pay for the new body she envisioned. The end would definitely justify the means. No doubt about it. If she could lose ten pounds in two weeks, there was no reason she couldn't lose forty pounds in eight. Who knows, maybe she'd be svelte by Christmas if she played her cards right.

She hopped into her hooptie, a dark blue, late-model

Chrysler with a fresh paint job, backed out of the driveway, and drove down Merrick Boulevard. She was tempted to stop by the Pathmark supermarket on the way for some frozen dinners since they were on sale but decided against it. She didn't want to be late for work again this week. It was hard getting up in the morning when the bed was holding you hostage.

Heather quickly found parking along Eighty-ninth Avenue, and thus avoided having to pay the municipal parking lot fee. With minutes to spare, she was behind the desk in the language and literature section, and her workday began. She spent most of the morning helping college students find books for their research projects. Thank goodness those days were behind her.

Before she knew it, it was lunchtime, and boy, was she starved. She microwaved her Lean Cuisine and headed for the lounge to join her coworkers. Most were watching soaps and greasing back. She slid a pill in her mouth and washed it down with diet 7UP. She tried to ignore the Popeyes chicken, Margarita Pizza, and burger aroma that permeated the room and concentrate on her roasted turkey and vegetables, but it was hard. Really hard.

"You sure you don't want some of this Popeyes, Heather?" Delta asked.

"No, thanks," Heather told her.

"Of course she doesn't," Wanda said. "She'd rather have pizza. She knows I have an extra slice right here with her name on it." Wanda was the fattest in the bunch. Everytime she sat down her knees spread like a wildfire, but she was as sweet as they come. "You're not trying to go Beyoncé on us now, are you?" she asked.

"Only if she can have the money to go with it," Delta shot back, and they all laughed.

Heather didn't answer. She realized that she'd have to distance herself from them if she wanted to stay on track.

Otherwise, her efforts would be sabotaged. She finished eating and decided to get some air to clear her head.

Jamaica Avenue was usually crowded around lunchtime and today was no exception. She window-shopped as she strolled down to Canyon's Health and Fitness Club, where Tangie worked. She was tempted to stop and inquire about a gym membership, but lost her nerve. Maybe one day she'd let Tangie talk her into it. It was a beautiful, Indian summer day, and secretly she envied all the skinny women floating around with their bare midriffs and piercings. Not that she wanted to expose her belly button. It just would have been nice to have that option.

A homeless man approached her for a quarter. She reached in her pocket. All she felt were bills. She gave him a dollar.

Becoming winded, she stopped in a little rinky-dink store for some water. They wanted three dollars for one sixteen-ounce bottle. Her throat was parched. She plopped down three bucks and headed back to work, her face glistening ever so slightly from perspiration.

Later that evening she arrived home to find her mother barbecuing in the backyard. It was a nice surprise seeing Leola Grey at that time of day since she usually worked the four-to-twelve shift as a neonatal nurse at Jamaica Hospital.

"Hi, boobie," Leola Grey said, kissing her only child. Newly divorced and unable to bear children of her own, Leola had adopted Heather when she was just one month old. She told Heather the truth as soon as her young mind could understand. Heather remembered the days when her mother worked two jobs to keep a roof over her head. Leola insisted it was well worth the sacrifice.

"Hi, boobie," Heather said. "No work today?"

"I've been working four weeks straight without a day off, and those double shifts are killing me. Today seemed like the perfect day to exhale. So here I am. Want a burger?" Leola asked.

"No, thanks. I'm on a diet, remember? Can't you tell I'm losing weight?"

"Of course I can, but you can't starve yourself."

"I'm not," Heather insisted. "But I am so sick and tired of all this." She gestured to her body and sat down in a lawn chair. "How come I have to be the fat one in the family? Everyone else can eat whatever they want and not gain an ounce. I suck down a glass of water and gain weight. Slim people are *so* privileged, and they don't even realize it. I'd do *anything* to be thin. *Anything.* It's not fair!"

"I know, boobie. I know. Nobody ever said life was fair, because it's not. Look at it this way. You weren't born slim, but you were born healthy. That's a blessing. Do you know how many sick babies I care for everyday? You're a good person, a kind person," she continued. "You have a glow that comes from within. On top of all that, you're gorgeous. There are plenty of skinny women around here looking like something the cat dragged in who would *love* to look like you. So count your blessings, kiddo."

Heather stood, went over to the grill, and hugged her mother. "Why don't you take a load off your feet, and I'll finish barbecuing."

"That's okay, boobie. I'm fine. You've been working all day. Sit down, I'll fix you a plate—chicken and salad, right?"

"Uh-huh. What d'ya want to drink?" Heather asked as she grabbed her purse and headed for the kitchen.

"Some iced tea is fine."

"Okay." Inside, Heather quickly opened the bottle of pills and popped two in her mouth as her mother came inside for salad dressing. With her back to Leola, she dropped the bottle in her bag and washed the pills down with a glass of water. "Boy, I'm hungry." Heather laughed a little nervously. "Let's eat."

3

Tangie

The faint smell of sweat stung Tangie's nostrils as she entered Canyon's Club. It was Friday morning and the gym was already packed. She nodded to a few coworkers on her way to the locker room. Once there, she locked up her purse and leather jacket before heading to the front desk to begin work.

There was a steady flow of members and prospective ones requiring assistance coming in to the gym. So much so that Tangie hadn't time to process the small stack of new applications from yesterday. To make matters worse, the scanner was out of order so all the membership cards would have to be swiped manually.

Aaron walked in smiling like a Cheshire cat, and handed Tangie his membership card to swipe. She could practically see his antenna stand up and salute her through his sweatpants. *Damn, why did I have to run into him today?* she thought. *I am so not in the mood.* He was such an arrogant SOB, but she had made the mistake of telling his personal trainer that he had an awesome six-pack. Now she'd never live it down. Most of the club's halfway decent members thought they were all that. They paraded around like they were God's gift to women. Give me a break. Most of them still lived in their mama's house.

Aaron muttered something under his breath.

"Did you say something?" she asked.

In response, he slowly removed the toothpick from his mouth and allowed his eyes to slowly feast on her generous cleavage before returning to her face. "Not a word."

She swiped his card and slapped it on the counter, shielding her assets with her cardigan.

"It's all good, baby. It's all good." He smiled to himself as he picked up the card, placed the toothpick back into his mouth and walked off.

Just then, the owner's granddaughter, Chase Martini, walked in, and Tangie rolled her eyes ever so slightly at Charisma's archrival. Chase looked like she was smelling dirty socks each time she entered the gym, like everyone was beneath her and her stuff didn't stink. Chase worked with Charisma and even though she was a part-time worker, she was a full-time slut. Their nickname for her was Miss Crappuccino because she practically lived across the street in Starbucks. She and her best friend, Loren Stampato, worked out virtually everyday and had the bodies to prove it. Then they would shower in the reserved bathrooms and hang out in Starbucks, hoping to pick up some dark meat before heading back to Long Island. Her grandfather, Stone Canyon, was one of the most racist mothers this side of the Mason-Dixon Line.

Tangie couldn't wait for the day to be over. She was seeing Blade Watson that night, and the minutes couldn't pass fast enough. It was their second anniversary and he said he had a surprise for her. As usual, she would have to pick him up because he didn't have a car. After all, he had just moved out of his mama's house and was still trying to get on his feet. Once a month Tangie had the weekend off, and this was it. She rushed out of there as fast as anyone in their right mind would, jumped in her car, and headed home to Springfield Gardens. The minute she walked through the door, she checked her machine for messages. Unfortunately, Blade hadn't called yet, but that didn't mean anything. He knew that she wouldn't be home until six-thirty, and it was just a little after seven.

Tangie put on a CD and headed for the kitchen to start dinner. Blade loved her cooking, or at least he said he did. A man would say almost anything to get a woman into bed—even if it meant lying through his teeth. She whipped up a dish of chicken parmigiana and placed the dish in the oven to bake.

Then she got out of her sweats and sneakers and ran her bath. She took the cordless phone into the bathroom and turned around and grabbed her cell phone too—just in case. The hot bubble bath relaxed her instantly. She was tempted to call Blade and engage in some steamy phone sex but decided not to. By eight o'clock he hadn't called. Eight-thirty—still no Blade. Now she was really getting ticked off. He worked nine-to-five and had promised to call her the minute he got off work. Nine o'clock—nothing. Finally, she called and left him two messages on his home phone and his cell. She might as well have been calling the man on the moon. It wasn't the first time she had been stood up by Blade. She was tired of his bull.

Tangie ate alone that night. With every mouthful, she vowed not to let him into her bed no matter what his excuse was. She cleaned up the kitchen and got ready for bed—more angry than disappointed. Tired of playing the fool, she drifted off to sleep.

Blade knew Tangie would be pissed off, being that it was their anniversary and all, but he was having too much fun scoping some blond chick two rows up at a Jay-Z concert out at Westbury. She was sitting with a girlfriend and every so often she'd glance back, hold his stare, and toss her hair. A definite tease, Blade thought as he watched her flirt with him. At one point, she caught his eye and slowly licked her upper lip before turning back around in her seat. She was definitely feeling him. Blade smiled to himself. He knew his stock was rising without even reading the *Wall Street Journal*.

Luckily, they caught up with each other outside in the parking lot and introduced themselves. He checked her out head to toe in one quick glance. She looked better up close with her full lips and deep blue eyes. Or were they contacts?

Blade was glad that he had come stag. No sense bringing sand to the beach. She quickly grabbed his hand and scribbled her cell phone number on his palm while her girlfriend tooted impatiently for her to get a move on.

Later that night, Blade worked as an exotic dancer, filling in for a sick coworker at the last minute. He oiled down his taut, spicy brown body until it glistened like gold. He knew he was all that as women stuffed his bikini with tips. His nickname was Razor Blade cause he was cut sharp and deep. He looked out at the crowd. Women of all shapes, sizes, ages, and color were present. Black, white, Latina or Asian—all women wanted the same thing, and he knew just how to serve it up. Gyrating, he delivered the goods until they were caught up in a frenzy. After the show, the club's owner stopped by and promised something extra for coming into work on his night off as Blade relieved his swollen bikini of tens and twenties. Damn, I'm good, he thought to himself as he headed out the door.

Tangie woke up Saturday morning in a foul mood, anxious to kick an imaginary dog. She checked both phones. Blade never bothered to call. The first thing she did was call Charisma and Heather. Thank goodness they were still on for later that night. It was times like these when she really needed her girls. They agreed to meet that night at Corn-bread and Caviar in Baldwin for dessert. Tangie got her household chores out of the way. Then she did her weekly shopping and stopped by the dry cleaner's before return-ing home. After a nice, long nap, she showered, dressed, and headed down Sunrise Highway to meet her friends.

As usual, Heather was the last to arrive. When she did, she joined Tangie and Charisma at the bar. Shortly there-after, the three were seated at a table, where they ordered cheesecake and coffee. While they waited for dessert to ar-rive, the waiter brought over a plate of hot cornbread and warm caviar butter for their enjoyment.

"How was last night's surprise?" Charisma asked Tangie.

"Hmph, the surprise was on me," Tangie admitted. "I am officially removing Blade from the T-spot," Tangie said, re-ferring to her little black book. It was a backup to her cell phone, which she had lost more times than she cared to re-member.

"Yeah, right," Heather said.

"I'm serious," Tangie insisted.

"I think you and Blade are just on hiatus," Heather told her.

"No, we're through," Tangie reminded her. "I know I've said it before, but have you seen *this*?" Tangie rummaged through her bag for her little black book and a pen. Then she drew lines through his name and number. "What a waste," she told them, shaking her head. "He was one of the best lovers to ever grace the T-spot. Definitely in the top three."

"But I bet his number's still in your cell phone," Heather insisted.

Tangie promptly found her cell phone and erased his numbers. "Satisfied?"

"Dag, she *is* serious," Charisma said. "So what brought about his fall from grace—this time?" she added.

Tangie filled them in on the latest. "I can't take it anymore. You're right. I deserve better. He's played out," she said between mouthfuls of buttered cornbread.

"You sure do, girl." Heather raised her glass. "Behind every successful woman is herself." They all agreed.

"All I wanna know is why I keep choosing the wrong men," Tangie said. "Remember Omar?"

"How could we forget?" Charisma said. "I mean, it's not everyday your boyfriend gets busted for passing bad checks."

"Yeah, and then get written up in the *Daily News*." Heather sipped her diet soda.

"And remember Victor?" Tangie asked.

"The mechanic. At least he kept your car running perfectly," Heather said.

"Yeah, mine and half the women in Queens." Tangie shook her head.

"Hey, what's his number?" Heather joked as their coffee and dessert arrived. They had requested three forks and one large plate with a slice of red velvet cheesecake, sweet potato cheesecake, and chocolate cheesecake.

"Enjoy," the waiter told them as they dug in.

"Thanks," they said in unison.

"Maybe you should take a break from men for a while and clear your head," Charisma said before sliding a forkful of red velvet cheesecake into her mouth.

"Take a break? Are you kidding me? It's a man's world. James Brown wasn't joking. Let's face it. Women with men are privileged," Tangie told them. "Everybody knows that."

"Take a break," Charisma insisted. "They're not going anywhere."

"It's funny," Tangie admitted. "I almost wish they were."

* * *

Somewhere around two AM Sunday morning, Tangie was awakened by the intrusive ringing of her telephone. She knew who it was before she even picked up. It was Blade.

"Tangie, you still awake? I'm coming over."

"Don't bother." She hung up.

He called right back. "Don't be like that. I need to see you, baby. I can explain."

She hung up the phone again, in no mood for his lame explanations.

Ten minutes later Blade was pounding on her door. At first she considered not letting him in. He could stay out in the cold for all she cared, but he was a loud drunk and the neighbors didn't need to know all her business. So, she let him in.

"I'm giving you five minutes," she said to him. "And don't even think about taking off your jacket."

"So it's like that."

"Four minutes and thirty seconds."

"Oh, you got jokes."

"Four minutes."

"Baby, I was working. You know I wouldn't miss a chance to get some of your good loving on purpose."

"Oh, and you couldn't call? Give me a break."

"Baby, don't be like that." He tried to take her in his arms, but she pushed him away.

"Time's up. Good night, Blade," she said, showing him the door.

Blade kissed her on the neck and slid his hand up her robe. She wasn't wearing anything underneath it. Angry, Tangie pushed his hands away. Blade slid his tongue into her mouth and kissed her nice and slowly, just the way she liked it. Before long she was kissing him back. He rubbed her breasts—first one, then the other. He squeezed her nipples ever so gently until they were hard. Then, he slid her left breast into his mouth. That's when Tangie let out a soft moan, and she knew he had her just where he wanted her. Again.

In one swift motion, he removed her robe, swooped her up in his chiseled arms, and carried her off to the bedroom. Within seconds, he had her sprawled out on the bed, watching him strip. He bent down. When his meat fell out of his boxers, she nearly came. She knew she had to have him. In the darkness, she reached for the box of condoms in her nightstand and made him put one on. She knew he'd oblige, willing to do almost anything to get some pussy.

He rolled her over until she was on top. Then Tangie pulled herself up and sat on his dick. Slowly, she rocked back and forth, enjoying every minute, every inch. He grabbed her tight ass as her breathing became heavier.

"You gonna come for me?" he asked her.

"Uh-huh," she said, her eyes closed, loving the sensation between her legs and not wanting it to end. Before long she was coming, and she lay back down on top of him, panting ever so softly.

He flipped her over on her back and finished what she had started. Within a few minutes, he had come too. They both lay back on the bed, catching their breath.

"Girl, you got game."

"You're not so bad yourself."

He got up and reached for his clothes, which he had left in a heap on the floor.

"I thought you were spending the night. I know you're not leaving," she said.

"Baby, I gotta go back over Tyrone's house."

"You're joking, right?"

"No. I'm not." He zipped up his jeans, fastening the belt buckle.

"If you leave, don't bother coming back. I mean it, Blade."

"Baby, your pussy is like Gotham City's police department. It sends out the bat signal when it needs some. I was just answering the call."

She grabbed a book on her nightstand and threw it at him, barely missing his head as he walked out the door.

4

Charisma

It was Thursday and Charisma had agreed to give her new boss, Nate Arquette, a taste of local nightlife. That morning he stopped by her office.

"Are we still on for tonight?" he asked her. They had already agreed to go dutch.

"Absolutely," she said. "I hope you don't mind if we take my car."

"Not at all. I've seen you maneuver."

"Tell me one thing, Nate. What kind of music do you like?"

"All kinds, but especially R and B and jazz."

"And what kind of food do you like?"

"Soul food, Caribbean, Italian, Chinese."

"Oh, you're easy," she told him, smiling.

"I'm easy?" he repeated.

"Uh-huh," she said. "I thought we might go to Regine's for dinner and then stop by Manhattan Proper afterward."

"You're the boss. I'm in your hands." He winked and they shared a smile. Charisma looked away first.

They worked until six before calling it a day. Charisma turned off her computer and headed to the ladies' lounge to freshen up. She wore a navy wool suit that showcased her assets—mainly her ample buns and generous breasts. She had tried on three different outfits before settling on that one, not wanting to convey the wrong message. She wanted to appear professional, yet feminine, and the navy suit was the perfect choice. Charisma reapplied her make-up and lipstick, thankful that Cinderella had just done her eyebrows days ago. She ran her fingers through her hair, spritzed on her favorite perfume, and was good to go.

Nate was waiting for her in the lobby and they left the building together. She hadn't bothered telling her coworkers that she and Nate were going out. She knew they'd find out soon enough. She was parked just up the block, and they walked the short distance to her car. It was a chilly October evening, and she was glad that she had put the lining back in her trench coat. She unlocked the doors to her Honda, and they got in. Nate immediately adjusted the passenger seat to accommodate his six-feet-plus frame.

Once again, Charisma showed him what a smooth operator she was as she skillfully made her way through rush hour traffic. Within half an hour they were pulling up in front of Regine's.

"I hope you're hungry," Charisma said as they got out of the car.

"Famished. I skipped lunch for this."

"Good. Get ready for the best steak in Queens."

"You know, there's plenty to be said for seafood, chicken, and pasta, but sometimes nothing takes the place of a nice, thick juicy steak."

"I know exactly what you mean."

They entered the dimly-lit steakhouse and waited for the hostess. It wasn't long before they were seated at a table for two. The waitress came to take their orders and returned shortly with their drinks—her apple martini and his scotch on the rocks. Their eyes met.

Finally Nate spoke. "So," he began. "How long have you been with Freeman?"

"Eleven years."

"And how have you been treated in those eleven years?"

"I enjoy my job, but I've been turned down for the last three promotions I applied for."

"Did you think you were the best qualified for the positions?"

"May I be frank?" she asked him.

"Absolutely."

"I may not spread 'em like butter, but I work my spreadsheets."

"I'm sure you've heard that it's not what you know, but who you know."

"Yes, and apparently sometimes it's who you do. So watch your back," she warned him.

"Off the record, I know all about the state of affairs—pun intended—at Freeman LTD and I was called in to do some housecleaning. On my watch, the best qualified will be rewarded," Nate said, draining his glass.

She returned his gaze, refusing to speak. The waitress returned with his medium well prime rib and her grilled chicken. For a moment, they ate in silence.

"Mmm, this steak is like butter." He cut her a slice. "Have some."

"No, you enjoy it," she said, slicing her chicken. "I'm fine."

They finished their meal and switched gears to talk of the new NBA season. Being a die-hard New Yorker, Charisma insisted that the Knicks had been completely revamped. That coupled with their securing the second pick in the draft choice practically clinched a play-off spot.

"Are you kidding me?" Nate asked her. "I respect your

hometown loyalty, but don't bet on it. I'm going with the Lakers and Miami. Dwyane Wade is no joke."

"Dwayne Wade is on the injured list. The Heat don't have a chance this season."

"But don't forget, it's early in the season. He has plenty of time to heal," Nate reminded her.

"Yeah, before he gets injured again."

"Don't jinx my boy, now. Your Knicks'll be lucky to reach five hundred, but if you have so much confidence in the Knicks, why don't we make a little wager. Are you in?"

"I'm listening," Charisma said.

"A frat brother of mine gave me two tickets to next Saturday's Knick game."

"Against the Lakers?"

"Exactly. Why don't you check your schedule, and see if you're free."

"What's the wager?"

"If the Knicks win, I'll buy you dinner. If they lose, you'll buy me dinner. Is it a deal?"

"Deal," she said.

They finished their meal at Regine's and headed to Manhattan Proper. Charisma took the Van Wyck Expressway to the Belt Parkway and ended up parking across the street from the Linden Boulevard nightclub. It was well after eight. Of course, at that hour the club was already packed. So Charisma and Nate headed straight for the bar. She ordered another apple martini, and he had a gin and tonic.

"So tell me more about yourself, Charisma," Nate said.

"Well, what would you like to know?"

"A woman as beautiful as you walking around single? What's wrong with the men in this city?"

"Did you ever think that maybe I'm single by choice?" she asked.

"Let me guess. You're one of those SBW's. Just what the world needs—another strong black woman."

"I detest that phrase. It's so . . . political."

"It is what it is. So why *are* you still single?"

"Maybe," she said, taking a sip of her apple martini, "I just haven't found the right man."

"So what's your type?"

"Got an hour?"

"I'm listening."

"I want a man who's sensitive, ambitious, hardworking, family oriented, has a great sense of humor, attractive, and last but not least, can be faithful."

"You don't want much, do you? And I bet he'd have to rock your world in the bedroom too, wouldn't he?"

"It wouldn't hurt." She smiled, stroking the back of her neck. "Now you see why I'm still single. It's a tall order to fill, and I'm not about to settle."

"Tall? Yes. Impossible? No."

First thing Saturday morning Charisma called Tangie and Heather to meet her at IHOP on Rockaway Boulevard in Five Towns. She hadn't been able to sleep much since she had taken her boss out the other night.

As usual, the IHOP in Five Towns was packed, but amazingly, they were all able to find parking. Unfortunately, they waited well over half an hour to be seated, but breakfast there was always worth it. Charisma ordered a stack of buttermilk pancakes, turkey sausages, and coffee. It was times like these she was glad she worked out on a regular basis. Tangie ordered a western omelet and Heather had egg whites.

"I thought we were meeting tonight. What happened?" Tangie asked Charisma.

"I took my boss out the other night. That's what happened," Charisma said.

"So how did it go?" Heather asked.

Charisma tilted her head back and slowly exhaled an imaginary cigarette à la Bette Davis. "I can't believe I'm even giving him a second thought. I must be crazy." She shook her head.

"Why?" Heather and Tangie said in unison.

"Why?" Charisma repeated. "It's a cardinal rule. Don't get your honey where you make your money. Especially when your boss is involved."

"There you go again, the world according to Charisma." Heather looked up as the waitress returned with their breakfast.

"I'm sorry, but I just can't go out like that. It's not my style." Charisma poured syrup on her pancakes.

"Just be open to the possibilities, Charisma. That's all we're saying." Heather dug inside her purse for her diet pills. She placed one in her mouth and washed it down with a couple of sips of water before starting breakfast.

"You need a *real* relationship," Tangie said.

"You know I'm seeing Dex," Charisma reminded her.

"Dex? Please. You and Dex are lovers. You have a lover, Charisma. You don't have love. There's a difference. I should know." Tangie chewed her omelet.

"For the last time, he's too close for comfort. He's off limits. Now, next topic." Charisma sipped her coffee.

Heather chose a different strategy. "Now just imagine we were clubbing one Friday night and this fine-looking brother walks up to you and offers to buy you a drink. He's not wearing a wedding band and neither are you. Do you mean to tell me you'd turn him down without giving him a chance?" Heather asked.

"No, of course not," Charisma admitted.

"That's what you're doing to your boss. He can't help it that he's your manager. Why punish him? You're two consenting adults. What you do on your own time is your own business," Heather insisted.

"And another thing," Tangie said, piggybacking off Heather.

"More people meet their spouses or hook up at work than anywhere else. So what happened on your first date?"

"It wasn't a date," Charisma corrected her. "I was just showing him around."

Tangie looked at Heather. "Correction, it was a date," she said to Heather. Continue," she told Charisma.

"We had dinner at Regine's and drinks at Manhattan Proper," Charisma said in between chewing turkey sausages.

"And that's the whole story?" Tangie grilled her.

"That's it," Charisma said.

"What time did you get to Manhattan Proper?" Tangie continued.

Charisma thought for a moment. "A little after eight."

"And what time did you get home," Tangie asked.

"Around ten-thirty." Charisma rubbed the back of her neck.

"Interesting," Heather said, smiling. "Sounds like a date to me."

"Okay, okay, I'll admit it. I had a good time," Charisma said, smiling.

"That's all we wanted to hear." Tangie returned her smile.

"Actually, it was fun. I had a better time than I expected. That's the scary part. Half of me is, don't you dare, the other half is saying go for it," Charisma admitted.

"So you know what you do?" Heather asked without waiting for an answer. "You go for it. What's the worst that can happen? Right, Tangie?"

"Right," Tangie agreed.

"A lot of help you guys turned out to be." Charisma shook her head as they finished breakfast. They left a tip for the waitress, put on their jackets, and paid the check. They left the restaurant and stood outside in the November air saying good-bye. Just as they were about to walk to their cars, a black Camry pulled up in the spot next to Charisma and out stepped Nate Arquette.

"Charisma, how nice." Nate was casually fine in a pair of freshly ironed blue jeans, an open collar denim shirt, a black leather bomber, and loafers.

"Hi, Nate. These are my friends, Tangie and Heather. This is my boss, Nate."

"Hi," they all said to each other as Charisma checked out her boss. Finally, she spoke. "We have to get going, Nate. You picked the right spot. Enjoy your breakfast."

"Thanks. Nice meeting you both." He looked at Heather and Tangie, smiling. "See you Monday, Charisma."

"Whew! What a reason to get up in the morning," Heather said under her breath as Charisma got into her car.

For the rest of the weekend, all Charisma could think of was her boss—as much as she hated to admit it. Sure, he was good-looking and charming, but men like that were a dime a dozen. And if she had a dollar for every man in New York who fit that description, she wouldn't need her 401(k) plan. Besides, one piece of candy in her candy dish was enough. And that slot was already filled—by Dex. And boy, did he know how to make her drool.

By the time Monday morning rolled around, Charisma was confident once again that she had everything under control. She found that it was easiest when she stayed out of Nate's way. She did that as much as possible. In fact, she managed to avoid him all morning long, up until lunchtime. It was then that he asked her if she wanted to join him and a few of the other coworkers for a bite to eat. It was a nasty day out, and they were all going down to the cafeteria.

"No, you go on, Nate," she told him. "I think I'll just stay here and read. I just started Jackie Collins's new novel last night, and I can't wait to pick up where I left off."

"Well, read on, Charisma. Read on." He smiled.

The afternoon flew by and before she knew it, it was time to call it a day. She always liked to freshen up before she left the office. You never knew who you might meet on the way home, and you never got a second chance to make a first impression. Unfortunately, Chase Martini, aka Miss Crappuccino, was in the ladies' lounge mirror as well, applying a fresh coat of war paint.

"Charisma, you should've joined us for lunch. We had a blast. Nate is awesome."

Yeah, I know. Your white behind thinks all black men are awesome. Instead, Charisma said, "I'm glad you had a good time."

"You know what your problem is, Charisma?" she said, tossing her blond hair.

"Here it comes, the world according to Chase."

"You like to act all nonchalant like you're not interested in Nate, but I know that half the women in this office have the hots for him—including you. At least I'm honest about my feelings."

"Do you know what your problem is?" Charisma didn't wait for an answer. "You waltzed in here like you're some freakin' princess, but you're nothing but upper-middle *ass*."

"Sounds like a personal problem to me, Charisma. Don't hate me because I was born with a silver spoon in my mouth and yours was what, plastic? And don't hate me cause I'm beautiful. Watch me make Nate mine just like I stole those two jobs you wanted from under your nose. Just make sure you take plenty of notes, though, because I work fast and I'm only going to show you once." She tossed her hair one last time, having perfected the official white girl's imaginary power move as she left. Charisma secretly hoped she'd snap her neck.

5

Heather

Heather drove out to Ashley Stewart in the Green Acres Mall. She was eager to try on some new clothes, having shed a whopping ten pounds. She walked through the mall checking out the other sisters—their hair, their makeup, their jewelry, their fashion sense. Some things came with a price tag, but when it came to style, Heather knew that hey, either you got it or you don't. And underneath her body by Häagen-Dazs was a svelte, young thing just itching to get out.

She walked into Ashley Stewart, fall and winter fashions all around her. A couple of sweaters caught her eye, along with a skirt and some pants. She was ready for the fitting room. Everything fit but the size eighteen black pants, which were a little snug in the thighs. She knew that within a month or so they'd probably fit perfectly, but for now she debated getting them. Her old black wool slacks were so tight that they practically squeaked when she walked. She felt like she could be in a *Seinfeld* episode. She looked at herself in the mirror one more time before getting dressed, trying to ignore her nose. It didn't work.

She was a few feet from the cashier, debating whether or not she should get the pants in a bigger size when someone called her name.

"Heather Grey. I thought that was you," an unfamiliar female voice said.

Heather followed the voice. "Ava Johnson. I haven't seen you, *oh my gosh,* since high school," she said. "And you chopped off your mane."

"I had to, girl. My life was too complicated." Ava was a petite, shapely, medium brown beauty with a short, black boycut. Her bangs fell just above her brows, emphasizing her wide-set eyes.

"You're still here in New York?" Ava asked her.

"Uh-huh."

"So how've you been?"

"Just fine," Heather said. "How about you?"

"Oh, I can't complain, but I'm starving. Wanna grab a bite to eat in the food court?"

"Sure. Let me pay for these first, and I'll meet you upstairs," Heather said. She stood in line for over ten minutes before leaving the store with her purchases, minus the pants. She took the escalator up to the second floor and spotted Ava in the center of the food court.

"Over here,"Ava said, waving to Heather. Ava's face hadn't changed much since Bayside High School. She still had that cute little nose and those adorable dimples.

Heather sat down opposite Ava and put her bags in the empty chair, anxious to take a load off her slightly swollen ankles. "Why don't I watch your bags while you get your food," Heather suggested.

"You sit. I'll get yours too. What's your pleasure?"

"Are you sure?"

Ava nodded. "It's no biggie. Why not?"

"Okay, I'll have a grilled chicken sandwich from Burger Hut and a diet Seven-UP."

"You want fries to go with that?" Ava asked her.

"No fries. I'm trying to get to where *you* are," Heather told her. "What were you doing in Ashley Stewart, anyway?" Heather reached into her wallet and pulled out a ten-dollar bill for Ava.

"I go in just to remind myself of how far I've come."

"How much did you lose?" Heather asked her.

"Seventy-two pounds."

"Amazing." Heather shook her head.

"Don't worry. Your day'll come," Ava said before going to get their orders.

Ava returned a few minutes later with Heather's order and a Wendy's double cheeseburger for herself. She barely had time to give Heather her change before sinking her teeth into her burger.

"I haven't eaten all day," Ava said, wiping her mouth with a napkin. "Once a week I treat myself. So what have you been up to since high school?"

Heather removed the grilled chicken from the buns. She searched in her purse for her diet pills, popped two in her mouth, and washed them down with diet soda. "Vitamins," she explained to Ava before continuing. "Well, I did four years at Howard, got a liberal arts degree, and came back to New York to get my master's. And you'll never guess where I'm working."

"Where?" Ava asked.

"The Queens Library as a librarian."

"Right off the avenue?"

Heather nodded.

"Get outta here. How many afternoons did we spend there working on term papers?"

"Tell me about it. Now I'm helping others do it."

"That's amazing. So is there anyone special in your life?"

"No, not at the moment. What about you?" Heather asked.

"Not unless you count my vibrator," Ava admitted, and they both burst out laughing.

"Girl, you are still crazy. You haven't changed a bit."

"You have," Ava said.

"How?" Heather asked, taking another bite of her chicken.

"You were so uptight in high school that tampons looked up to you." She laughed.

"Stop it," Heather said, laughing.

"You were. What's your guiltiest pleasure now?"

"Red Lobster biscuits. One day I got so depressed I went to Red Lobster, ordered a dozen to go, sucked them down, and got sick as a dog."

"Girl, my cheddar biscuits are so good, I expect Red Lobster to show up on my doorstep and serve me with papers any day now."

"I better watch my back with you," Heather joked, taking one last gulp of her soda.

"Let's keep in touch." Ava whipped out her cell phone and Heather did the same as they exchanged numbers.

A week later Heather was busy at work when she had an unexpected visitor—Ava had stopped by to have lunch.

"I hope you don't mind," Ava said. "I thought you might wanna have lunch."

"Perfect timing," Heather said. "Let me grab my coat." She disappeared behind one of the doors designated for employees only and returned with her black leather swing coat.

They decided on Margarita Pizza, one of the best pizzerias in all of Queens. As crowded as it was, Heather managed to get two seats in the rear while Ava waited for their piping-hot slices to come out of the oven. Heather took a swig of the bottled water she kept in her purse, hoping to quiet her growling stomach.

Heather only ate one meal a day and some days it was

pure torture, but in the end it would be well worth it. She wanted that size eight body so badly that she could taste it as much as the cinnamon Altoid she had just eaten. In fact, that's what she was visualizing when Ava came with their pizzas.

"Whoever or whatever it is must be good," Ava joked.

"Trust me. It is," Heather admitted and left it at that. "So you never told me what you've been up to since high school."

"I graduated from York College with a degree in accounting, and I've been working at Zales ever since. I used to work in Queens Center, but now I'm right across the street. You should come down and pick out something. I have a great discount."

"Thanks, maybe I'll take you up on that," Heather said as she took another bite of her pizza. "Do you ever run into anyone from Bayside? Remember Walt? Oh, what was his last name?"

"You mean Walt Sample from the varsity basketball team? Oh, he just made partner at some big-time law firm in Chicago."

"I had a huge crush on him," Heather admitted.

"Please, half the female student body was feeling him." Ava wiped her mouth with a napkin. "And the other half was sleeping with him."

"Which half were you in?" Heather asked.

"I'll never tell." She grinned. "But we wore out the cushions on the backseat of his hooptie," Ava whispered.

"You are so bad." Heather checked her watch. "I better get going." They both stood, ditched their paper plates in the garbage and headed for the door.

"Looks like it's starting to rain. I should've brought my umbrella," Heather said.

Ava fished in her bag for hers. "I have mine. I'll walk you back."

"It's so out of the way. Are you sure?" Heather asked.

"It's no problem," Ava insisted.

They walked out of Margarita's as it was just beginning to pour. Ava opened her umbrella, and they huddled together in the rain. Her wrist accidentally dropped and her fingers brushed against Heather's breast. She quickly apologized, and Heather accepted her apology. Funny thing, though, Heather wasn't quite sure it was an accident.

Heather's car died two blocks from her house that evening. She walked home in the pouring rain without an umbrella. Her naturally curly hair was totally soaked. Once inside, she took a hot shower and got into some dry clothes. Heather called Charisma to see if she could pick her up that night since they were all meeting for dinner at Heather's favorite spot, Cabana. It was a little Spanish restaurant in Forest Hills. Parking was always at a premium there, so usually they'd all ride in one car. If no parking spots were available, they'd park in the lot and split the cost three ways. That night they were lucky. A car was pulling out just as Charisma turned onto Austin Street.

Tangie hopped out the car, dashed into the restaurant, and quickly gave her name to the hostess. The place was packed, but that was the norm, especially for a Friday night. They waited at the bar for about forty minutes before their table was ready.

Once seated, they ordered a pitcher of sangria. The waiter returned with the sangria and the menus. After their usual toast, they sat back and enjoyed the ambiance. They loved the fun, lively atmosphere. There was an element of electricity in the air that could not be denied. Even though it was a Spanish restaurant, all kinds of patrons—Latinos, blacks, whites, Filipinos, Asians—frequented the hot spot.

The waiter returned shortly and gave them a description of the specials that night—in Spanish, of course. Except for a few words here and there, they had no idea what he was saying. He appeared very patient, and then described the dishes in English as well. They skimmed over the bilingual menu and made their choices. Finally, he returned with their appetizers of little beef turnovers and thinly sliced plantains.

"I can't believe my car conked out on me again on my way home from work," Heather began. "I ended up walking home in the rain." She rolled her eyes, shaking her head in disgust.

"Why don't you just buy another one? It doesn't have to be brand new," Charisma reminded her.

"I wish I could," Heather told her. "But plastic surgery doesn't come cheap, and I can almost taste that nose job."

6
Charisma

Charisma rushed home Wednesday night to get ready for Dex. He had just gotten back in town and was coming by straight from the airport. She took a long, hot bath in Cinderella's Wishes Sugarbutter bath crystals before moisturizing with the body butter. She smelled like a dream as she slipped into a sheer black teddy and waited for the fireworks to begin.

Dex called a little after six to say he was in a cab, stuck in traffic at JFK. By seven they were in each other's arms.

"I missed you," he told her as she greeted him at the door.

"How was your flight?" she asked.

"Smooth, but long."

"Hungry?" she asked him.

"I think *he's* hungrier than *I* am." He took off his coat and dropped his luggage by the door and took her in his arms. For a few moments, there was nothing but silence as their mouths got reacquainted.

"You always smell so good." He held her tight, burying

his face in her neck. "I've been thinking about you all week."

"I know the feeling." She held him close, massaging the back of his neck with her right hand. Then she grabbed him by the hand and led him into the bedroom. "Come on."

They quickly made their way onto her queen-sized bed, where he practically tore off his shirt while she unbuckled his belt. Standing, Dex then unzipped his pants, removing them along with his boxers, shoes, and socks. He stripped Charisma of her teddy in two easy motions. Moaning, she leaned back into the pillows as he milked her tits—first with his hands, then his mouth. She got hotter and wetter watching him slide his tongue down her body until he reached her throbbing honey nugget. Her breath got caught in her throat as he teased her favorite hot spot with his tongue, stroking it and massaging it stiff until she could stand it no more. Her entire being exploded. He made his way back up to her lips.

Finally, they lay on her bed with only a Trojan between them. Dex sat up, beckoning Charisma to join him. She stood over him and gently eased herself down, facing him. Grinning, Charisma spread her legs, marveling at why she had nicknamed him Mr. Goodbar as she wrapped her legs around his middle. He rocked her world—first nice and slow and then hard and fast. She bit his shoulder, trying to stay in control. Finally, they both came, momentarily paralyzed with passion, before collapsing onto the bed. Covered in sweat, they both laughed as he leaned over and lightly kissed her on the mouth. Anything else would have taken too much energy. He took her in his arms and told her how glad he was to see her.

They drifted off to sleep and somewhere past ten Charisma's phone rang, awakening them both. It was a wrong number. Dex got up and dressed, then called a cab.

"I hate having to leave you," he said. "I have an early meeting tomorrow. I know we've discussed it before, but I want you to move in with me."

"You know I can't do that."

"Why not?" He kissed her gently.

"Because," she said. "You don't have enough closet space for my shoes." She laughed.

"You're right about that, but I'll add a wing just for your shoes. Stay in bed. I'll let myself out."

"No, that's okay." Charisma reached for a robe and walked him to the door. He kissed her one more time before grabbing his coat and luggage, and heading out the door. They promised to get together again real soon.

Charisma took a shower before retiring for the night. She too wanted to be fresh and rested for the workday tomorrow.

First thing Thursday morning Nate stopped by Charisma's office. She was busy reading her e-mail for the day's assignments. Sensing his presence, she looked up.

"Good morning, Nate,"

"Good morning, Charisma. Are we still on for Saturday night? You know the Lakers are in town."

"That's right. How could I forget?"

"I hope you cleared your calendar for me."

"Consider it done," Charisma said simply.

"The game starts at seven-thirty. So, I'll pick you up around . . . six?"

"Sex will be fine—I mean six will be fine." She reddened. "Here, let me give you my address." Charisma jotted down her address and easy directions. He slipped it inside the upper-left inside pocket of his suit as he left her office.

"Good morning, Nate. Love your aftershave," Chase said as she walked by.

"Thanks." Suddenly his phone rang, and he sprinted back to his office, leaving Charisma and Chase behind in a staring match.

"For someone who's not interested, it sure didn't take you long to slip him your number," Chase told Charisma, expecting a response. When none came, she tossed her hair and walked away.

After work, Charisma stopped at the mall for a little retail therapy. The moment she walked onto Macy's second floor, she went into shoe shock. She walked out with a pair of burgundy suede peep toe pumps and some black satin dressy sandals. So much for zeroing out her Macy's charge.

When she got home there was a package waiting for her. Home shopping was one of Charisma's guilty pleasures. She tore open the package, revealing a pair of tiny, heart-shaped diamond stud earrings. She headed for the bathroom to sterilize the earrings with alcohol before putting them in her earlobes. They were exquisite. She loved earrings, bracelets, rings, ankle bracelets, toe rings, and an occasional necklace. The list went on and on. Jewelry, clothes, shoes. Every week there was at least one new addition to her home. She was a true shopaholic. That's why her monthly American Express bill was sky-high.

The girls met Friday night at Red Lobster. After they ordered dinner and their drinks arrived, they raised their glasses in the usual toast.

"So what's happening on the *job?*" Tangie asked Charisma.

"Who's happening is more like it," Heather added.

"You got that right." Tangie laughed.

"Well," Charisma began. "Tomorrow night's the game."

"What game?" Tangie and Heather asked in unison.

"Remember I told you he's taking me to the Garden?" Charisma sipped her Miami Vice.

"No," Heather and Tangie said.

"Well, anyway, he bet me dinner that the Lakers would slaughter the Knicks. Only he doesn't know the Knick's are gonna put a hurtin' 'em." She laughed.

"How long has he been working with you?" Tangie asked.

Charisma thought for a moment. "Since early October, why?"

"You two are finally dating. It's about time," Tangie said, reaching for her glass.

"We are *not* dating," Charisma insisted. "We're just going to a game."

"And dinner," Heather added.

"And dinner," Charisma admitted, smoothing down the hair on the back of her neck. "But that's it. Then he'll go home to his house, and I'll go home to mine."

"Not if you both play your cards right." Heather grinned.

The waitress returned with hot cheddar biscuits. Tangie said grace, and they dove right in. Even the eternal dieter, Heather couldn't wait to sink her teeth into them.

"Mmm," she moaned. "I forgot just how good these are." The look on Heather's face was one of pure joy.

"I know, girl," Tangie said. "Just enjoy it."

"Did I tell you guys I got hit on by this woman I went to high school with?" Heather asked.

"Uh-uh," Charisma said.

"Yeah, she was really smooth with her stuff. I ran into her shopping one day, and a couple of days later she met me for lunch. It started to rain so she whipped out her umbrella. Anyway, we were huddled together walking down Jamaica Ave. She was holding the umbrella with one hand, and she had her arm around me trying to keep me dry. Then her hand kind of drops and grazes my breast."

"How do you know it wasn't an accident?" Charisma asked.

"Cause it lasted just a *little* too long, and she couldn't

look me in the eye afterward. And would you believe she actually blushed?"

"Well, you know what they say. Once you have a woman, you never go back," Tangie said.

"That's what they say," Heather agreed.

Charisma was up bright and early Saturday morning. She threw on a royal blue sweat suit and headed for Daisy's for her weekly shampoo. Normally, she went on Sundays after church, but since she was going out that night with Nate she wanted to look her best. It was a few minutes till nine. She parked right across the street from the salon and fed the parking meter. The salon was not yet packed.

"*Hola*, Charisma," Daisy greeted her as she walked through the door. Daisy was a friendly Latina with beautiful brown eyes and an infectious laugh.

"*Hola*, Daisy," she said in return.

"*Que quieres?*" Daisy asked her

"Just a wash and curl," Charisma told her, hanging up her jacket on the coatrack and heading toward the rear.

"Maria, *Charisma quiere shampoo,*" Daisy said.

Maria, a young Puerto Rican brunette, wiped out a chair and motioned for Charisma to have a seat. She shampooed her hair three times before applying a deep conditioner and placing her under the dryer for a few minutes. Charisma used that time to flip through a magazine and refed the meter. Before she knew it, it was time to be rinsed out. Daisy always blow-dried and styled Charisma's hair no matter who shampooed and conditioned her, shaping up a male customer before turning her full attention to Charisma. Customers poured in. The Saturday rush had begun. Daisy trimmed and put the finishing touches on Charisma's do. Finally, Daisy swung her around in the chair and positioned a mirror behind her so that she could see her hair from various angles. Charisma was satisfied. She paid Daisy and tipped Maria. She walked out of Daisy's ready for a Dark and Lovely ad.

She stopped by When We Were Queens on her way home to have Cinderella do her eyebrows. She lucked up at Cinderella's too. Nobody was there yet. She was Cinderella's first customer. Cinderella gave her sister-friend a kiss on both cheeks, and Charisma sat down in the chair.

"Look at you. You must have a hot date tonight." Cinderella smiled. "Call the cops," she said, adding her trademark line. Cinderella cleaned her brows before applying hot wax.

"No, I'm just going out with my new boss," Charisma told her. "He's new in town so I'm kinda showing him around."

"So where are you going?"

"Actually, he's taking me to see the Knicks tonight."

"Oh yeah? What's he like?"

"He seems like a nice guy."

"Okay."

"Too bad he's my boss. I don't think I could ever get involved with someone I work with."

"Why not?" Cinderella asked her.

"Why not? Because when it's good, it's very good. But when it's bad, it's terrible."

"Well, you know, sometimes we expect God to come one way, and he comes from a totally different direction." Cinderella smiled, revealing her beautiful white teeth. "Time will tell, my queen," she sang, removing the strips from Charisma's brows. Then she picked up her tweezers and the plucking began. She shaped them like the professional she was, proving once again why she was the best in town. She gave Charisma the mirror to review her handiwork. Her eyebrows were arched just the way she liked them.

"Mommy was in yesterday on her way to Pathmark to do some Thanksgiving shopping. She's so beautiful. She asked me to introduce you to someone real nice," Cinderella told her.

"My mother's something else."

"Charisma, she just wants you to settle down and have a family. She just wants to see her little grandbabies."

"I know, Cinderella, but I'm not ready to get married. Not yet."

"How's Dex?" she asked.

"He's okay."

"You know something? You deserve all of God's blessings. You are so precious, and I don't want to see you waste yourself on anybody. God has someone special just for you. You'll see."

Charisma was just a touch nervous as she got dressed for an evening with her boss. She couldn't decide what to wear. It wasn't really a date, she reasoned, but she wanted to look good nonetheless. She tried on at least three outfits before settling on black leather jeans and a black suede shirt.

She applied foundation and bronze eye shadow on her lids and then ended up dropping eye shadow all over her bathroom floor.

"Dag," she said, bending down to wipe up the mess. Why was she so uptight? It was only a night out at the Garden. She looked in the mirror and took a few cleansing breaths to calm herself. She finished applying makeup just before the doorbell ran.

Nate was right on time, casually dressed in black as well.

"Come on in," she said with a smile. "Make yourself comfortable. I'll be ready in a minute. Can I get you anything?" she asked from the bathroom.

"No, I'm fine. Nice place," Nate said, looking around. The chrome-and-glass furniture was dust-free and devoid of fingerprints while her bookshelf boasted the latest bestsellers. Nate sat down and waited patiently. Charisma took another five minutes before she was good to go. She couldn't help but notice that his eyes lit up when she entered the room, and for some reason that secretly pleased her.

They decided to take his car into Manhattan. It was high time he learned the city. They took the Belt Parkway to the Van Wyck, eventually ending up in the Midtown Tunnel. It was a lovely, crisp night, and they enjoyed the ride.

Before long they were a few blocks from Madison Square Garden, pulling up into a garage. They got out of the car, and the parking attendant did the rest.

"You could probably be a New York cabbie on the side," she told him.

"And you could probably be *my* boss," he said, referring to her driving skills that first day. They both laughed.

The line for the basketball game wrapped all the way around the block. New Yorkers were tough cookies, and it took more than a half-hour wait in the cold to discourage them from supporting the home team. After about another fifteen minutes outside the line began to move, and the warmth that greeted them at the entrance to the Garden was much appreciated.

With the help of an usher, Nate and Charisma found their seats, and they weren't too shabby, either. They were seated about eleven rows behind center court.

"Great seats," she said, leaning toward him.

It wasn't long before someone came around to take their order. Nate ordered a beer, and Charisma a 7UP. Nate refused to let Charisma buy her own drink. "Save your money," he told her. "You'll need it when the Knicks lose, and you buy me dinner."

She threw back her head and laughed as the pregame show began. "Don't you know those are fightin' words? And practically everyone in here has my back so I suggest that you watch yours."

"I see you New Yorkers are a confident bunch." He grinned.

"Sometimes modesty's overrated, so we just cut to the chase."

Finally, the pregame show ended and the Los Angeles Lakers were introduced amidst a chorus of boos. Then the announcer introduced the New York Knickerbockers and the crowd went wild. Nate gave Charisma a smirk.

"Let the games begin," she said simply at the opening tip-off. Charisma knew her basketball. Not only was she familiar with the players on both teams, she also knew the referee's signals. At one point, she and 95 percent of the Garden disagreed with one of the calls, and they let their displeasure be known. Kobe made two foul shots off the call. By halftime the game was tied at fifty-nine.

Nate headed for the men's room while Charisma stood and stretched. It was hard to tell who'd be buying whom dinner after the game. By the time Nate returned the third quarter had already begun.

He looked up at the score. "Damn!" The Lakers hadn't scored in the last five minutes, and the Knicks were ahead by seven. When Stephon Marbury hit a three-pointer from downtown giving the Knicks a ten-point lead, the Lakers had no choice but to call a time out. The crowd was on their feet, giving the Knicks a standing ovation. The Garden was on fire, and the Knicks were unstoppable. They beat the Lakers 107–92.

Charisma looked at Nate without saying a word. Nate returned the look and laughed.

"You win," he said simply. "I guess it's time to pay up. Where would you like to eat?" he asked as they slowly left the Garden.

"How about Mustang Sally's?" she suggested.

"Your wish is my command," he said. "Lead the way."

It was a perfect autumn night for walking in the city. Charisma loved Manhattan. No other place in the world could compare. When she was a teenager, she dreamed of going to France. She'd be the toast of Paris and would shop at all the high class boutiques along the Champs-Elysées. Her father promised to take her there one day. When Charisma grew up, she discovered the city and told her friends that she'd take Manhattan, preferring the city that never sleeps to the City of Lights.

Surprisingly, they only waited twenty minutes for a table. The place was packed after the game, but the turnover was fast. They slid into a booth and ordered drinks. It was a martini night. Nate ordered apple martinis while Charisma drank chocolate ones. By the time the appetizers came around they were both mellowing out and enjoying each other's company.

"You are just full of surprises, aren't you, Miss Dearborn?"

"Whatever do you mean, Mr. Arquette?"

"Well, I mean you have beauty, brains, and you know all about basketball. What more could a man possible want? You must have a deep, dark side. Am I right?"

She tilted her head to the right and circled the rim of her martini glass with her finger. "Doesn't everyone?" she said, shrugging.

"Let me guess. You go around slashing men's tires if they beat you out of a parking spot."

"Only if I'm late for work and the new boss is due that morning," she added. "But enough about me. Let's talk about you."

"Okay. What would you like to know?"

"You probably haven't lived here long enough to establish a relationship, but there has to be someone in your life. Are you into long-distance relationships?"

"Not me. I had one right after college, and I promised myself never, ever again. It's like setting yourself up for failure. It's a no-win situation. Why bother?"

"Okay, then you must be into Internet sex."

"You must be kidding?" He laughed.

"I just can't imagine how a man like you can be walking around unattached. I mean you have a good job. *With* dental benefits," she stressed, laughing.

"With dental benefits," he agreed.

"You seem to have a lot going for you. What's the deal?"

"Well, if you gave me the chance to wear you out in the bedroom, maybe I could prove to you that I'm your Mr. Right," he said, referring to an earlier conversation that they had had. "But that's strictly off the record."

Charisma was caught completely off guard. For a minute their eyes locked, and they sat in silence. Finally, she looked away.

"I shouldn't have said that. I'm sorry," Nate apologized.

"That's a tempting offer," she said, smoothing down the hair on the back of her neck, her face flushed with excitement. "But just like you don't do long-distance relationships, I don't do my bosses."

As if on cue, the waitress arrived with their piping-hot pizza.

7

Tangie

Tangie had been in the gym for about an hour when she was called to the front desk. Before she even made it all the way up there, she could see him standing there. It was Blade. Blade was a regular at the gym, working out a good five days a week. Tangie wished that he would just go on with his workout and let her be, but it wasn't that simple.

"Tangie, we need to talk," he began.

"Really? About what?"

"Are you still mad at me?"

"No, I'm not mad at you. I'm through with you. And would you mind not making a scene? I work here."

"Calm down, Tangie. Nobody's trying to make a scene, but I told you. I was at work the other night. Don't fault a man for making a living."

"Don't even *try* it," she said, referring to his lame attempt to flip the script. "I am sick and tired of being at the bottom on your list of priorities. You told me you were coming by for our anniversary. I planned a nice evening for us, and you show up at two AM Sunday morning like I'm just an afterthought or something. Find someone else to be your doormat. I'm through." Without so much as a backward glance, Tangie walked away.

When she arrived home that evening, Blade was standing on her front porch with a dozen red roses. *How trite. The man doesn't have an original bone in his body.*

"What are you doing here, Blade?" she said, the tiredness evident in her voice.

"I wanna take you out to dinner."

"Why?"

"I know you're tired, and I just wanted to do something to make your life a little easier."

"You should've thought of that two years ago."

"Tangie, please. I'm really trying. And it's cold as hell out here."

She looked into his eyes and decided to hear him out. "So where are you taking me?"

"Name the place."

"I'm not changing my clothes," she told him.

"How about the diner?"

"Fine."

She put her house keys back into her purse and got into the car. "So whose car did you steal?"

"It's a rental," he admitted as he started the ignition. They drove the short distance to the diner in silence. It was only after the waitress took their orders that they spoke.

"I've been doing a lot of thinking about us lately," Blade began. "And I really want this relationship to work."

"Why do you suddenly want this relationship to work?"

"Because you're important to me." He sat in silence for a moment as the waitress returned with their meals. "I don't want to lose you, baby." He reached out for her hand and brought it up to his lips. "I need you, baby." He stared at her intensely and a tear formed in the corner of his eye. "Please, baby, I promise to be a better man."

"Do you promise?" she asked.

He nodded slowly, unable to speak.

She returned his glance and a tear welled up in her eye as well. "Let's go home," she said simply.

"Life never turns out the way you plan it," Tangie said to Charisma as they sat in Tangie's living room, listening to Mary J. Blige. "I mean, I thought that by thirty-four I'd have a few years of marriage under my belt and at least one crumb snatcher on my hip. But here I am miserably single. Go figure."

"Tangie, you have plenty of time for that. Trust me. You still have your whole life ahead of you. We both do."

"I'm not cut out for this, Charisma. I'm meant to be part of a couple."

"And you *will* be when the time is right."

"See, that's why I can't understand why you're not giving Nate more play. You know he wants you. All you and Dex have are weekly drive-bys with no strings attached."

"And that's enough for me," Charisma said.

"You think like a man. Don't you want to plan a wedding and be princess for a day?"

"Are you kidding me?" Charisma laughed. "I was *born* a princess. You're starting to sound like a desperate woman."

"I need a drink," Tangie said, getting up to make a batch of chocolate martinis.

"I think we both do," Charisma said.

Just then the phone rang. "Will you get that?" Tangie yelled from the kitchen.

"Okay," Charisma shot back.

It was Heather, apologizing for not being able to make it over that night. She had to work late but wouldn't miss their breakfast date on Saturday.

"That was Heather," Charisma told Tangie as she returned from the kitchen bearing a tray with a pitcher of wicked martinis and two glasses. Tangie poured them both a glass and laid back on the sofa just as the phone rang again. Tangie checked her caller ID.

"Hello?"

It was Blade.

"Hi, baby. How's it going?" She paused, listening to his response. "No problem, take your time. Charisma and I are just hanging out. See you later. Okay, bye."

"You should've let your machine pick up. Make him wonder where you are sometimes. I think you're too available to him," Charisma said.

"No, I don't want to start playing games, and he's been on his best behavior lately."

"Really?"

"I know. Hard to believe, right?" Tangie asked.

"Exactly," Charisma said, making a dent in her first martini.

Confident that Tangie was home and staying *out* of trouble, Blade was ready to get *in* to some. His finger had been itching to hit Blondie on her cell phone ever since he first met her. He worked out an extra hour at the gym just to release some of that nervous energy. Luckily it was Tangie's day off, and he could concentrate on other things.

He checked his watch. It was a little after seven. He gave her a call. Her phone just rang and rang. Funny, he didn't even know her name, and it never occurred to him that she could have given him a fake number. It wasn't even a thought; as good as he looked that night at the concert, please.

Finally, she picked up. "Hello?"

"What's up, baby?"

"Who is this?" she asked.

"It's Blade. We met at the Jay-Z concert. You gave me your number."

"Hey, brown sugar." She smiled. "I was wondering when

you'd call. I was beginning to think you'd forgotten about me.'

"Forgotten about you? I may not know your name, but I definitely got your number."

"And what would that be?" she asked.

"I think we have a definite vibe going on. I mean, we're both feelin' each other. Am I right?"

Her response was a throaty laugh.

"I can't get you out of my mind. When can I see you?"

She paused for a moment. "What are you doing tomorrow night?"

"Gettin' with you, I hope. Just say where, and I'll be there."

"How about the Sandbox in Hempstead?"

"On Peninsula Ave?"

"Yeah, let's meet there tomorrow night around ten?"

"That'll work," Blade said simply, praying he could get someone to cover for him at the G-Spot as he made plans to get into hers.

"Great, see you then," she said.

"Hold up. Hold up," Blade said. "What's your name?"

"Chase," she said.

"Chase," he echoed. "I like that."

"See you tomorrow night."

"Aight."

Blade quickly dialed his buddy Jason to fill in for him tomorrow night. Jason couldn't but thought that maybe Alec could. He was right. Alec needed to make some extra cash and was more than willing to help Blade out. Blade could already feel a rise at the thought of new meat on his table.

Blade spent the next day working out at the gym and washing his newly acquired ride. He even stopped by his barber for a fresh cut. Then he came home, took a nap, showered, and got ready to meet Chase.

He got to the bar around ten-fifteen and scoped out the

place from the parking lot before heading in. It was packed even for a Friday night. He stood at the bar and ordered a beer, checking out the clientele—mostly white, sprinkled with a few blacks.

His cell phone vibrated. It was probably Chase, he thought as he retrieved it from the inside of his jacket pocket. Nope, it was Tangie. He wasn't in the mood for Tangie, not tonight.

He let his voice mail pick up as he took another sip of beer. Another ten minutes went by and no sign of Chase. He ordered another beer. Was she playing games? He'd give her a few more minutes, and then he'd bounce. It was already after eleven. He finished his beer, paid the bartender, and prepared to leave. Just as he stood he felt a pair of hands on his shoulders.

"Going somewhere?"

He turned. It was Chase.

Blade broke out in a grin. "Playing hard to get?"

"Not me." She smiled mischievously. Just then a stool opened up and she sat down next to him.

"So what's the hot drink around here?" Blade asked her

"Mojitos. Buy me one?"

He laughed. "I wouldn't have it any other way," Blade said, signaling the bartender. "Let me have two mojitos," he told him.

The bartender looked at Blade first and then Chase—apparently not thrilled to see them coupled up. He rolled his eyes ever so slightly, prepared their drinks, and returned with them momentarily.

Blade took a sip of his drink. "Excuse me a minute. I'll be right back," he said, heading for the men's room.

Chase ran a perfectly manicured hand through her blond locks. The bartender moved in on her.

"So what's up with you and Mandingo?" he asked.

"What's it to ya?" she shot back.

He shook his head, mumbled something under his breath, and walked away.

Chase recalled as a twelve-year-old being in a drugstore with her mother. A black guy asked the pharmacist for extra-large condoms. The pharmacist had told him no, just what was on the shelf. He turned to the other pharmacist and asked, his voice dripping with sarcasm, "What the hell does he want, a freaking garbage bag?" Chase hadn't understood then, but she understood all too well now. White men were good for wining and dining her, but when her body ached, only a brotha would do. She silently prayed that Blade would deliver her.

As if on cue, Blade returned from the men's room. "I think it's time we get this party started." He winked.

Chase checked her watch. "And not a minute too soon," she said, her lips curling into a wicked smile.

"Why the hell isn't he answering his cell?" Tangie said to Charisma and Heather as they sat on the floor of Tangie's living room, eating Jamaican beef patties.

Tangie had stopped by Wilson's West Indian Bakery on Guy R. Brewer Boulevard across from Rochdale on her way home from work for the spicy treats. She had bought a dozen, knowing how much they all loved them. They were easily the best she had ever tasted, bar none. Even Heather wolfed down two.

"I have been calling that man all freakin' day. I am fed up with his crap. I've had it up to here." She motioned to her chin.

"I thought you erased his numbers from your life," Charisma said.

"I did, but I can't help it if I have a memory like an elephant," Tangie shot back.

"Why do you let him drive you crazy?" Heather asked. "You know how he is. You should be used to him by now."

"I know, but I thought this time would be different. I thought he had changed."

"Sweetie, I know you want to believe in Blade, but one tear does not a changed man make," Charisma said.

"For all you know, he sprinkled some salt in his eyes when you weren't looking." Heather said, laughing and Tangie rolled her eyes.

"He knows how to play the game. Don't underestimate him," Charisma warned. "And what you have with Blade right now is as good as it gets. He'll never try to wine and dine you again. He's already got you."

"You're such a male basher," Tangie told her,

"No," Charisma insisted. "But it's time you learned how the game is played,"

Tangie reached for her cell and dialed his number once again.

"Starting now," Charisma continued. "Tangie, put the phone down. There is no reason you should be blowing up his phone like that. You've called him a good five times in the last half hour. Enough already. If he hasn't answered by now, he ain't answering. Don't you get it?"

Reluctantly, Tangie flipped her phone shut.

"Good girl," Heather said, rubbing her back.

"Attagirl," Charisma agreed. "Remember, behind every successful woman is herself."

Tangie sighed. She wasn't feeling it.

Blade had gotten Tangie's messages—all eight of them, not to mention the missed calls and hang ups. He laughed to himself. Everybody wanted a piece of sweet daddy, but Blade was busy kicking it with Chase. They had gone out drinking that night. She was fired up and couldn't keep her hands off of him so they got a room.

He had barely closed the door before she was all over him. Chase slid her alcohol-flavored tongue in his mouth and kissed him hard. Somehow, they found their way to the bed, where she unbuckled his belt and undid his pants. Just as she unzipped his fly, Blade flipped her onto her back and unbuttoned her sweater, revealing a little black lace bra that opened in front. He then proceeded to remove her jeans, revealing a matching thong. He smiled to himself as he feasted on her curves, but Chase wanted more than just an appreciative glance. She unhooked her bra, burying his face in her twin peaks. His mouth quickly found her strawberry nipples, and he sucked on them until they were big and hard. A slight moan escaped her lips as she slid out of her panties.

Blade stood and quickly undressed, fishing for a rubber to cover his now rock-hard dick. Chase grinned in anticipation and spread her legs invitingly as he returned to the bed and slid a finger inside of her, enjoying the wetness of her pussy. He climbed on top. When neither of them could stand it anymore, he entered her and rested for a moment. No matter how many women he had been with, there was never anything like that first dip in a new sauna. It was the thrill of victory. Lil' man couldn't stay away from those steam baths if his life depended on it. It was an obsession that kept Blade in trouble time and time again. On the other hand, it served him well. Real well.

He turned his attention to fucking the hell out of the blond pussy underneath him, enjoying her just as much as she was enjoying him. Chase was a loud one. Finally, her body began twitching in the spasms that let him know his mission was successful. He let go himself and came too, collapsing in a pool of sweat, thoroughly exhausted. He lay silent for a moment, his chest rising and falling as he tried to catch his breath.

Chase climbed on top of him. "Mmm," she purred softly.

"You are something else. You know that?" he said.

She smiled and snuggled up to him as he rubbed her back.

"Ready for some more?" Chase asked.

In response he grabbed her ass and rolled her right over. She laughed, definitely ready for more.

Stone Canyon wondered where the hell his granddaughter was as his family prepared for Sunday Mass. She knew how important it was to him, and yet she tried his patience at least twice a month. When she left the house last night for God only knows where, didn't he remind her to be home in time for church? And didn't she assure him that she would? It was already after seven and she was nowhere in sight. He called her cell phone. No answer. Next, he tried calling her best friend Loren, who had obviously been sleeping.

"Hello?" she said, her voice groggy with sleep.

"Loren, this is Stone Canyon."

"Yes, Mr. Canyon." She cleared her throat.

"Have you heard from Chase?"

"Uh, yeah," she lied. "She just left. We went out last night and got back really late. She spent the night here."

"Okay, Loren, sorry to wake you."

"No problem, Mr. Canyon, buh-bye."

Loren disconnected and immediately dialed Chase. Chase picked up on the fourth ring, awakened by Loren's ring tone.

"Yeah, what's up?" Chase asked.

"Your grandfather just called here looking for you. Where the hell are you?"

"I'll explain later," she said simply. "What did you tell him?"

"That you crashed at my house last night, and that you had just left."

"Shit," Chase said, jumping up out of bed. "I already missed Mass last Sunday. What time is it?"

"Seven-fifteen."

"Well, playtime's over," she said, searching for her panties. "Thanks for covering for me. I owe you."

"No problem. Just get your buns home."

"I'm leaving now," Chase said, diving into her black jeans and looking for her left shoe. Where the hell was it?

Blade stirred just as she hung up. He tried to pull her back to bed.

"Gotta go, babe. I am so late it isn't even funny." She kissed him quickly on the cheek, grabbed her purse and keys, and headed out the door.

Stone knew it was time to start keeping tabs on his granddaughter—again. Chase had always been a wild child, but lately she was taking it to a whole new level. She'd come home at all hours of the night, or not at all. And he didn't believe she was spending all that time with her girl-friend Loren, either.

Whatever meetings he had that day would have to be rescheduled. He was already late for his appointment with Johnston's Athletics Equipment and time was money. Thank goodness his driver was waiting for him as he left the building.

Stone was just about ready to open his fifth health club. He met Nico Antonelli, his corporate attorney, downstairs and together they closed the deal. Though only thirty-five, Nico was a brilliant attorney, and Stone was lucky to have him on his team.

Two hours later, the two were back in Stone's office sip-ping champagne. "I'd love to see the look on the face of that loan officer who turned me down. What was his name again?" Stone asked.

"Dearborn," Nico said.

"That shithead," Stone said, refilling their flutes. "Why don't you come over for dinner tonight? My granddaughter would love to see you."

"You know Chase is too wild for me," Nico admitted, draining his glass.

"One day my granddaughter will come to her senses. I'll get you in the family yet." He winked.

As if on cue, Stone's secretary, Juana, entered with her steno pad ready for dictation. Familiar with the routine, Nico grabbed his coat and briefcase and prepared to leave. Stone stood as well and walked his attorney to the door.

"Good job," he told him, firmly shaking his hand.

"Give my regards to the family."

"Take care, Nico."

Juana and Stone both waited for the elevator to close before she locked the office door. Stone took her in her arms. She stroked his head, loving the feel of his white mane. For a seventy-two-year-old man, his hair was remarkably thick, and their passionate kisses always warmed up his steel blue eyes, something that his wife Lola hadn't done in years.

Juana had been his mistress for more than five years. He took care of her rent and expenses in exchange for the best sex he'd had in years. At forty-one, Juana wasn't some starry-eyed bimbo expecting her Mrs. degree. She knew that she was simply a diversion for her boss and that he would never leave his wife. But she was willing to stay with him as long as both their needs were met.

Juana freed her French twist as their two bodies riveted toward the blue leather custom-designed sofa that exactly matched his eyes. The sofa was imported from Italy, and he had had the deliverymen return it twice before the furniture store landed the perfect shade. Juana paused for a moment to retrieve a blanket from the closet to cover the sofa. Within minutes the Valentino suit and silk blouse he had bought her on one of their shopping sprees in Manhattan joined his in a heap on the carpet. It wasn't long before they were working it out on top of the blanket. She rode him like a bronco, rolling her hips with the same intensity that she rolled her *R*'s. It wasn't long before he was totally spent, and they lay satisfied on the sofa.

They dozed off for a minute until they were awakened by the phone. A completely naked Juana jumped up to answer it while Stone's eyes followed her ripe body admiringly.

"Just a minute, Mr. Caparelli." Juana handed the phone to Stone.

"Yes, Zynk," Stone said, rising and wrapping the blanket around his waist. "Okay, I'll meet you at O'Neil's in half an hour," he said before hanging up.

Thirty minutes later Stone and Zynk were seated at a table in O'Neil's Pub and Steakhouse. Zynk was a private investigator, and Stone had hired him to keep tabs on Chase. They ordered drinks and got straight to the point.

"So what did you find out, Zynk?"

"Well, Mr. Canyon, your granddaughter is a very busy lady. Seems like she has a new friend." He reached into his jacket pocket and removed an envelope, which he handed to Stone.

Stone opened the envelope, revealing photos of Chase and some black guy going into and coming out of a bar and then into a hotel.

"Who is he?" Stone asked.

"Blake Watson. They call him Blade."

"Blade, huh? Nothing surprises me anymore. What does he do?"

"He an exotic dancer at some club called the G-Spot."

"It figures. Do you think he knows how much she's worth?"

"I'm not sure, Mr. Canyon, but I will say they hit the hotel about twice a week. And a couple of times they made out in the back of his car. Apparently, they've been seeing each other hot and heavy for almost a month now."

Stone shook his head in disgust. "Please spare me the details. My granddaughter is going to give me a heart attack yet." He took a sip of his vodka.

"So what's the next move?" Zynk asked.

"I want you to set up an appointment between this Blade character and me. There is no way I'm letting this shithead mess over my granddaughter, and I sure as hell don't need the publicity. Everybody has a price. I'll write him a check with enough zeros to cover his."

Tangie hadn't seen Blade in weeks, and it hurt. She was beginning to think there was someone else. He didn't return her phone calls or he was always working. She didn't wear rejection very well. She never had.

Tangie got to the gym early Tuesday morning, surprised by Blade's presence. He was in the back lifting weights and didn't see her at first. It was only when she stopped in front of the women's locker room to speak to a coworker that he caught her voice and walked over to her.

"What's going on?" he asked her.

"Hey," she said coolly.

"Listen, I want to see you tonight. Are you busy?"

"I'm not sure. What did you have in mind?" she asked.

"I have a business appointment this afternoon, and I thought if everything goes well maybe you could come by and I'd make us dinner. How does that sound?"

"Sounds doable."

"It sure does," he agreed. "What time do you get off work?"

"Six."

"Why don't I call you when I get in?"

"You do that," she said, feeling his eyes on her butt as she walked away.

8

Heather

Heather worked late at the library Wednesday evening. It was her second late night that week, and she felt like she was coming down with a cold. Thankfully, she was off the next couple of days so she took her schedule in stride. She clocked out. Forty-eight hours of sweet freedom before she returned to work.

By the time she left work, visions of a hot bubble bath were what navigated her home and into the tub. She eased into the water, feeling like the original Calgon lady.

Afterward, she checked out her body in the bathroom mirror. She turned, viewing herself from various angles, covering her nose with her fingers. Shit. Apparently, all the eating she had done lately was catching up with her. She stepped on the scale, looking over her pouch down to her toes. Damn, she was back to her pre–diet pill weight. Twenty pounds down the drain. She kicked the scale back into the corner, turned off the light, and shut the bathroom door.

Heather went straight to bed, but her stomach wouldn't let her sleep. Should she or shouldn't she? She tossed and turned for a while until her cravings won the battle. Hell, if it was too late for dinner it only meant it was time for a late-night snack.

She headed for the kitchen. With one hand she grabbed the half pound of ground beef from the bottom shelf of her fridge while snatching a small onion with the other. She closed the door with her leg. Heather reached under the microwave shelf for her George Foreman, placed it on her counter and plugged it in. She quickly seasoned the meat and chopped up the onion before mixing it up in the bowl. By then the grilling surface was hot, sizzling as it met the beef. She reached for a saucer and the bag of potato buns in the bread box.

She slid the burger on the bun, topped it with a red onion ring and a dab of hickory and brown sugar barbecue sauce. Heather hadn't eaten all day. She started to pop a diet pill into her mouth, but who was she kidding? Instead, she threw the half-used bottle in the trash. Nothing but net. She smiled as she bit into the juicy burger, the sweet, tangy sauce oozing ever so slightly from the corners of her mouth. She lapped it up with her tongue. It didn't get much better. She washed the burger down with a glass of raspberry lemonade, suddenly wide awake, then headed into the living room and grabbed the remote. *Waiting to Exhale* was on. She made a quick trip to the kitchen and snatched the package of chocolate chip cookies off the counter. Heather ate an entire sleeve of cookies before the first commercial. Then she conked out on the couch.

The next morning Heather cleaned her basement apartment and did laundry before stepping one foot outside her door. It was a brisk November day, worthy of a turtleneck and leather jacket. On second thought, she went back home and grabbed a scarf. She was susceptible to colds at the drop of a hat. She spotted a neighbor watching her as she sashayed down the block to her parked car. She was tempted to walk backward as much press her behind got. She always caught him checking her out. Unfortunately, so did his wife. His tongue might as well have been hanging out his mouth. Men, could they be any more obvious?

The mechanic had given her car a clean bill of health when she picked it up from the shop the other day. With the car seat pushed all the way back, she eased into her late-model coupe. With all the heavy eating she'd been doing lately, she had developed a steering wheel gut. Apparently, the diet pills were useless if she continued to eat like a pig. She still couldn't believe she had regained twenty pounds. It was back to the drawing board. Luckily, her car started right up. She hated spending the money on a new alternator, but it was either that or the bus. She headed for the Green Acres Mall to pay her Ashley Stewart bill. Ever since her payment got lost in the mail about six months ago, she paid in person. She worked too hard for her money to blow it on late fees.

The parking lot was full. Maybe her New Year's resolution would be to start parking farther away from her destination, but for now she lucked up with a spot a few feet from the entrance.

Though surrounded by new holiday merchandise, Heather grit her teeth, paid her bill in full, and walked out the store. She checked her watch. It was too early for lunch, but a Dunkin' Donuts coffee coolatta would more than hit the spot. She knew it was a bad move on her part, but maybe if she cut back for the rest of the day she'd be okay. Walking to the center of the first floor, she caught a glimpse of her reflection in a mirror before riding the escalator up. Even without a stitch of makeup, she seemed to invoke the wrath of a female passerby or two. They rolled their eyes as they crossed her path. It didn't seem to matter that an extra sixty pounds padded her girth, their stares were still icy.

As usual, Heather zoned the women out, focusing instead on walking down to Dunkin' Dounuts. She got her hazelnut-flavored drink, found a seat in the food court, and took a load off her feet. She closed her eyes as the coffee crept down her throat, glad she'd had it made with real cream instead of watery skim milk.

Heather sucked down another mouthful with her French manicured fingertips gently grasping the straw. She stirred her coolatta slowly, her mind drifting to her car. Lord only knew how much she needed a new one, but she hated another expense. At least her car was paid for. She had more than the recommended twelve months of living expenses saved in her bank account, but that was beside the point. She just wasn't ready for another bill.

She was so engrossed in her thoughts that she barely noticed the man standing over her until his shadow became evident, hovering on the table.

She sneezed unexpectedly, giving him the perfect opening.

"Bless you," he said simply. "I couldn't help noticing you from across the way." Heather looked up at him. He was about five feet nine with heavy eyebrows and a full beard, dressed in cords, a crewneck sweater, and a leather jacket. He handed Heather a business card inscribed A+ SIZE MODELING AGENCY.

He looked familiar. Where had she seen him before? Then it dawned on her.

TV One had recently done a show on the plus-size modeling industry.

"I know you've heard this before, but you look amazing. Ever consider modeling?"

"Oh sure, every night as I nuke the Häagen-Dazs," she assured him.

"You laugh, but I'm serious," he said. "Do me a favor. When you drop forty pounds, give me a call. I'll be waiting by the phone." He smiled. "Better yet, make that twenty pounds, as good as you look."

"Whatever," Heather said under her breath as he walked away. She shook her head. How long had she been waiting to be "discovered" by an agent? Too long. But she didn't have the chutzpah to sashay herself down to a modeling agency in the city and take her chances. She was too afraid that they'd laugh her big fat ass all the way back to Queens. And now look what happened. Twenty pounds. Twenty freakin' pounds. Why couldn't their paths have crossed last week? Was life fair or what? She drove to Red Lobster and ordered a dozen cheddar biscuits to take out. Unfortunately, they didn't make it home. That night as she stared at her reflection in the mirror—nose and all—she made a decision. Slowly, she leaned over the toilet and stuck three fingers down her throat. The rest was easy. It would be her little secret.

Later that week, Heather dialed Charisma and Tangie for a threeway about getting together that night.

"Let's have dinner at Cabana," Charisma suggested.

"Cabana?" Heather whined. "They have to practically roll us out the door every time we eat there. Thanksgiving'll be here before you know it. How about Manhattan Proper for drinks?"

"Okay, Heather. We'll do Manhattan Proper," Tangie said. "You need me to pick you up?"

"No, I'm good," Heather reassured her.

"Meet you guys there at seven?" Charisma asked.

"Seven's good," Heather agreed before hanging up.

Apparently, it wasn't. Tangie and Charisma waited over half an hour for Heather to show that night.

"That damned car," Tangie said. "I knew one of us should've picked her up."

"I'll call her cell phone." Charisma dialed Heather's cell phone. "I'm just getting her voice mail." Chrisma shook her head.

"I hope she's not stranded somewhere." Tangie reached for her wineglass.

"Let me call her house. Maybe she hasn't left yet. It's ringing," she told Tangie. "Heather, we're at Manhattan Proper waiting for you. It's something to eight. Call us when you get this message."

"Hello?" Heather yawned.

"Heather?" Charisma said. "What's wrong? Were you sleeping?"

"What time is it?" Heather asked her.

"It's a quarter to eight."

"Oh, my gosh. I'm so sorry. I came home and took some cold medicine, and I guess it knocked me out."

"Well, stay home and get some rest, Heather. We'll talk to you tomorrow."

"Okay, Charisma. Bye."

"What happened?" Tangie asked Charisma.

"She's all right. She was asleep. She took some cold medicine, and it made her drowsy." Charisma popped a couple of peanuts in her mouth.

"Oh, okay. I'm starving. Let's eat something and call it a night," Tangie said.

"Good idea. I have an early meeting tomorrow. You wanna hear something funny?" she asked without waiting for an answer. "I've been debating whether I should invite Nate over for Thanksgiving dinner."

"Are you cooking?" Tangie asked.

"No, my mother's having Thanksgiving dinner, and I thought that maybe if he didn't have plans he could have dinner with us."

"Do it," Tangie pleaded. "The holidays are the perfect

time to get together. Wait a minute. Didn't you say he has a son?"

"Yeah, he has a teenaged son. Maybe he's already made plans to spend Thanksgiving with him," Charisma said.

"Ask him anyway," Tangie insisted. "Plans change."

"I don't know. You know Dex always comes by."

"So, the more the merrier. Wait a minute, Charisma. Don't forget," Tangie said, raising her glass. "Behind every successful woman is herself."

"I must be crazy to let you talk me into this." Charisma shook her head.

Heather spent the following Monday at the main branch of the New York Public Library in Manhattan. She took the E train to Times Square and walked a few blocks to Fifth Avenue. She had stood all the way from Jamaica Center Parsons Archer to Forty-second Street, and no matter how comfortable her shoes had started out, the low-heeled leather sling pump was rubbing against the corn on her right pinkie toe. She double-checked her purse to make sure she hadn't forgotten her toothbrush and whitening toothpaste. She had done a lot of research lately on bulimia, and the advice was all the same: Take special care of your teeth to prevent gray or yellow teeth from tooth erosion. Also, stomach acids in vomit eat away at tooth enamel and cause bad breath. The last thing Heather wanted to do was to offend anyone with her breath.

Compared to the Queens Library in Jamaica, where she worked, the Manhattan library was like a universe of knowledge. From the moment she hurried up the stairs guarded on either side by statues of the landmark lions, she felt like she was entering the halls of wisdom.

Heather removed her coat and draped it over her left arm. As instructed, she signed in at the front desk. Her ID badge, clearly displayed, hung around her neck. She road the elevator to the firth floor and found room 503.

The class was mandatory for all library personnel, and though most employees were fortunate enough to be taught in their home branch, Heather was unlucky enough to have to schlep to Manhattan that day. There were approximately one hundred people in the class and after introducing herself the lecturer asked everyone to move up as close to the front as possible, filling in all empty seats. Heather chose an aisle seat.

The lecture lasted for three hours and then they broke for lunch. She walked to the nearest bank of elevators and waited along with the others. Four elevators passed before she would get one, and even that elevator was packed to the gills. Heather left the building and walked around the corner to the Bryant Park Grill.

She didn't beat the lunch crowd and had to wait fifteen minutes for a table. The waitress brought her a glass of water, with which Heather washed down her diet pills. When she returned to take Heather's order, she took one look at the menu and ordered a slice of chocolate-layer cake and coffee. She checked out her surroundings. The skinny minis, as she called them, were in rare form, looking as though they had just stepped out of the pages of *Vogue*. Then again, considering that she was in Bryant Park, home of New York's Fashion Week, some of them probably had.

Heather didn't know what made her eyes widen more—the sight of *Black Enterprise*'s Ed Gordon walking past her table or the arrival of her lunch. In either case, presentation was everything and the combination nearly took her breath away. Certain that she'd never sample his succulently full, juicy lips, she resolved to enjoy her meal in between stealing glances at his impressive form. The cake, which sat a full five inches high, was simply mouth-watering with chocolate shavings galore. Heather cleaned the last morsel of chocolate from her plate like it was the most precious commodity on earth. So much for saving some for manners.

She left the restaurant, straining her neck for one last glimpse of Ed Gordon, but he was nowhere to be seen. It was just as well. He'd probably never give someone like her a second thought anyway.

She took one last backward glance as she left the establishment and ran smack into a passerby on the sidewalk. She was more startled than he was.

"Oh, my goodness, I'm so sorry," she said as they both got their bearings.

"Wait a minute. I know you. We met in the Green Acres Mall, right?" he asked. "I'm from the modeling agency."

"That's right," Heather agreed.

"My name's Don."

"I'm Heather," she said simply.

"How are you?" he asked.

"I'm fine, just running a little late."

Here, take another card," he said, extending his arm. "And don't forget to give me a call when your're ready for a career change. It's all up to you."

She took the card and hurried back to the library.

Against her better judgment, Heather spent Tuesday night grocery shopping. Pathmark was open twenty-four hours a day, and apparently half of Springfield Gardens was there too in preparation for Thanksgiving. A cute-looking guy followed her up and down the aisles, trying to make eye contact. When he got up the nerve, he introduced himself as Jamal and gave her his home number. She took his number, promising nothing. His eyes lit up nonetheless. In the frozen food department two women were fighting over the last thirty-pound turkey, even though management assured them that more would be delivered the next day. From the looks of the checkout lines, you'd think they were giving food away. Heather made certain that she stuck to her grocery list. By the time she walked out the door, the thought of a hot bubble bath was the only think that kept her sane. That and the box of chocolate chip cookies she'd be devouring later that night before she embarked on her secret ritual.

Her mother was working a double shift at the hospital and wouldn't be home until Wednesday evening. Since Heather was only working half a day, she agreed to start the cooking. Thanksgiving was easily her favorite holiday. The thought of turkey and dressing, macroni and cheese, greens, mashed potatoes and gravy—not to mention a slew of delectable desserts—always put a smile on her face.

They were expecting ten for dinner. She looked forward to seeing her family. Even though Heather was adopted, she never thought of them as anything less than that. Heather never told another living soul except Charisma and Tangie about her birth. They were the closest she had to sisters. It was nobody else's business.

By the time she got to bed that night, it was after midnight. She tossed and turned and barely made it to work on time. It was a quiet day at work since most people were home cooking and baking. The four hours that she worked crept by like a centipede crawling against a windstorm. Her zebra-print slingpumps hurt so badly that she felt like her feet were dying a slow death. Now she remembered why she hadn't worn them in years. It was a relief when noon came and she could wish her coworkers a happy Thanksgiving—especially since she wasn't due back until Monday.

Feeling like steak knives were eating away at her feet, Heather crept to Hillside Avenue where her car was parked. She slipped off her shoes and exhaled. Thankfully, the car started right up, but traffic was a nightmare. Everybody and their mother must have left work early that day.

The minute she arrived home, she threw her shoes in the hamper. That way she wouldn't be tempted to wear them again. At least not anytime soon. She handled her business in the bathroom, making certain to brush and rinse thoroughly with mouthwash. She examined her teeth carefully in the mirror. Thank goodness, they still looked the same. Then she walked upstairs. Her mother was already in the kitchen making the dressing.

"Hey, Mom." Heather grabbed a bottle of water from the fridge and plopped down at the kitchen table. Her mother was busy chopping green peppers, onions, and celery. The sweet potatoes and cornbread were already baking.. Even though the food processor sat right in the cabinet above her head, Leola chose to cook the old-fashioned way.

"Hi, boobie." Leola stopped just long enough to lean over and exchange a kiss with her daughter before returning to the tasks at hand.

"How was your day?" Heather asked.

"Those double shifts are a killer." Leola shook her head. "Thank God I'm off the next couple days. I just may sleep all day Friday. I'm exhausted."

"Here, I'll take over. You go get some rest." Heather shooed her mother away.

"Boobie, you're tired too," Leola said.

"I can handle it. You taught me well, remember?"

"Okay," Leola said. "I'm just going to take a quick nap. Call me if you need me."

"Okay, Ma. Go get some rest. Everything's under control."

"Call me if you need me." she said again, yawning as she retired to her bedroom.

Heather finished chopping up the veggies and took a skillet out of the bottom cabinet. She put a small amount of oil in the pan and proceeded to cook them until they were tender. She checked the cornbread to make certain it was browning nicely. When the sweet potatoes were done, she pulled out the mixer and added all the ingredients for the four pies. After washing the greens several times, she added them to the pot of smoked turkey to cook.

Heather took a quick break before starting on the cakes. She sat down at the kitchen table and pulled up a chair upon which to elevate her slightly swollen ankles. It would be a long night, but at least she could save the macroni and cheese and mashed potatoes until the morning. That way they wouldn't dry out. Heather got up, went to the fridge and then the cupboard. She placed all the ingredients for the cakes on the table and the counter. Next, she oiled and floured the pans. She mixed the batter for both cakes and poured it into the pans, saving just enough batter on the spoon for a double reward. She loved licking the spoon as a little girl. Some things never changed. Once the cakes were in the oven, Heather busied herself cleaning up the kitchen. Her mother taught her to clean up as she went along so there really wasn't much left to do.

Next, she dusted and vacuumed the living room and dining room. She also cleaned the bathroom. The aroma of the cakes baking in the oven put a smile on her face, and she was able to finish mopping the kitchen floor. By the time she finished cleaning her mother's house, it was after one AM. Sweating, she eased herself down the basement steps to her apartment, her knees creaking from the household workout. She took a two-minute shower and passed out as soon as her head hit the pillow.

Heather woke up Thanksgiving morning to the aroma of roasting in the oven. She made a quick call to Charisma before getting up. She was still upset about the twenty pounds. She could have been halfway to a modeling contract. She could kick herself. Charisma assured her that if she did it once, she could do it again. The world wasn't over. Heather had to laugh at that one. She hung up, comforted. Charisma would make a good mother one day. She got up, put on her robe, and headed upstairs to her mother's kitchen. Leola was pouring herself a cup of coffee.

"Good morning, sweetie. Want some coffee?" she asked her daughter.

"Sure," she said. "You're up early."

"I got up around five and put the turkey in the oven. It feels so good to have the day off." She handed Heather her coffee then opened the oven door to check on the turkey.

Heather added milk from the fridge and sweetner to her coffee before sitting down at the kitchen table. "Looks like everything's under control."

"Uh-huh. Let's see, all I have to do is make the mashed potatoes and gravy and macroni and cheese, and I think that's it. You've been a big help, Heather. I tasted the stuffing. It's delicious. I couldn't have done a better job myself, and the cakes and pies look scrumptious."

"Where are they anyway?" Heather asked, looking around.

"Oh, they're all on the dining room table." Heather got up to view her handiwork. Her mouth watered at the sight of the pies and cakes. "Was that one of Grandma's tablecloths?" she asked as she sat back down.

"Um-hmm." Leola was peeling white potatoes.

"Wow, it's in great shape. How old is it, anyway?"

"Let's see. Mama must have bought that when I was in junior high. So we're talking a good forty years."

"A family heirloom," Heather added.

"You'll treasure the things your mother's given you. Especially when she's gone," Leola said simply.

By three o'clock the guests started arriving at the Greys' house. Heather's Uncle Frank and Aunt Joan were the first to arrive, followed by her cousins and their husbands and kids. Bored with the adults, the kids quickly decided to camp out in the den and play video games. When dinner was served, the kids had their own little table while the adults had theirs.

Heather enjoyed turkey and all the trimmings and cut herself some cake and pie for later. She was headed over to Charisma's parents' house and would probably have dessert with them. There was no way she could pass up all these homemade goodies.

"Sissy, you got any ice cream to go with this sweet potato pie?" Heather's Aunt Joan asked her mother.

"I'll get it," Heather said, heading for the kitchen. She returned with three gallons of ice cream—butter pecan, chocolate, and good ole vanilla.

Aunt Joan grabbed an ice cream scoop and dug right in, heaping several scoops on top of her sweet potato pie. "Aren't you having any, Heather?" she asked her niece.

"Maybe later," Heather told her as she checked her watch. "I'm headed out to see some friends. You remember my friends Charisma and Tangie?"

"From college? Of course. Well, in case we're gone when you get back, give me my sugar now." She hugged and kissed her niece.

Heather headed downstairs to rid herself of the Thanksgiving dinner. She evaded the mirror, unable to look herself in the eye. She hated having succumbed to this. It was humiliating. Then again, maybe if she had thought of this sooner, she'd have more control over her weight problem. She took a deep breath and leaned over the commode. Then she changed her mind. She might as well wait until after she returned from the Dearborns.' That way she could kill two birds with one stone.

9

Charisma

"So how'd your date go with Nate?" Tangie asked Charisma over drinks and hors d'oeuvres.

Charisma opened her mouth to protest, then shut it.

"Thank you," Tangie said. "At least you're no longer in denial."

Charisma gave her a quick rundown of that night, including his candid remark over dinner about possibly wearing her out in the bedroom and being Mr. Right.

"Girl, I bet if you gave him a piece it would blow his mind." Tangie laughed.

"I've looked at this from every angle and the bottom line is the same. When an office romance is good, it's very good. But when it's bad, it's extremely bad. And I can't afford to take that chance. I need my *job*." Charisma shrugged.

"Don't we all?" Tangie said nonchalantly.

"Well, I don't see you kickin' it with your boss," Chrisma said.

"Have you seen my boss?" Tangie asked. "Stone Canyon is a worn-out racist. But back to you, stop being so noble. If you want him, go for it."

"I have too much to lose." Charisma ran her hand through her hair.

"Not really. He has more to lose than you do," Tangie said. "What can Dex offer you but great sex? What *has* Dex offered you but great sex?"

"You know Dex wants more. I'm the one who's not ready for marriage."

"At least not with him," Tangie reminded her.

"But you don't know what Nate has to offer. Maybe he's not even interested in a relationship. Maybe he's just after a good time," Charisma insisted.

"Anything's possible," Tangie admitted. "But I don't think so from what you've told us. I think he's really feelin' you. And because he's a gentleman, he's trying not to rush you. You know how Miss Crappuccino loves our black men, and you're ready to just hand him over to her on a silver platter? Charisma, so help me, if you blow this one, I better not hear a peep out of you about shoulda-woulda-coulda."

Charisma thought for a moment and took another sip of wine. "I don't know, Tangie. Maybe deep down inside I'm afraid of happiness. Maybe I don't think I deserve to be happy in the traditional way. Maybe on some level we all fear commitment. When's the last time any of us has had a real relationship?"

"I'm not afraid of commitment," Tangie insisted. "Men are just dogs—black, white, well-bred, ghetto, mutt, pedigree. They're all dogs—two-legged, dysfunctional dogs."

"No, you mean three-legged, and it's that third leg that gets them and us into trouble every time." Chrisma laughed and Tangie joined in.

Charisma went in to work Monday morning with the intent of asking Nate over for Thanksgiving dinner that Thursday. She caught up with him in the break room pouring a cup of coffee.

"Good morning, Charisma," he said with a smile.

"Good morning, Nate." She returned his smile, pleased that he was wearing her favorite suit. Charisma loved the way he looked in his gray pinstripe. She took it as a good omen that maybe he'd accept her dinner invitation.

"Ready for Thanksgiving?" she asked simply, adding cream to her coffee.

"Absolutely. I'm going to San Diego to see my son. I can't wait. I haven't seen him since I moved here."

"That's great. How old is he?"

"Sean's fifteen, and he's as tall as I am. He's a great kid."

"Nice. Have a wonderful time. I'm glad you won't be alone. I wanted to invite you over for Thanksgiving, but I'm glad you'll be with family."

"I appreciate your offer. So what are you doing, Charisma? Are you cooking?"

"I'm going over to my parents', but I'm taking a couple of dishes."

"I bet you're a good cook." He took a sip of his coffee, looking into her eyes. "Hopefully, one day I'll find out."

"Maybe one day you will." She smiled.

As if on cue, Charisma sneezed just as Chase Martini tipped in, her royal blue stiletto heels the exact shade as her suit. "Must be the fumes in here," Charisma said, fanning herself from Chases's daily overdose of the latest designer frangance.

Nate got back to business. "Chase, I need to see you in my office about the Grant account. The Grant brothers just called for status. I told them I'd have some figures for them before noon."

"No problem," Chase said as she and Nate left the break room together. If her slit had been any higher it would have cut her throat.

Well, so much for inviting Nate over for Thanksgiving dinner. Now it was safe to ask Dex. He loved having her with him on the holidays or at least stopping by afterward and hanging out with her folks. She went back to her desk and dialed his work number. He picked up on the fifth ring just as she was about to hang up.

"I know your mother's having Thanksgiving dinner, but I thought you might want to stop by for dessert," she told him.

"I'd love it even more if you came with me to my mother's. My brothers'll be there with their wives, and I'd love to show you off, but dessert's good," he told her.

"Great. I'll see you Thursday."

Next, Charisma quickly dialed Tangie. "I have good news."

"What's that?" Tangie asked.

"I invited Nate over for Thanksgiving dinner, but he can't make it. He's going to spend Thanksgiving with his son in San Diego so I'm off the hook."

"So much for the Thanksgiving massacre. Dex would've kicked Nate's behind."

"Don't be so sure," Charisma said.

"You're gonna stand by your man, huh, lady?"

Charisma shook her head. "Don't start, Tangie. I am *not* in the mood. I'm just relieved to be skipping all that drama."

The next couple of days flew by as Charisma did her last-minute grocery shopping and errands for Thursday. Wednesday afternoon, just as she prepared to leave work, Nate stopped by to see her.

"All set for tomorrow?" he asked her.

"Not hardly. I have to go home and start making the cakes and lasagna. JFK must be a madhouse. What time's your flight?"

"Would you believe my plans have been canceled? I just got a call from my ex-wife. My son's grandmother had to have emergency surgery so he and his mother drove up to Oakland to be with her. So if your invitation still stands for tomorrow . . ."

"Absolutely," she said, wondering how Dex would react to Nate, but she couldn't uninvite either of them. "Dinner'll be around five."

"Can I bring anything?"

"Just yourself." She gave him easy directions to her parents' home and told him she'd look forward to seeing him there.

The minute she got home Charisma called Tangie and Heather and told them about the change in plans.

"I just hope I'm there in time for the cockfight," Tangie said, laughing.

"I knew I shouldn't have let you talk me into this," Charisma said.

"Charisma, breathe. I wish I had one man interested in me, let alone two. Miss Diva, you better count your blessings and have some fun with it," Heather told her.

"You know how jealous and possessive Dex can be. All Nate has to do is look at me the wrong way, and it's on. And lately Dex has been talking about moving in together. So he's gonna put two and two together and come up with eleven. But you guys are welcome to stop by and watch the fireworks if you're feeling a little sadistic," Charisma told them.

"Girl, we wouldn't miss this for the world," Heather said.

"Wish me luck," Charisma told them.

Luck," Heather and Tangie both said before hanging up.

Charisma slowly exhaled and poured herself a glass of white zinfandel before taking a quick shower, changing into sweats, and getting busy in the kitchen. It was going to be a long night. Somewhere after midnight, Charisma was awakened by the sound of her phone ringing. It was Dex.

"Hey, Miss Lady, mind if I stop by?" he asked her, his speech slightly slurred.

"What time is it?"

"Twelve-twenty. Can I come by?" he repeated.

Charisma yawned and opened her eyes, hesitating slightly before answering him. "I'm really exhausted, Dex. I've been up baking and cooking for hours. Can't it wait till this evening?"

"Baby, I need to see you now. I just wanna hold you in my arms and feel you next to me. I promise I won't stay long."

Charisma thought fast. Maybe if she let Dex come over tonight, he'd feel no need to come by after Thanksgiving dinner. "Okay, come on by," she said simply before hanging up. She quickly headed to the bathroom to wash and brush her teeth.

He was there within minutes. "Gosh, you even smell good." He tickled her neck with his nose. "It should be against the law for a woman to get up looking so fine," he told her as he took her in his arms. "I missed you so much, baby." He sat on the sofa and pulled her toward him. "Come sit on my lap."

"Boy, you're sure in a good mood." She yawned. "What 'cha do today?"

"My brothers and I went out for drinks, and they were all bragging about how special their wives are and how they wouldn't trade their marriages for the world."

Charisma could tell it was going to be one of those nights. She knew that whenever he got around his brothers, he ended up putting the pressure on. But the truth was she just wasn't ready for marriage. Sure, she cared for Dex, but she enjoyed her freedom too much to settle down. For the umpteenth time, she tried to make him understand.

Finally, he asked her, "Is there somebody else?"

"No, there's no one else, Dex."

"Then, you're not making any sense. Don't we have a good time when we're together?"

"Yes."

"And don't I make you laugh?"

"Yes."

"And don't I take care of business in the bedroom?"

"Yes."

"So, what's the problem? What more do you want? Don't you know I'd give you the world? Maybe you're the one with the problem."

Charisma got off his lap and stood, pulling her robe closer to her. "I care about you, Dex. I really do. Yes, we laugh and have a good time. Why can't that be enough? Why must you push and push and push?" She ran her fingers through her hair.

Dex sobered up. Finally, he stood too and grabbed her from behind. "Baby, I'm gonna wine and dine you till you beg me to marry you. And that's a promise. Lord knows you don't need any more beauty sleep, but I'm gonna let you get some anyway. I'll see you tomorrow."

"Okay, Dex," she said simply, taking his hand and leading him to the door. He kissed her on the forehead and left.

First thing Thanksgiving morning Charisma got up and fixed herself a cup of coffee. While enjoying the sight and aroma of the cakes she had baked last night, she turned on the Macy's parade. When she was a little girl, her father would take her and her brother Eric down to the city to see the big, colorful floats until she got lost in the crowd of people when she was seven. After that, the Dearborns never went farther than their living room to watch the Macy's Thanksgiving Day parade.

Heather called, still boo hooing about her weight gain. She was suffering from the shoulda-woulda-couldas. She was petrified about putting on even more pounds. Sometimes, she dreaded the holidays.

"You know Thanksgiving is just the beginning," Heather whined.

"Heather, it'll be okay," Charisma told her. "Just drink lots of water beforehand and don't gorge yourself on sweet potato pie."

"Yeah, and macaroni and cheese and dressing, and lemon coconut cake. . . . I can go on and on. I don't stand a chance."

"Heather, if you lost it once, you can do it again. The world isn't over. But, if you really can't resist temptation and you wanna skip my parents' house, it's okay."

"And miss bachelor number one meets bachelor number two? Are you kidding me? I wouldn't miss it for the world," she said.

"Don't remind me."

"I think you better talk to your girl."

"Why, what's up?"

"She's back with Blade."

"You gotta be kidding me," Charisma sighed.

"Not only that, but he wants to move in with her."

"What? Are you serious?"

"As a root canal."

"I'll talk to you later. Let me call Tangie and see if she needs to be committed." Charisma got up from the sofa and poured herself another cup of coffee before calling Tangie. She ended up leaving a message on her answering machine and enjoying the last hour of the parade.

Dinner wasn't until five, but she decided to hop in the shower and head over to her parents a little early to help with last-minute preparations. Just as she finished showering, the phone rang. She grabbed her bathrobe, dripping water along the way.

"Hey, girl, what's going on?" It was Tangie.

"I can't believe you're back with Blade."

"Heather has such a big mouth!"

"You're crazy."

"I knew you wouldn't understand."

"Hmmph. What's to understand?"

"No, you did not."

"Tangie, you could do so much better than Blade."

"Charisma, you've had your choice of guys since we were five years old. Some of us aren't so lucky."

"What school did you go to? Don't even try it."

"Look, Charisma, men treat you like a freakin' princess. You crick your little finger and they come running, ready to wine and dine you. Your every wish is their command. Men save their best side for you, and their backside for me. Right now you have one man who wants you and another just itching to get with you. And you're still not satisfied, Miss Prima Dona."

"If men act like dogs around you, it's because you let them."

"Are you saying it's my fault?" Tangie asked.

"I'm saying that we teach people how to treat us. Stop treating these men like they're the prize. *You* are the prize, Tangie. Not them, *you* are, Tangie."

"I know, Charisma. I know. Everything you've said to me, I've already said to myself."

"Then, enough said. See you later?" Charisma asked her.

"Whatever."

Hours later, Charisma was busy making homemade biscuits in her mother's kitchen. Jena Dearborn saw the tension in her daughter's face right away.

"Wanna talk about it?" she asked her.

"What d'ya mean?"

"You've been slamming that poor oven door like there's no tomorrow. I carried you for nine months. You think I can't tell when something's on your mind?"

"I guess I'm a little nervous about Dex meeting Nate."

"Why should you be nervous? Nate is just your boss, right?"

Charisma didn't say anything.

"Right?" Jena repeated. She paused for a moment. "Charisma?" she said softly. "Talk to me. What's going on? You know I try hard not to meddle in your life, but is Nate more than just your boss?"

"No," Charisma said. "But I'm attracted to him."

"And how does he feel about you?"

"The same."

"He's not married, is he?"

"No."

"So what's the problem?"

"He's my boss!"

"I know that."

"I just don't know if I'd respect myself in the morning."

"Well," Jena said as she walked through the swinging door and put the last few dishes on the dining room table. "Time will tell."

As if on cue, the doorbell rang. It was Nate. Charisma welcomed him into her parents' home and took his coat. Jena, the consummate plant lover, thanked him for the lovely houseplant he had brought. Ellis Dearborn shook Nate's hand and looked him squarely in the eye. Standing several inches shorter than Nate, he wore a royal blue sweater that set off his salt-and-pepper gray hair and camouflaged his love for his wife's cooking. The two joined his son Eric in the basement to watch the football game.

Half an hour later Jena called down to the men and told them that dinner was ready. They were having a hard time pulling themselves away from the television. Finally, after three *coming honey*s Ellis, Eric, and Nate made their way up to the dining room. Ellis was obviously ticked off about losing money in the office pool. Thanksgiving was one of the few times of the year that he gambled. As a loan officer, he was mindful of his spending habits. Jena turned the stereo down. They sat down at the table and Ellis said the Thanksgiving grace as they joined hands. He thanked the Lord for his family's good health and the food they were about to eat. They were a family blessed with plenty of love and a warm home. They were truly privileged.

Finally, it was time to eat. Carved turkey, ham, and roast beef took center stage on the dining room table, surrounded by cornbread dressing, macaroni and cheese, potato salad, a mixture of mustard and turnip greens, string beans, cranberry sauce, and buttermilk biscuits. They chowed-down like there was no tomorrow.

Charisma had second helpings of almost everything. Thanksgiving and Christmas were two days out of the year when she ate like a pig, kicking her eating plan to the curb. Jena insisted that everyone help themselves to more. There was plenty of everything, and they ate up.

"So how do you like New York, Nate?" Ellis asked.

"Well, it's a big difference from San Diego, especially weatherwise," Nate answered.

"You can say that again," Jena added. "New York winters can be brutal."

"So I've heard," Nate said. "I'm dreading it already."

"I know what you mean," Ellis admitted, shaking his head. "I've been here all my life, and I still dread them."

"I bet you're a big Lakers fan," Eric said, adjusting his Knicks baseball cap. Eric had Ellis's height, smile, and warm brown eyes.

"No doubt," Nate answered. "I'm as big a Lakers fan as your sister's a Knick fan."

"Aww man, you got it bad then, cause there is no hope for my sister," Eric said.

"Did she tell you I had to buy her dinner after I lost a bet at the Garden?" Nate asked.

"Yeah, that sounds like my sister. Always looking for a free meal," Eric said.

"Don't listen to him, Nate," Charisma said good-naturedly. "He's just mad because he can't get good seats to any of the games."

"Next time I get tickets, I'll give you a call," Nate told Eric.

"Cool," Eric said.

Jena looked at the others. "Anyone ready for dessert?"

They all shook their heads, completely stuffed. Dessert would have to wait.

"Let's finish watching the Eagles whip the Cowboys' behind," Ellis said to his son and Nate. "I bet the guys at work that Philly would win by six. Honey, dinner was magnificent." He gave Jena a quick peck on the cheek before heading back downstairs to enjoy the big-screen TV and fully stocked bar while Charisma and Jena cleaned up the dining room table and loaded the dishwasher.

"So what'd'ya think of Nate?" Charisma asked her mother once the men were no longer in earshot.

"Well, one thing for sure, you'd have some beautiful children."

"Mother, I'm serious."

"So am I."

"Never mind. Forget I even asked."

"Okay, especially since you're not interested, right?"

In response, Charisma looked at her mother and winked.

Jena sighed, shook her head and smiled.

They put the cakes and pies on the dining room table along with plates and forks before settling in the living room. The doorbell rang. It was Tangie and Heather stopping by to share some holiday cheer.

"Come on in," Charisma told them, taking their coats.

"Is Dex here?" Tangie whispered.

"Not yet. Nate, Daddy, and Eric are in the basement watching the game." Charisma took Tangie aside. "Listen, I want to apologize for being so hard on you earlier today. I said somethings I shouldn't have."

"Don't worry about it, girl. And he is *not* moving in. You were just keeping it real." Tangie gave her a warm hug before they rejoined the others.

"Your timing is perfect. We're just getting ready for dessert," Jena said.

"Mrs. Dearborn, we can smell your sweet potato pie from around the corner," Heather said.

"I made that pound cake you love so much, Heather, and Charisma made red velvet cake." Jena smiled.

"You two make it so hard for a full-figured sister." Heather shook her head. "But I'm trying to watch it."

The men returned from the basement, talking football.

"Hey Heather, Tangie," Ellis said. "Good to see you. Happy Thanksgiving." He kissed them both on the cheek.

"Long time no see Tangie, Heather," Eric said giving them both a hug.

"Nate, you remember Tangie and Heather?" Charisma said.

"Of course. Nice to see you both again. I think we met at IHOP one day." Nate smiled.

"That's right," Tangie said. "How've you been, Nate?"

"Fine, thanks. Just getting used to the city that never sleeps," he said.

"Are you guys ready for dessert?" Jena asked.

"I'd love some," Nate said.

"Me too," Eric said, heading for the dessert table.

"Charisma, get Nate some dessert," Jena said as she got up to get dessert for her husband.

Charisma and Nate went into the dining room, and she cut him a nice, big slice of red velvet cake.

He slid a forkful into his mouth. "Mmm. Did you make this?"

She nodded.

"I knew you were a good cook. It's written all over your sweet . . . body," he whispered softly in her ear. He was so close his breathing tickled the hairs on her neck.

She could barely resist him.

"What's in the frosting?" he asked.

"Cream cheese, coconut, and pecans," she said.

"It's delicious." He took another bite. In his haste, he accidentally dropped the fork. The cake landed first on his sweater, and then on the carpet. "You see what your stuff does to me?" he whispered. "I can't help myself." They looked at each other and burst out laughing. Nate knelt down and cleaned up the floor.

"Come on. I'll clean you up," Charisma said, leading him into the kitchen. She wet a paper towel and gently dabbed at his turtleneck until the spot of frosting disappeared. "There, all gone," she said simply.

He took her in his arms and kissed the tip of her nose. She wiggled free.

"Why are you fighting this?" he asked.

"Let me go or I'll scream." She grinned.

"Go ahead. Scream."

"Help," she said barely louder than a whisper. They both burst out laughing again.

"You're such a tease."

Charisma and Nate headed back into the living room to join the others, still laughing. Startled, Charisma was caught off guard as her eyes met Dex sitting on the sofa. Her smile vanished instantly.

Dex jumped to his feet, put his arms defensively around Charisma, and planted a kiss firmly on her cheek. "Hey, baby."

She wiggled free, rubbing the hair on the back of her neck. "Dex, this is my boss, Nate Arquette. Nate, Dex Spencer."

The two shook hands. "How's it going, man?" Dex asked, giving him a quick once-over.

"It's going well," Nate said. "I can't complain. I'm new in town, and Charisma was nice enough to invite me over for Thanksgiving dinner."

"Yeah, if there's one word you can use to describe my Charisma, it's *nice*," Dex agreed, throwing her an odd look.

The three stood in silence for a few moments. Dex eyed Nate suspiciously.

Nate eyed Dex suspiciously. Tangie, Heather, and Charisma exchanged glances. Charisma rolled her eyes in response. If looks could kill, somebody would be on death row, but who?

10

Tangie

Tangie checked her watch. She had gotten home from work over an hour ago and still nothing from Blade. She made sure her cell phone was on. No messages from Blade, but she did have one from Charisma and Heather. They were headed to Cabana for dinner and wanted to know if she'd join them.

Tangie called Charisma. "I'm starving, and I need to get out of the house. Can you pick me up?"

"Sure. Be ready in half an hour?" Charisma asked.

"Okay." Tangie took a quick shower and changed into a pair of jeans and a long-sleeved black shirt. She spritzed herself with her favorite perfume and added just the right amount of makeup.

By the time they reached the restaurant, the wait was over an hour, typical for a Friday night. So they strolled along Austin Street, window-shopping until Charisma spotted the perfect little black dress in the Ann Taylor Loft. Naturally, she had to try it on. It fit like a glove, but unfortunately, she had changed purses and didn't have any credit cards with her.

Heather and Tangie both fished through their purses until Heather found her American Express. "Jackpot," she told Charisma.

"Thanks," Charisma said, handing Heather the dress. "I'll pay you back."

"I know, girl. Your credit's good with me." Heather got in line and paid for the dress. They got back to Cabana just in time to be called by the hostess.

They were seated in the cozy little restaurant and ordered drinks.

"You know what I need?" Tangie said. "A vacation. Let's all go away for a few days. Anywhere hot," she continued. "I just want out of New York."

"I know the feeling," Charisma agreed. "Dex is getting on my nerves. I can't breathe. So if you're serious, I'm in."

"You two go and enjoy yourselves. I have too much on my plate right now," Heather said as the waiter returned with a pitcher of sangria and poured their drinks.

"It wouldn't be the same without you," Tangie insisted.

Heather sighed. "I have bigger fish to fry, but I'll see what I can do."

After a smooth, two-and-a-half-hour flight, Tangie, Charisma, and Heather landed in South Beach. It was hot and sunny, and the balminess did them all good. Tangie immediately tried calling Blade. She left a message asking him to return her call. They checked into the Colony Hotel, and Tangie and Charisma immediately slipped into their bathing suits. Heather, on the other hand, was still self-conscious about her weight.

"I look like a stuffed frog in this getup," Heather decided.

"Stop it, Heather," Charisma said.

"That's easy for you to say, Miss Size Eight." Heather struggled to get into her one-piece.

"Think of it this way," Tangie began. "You will never see these people again in life. So what are you worried about?"

Heather shook her head at them both. "You will never understand what it's like to be me. I'm like a rump roast next to two celery sticks."

"No, babe, you're just a whole lotta woman," Tangie said.

"I see men checking you out all the time," Charisma told her.

"But you're so obsessed with your weight you don't see it." Tangie shook her head this time.

"I'll bet you ten dollars that someone'll try to pick you up before we leave," Charisma said.

"Deal," Heather agreed as they headed out the door.

They rented chairs and umbrellas and spent all day on the beach. It wasn't long before their New York iciness melted away.

"I need some gum," Tangie said to anyone who was listening.

"Look in my bag," Heather said, not willing to move a muscle.

Tangie leaned over and grabbed Heather's bag, finding gum and mints. "Wow, you bring a toothbrush and toothpaste to the beach? Check her out," Tangie said to Charisma.

"We must be amateurs." Charisma shook her head.

"Don't hate," Heather said, laughing.

Two persistent guys tried to talk Tangie into entering a wet T-shirt contest. Tangie insisted she was not interested. Finally, they left her alone, but not before taking one last lingering look at her impressive cleavage. Apparently, half the men on the beach thought Heather was Latina, sprinkling their rap with just a dash of English as they poured on the charm. Tangie, Heather, and Charisma relaxed under the sun until the rumbling thunder and pouring rain forced them inside. They quickly peeled off their swimsuits and changed into shorts.

"I'm starving. What's for dinner?" Heather asked.

"Let's try Wet Willie's," Tangie said as she lay across the bed, thumbing through the restaurant guides.

"Let's order room service," Heather suggested.

"Room service? We might as well be at home eating. Let's get out," Charisma insisted.

"Why don't you guys go ahead, and I'll eat in?" Heather was comfortable right where she was.

"Okay, why don't we all go out tonight and do room service tomorrow night?" Charisma said.

"You drive a hard bargain. You better be glad I love you." Heather reluctantly got up and hopped in the shower first. She took so long in the bathroom that they were afraid she had drowned. She changed into a golden yellow floral halter sundress. Her long, curly locks, which were beginning to dry, only added to her lushness.

"Yuh know, for someone who wasn't feeling getting out, you sure look like you're after some male attention," Charisma admitted as she and Tangie finished getting dressed.

They walked into Wet Willie's and immediately found a seat upstairs in the open balcony. Charisma ordered a chocolate martini, Tangie had a Miami Vice, and Heather ordered sparkling water.

"On second thought, I'm on vacation. What do *you* suggest?" she asked the waiter.

"Call a Cab is our most popular drink," he suggested. "I guararantee you'll love it. It's sneaky, but it's good."

"I'm game," Heather admitted. "Oh, and a bottle of water, please." She needed to take her diet pill.

"Coming right up," he agreed.

Tangie looked around, bouncing to the music. "Vacations are a beautiful thing. Whose idea was this anyway?"

Heather and Charisma just looked at each other.

"Oh, yeah, it was mine. Brilliant." Tangie grinned. The

waiter returned with their drinks. Tangie raised her glass. "Behind every successful woman is herself."

"I know that's right," Heather and Charisma both said, sipping their cocktails. The waiter returned about ten minutes later with their meals.

Tangie said her grace. "I am so glad there's no testosterone sitting at this table," she said, cracking open a lobster and dipping it in butter. "Talk about sweet meat. There's no way I can eat like a lady and do this meal justice."

"You have to taste these crab cakes," Heather said. "They are *so* fresh."

"Good?" Charisma asked, enjoying her coconut shrimp.

"*Good* doesn't even begin to describe it." She cut one in half and put it on both of their plates.

"Mmm," they both said.

Charisma didn't say another word until she had cleaned her plate. "I am stuffed," she finally said, leaning back in the booth. "I don't even have room for dessert."

"You know me. I always save room for dessert," Tangie admitted. "Wanna join me, Heather?"

"Is water wet?" Heather smiled.

The waiter came to clear the table and leave a dessert menu. A few minutes later he returned. "So what'll it be, ladies?"

Tangie and Heather decided on one slice of key lime cheesecake and two forks.

"And what would you like?" He smiled at Charisma.

"Nothing for me," Charisma said. "I can't eat another bite."

"All right," he said before leaving.

"So what are we doing tonight?" Charisma asked Tangie and Heather.

"You know there's a couple of clubs in the hotel," Tangie said.

"You guys go ahead. I think I'll just crash," Heather decided.

The waiter returned with cheesecake and three forks. "I know it's a woman's prerogative to change her mind. Enjoy, ladies."

Charisma had to laugh as she sampled the dessert. It was delicious, almost unconscionable, and before long, history. They left the waiter a nice, big tip.

The next morning they got up, had breakfast, and hit the beach. There wasn't a cloud in the sky, and it promised to be a picture-perfect day. They got three lounge chairs and umbrellas and slathered sunblock all over their bodies. They had iPods, books, magazines, and not a care in the world as they soaked up the sun. Tangie and Charisma finally went for a dip in the ocean while Heather lounged in her chair.

Sensing someone's presence, Heather opened her eyes to find a well-groomed chocolate stud standing over her.

"You take my breath away, baby," he said, shaking his head.

Heather propped her shades on top of her head.

"You have the most sensuous legs in the Western Hemisphere." He walked away as Heather pulled the sunglasses down over her eyes, her lips curling into a slight smile.

"What are you smiling about?" Charisma asked Heather as she returned from the ocean and grabbed her towel to dry off.

"Oh, nothing," Heather said lightly.

"You are a lousy liar." Charisma laughed. "And by the way, you owe me ten bucks."

"He didn't try to pick me up," Heather insisted.

"That was a down payment. He'll be back to finish the job later. Trust me," Charisma said. "Pay up, sister."

"Win your bet already?" Tangie asked Charisma, sliding back into her lounger, her body soaking wet.

"I'm just about ready to collect. Right, Heather?" Charisma laughed.

"Whatever." Heather sighed, getting up for a quick dip.

"This is the life," Tangie remarked as she gestured to the bartender for a drink. He took their orders and returned shortly after with their drinks.

Like true ladies of leisure, they spent the entire day on the beach. Then, they turned in the towels and umbrellas, gathered up their things, and went back to their room.

Tangie tried calling Blade. He picked up on the sixth ring. There was a lot of commotion in the background.

"Blade?" Tangie said, straining her ears. She heard a woman's laughter in the background. It was vaguely familiar, but she couldn't quite place it.

"Give me the phone. Give me the damn phone," he said before they were disconnected.

"Bad connection," she told them. "I think I'll just chill tonight."

"Me too," Charisma and Heather agreed.

Tangie took one of the longest showers ever. Finally, she emerged from the bathroom with a frown on her face.

"I have two gray hairs," Tangie told them.

"Oh please, I have plenty," Charisma admitted.

"Hello, I'm not talking about on my head. I may have to do the male thing and shave it all off. A Brazilian sure beats the alternative," Tangie said.

"Ouch," Heather laughed as she picked up the phone to order room service.

On their last night in South Beach, Heather ran into the chocolate stud from the day before. Ian convinced her, Tangie, and Charisma to join him and the fellas at Mango's. He didn't have to twist their arms. He and his two friends seemed nice enough, and they were perfect gentlemen.

Male and female exotic dancers gyrated on bar tops as patrons indulged in vertical sex on the dance floor. While Charisma and Tangie danced with Ian's friends, Ian had Heather all hemmed up at the bar. Tangie motioned to Charisma to check out Heather. Heather didn't seem to mind her size that night. Some men preferred thick women. Apparently, Ian didn't mind one bit. They all had a good time. Ian was trying to get Heather's number, but she refused to give up the digits. She did, however, pay Charisma her ten bucks.

Stone checked his watch again as he sat in the Flagship Diner off Hillside Avenue awaiting his granddaughter's latest obsession. He ordered coffee and waited. Blade was already fifteen minutes late. Typical, Stone thought. As usual, those people had no concept of time. None whatsoever. You'd think that he'd be on time, considering Stone was meeting him in his own neighborhood. No such luck.

Blade finally showed up a full twenty minutes late. He sat down and ordered coffee, apologizing for his tardiness. Stone took a long, hard look at him and wondered what in the world Chase saw in him. Must be that damn forbidden-fruit syndrome, again. Stone knew what had to be done and was willing to make him a deal.

The two men sat across from each other in silence, neither of them having touched their coffee. They quickly sized each other up. Stone got straight to the point, prepared to let his wallet talk for him. He reached into the breast pocket of his blazer and pulled out a white business-sized envelope.

"Mr. Watson, I want you out of my granddaughter's life. I'm prepared to offer you a substantial amount of money to do so." Stone placed the envelope on the table.

Blade stared at the envelope for a moment before picking it up to view its contents. Inside was a check that could very easily null and void his financial woes. He placed the envelope back on the table before speaking.

"Keep your damn money," Blade began. "You don't have enough money to buy me."

"You haven't seen my bottom line," Stone chuckled.

"I'm not for sale."

"We're both men. Let's cut to the chase, excuse the pun. Hell, I know a good piece of pussy can make you feel like a million bucks, but let's not be ridiculous. Didn't your father ever tell you the story of the raccoon on the train tracks?"

"No." Blade shook his head.

"Well, there was this raccoon walking down the middle of these train tracks singing his heart out when he hears a train approaching. Luckily, he starts running and just barely makes it off the tracks before the train speeds by. Thank God. He's a little shaken up, but he's safe. He starts singing his little happy song again, until he notices something isn't quite right. He looks back and realizes that an itty-bitty piece of his tail is missing. It's on one of the tracks. Damn. He needs this little piece to glue back on to his body. He hears another train way off in the distance, but he knows he can make it back in time. He runs back to the train tracks and snatches up the piece of tail with his hot little hands. Just then another train comes by and runs over his whole head. Do you know what the moral of that story is, Mr. Watson?" Stone asked.

"Don't lose your head over a little piece of tail," Blade said, bored.

"I knew you were an intelligent man." Stone smiled. "Take the money and make it easy on yourself."

Blade picked up the envelope again and immediately put it back down.

Stone eyed the piece of crap in front of him. Nothing was more pitiful than an indecisive man.

"Give me the damn check," Blade said, annoyed.

"Now you're being smart. If I hear that you've so much as called my granddaughter, you will curse the day you were born. Is that clear?"

"I hear you."

"Good. Don't make me lay eyes on you ever again." Stone stood and walked out the door, his coffee untouched. Secretly, he was amused. He had been prepared to go higher, but he had gotten off dirt-cheap.

Blade watched Stone leave as he slid the envelope in his jacket pocket. Easy money was the best kind. He'd kiss his debts good-bye, and if he was lucky, see Chase too. Nobody told Blade what to do. Nobody. Especially not Stone Canyon

Blade walked up to the teller's window of the National Bank and endorsed Stone Canyon's check for deposit into his checking account. He would have loved to bank it with his meager savings, but he was in so much debt that he'd have to start writing checks the minute it cleared. Not that he could afford to wait even that long. Blade's eyes grew to the size of golf balls as he glanced at his copy of the deposit slip that the teller returned to him. He had never had so much money in his account at one time, but if he played his cards right the possibilities were endless.

He breathed a little easier as he drove off, waiting until after he passed the local police precinct before picking up his cell and dialing Chase Martini's number. Let's see who gets the last laugh, he said to himself, thinking about his deal with Stone Canyon.

Chase picked up on the fourth ring. "Hello?"

"Hey, it's Blade. What are you up to? I need to see you."

"Oh yeah?" she laughed. "I thought you had deserted me. What's going on?"

"I've just been busy, ya know? But I've been thinking about you day and night. When can I see you?"

Chase laughed again. "I don't know. You tell me."

"Why don't we meet tonight in Queens at Manhattan Proper?"

"Why the change?" she asked.

"I'll explain when I see you. How's nine o'clock sound?"

"I have an early day tomorrow. How about seven?"

He hesitated slightly. "Okay, that'll work."

"See you tonight."

Blade hung up, relieved. Maybe his plan would work after all.

Stone checked his personal account that morning from his office and discovered that Blade had finally deposited the check. It had taken a full thirteen days. Could someone named Blade possibly have scruples? Not in this lifetime, Stone thought to himself. The private investigator assured him that Chase's whereabouts seemed back on track. And thank goodness that no matter how late she hung out with her friends Saturday night, she attended Sunday morning Mass with the family. At long last, Chase was finally getting her priorities straight.

Appearances were everything, which was why he came home every night to his wife Lola. He even slept in the same bed with her, even though they hadn't had sex in years. Lola knew about his "Spanish taco," as she called Juana. How the hell she found out he couldn't imagine, but women had a sixth sense about these things. Why, her intuition alone could make a blind man see.

Why had he married Lola in the first place? She had what one would call class and traveled in the right social circles. She was a debutante. She attended all the right schools. Her parents had the right connections. He was the dashing, slightly older man to her innocence. So when the opportunity presented itself, he did what any other red-blooded, money-hungry American male would do. He snatched her up quickly, eloping without even a hint of a prenup. Back then he could barely afford the puny diamond he placed on her hand, but being the lady she was, she wore it proudly. He made sure she pushed out a baby, their only child, a daughter named Sloane, the following year to secure his future. After that, he was set. His father-in-law saw to it that he made the right contacts and before long, the first Canyon's Club opened. That was almost fifty years ago. Her parents had both since died and passed on the bulk of their fortune to Lola. Lola was well-off in her own right, but when she and Stone argued she never let him forget how he owed his success to her family. And that if it hadn't been for her, he'd still be a used-car salesman.

Stone called Juana into his office. "Get Zynk Caparelli on the phone for me, will you?" he said, knowing full well that he just wanted to gaze upon her lush, ripe body. She knew the game, smiling at him as she turned to walk back to her desk.

Within moments, Zynk was on the phone.

"That bastard Blade finally cashed the check," Stone told him. "I want you to continue the surveillance, and I want weekly reports. I still don't trust him."

"No problem, Mr. Canyon."

"Great. Keep me posted."

"Will do."

Blade pulled into Manhattan Proper's parking lot, looking for Chase's ride. When he realized she hadn't yet arrived, he sat in his car for a moment debating whether or not he really wanted to continue seeing her. If he wasn't careful, he could wind up in a lot of trouble. He was playing hardball with the big boys, and he could easily get burned. Was he ready to take that risk? Was she worth it? On the other hand, maybe he could cash her in for an even bigger paycheck. He might get the shit kicked out of him in the process, but there was a price to pay for everything.

He looked up and into the headlights of an approaching car. It was Chase in her shiny red Porsche. She pulled up right beside Blade, who got out of his car and approached hers.

"What's going on?" he asked, leaning over the driver's side.

"You tell me."

"I thought maybe we could hop in my car and drive to someplace private."

"Like where?"

"You name the spot."

"This isn't exactly my neighborhood. You know?"

"I know. Why don't we have a drink here first and then decide what we wanna do?"

"Okay," she agreed as she opened her car door and got out.

Blade gave her a quick hug and possessively placed his arm around her shoulders as they crossed Linden Boulevard and entered the club. He paid at the door and they found seats at the bar. She ordered a cosmopolitan while he had a rum and Coke. They kept the drinks coming that night, and as they staggered across the street to the parking lot hours later, Blade decided to drive them someplace quiet and secluded. He had spent practically all of his money on drinks and didn't quite have enough to spring for a room. Chase, too wasted to object, even handed over the keys to her car. She slid into the seat next to him and off they went. He had never driven a Porsche before and boy, was he loving it.

On more than one occasion, she begged him to slow down. "What are you trying to do, get us both killed?"

"Relax," he told her. "I know what I'm doing."

"Pull over," she demanded as he ran a second red light. "We're almost there."

"I don't care. Pull over now," she insisted.

The car in front of them came to a sudden stop, forcing Blade to slam on the brakes. Unfortunately, Blade couldn't stop in time and ran smack-dab into the back bumper with such force that both their air bags deployed.

"Shit," he said as he got out the car to assess the damage done.

Chase blacked out momentarily. When she came to, Blade was in the street talking to the other driver.

"Look what the hell you did to my car," she yelled at him as she exited from the passenger side. She felt a sudden, sharp pain shooting from her neck down to her shoulder and stiffened instinctively.

The other driver was calling 911 on his cell phone. Blade tried to convince him that it could all be handled without getting the authorities or their insurance companies involved, but he didn't want to hear it. About five minutes later, the cops showed up and reports were filed.

Blade didn't know what was worse—that he was charged with a DWI or that he'd just gotten busted with Chase. Evidently, she knew nothing of his deal with Canyon.

When Stone found out about the car accident, his first reaction was, what the hell was Chase doing in Jamaica at one o'clock in the morning? He hated calling his attorney, Nico Antonelli, at such a godforsaken hour, but then again, that's why he was on retainer. Nico took care of everything, including driving Chase home from the emergency room.

The first thing Stone did when his bank opened was to stop payment on Blade's check. There was no way in hell he'd allow him to spend so much as a penny of that money. Stone would rather rot in hell first, and he wasn't through with Blade yet. Not by a long shot.

Chase spent the next few days visiting specialists to treat her whiplash and recuperating at home. One morning before leaving for the office, Stone summoned his granddaughter to his study.

"What the hell were you doing in Jamaica of all places at that time of night?" he asked her.

"I was hanging out with a friend?"

"A friend? Apparently, you use the term much too loosely."

"You don't even know him, Granddad."

"I think I know him a little better than you do, young lady."

"You know Blade? You know Blade?" she repeated.

"Take a look at this, and tell me how much of a friend he really is?" He handed her an envelope.

She just stared at it.

"Go on, open it. Let's see how close you and Blade really are."

She opened up the envelope and pulled out a check from her grandfather's private account made payable to Blade for ten thousand dollars. She turned it over. It had been endorsed by Blade.

"What the hell is this?" she asked.

"I offered your *friend* ten thousand dollars to stay away from you and he practically broke his neck signing on the dotted line. Evidently, you don't mean very much to him. You're just a meal ticket. Next time you go slumming, watch out for the street urchins.

Tangie couldn't remember the last time Blade had actually called her. She did the math and didn't like the results. Apparently, somebody else was answering his booty calls. She knew there was another woman. There was no other excuse for his absence. Then one day a coworker confirmed it. He was seeing Chase. Her mind flashbacked to that night in South Beach. It was Chase's laugh she had heard on Blade's phone.

Tangie went home that night and cried. She cried until there was nothing left to shed. Then, she picked up the phone, called Charisma and Heather, and cried some more.

"Guess who Blade's seeing?" she asked them. "That bitch, Chase."

"Martini?" Charisma asked.

"Yeah, that's the one."

"Wow, I'm sorry, Tangie," Heather said.

"It's not *your* fault," Tangie told them. "Would you believe I tried calling him everyday from South Beach? I'm such a fool."

"No, you're not. You're just a woman who gave her heart too quickly. We've all been there. It's in our genes."

"Yeah, well, I should've kept him out of my jeans," Tangie said, trying to joke about it.

"Have you confronted him?" Heather asked.

"No, not yet. He'll come around when he wants some, but we are so through. I gotta go. I'll talk to you guys tomorrow."

"Get some rest. Call us if you need us," Heather said before hanging up.

When Blade showed up on Tangie's doorstep a few nights later for a little TLC, she was ready for him.

"Come on in," she told him. "I've been expecting you." She kept it light.

"Oh, really?" Scratching his head, he walked in and sat on her sofa.

"Uh-huh. I was wondering when you'd show up. Why haven't you called me lately? Did you lose your cell phone?"

"You know how it is. I gotta hustle, baby. I've been real busy. I just made ten thousand dollars." Blade smiled.

"Well, I'm glad you made time for me."

"Don't even go there. You know you're my boo. I always have time for you," he said.

"Really?" she asked.

"Yes, really. Where have you been?"

"What do you mean, where have I been?"

"Look at you, all tanned and whatnot. Where you been?"

"Oh, *now* you suddenly care? I've been on vacation. Where have you been? I've been calling you and calling you. I'm lucky if I get your voice mail."

"If you must know, I was in a car accident."

"Well, it looks like you walked away without a scratch. Lucky you."

"Yeah, lucky me. Listen, Tangie, I didn't come here to argue with you."

"Then why did you come?"

"I missed you, boo."

"Cut the crap. I've had enough. I'm releasing you, Blade."

"What?"

"It's over, and I know all about you and Chase."

"That bitch means nothing to me. Trust me. She's just a thang. I don't want to lose you."

"You already have. For two years I've put up with your crap. You schedule me into your life like a dental appointment, or like I'm the other woman on the side. But it's not all your fault. All this time I thought you were my knight in shining armor, but you're not. You're just a man. And at times you're a mean, spiteful, arrogant, pitiful man. I'm sorry I had you on a pedestal like you were something more. You didn't deserve to be there, and you proved it. I did you a disservice, but I also did myself a disservice for giving you so much power and control over my life. Well, now I'm taking my power back. You're not responsible for my happiness. So I'm giving you a gift—the gift of good-bye."

"The gift of good-bye? What the hell is that? You've been watching too much Oprah. Is that a joke?"

"No, you are," Tangie said. "Now get the hell out of my house."

"Okay, Tangie. I'm leaving, but I'm not going away."

Tangie slammed the door in his face and went back to bed. She doubled her Kegel exercises and looked forward to a good night's sleep.

11

Heather

Heather stepped on the scale one morning before going to work. She was ten pounds lighter. Apparently, her diet pills and her nightly ritual were beginning to pay off. With pep in her step, she sashayed down Jamaica Avenue during lunch. Heather caught a glimpse of her reflection in the Golden City Jeweler's window. She waved at Sammy and David as she walked by.

"Heather?"

She turned around. It was Ava. "Hey Ava, how's it going?" Heather asked her.

"I'm good," she said simply. "Where're you headed?"

"The food court for a salad. How about you?"

"I don't know what I'm in the mood for. Do you eat a lot of salads?"

"Just trying to keep the weight down," Heather said simply.

"You need to try something different." Ave checked her watch. "Let's go to Patty World. They have the best brown stewed chicken in the neighborhood."

"Never been there before."

"Really?" Ava asked. "Time to broaden your horizon, babe. Come on."

"Okay, I hope I like it." They turned around and began walking in the opposite direction.

"You've never had Jamaican food before?" Ava asked.

"Just beef patties."

"Where have you been? You can't be a New Yorker."

"Not originally. We moved from Michigan when I was seven."

Heather wished she hadn't left her hat at work. With just a hint of snow in the air, the air was so brisk that her ears were not just stinging, they were practically singing.

When they reached the tiny restaurant, spicy aromas tickled Heather's nostrils and Ava smiled at the sight of her reaction. Ava ordered the curry chicken while Heather tried the brown stewed chicken.

"Here, taste this," Ava said, sharing her chicken. Heather was hooked. Her waistline would be in trouble if she didn't watch it. She had found a new lunch spot and said as much to Ava.

"Stick with me, chickylicky, and we'll go places." Ava winked, taking a sip of ginger beer.

Bored to the gills, a few days later, Heather called Jamal, the guy she met grocery shopping in Pathmark a couple of days before Thanksgiving, and left a message on his answering machine. Since her phone number was blocked, she didn't worry. She had no way of knowing, but Jamal betrayed the brotherhood and hung around the house for three nights afterward hoping to catch her next call. Heather, however, had a game plan of her own. There was no next call.

Unbeknownst to her, Jamal had a game plan too. His buddy was a security guard at Pathmark. After describing Heather to a T, he put out an APB and a week later got the call. He hustled on over to Pathmark and spotted her in the parking lot as she was loading her groceries in the trunk. Heather slammed the trunk shut and ran smack into Jamal just as she turned toward the driver's side.

"Oops, sorry," she said, at first not recognizing him.

"Heather?" He feigned surprise.

"Hey, I know you."

"It's Jamal. We met inside a couple of weeks ago. How've you been?"

"Fine," she said simply. "And you?"

"I'm good. Just waiting for your call," he admitted. "Why don't you just give me your number and put me out of my misery?"

Heather took a long look at him. He really was a cutie with his Caesar haircut, his faint beard, and the smoothest chocolate skin she had seen in years. "I hope I don't live to regret this." She toyed with him, her head cocked ever so slightly to the side.

"This is your lucky day. Ever been to Vegas?" he asked.

"Why?" she said, laughing.

"You just hit the jackpot."

Heather gave him her cell number, which he quickly placed in his BlackBerry. "We'll see about that." She got into her car and started the ignition, driving off with the reflection of Jamal, still grinning, in her rearview mirror.

Before she even got home that night, he called. "I just wanted to make sure you didn't give me a bogus number. I know how you sisters operate."

"Only when necessary," Heather admitted.

"Then I just hit the lottery," Jamal surmised.

"Imagine that," she laughed before hanging up.

That weekend Heather and Jamal went out on their first date. She insisted on going Dutch, but he wouldn't hear of it.

"You might as well have Monopoly money in your wallet. It's no good tonight," he told her as they had dinner at the Cheesecake Factory.

She rolled her eyes ever so slyly.

"Deal with it," he added.

That was just the beginning. Heather and Jamal went out every night for the next week. Each night Jamal insisted on paying. Each night Heather ate like a little bird, but behind closed doors she gorged on pork chops, macaroni and cheese, and ice cream. They saw movies, went to a comedy club, and just hung out in Manhattan. Then, Jamal started buying things for Heather—things that didn't require sizing like earrings and bracelets.

When she protested, he hugged her unexpectedly, catching her off guard.

"Wow, you smell good. What are you wearing?" he asked.

"I can't tell you *all* my secrets." She grinned.

The next day Jamal bought her a gift set of her favorite perfume, body lotion, and shower gel. It was almost as though her every wish was his command.

"How'd you know?" she asked.

"I have my ways," he said simply.

"You don't have to do all this."

"I know. I *want* to."

"Jamal, you're scaring me. I barely know you."

"You deserve to be wined, dined, and devoured," he said lustfully. "And I'm just the man who'll do it."

"I called you three times last week," Charisma told Heather. "And all I got was your answering machine."

"What have you been up to?" Tangie added.

"Didn't I tell you? I met someone. I've been kinda busy," Heather said between bites of her egg-white omelet.

"Details," Charisma insisted.

"His name is Jamal and would you believe I met him at Pathmark? I've seen him just about every night this week. And he loves buying me things," she admitted.

"Already?" Tangie asked. "Sounds intense."

"He is," Heather said.

"And you?" Charisma asked.

"Not me." Heather looked at her sideways.

"I bet that's driving him crazy," Charisma laughed.

"Hey, behind every successful woman is herself," Heather said.

"Just make sure that stalker Cole isn't behind you." Tangie shook her head.

"Don't even mention his name," Heather warned her. Cole was the nut who staked out her house, her job, anywhere he thought she might possibly show up to talk to her. "See what happens when you feed stray dogs? That's why now I treat 'em rough and tell 'em nothing."

"Hey, whatever works," Tangie told Heather. "Are you gonna eat your bacon?"

"Here, you can have it." Heather handed her the saucer. "I do not need these extra calories as big as my butt is, and it's the holidays too."

"I know what you mean, but I keep telling you, Heather, you gotta hit the gym. Just come one time. I'll even work out with you," Tangie promised. "Get that butt moving."

"And be part of the butt parade? I'll get back to you," Heather said.

"Never mind. I know what that means," Tangie sighed.

The following week Heather's car died. She was on her way in to work Friday morning when her car took its last breath. She was on Springfield and Merrick when it stalled. She tried the ignition, but it just wouldn't turn over.

Heather put on her hazard lights, reached for her purse, and fumbled inside for her cell phone. She called the library, letting them know her car had died. What the heck was she going to do?

Just as she was about to call AAA, two men in blue overalls got out of a red truck, knocked on her window, and offered to give her a jump. Thank God for miracles. Lord knows she didn't have AAA money, not this week, anyway. The two men pushed her through the intersection and to the side of the road directly behind their truck. Then they turned their truck around so that the two front ends were only a foot apart. They quickly got the jumper cables from the truck's rear and fastened the cables.

Heather gave the car a little juice, and it started up in no time. She offered to give the men a few dollars, but they wouldn't hear of it. Before long, she was safely at work, but she had to stay late to make up the time she had missed that morning.

As she left the building and walked to her car, she silently prayed that it would start. Unfortunately, it did not. She sat in the darkness for a moment, her forehead pressed against the steering wheel as more fortunate drivers whizzed by. Who would she call? Her mom was working until midnight and Charisma was too far away. She dialed Tangie's job. She had left an hour ago. She tried Tangie's cell phone. It went straight to voice mail.

After a long sigh, she called Jamal. "Jamal?" she practically cried. "I'm stranded outside of work." That's all she had to say.

"Stay put. I'm on my way."

She put on her gloves and waited. She could have called a cab or hopped on a bus, but she didn't want to just leave her car on the street. In the meantime, she called AAA. Jamal arrived first. She was never so happy to see him. He parked his car behind hers and got out.

"You are a sight for sore eyes," she said, leaning over and

opening the front passenger door. She gave him a big hug once he was seated.

"How's it going?" he asked her, getting in and kissing her gently on the cheek. "Here, I stopped and brought you some hot chocolate." He removed the large cup from the Dunkin' Donuts bag and handed it to her.

"Thanks, you're such a honey. I knew I could count on you." She took a sip. It was the perfect temperature. "Mmm. Would you believe this is the second time this car stalled today? Unbelievable, but I called AAA. They're on the way."

They sat in silence for a moment until Jamal spoke. "We can go sit in my car if you want. I have heat and music."

"Heat and music, huh? That's one helluva combination. I'm down," Heather admitted, her nose beginning to run.

Just then the tow truck pulled up. "Thank goodness," she said as they got out of the car.

They tow-truck operator tried to start the car's engine, but it was dead. He then got out of Heather's car and asked her where she wanted her car towed to. Heather often had her car serviced at Big Apple Tire on Baisley Boulevard and 166th. The tow-truck operator took Heather's AAA membership card and ran her car through the machine. A few minutes later he gave her a receipt and began hooking up her car to his truck. Minutes later, her car was history as she watched both vehicles disappear in the distance.

Jamal turned to Heather. "Hungry?" he asked.

"A little."

"What are you in the mood for?"

"I don't know. What do you feel like?"

"We can eat out, get take-out, or I can whip up something at my house."

"You cook?" she said, stifling a yawn.

"Don't act so excited. I make some mean turkey burgers."

"Really?"

"Really. It's settled. You're coming home with me."

"And then you'll take me home?"

"Yes, and then I'll take you home."

Jamal drove off and headed home. Traffic was bearable for a Friday night, and in no time they were pulling up to his second-floor rental. By now it was after eight and Heather's stomach was growling big-time.

"Oops, excuse me," she said to Jamal, embarrassed that he'd heard her stomach music.

"Please, don't worry about it. Chef Jamal has just the thing for you." They climbed the stairs to his domain. "Make yourself at home," he told her as he switched on the living room lights and unzipped his leather bomber jacket.

"All righty," Heather said, looking around at the black leather sofa and giant-screen TV. It was definitely a bachelor pad.

"Sit down. Can I get you anything?" he asked her as he returned from the kitchen, drying his hands on a paper towel.

"No, I'll wait," she said, sitting on the sofa.

Jamal went in the back and changed into a T-shirt and sweats. He popped a CD in the stereo and Ne-Yo fillled the air.

"Can I help?" she asked him.

"No, everything's under control."

Heather found that to be an understatement as they sat at the kitchen table half an hour later. Jamal had prepared turkey burgers smothered with onions and peppers, yellow rice, and broccoli.

"You got skills," Heather told him as she took another bite of the burger. She knew she should have skipped the potato bun, but she couldn't resist.

"I do 'aight," he said, chewing on a broccoli stalk and they both laughed.

"Your friendship might put a hurtin' on my diet."

"Hold still." He leaned across the table and removed a grain of rice from her lower lip. "Now you're perfect."

Heather blushed. "Trust me, there is nothing perfect here."

"Well, I like 'em thick."

"Is that right?"

"You'll see." Jamal gazed deeply into her eyes.

Heather stood. "Why don't I clean up the kitchen," she said, more as a statement than a question.

"No, no, no. You go chillax, and I'll clean up." He shooed her out of the kitchen.

Heather was so exhausted that she didn't even protest. She sat back on the sofa and drifted off to the clanking of pots and pans and running water. She turned ever so slightly when Jamal gently shook her.

"Heather?"

She barely budged.

"Heather?

When she didn't wake up, he took a blanket from the closet and draped it over her body and returned to his bedroom to watch the Knick game. They were playing on the West Coast, and he tuned in just in time for the opening tip-off. Jamal removed his T-shirt and sweatpants before sliding under the covers of his full-sized bed. Only the light from the television invaded the room's darkness.

Halfway through the first quarter, he heard Heather stirring from the living room. A moment later there was a knock on his slightly ajar door.

"Jamal?"

"In here."

She pushed the door open. "I guess I fell asleep."

"It's all right. You had a long day. Come here." He motioned. "I'll give you the best seat in the house."

Heather hesitated only slightly. "I have a cop friend on speed dial."

"Hey, come check out this game. The Knicks are leading. You don't see that too often."

"Okay, but watch yourself."

"Don't worry. I know you're quick on the draw," he said, referring to her speed-dialing technique as he sat up in bed.

"And don't you forget it," she said as she plopped down on the bed next to him.

"Cold?" he asked.

"A little."

"Here, get under the covers."

She glanced at him sideways. "You must take me for an amateur."

"You know me better than that." He grabbed a pillow with one hand and placed it behind his head, his triceps catching Heather's eye.

"If I weren't a gentleman, I wouldn't have rescued you tonight and offered to drive you home when you're ready. I mean the offer still stands. I can take you home now if you like."

"I'll let you know when," she said, sneaking a peak at his boxers before lying down next to him.

"Comfortable?"

"Uh-huh," she said as she laid on top of the covers.

"Your clothes'll be wrinkled by morning," he warned. "There's a robe in the bathroom behind the door if you like."

"Who said I'm spending the night?"

"My bad," he said and they both laughed.

"Where's your bathroom?" Heather asked on second thought.

"Down the hall, second door on the left."

"Be right back." She slid off the bed and headed down the hall. A white terry cloth robe hung behind the bathroom door. A wicked smile formed on her lips. She removed her shoes, panty hose, and cardigan and kept on her sleeveless tank and skirt. Then she tried on the robe. It was long enough to conceal her skirt. Perfect. She sashayed back into Jamal's bedroom and stood at the foot of his bed. Evidently, just the vision of her in a robe with nothing on underneath bought a smile to his face.

"So you like 'em thick, huh?" she asked him.

"Oh yeeeah." He grinned. "I like 'em thickalicious."

Imagining herself as an exotic dancer, Heather did a little dance, her eyes fixed on his. She opened the robe and his grin disappeared before the robe hit the floor. When she started removing her top and skirt, the grin reappeared. His breathing deepened by the time she stripped to her bra and panties, teasing him with her gyrations. She squeezed her breasts gently as she licked her lips, rolling her tongue around the perimeter of her mouth.

"Damn," was all Jamal could say. Heather grabbed the sides of her panties and pulled them down ever so slightly, ever so slowly, feeling his eyes glued to her body. In one quick motion, Jamal cut the distance between them in half. They both laughed as he wrapped his arms around Heather's ample body and gently unhooked her bra. The sight of her bare breasts nearly took his breath away. He reached for the light switch to get a better look.

"No, don't," she said, pulling his hand away from the wall. He flipped the switch on anyway. "You are so hot. I just want to see all of you."

Men were all alike. Disgusted, Heather bent down and picked up her clothes from the floor. "I'm ready. You can take me home now."

12

Tangie

Tangie was convinced that there were four personality types of men in the world: the diplomat, the military, the clergy, and the politician. She said as much to Charisma and Heather one night over Charisma's delicious carrot cake.

"So what type was Blade?" Heather asked.

"He was hotheaded but great in bed," Tangie decided. "What a combination. I don't know which one of his heads was hotter. He was straight-up military-thug."

"All military men aren't thugs," Heather insisted.

"No, but most thugs have a military-type mentality," Tangie said.

"Oh my goodness, she's even starting to sound like a therapist." Heather shook her head.

"Don't hate me cause I'm analytical," Tangie replied.

"When did you become so analytical?" Charisma asked as she got up from the kitchen table to fix some herbal tea to go with the carrot cake. She put the water on to boil and placed a box of assorted teas on the table along with cups, saucers, plates, utensils, sugar, and milk for Heather. Heather always had milk in her tea. It didn't take much time for the teakettle to start whistling, and before long they were all enjoying Charisma's homemade cake and soothing tea.

"What can I tell you?" Tangie shrugged her shoulders. "I'm just keeping it real."

"Okay, but you can't be analytical without being anal," Charisma told her.

"That's not true," Tangie said.

"Of course it is," Charisma insisted.

"Anyhow, I just wish I knew why I'm always attracted to the same type. Maybe if I changed my type, I'd have better luck with men," Tangie said.

"Heather, when Tangie and I were in third grade, she had her first big crush on a guy who used to steal people's lunch money. What was his name, Tangie?"

"Robin Hood?" Heather joked.

"Ryan. Ryan Garnett," Tangie said reluctantly, shaking her head.

"And when we were in the fifth grade, who did you like?" Charisma asked Tangie.

"Dustin Simms," Tangie said, yawning.

"And what was he suspended for?" Charisma asked.

"Bringing pot to school," Tangie answered.

"And what about sixth?" Charisma continued.

"Enough already," Tangie said.

"Well, if you keep doing the same thing, how can you expect different results? Maybe it's time to change your game plan and give up the roughnecks," Charisma advised her.

Tangie thought for a moment. "Maybe you're right, Charisma. Maybe I should try a diplomatic type or someone with a political mind set."

"What's the difference, Tangie." Charisma yawned.

"Diplomats are levelheaded leaders. They're good providers. Politicians know the players on both sides of the fence. They're good protectors," Tangie explained.

"Just stay away from the clergy," Heather warned. "As many tricks as you have in your bag, you'd both probably burn in hell." They all laughed.

"But seriously, where did this theory on men come from?" Charisma asked.

"Just something I came up with on my own," Tangie admitted.

"Maybe you have too much time on your hands," Heather sighed.

"Maybe one day I'll write a book."

"I can hardly wait," Heather said, shaking her head.

"You can laugh all you want to now, but when I become a best-selling author, we'll see who gets the last laugh," Tangie told them.

Tangie was grateful that she hadn't run into Blade at the gym, but her luck was about to run out. Tangie checked her watch. It was almost seven PM. She was meeting Charisma and Heather at Macy's in about an hour. She had just enough time to grab her belongings from the locker, sign out, and hit the streets. Thank goodness she had had another uneventful week, which translated into no Blade sightings.

As she made her way to the underground garage, her heart sank. Parked three cars down from hers, sat Blade in an SUV, his window rolled down. Apparently, his finances were looking up. She tried to shield herself behind another car, but not before he spotted her. He and something were all hugged up in the front seat. Tangie had seen her working out at the gym on more than one occasion. She wasn't all that.

"Whassup?" He nodded to Tangie as their eyes met.

"Hey," she said simply as she walked to her car. She couldn't drive away fast enough. As she sped down Jamaica Avenue, her heart returned to near normal. She stopped at a light, whipped out her cell phone, and speed-dialed Charisma. "Well, he didn't waste any time," Tangie told her.

"Most men don't."

"She wasn't even his type."

"Please, anything with a hole is his type."

The cars behind her honked their horns as the light turned green. "Shut up," she snapped. "Listen, I'm on my way. I'll be there soon." Tangie flipped her phone shut.

Traffic was such a nightmare along Sunrise Highway that even Heather beat her to the mall. By the time Tangie met up with them in the shoe department, she was totally ticked off. Charisma had filled Heather in on Tangie running into Blade and his latest in the parking lot.

"Isn't it amazing how women want variety in everything—clothes, jewelry, lipstick, shoes—God, knows shoes—but we spend practically our whole life searching for the One. Well, when the hell am *I* gonna find the One?" Tangie picked up a six-inch stiletto. "And why the hell are heels so damn high these days? Huh? Give me a freakin' break!"

Several customers turned to look at her, but she didn't give a damn.

"Let's get the hell outta her before I really explode," Tangie warned them.

Charisma gave Heather a look.

"Let's get outta here," Heather said, getting up from a chair.

"Okay, let me pay my bill," Charisma said, walking to the register.

"I could use a drink," Tangie said.

"We know," Heather agreed

"Applebee's?" Tangie asked them both.

"Sounds good to me," Charisma agreed as they took the escalator down to the main floor. "I'll drive," she said as they walked out the door. They found her car and piled inside for the quick ride to the restaurant. They were seated at a booth immediately.

"I am *so* broke," Heather admitted as she opened the menu. "I'm still paying off South Beach, and I need a good used car like yesterday. I can't take it anymore."

"We got cha'," Tangie said. "Order away."

The waiter returned to take their orders. They ordered drinks and two plates of appetizers. Even Heather stuffed her face. By the time the second round of drinks arrived, Tangie was laughing like she hadn't a care in the world.

"So what did Blade say to you?" Heather asked.

"Who?" Tangie asked as she sipped her drink. "You know what we oughtta do tomorrow night?" she asked without waiting for a response. "Let's go clubbing. I am *so* over Blade. It's time I really get back in the game and see what's out there."

"Friday's payday. Can a sister hold out till then?" Heather asked Tangie.

She nodded.

"Then count me in." Heather said.

Tangie couldn't wait for Friday night. In spite of her ranting and raving in Macy's earlier that week, she slipped on her four-inch heels and strutted out the door. Charisma picked up Heather first, then swung by Tangie's on her way to the city. Friday-night traffic was no surprise. It wasn't crazy; it was bearable until they crossed the Fifty-ninth Street bridge. City traffic was atrocious. It was a mild, winter night, and everybody and their mother was out. Charisma refused to pay the garage thirty dollars for a few hours of parking. So she rode around in circles until she lucked up and found a spot. It was a few blocks from the club, but at least it saved them thirty bucks.

There were a slew of guys hanging out in front of the club, but none of them were head-turning material. Charisma and Heather walked in with Tangie leading the way. They checked their coats and headed for the bar.

They hung out at the bar for a while, scoping the club for men. Tangie made eye contact with a guy across the dance floor. It was amazing how a dark room could play tricks on one's eyesight. She gave him a quarter-of-a-tank smile. He left his entourage and sauntered over anyway.

"I'm Bryce," he introduced himself, shaking her hand.

"Tangie," she said simply.

"Nice to meet you. Wanna dance?"

"Sure, why not?" She said rolling her eyes at Heather and Charisma as they walked to the dance floor. It was only a dance. He smiled, and she noticed his teeth. She had never seen an arrangement like that before, and they each had a direction all of their own. They danced to a couple of songs until the DJ decided to slow things down, at which point Tangie said she needed a drink.

Bryce insisted on buying her one, but she refused his offer. They found seats at the bar. Tangie gave Bryce a quick once-over, stopping at his feet. His black shoes matched his black pants and charcoal gray sweater, but they were like two sizes too big. There was a large gap around his heels. Apparently, he thought big feet would give him an in with the ladies. Well, not this lady, she thought to herself. She wondered how he had lasted on the dance floor without tripping over his own feet.

"Well, Bryce, it's been real, but I gotta go."

"Why don't I give you my number, and we can get together sometime."

"Let's not," she told him before standing up and walking away. No use leading him on.

Twenty minutes later Tangie told Heather and Charisma the truth. "I thought I was ready for all this, but I'm not."

"Nothing before its time," Charisma said simply, reassuring her.

"You could bump into the man of your dreams at the coat check, and it wouldn't mean a thing," Heather added.

"You're right," Tangie said simply. "Let's go home."

Tangie was dreading Monday morning. She was scheduled to be a recruiter for the gym at the New York job fair in the city, where over one hundred companies would be represented. Thank goodness it was just for one day. She got up extra early to dress for success, apply makeup, and do her hair. She caught the Long Island Railroad and transferred to a bus, but luckily, she made it to the Jacob Javits Center without a hitch.

Katie Wong, her partner from the gym's Flushing branch, had already arrived. Katie was a young, friendly Chinese girl, who had already begun setting up pamphlets and applications. The two hit it off instantly. Neither of them was thrilled to be there, but they made the best of a bad situation, talking a mile a minute. Reluctantly, Tangie changed from her sneakers to a pair of navy suede pumps, which were the exact same shade as her business suit. Katie held out until the last possible minute—8:59, to be exact—before she abandoned her flats for heels. Habitual sneaker wearers, they both dreaded the guaranteed eight hours of torture they knew their feet would endure, but appearances were everything while they were at the fair.

Since their booth was situated at the rear of the floor, it took some time before they saw their first prospect. She was a college graduate with a degree in accounting. Tangie took her résumé and she took pamphlets about career opportunities at Canyon's Club.

As the morning progressed, Tangie and Katie became flooded with a constant flow of applicants. Somewhere around noon there was a lull, and they both got the chance to catch their breath. Tangie looked around to check out the other booths. They were just as busy as she had been.

She stood for a moment to stretch her legs, catching the eye of the man in the booth across from her. She couldn't help but smile slightly before returning to her seat. She glanced up at the banner hanging above his booth. He was recruiting for the FBI, but after every few applicants, he would glance in her direction.

Tangie checked him out on the sly. He sported a fresh-shaved head and a navy pinstriped suit. Nice. Apparently, he thought the same about her because around lunchtime, he strolled over to her booth and invited her to lunch.

"Hi, I'm Tony. Excuse me for staring a moment ago, but I couldn't take my eyes off your . . . pumps." He grinned.

Blushing, Tangie knew she was already in trouble. "I'm Tangie."

"Nice to meet you, Tangie," he said, shaking her hand and holding it just a bit longer than necessary. She didn't mind at all. They stood for a moment, enjoying the view, neither speaking.

"Do you like seafood?" he asked her.

"I love it."

"Have you ever been to Presto's?"

"No, would you like to take me there?" She laughed.

Tony laughed too, rubbing his chrome dome with one swift stroke of the palm of his hand.

Secretly, the gesture drove her wild.

"Yes," he said, grinning.

"Lead the way," Tangie said, grabbing her coat. "I'll be back in time to relieve you," she told Katie.

"Take your time," Katie said, smiling, looking from one to the other.

Tangie and Tony walked a few blocks to the restaurant, the winter air brisk and fresh. As much as Tangie loved the city, she didn't miss working there anymore. It was just too congested.

Surprisingly though, the restaurant wasn't crowded. They were seated right away. Tony and Tangie flipped open the menus and checked out the lunch specials.

"The shrimp scampi is all that," Tony recommended.

"Would you believe I've never had shrimp scampi, but I'm feeling adventurous," Tangie admitted. "Shrimp scampi it is," she told the waiter.

"Make that two," Tony agreed.

Tangie checked her watch and ran her fingers through her hair. She hoped her hair wasn't too windblown.

"So, how long have you been with Canyon's Club?" he asked.

"Eight years."

"Is this your first job fair?"

"No, it's my third. How about you?"

"I have been to more job fairs than I care to remember."

"So, how is it working for the FBI?"

"Well, I travel a lot, and there's never a dull moment. I'm probably one of the few people who can honestly say that I love my job."

The waiter returned with their lunch. It was piping hot and smelled divine. They waited for their meals to cool. Tangie quickly said her grace, and when she opened her eyes, Tony was smiling.

"Do you always bless your food?" he asked.

"Since I was a little girl. Some things stay with you."

"I think it's wonderful."

They began to eat. "You're right. This is good," she admitted.

"So what does Tangie stand for?"

"Tangela."

"Tangela," he said slowly, putting his fork down. "I like that. Mind if I call you Tangela?"

"That's my name." She grinned, taking a sip of bottled

water. She liked the way her name rolled off his tongue. She shook her head. "This shrimp is really good."

"I guess our first date was a success, but for me the only thing missing is your phone number."

"Well, that should be a piece of cake for you, Mr. FBI."

"Yeah, and I have one helluva sweet tooth." He winked at her.

13

Charisma

Charisma was ticked off with Dex. Ever since Thanksgiving, he had been sniffing around her like a puppy. He was constantly dropping by her house unannounced to the point where she had to forbid him from coming by without calling first. It was getting ridiculous. When she stopped answering her doorbell, he realized that she meant business. He called her one night and told her he was coming by. He didn't ask her. He told her. That's when she decided enough was enough.

"What time did you leave work today?" he asked the minute he walked through the door.

"What?"

"You heard me. What time did you leave work? Seems like you've been working a lot of overtime."

"Not that I owe you an explanation, but I'm working on a special project."

"Yeah, boning your boss. It must take a lot of energy. Let's see. Where do you begin? There's the conference room, the ladies' lounge, and let's not forget his desktop.

That's like the headquarters of the entire operation. Am I right?" he asked with disgust.

"You oughtta quit your day job and head for Hollywood cause you'd make one helluva writer," Charisma said.

"And we both know you have one helluva sweet ass, don't we. You been giving my stuff away? Huh?"

"You're crazy."

"Well, I don't share."

"You should know by now that I'm a one-man woman."

"I saw you two were checking each other out on Thanksgiving and the guilty look on your face when you saw me. You must think I'm stupid. Don't insult my intelligence, okay?"

"I said nothing is going on. Now, if you're looking for something, I'll make sure you find it."

"Are you threatening me?"

"Look, I don't have time for this, Dex. I really don't. It's been a long day, and I don't feel like arguing. So if you don't mind, my bed is calling me."

"Yeah, and I bet your boss's is too."

"Good-bye, Dex." Charisma walked to the front door, opened it, and waited for Dex to walk through. She wasn't in the mood for his crap tonight, especially when she had a meeting first thing in the morning.

Charisma got to work bright and early. She rode the elevator up with Nate, but he barely said more to her than a polite good morning. She noticed that he had turned rather cool toward her ever since Thanksgiving. Was he avoiding her? No more laughing and joking around and no more "dates." It was now strictly business, and their conversations were limited to work. Then again, maybe he was just flipping the script and playing hard to get. Men were famous for that.

Charisma poured herself a big cup of coffee before heading into the conference room for her first meeting of the day. It was only thirty degrees outside when she woke up that morning, and the fresh, hot brew hit the spot. She couldn't believe how the temperature had dropped overnight, but winter was definitely here. No more cute little leather jackets. It was time for cashmere sweaters and fur.

After the staff of Freeman LTD was seated, Nate walked in. Miss Crappuccino was close behind, flirting with the boss as usual. Evidently, something got her in to work early that morning.

"How much you wanna bet she's baiting her trap?" Lauren leaned over and whispered in Charisma's ear.

"With what?" Charisma whispered back. "Dark meat has *so* much more flava."

Nate took his seat at the head of the conference table and the meeting began. "I just received an e-mail from our corporate office. Unfortunately, we've lost the Emerson account. Apparently, Emerson felt that a larger marketing firm with more resources would be to his advantage. So, of course with the loss of that account comes a loss in projected revenue."

Charisma's eyes scanned the room. Everyone seemed absorbed in what Nate was saying. He made eye contact with many but avoided hers. She watched him from across the room, her eyes settling on his lips as he spoke and wondering what it would be like to . . .

The meeting lasted another half hour and included a PowerPoint presentation of the company's goals for the coming year. Concluding, Nate stressed the importance of maintaining their reputation of excellence.

The meeting ended, and Charisma returned to her office. Just as she was about to read her e-mail, the phone rang. In her haste to answer the phone, she knocked over her cup of coffee, spilling it all over the papers on her desk as well as her lap. She was wearing a turquoise wool suit. She jumped up and grabbed some tissue to mop up the mess with one hand and picked up the phone with the other.

It was Nate.

"Yes, Nate."

"Charisma, I need to see you in my office."

"I just spilled coffee all over myself. Can you give me a second?"

"Sure, I'll see you in a few."

She headed straight for the ladies' lounge to blot out the coffee from her skirt before it stained. Then she took a handful of damp paper towels back to her office to clean her desk. Finally, she went in to see her boss.

"Close the door, Charisma." She did as she was told and sat down.

Nate was seated behind his desk with his elbows resting on the arms of the chair, clutching his hands as though he was about to crack his knuckles. He looked at her for a moment without speaking.

"How's it going?" he asked.

"Fine."

He got up from his seat and walked over to the front of his desk, where he sat down with one foot dangling in the air. He chose his words carefully.

"I think we've been playing this cat-and-mouse game long enough. First, you play hard to get, and I chase you. Then, I act uninterested and all business, and you're drawn to me even more. We're two adults. Let's be honest with ourselves and each other and admit that there's something between us."

"Nate, I don't know what to say."

"You don't know what to say, Charisma? Please, let's cut the bull. Okay? You want me just as much as I want you. We both know that. Stop acting like a child and start acting like my woman. How's that love of your life, by the way? What's his name again, Dex?" He smirked.

"I don't have to take this," she said, getting up to leave.

He caught her just as she reached the door, his hand covering her hand that covered the doorknob. Nate turned Charisma around to face him. He rested his back up against the door and pulled her toward him.

He smelled so damn good. It was intoxicating. Of course, she was attracted to him too. *Why was she fighting it?*

"Then do *this*," he said, his voice husky.

Charisma put her hands on his shoulders and looked up into his eyes. He held her so close she could barely breathe, and yet her heart was racing a mile a minute. His lips were only inches from hers.

Who the hell am I kidding? she asked herself, ready to give into her desires.

Just then the phone rang, ruining the moment and snapping Charisma back to her senses.

"Damn!" he said simply, releasing her and sprinting back to his desk. He answered the phone, motioning for Charisma to stay.

She shook her head, and he put the caller on hold.

"This isn't over, Charisma."

"That's what *you* think. I hope you enjoyed yourself, Nate, because this will *never* happen again. E*ver*."

"Not only will it happen again, Charisma, it'll happen sooner than you think."

"You're a trip," she said, shaking her head and leaving him to his phone call.

Charisma steered clear of her boss, making certain that their only interactions were job related. She spoke only when spoken to and did her very best to stay out of his way, but one evening as she prepared to leave, he cornered her in her office. Everyone else had gone home for the day.

"How's the Madison account coming along?" he asked, sliding both hands in his pockets.

"It's right on schedule, Nate."

"Excellent. We need to talk. You've been avoiding me, Charisma. We need to talk."

"About what?" she asked as she packed up her briefcase, her back to him.

"About us."

"What us? There is no us."

"You are in serious denial. Why are you fighting it? It's just a matter of time before we get together."

Charisma turned around to face him. "Nate, let me explain something to you. I have a man."

"And when's the last time you've seen him?"

She hesitated just slightly. "That's . . ."

"That long, huh? Who are you kidding, Charisma? I know he does it *to* you, but he doesn't do it *for* you. What you need is a *real* man."

"And I take it you're that man? You see this?" she asked, feeling the outline of her body with her hands. "Let me just say that you will never, ever taste this."

Nate began to laugh, a deep, hearty laugh. "Sweetheart, never is a long time. You enjoy your evening."

Charisma arrived home late that night took a nice, long shower. She made the water as cold as she could stand it and then headed off to bed. Before long she was out like a light.

Charisma walked along the beach in the moonlight. She paused for a moment while Nate spread the blanket onto the sand. They were alone with the ocean. He sat down first and beckoned for her to sit on his lap. She wore only a white tank top and a full, island print skirt that grazed her legs just bellow the knee. Obliging, she sat in his lap, and he covered them both with a second blanket. With one swift motion, he slid his hand underneath her skirt and unzipped his fly. She repositioned herself on his lap until they were both satisfied. Kissing, they gently rocked to the sounds of the ocean. Yet, at the same time, they were oblivious to them. He held her close and buried himself in her neck, loving the scent of her hair. Then, he slid his arms underneath her top, massaging first her strong back and then her breasts, one at a time. He bent down and slid one breast into his mouth, loving the taste and fullness of it. Before long, she was panting and they were both rocking underneath the blanket. He stiffened as he came while her cries of pleasure rolled out to sea with the waves. . . .

Charisma woke up with a jolt. Her nightgown was soaked, clinging to places she tried to deny. Shamefully, she ran her hand through her hair in an attempt to catch her breath. Still flushed, she got up and headed for the bathroom. Then she thought better of it. She couldn't dare to face herself in the mirror.

Luckily, the alarm clock went off a little over an hour later and she had other things to occupy her time—like getting ready for work. Then she realized that she'd have to see *him*. And in an office the size of theirs, there was no place to hide.

She decided to go nondescript. She'd wear a pair of black wool slacks and a black cashmere turtleneck. She refused to wear anything that would draw attention to her person. She didn't want his eyes feasting on her body any longer than necessary.

Charisma drove to work and circled the building twice looking for a parking spot. She was hoping that her boss's car would be nonexistent and that he'd decided to take the day off. As luck would have it, though, they ended up sharing an elevator. It was just the two of them. So she pretended to be engrossed in the morning paper to discourage any attempts at conversation. Unfortunately, it didn't work.

"Was it good for you too?" he asked her point-blank.

"Was what good for me?"

"The dream you had about us last night. It must have been hot because you look positively radiant this morning."

Her answer was a swift slap across the face.

"I take it that means yes." He grinned, rubbing his stinging cheek.

As the elevator door opened, she stepped off, fuming. Why hadn't she had a quick comeback for his arrogance? Now she felt like an idiot. If she left early, she'd feel like a fool, and if she stayed the entire day she wouldn't be able to look him in the eye. It was a no-win situation.

Charisma wondered if her coworkers were aware of any sexual tension between her and Nate. If they were, they kept it to themselves, and Chase was probably too busy plotting and scheming herself to pay Charisma any mind.

Charisma worked all day on the Madison account, tabulating data from various demographics. The report was due by close of business Friday, and it was already Wednesday. She stopped at five PM, too exhausted to work any overtime. She wanted nothing more than to curl up with a hot cup of homemade cocoa and get some much-needed rest. Funny, as she drifted off to sleep, her last thought was whether or not she had remembered to lock her computer.

A well-rested Charisma got to work bright and early Thursday morning. The first thing Charisma did was check her computer. Dag, she *had* forgotten to lock it, but from the looks of her files, everything appeared to be untouched. She headed for the conference room and put on a fresh pot of coffee. It was an unwritten office rule that whoever got in first made the coffee.

By the time Charisma returned to her office, she realized that she wasn't the only one in. Evidently, Chase had made it in early as well. Normally, she worked from ten AM to four PM on Thursdays, but apparently, something had gotten her up early that morning. Charisma chose to ignore Miss Crappuccino.

There was still much to do on the Madison account. When Charisma accessed the file, the data looked strangely unfamiliar. Her flying fingers began typing a mile a minute. Someone had deleted all her hard work, and the report was due Friday. Damn, how could she have been so careless? And what the hell was Chase doing in so early?

"We need to talk," Charisma said.

"I'm busy," Chase said without giving her so much as an acknowledging glance.

"Like hell you are. I know you've been in my files."

"What?"

"You heard me," Charisma said.

"Prove it."

"You think that by making me look bad, Nate'll reassign the account to you, and you'll be the new golden girl around her."

"Correction, sweetie. In case you haven't noticed, I already am golden. You're the one struggling to get to my level, and that next promotion you've been eying? It's mine too." She laughed.

If there was one thing Charisma hated, it was a smug white chick. She was ready to slap her silly. All she saw was red. "You just crossed the wrong woman. Watch your back, bitch."

"Hmph, is that a threat?" Chase asked.

"Like I said, watch your back."

"Oh, go back to Africa," she said under her breath.

"What did you say?" Charisma asked her, getting up in her face.

"Go back to Africa."

"As much black meat you've had lately, I'm surprised

you're still here. Don't think I don't know about you and Blade."

"Please, if your best friend were a real woman, her man wouldn't have been breaking his neck to share his benefit package with me now, would he? And, *mama mia*, what a package it was."

"Let me remind you of something, cavewoman. Your people were crawling around caves when my people were kings and queens."

"Well, you're certainly not a queen now, are you?" Chase smirked.

Charisma walked out fuming. She returned to her office, her flying fingers attempting to reinput all the lost data that Chase had deleted, but time was not on her side. By three-thirty that afternoon, her report was only a quarter done. Nate stopped by to inquire on the status of the account since it was due by the next day, and he had a meeting with Bob Madison first thing Monday morning.

Charisma couldn't decide if she should blow the whistle on Chase or not, but she did admit to Nate that she was behind schedule.

"Let's cut to the point, Charisma. Will the report be ready tomorrow?"

She hesitated slightly. "I hope so, Nate. I'm working as hard as I can."

"You hope so? Charisma, if you couldn't handle this project, you should have informed me immediately. There is no excuse for this. None. And now, all of our asses are on the line. You know this is one of our biggest accounts." He picked up the phone and dialed his secretary. "Get Chase in her immediately," he said before hanging up.

A few moments later, a doe-eyed Chase walked into Charisma's office.

"Chase, I need you to help Charisma with the Madison account," Nate told her.

Charisma gave her a blank stare as Nate continued. "This project is due tomorrow. Chase, I know you're due to leave shortly, but is there any possible way you can work until five?"

"Of course, Nate," Chase said. "We're a team. I'll do whatever needs to be done. In fact, when Charisma mentioned to Lacy that she was behind schedule, I began a preliminary report myself. I just didn't want to step on anyone's toes."

"I appreciate your initiative, Chase," he said before turning back to Charisma's desk. Nate picked up the phone and dialed his secretary again. "Get Lacy in here," he told her. Moments later, Lacy had joined the group.

"Lacy, did Charisma tell you anything about the Madison account?" Nate asked her.

Lacy the office gossiper, refused to look in Charisma's direction. "Just that she was having trouble and that she probably wouldn't meet the deadline."

"You are *such* a liar," Charisma told her, realizing that she and Chase were in cahoots. Apparently, all her skinfolk weren't her kinfolk, as her grandmother used to warn her.

"Unfortunately, Miss Dearborn, I don't have the luxury of figuring out who's lying. Chase, have your figures been verified?" he asked.

"Absolutely. In fact, I double-checked them this morning," she told him smugly.

"Great. Chase, I want you to take over the account and Charisma, you assist her. I want hourly updates on your progress. Is that clear?" he asked them both.

"Yes," they both agreed.

"Charisma, I have the updated test-market results on my desk." Chase feigned helpfulness, putting her hair behind her left ear. "Why don't we start with that?" Chase asked innocently in front of Nate.

"Fine," Charisma answered, throwing imaginary darts into her back. "Nate, I've worked hard on this account from day one, and you're just going to hand it over to Chase? That's *my* account."

"Not any more, Charisma," Nate said before returning to his office. Charisma was the last employee to leave that night. After the day's events she realized that she had just kissed her chances for a promotion good-bye.

Charisma worked down to the wire on Friday. Chase, who normally worked half a day on Fridays, stayed for the duration after making certain that Nate knew she was sacrificing her personal time for the good of the firm. She insisted that she'd do whatever it took. *Yeah, whatever it takes my ass,* Charisma thought.

Charisma soon caught on to her game. Chase was merely spoon-feeding her results that Charisma had initially tabulated herself. She had stolen the findings, and now she was spoon-feeding them back to Charisma as her own. And Nate was impressed with Chase's speed and accuracy. If he only knew. . . . By five o'clock all the data was restored and the report was miraculously completed. Everyone breathed a sigh of relief. Charisma just wanted to get the hell out of there.

She had an after-work appointment for a manicure at Hot Tips Nails Salon in Rochdale Village, and then she and Tangie were meeting at Cabana for drinks. Eventually, two seats opened up at the bar.

"Girl, you look whipped," Tangie said.

"Yeah, tell me about it."

The bartender took their orders and returned with their drinks—two apple martinis. Charisma proceeded to tell Tangie about her week.

"Why didn't you speak up?"

"I didn't have any proof. It would have just been her word against mine."

"But still, Nate could have checked the times you two

signed in and out or something. She made you look like a fool."

"It gets better. Chase told him that I had confided in Lacy about being behind schedule, and then Lacy corroborated her story."

"Oh, they set you up big-time."

"Please, in that office a sister will cut you just as quick as Goldilocks will. There's no loyalty amongst the sisters. It's every woman for herself. I blame Chase. She was the mastermind, but like they say, payback's a bitch."

"What did you have in mind?"

"Karma will put her behind in check. She will curse the day she crossed my path. She messed with the wrong sister. Now, you see why I don't trust them? They'll smile in your face and stab you in the back every chance they get."

"Let me play devil's advocate for a minute. Would you have preferred being betrayed by a black coworker?" Tangie asked.

"I don't know, but I am just sick and tired of the whole game. I'm tired of their arrogance and the way they look down their noses at us like they own the world and belong to some kind of privileged sect."

"Wow, I haven't seen you this angry in a long time."

"And trust me. It's not over." Charisma sipped her martini. Slowly.

Tangie thought for a moment. "Well, you know how I feel about her. Between the two of us I'm sure we'll have no problem settling the score. Count me in."

A smile crept onto Charisma's face. "Deal."

14

Heather

Heather had put it off for as long as she could. Charisma and Tangie had told her it was time. Jamal thought it was time. Even the mechanics at Big Apple Tire had told her it was time. One day she woke up and realized they were right. It was time to buy another car—not a new one, but a better one.

It wasn't an easy decision for Heather to make. Lord knows, she had been putting it off for quite some time. Giving in made her feel as though she was drifting off track, losing focus of her goal to undergo plastic surgery. She tried to tell herself that she was just taking a slight detour for the sake of pure necessity. She wasn't abandoning her dream of a new nose—she was merely postponing it.

With that in mind, she left work early one afternoon and drove up to the Nemet showroom on Hillside Avenue for a car. Her mother had offered to accompany her, but being fully aware of the value of a man's presence at times like these, Heather opted to have Jamal meet her there instead. He was more than willing to oblige. In fact, he was there waiting for her when she arrived.

The salesman immediately took them to see the most expensive vehicles in the showroom. Heather wasn't interested. He promptly took her to the outside lot to check out the less expensive models in his inventory. All Heather needed was four wheels to get her from point A to point B. Bells and whistles need not apply. It was bad enough that she had to cut into money "nosemarked" for her surgery. Even though she planned on taking out a loan with the credit union, she still needed to put 10 percent down. Thank goodness the trip to South Beach was finally paid off. Less than a week later, Heather was sporting a new, black late-model Mazda. Though it had clocked 31,000 miles to its name, it was brand spanking new to her, especially compared to the guzzler she had just unloaded.

Whenever Heather got behind the wheel of the Mazda, she tried not to hate herself for selling out. She had to convince herself that the nose job was still in her future—a more distant future—but the future nonetheless. Each time she looked into the rearview mirror, she purposely avoided her nose and prayed the how-long prayer. Lord, how long will it be before I trade in this sorry excuse for a nose and start living up to my full potential in the looks department? She was already working on her weight. So, it was just a matter of time before her body was tight. The sad part of the transformation was that even if she lost every excess ounce of flesh that clung to her body, she'd still look a mess with her current nose splashed across her face. She'd just have to re-finagle her finances. Again.

"Wow, I never thought I'd see the day when you'd pick *us* up," Tangie admitted to Heather when she picked her and Charisma up for a girls' night out.

"Tell me about it," Heather agreed. "And there's nothing like a new set of wheels to restore your peace of mind. I mean, just the possibility of breaking down in the middle of traffic everyday raised my blood pressure twenty points. It was incredible."

"I know how much you wanted that nose job, but I think you made the right decision," Charisma told her.

Heather kept her eye on the road. She checked her rearview mirror, making certain that her glance didn't linger on her nose. "I hate to admit it," she said. "But it was worth it."

"I never thought your nose was that bad," Tangie said from the backseat. "It has character."

"Character?" Heather laughed. "That's like telling a mother that her baby's not *that* ugly."

"Your nose is unique, Heather," Tangie said. "It's part of who you are. Don't just ditch it for a new and improved model. Do that to your car, not a body part."

Heather nodded to shut Tangie up, but it went in one ear and out the other. She drove down Queens Boulevard, catching almost all the lights. She circled around a couple of blocks a few times in search of a parking spot, but had no such luck, then ended up parking in the lot. Outside it was cooler than expected. Sometimes the weatherman's predictions were off. They walked to the Midway, wishing they had worn heavier coats. Tyler Perry's movie was sold out. They ended up seeing something else instead.

Afterward they hit Cabana for a late-night snack. They gorged on steak, chicken, and black beans and rice, leaving no room for dessert. Heather listened to Tangie rant and rave about getting home to see if Tony had called her. Secretly, Heather couldn't wait to get home to her bathroom and undo the night's damage.

Ashley Stewart was packed with holiday shoppers like all the other stores in the mall that Saturday. Heather wasn't in the mood for crowds, but since she was scheduled to work late practically every night next week, this was the best time to come and pay her bill. The store was stocked with festive holiday merchandise, and Heather was more than tempted to purchase a few items. She realized, however, that if she waited a little longer, she'd be able to purchase an even smaller size. So she waited, but that didn't stop her from going through all the racks and daydreaming how she'd look in all the clothes. She especially loved the black velvet camisole top and matching pants and the red satin dress.

Maybe it was the purging or maybe she was just coming down with something. In any event, Heather was exhausted, but not too tired to hit a few of the jewelry stores. She told herself that she was just looking. That she didn't need any more jewelry. If the truth be told, though, she always made room for just one more piece.

Heather walked in the door and spotted the most adorable pair of brushed satin gold hoop earrings. It was love at first sight. She knew they were made for her even before the saleslady took them out of the display case. Heather oohed and aahed. She had to have them. No doubt about it. Unfortunately, she had left her checkbook and ATM card at home. She did, however, have her good ol' American Express card. Problem solved.

She waltzed out of the store and smack-dab into a shopper. She apologized quickly, eager to get home and eat. Her growling stomach embarrassed her. She hoped it wasn't audible. She thought about going up to the food court, but then it would take that much longer to try on her earrings at home. Vanity won out. She went home.

Halfway home Heather reached for her purse on the passenger seat and unzipped it with one hand. She grabbed the steering wheel with both hands to steady herself. She was just a bit light-headed. The car swerved ever so gently as she grabbed her wallet, checking for her American Express. *Where was it?* Without taking her eyes off the road, she felt the contents of her bag, her hands now trembling.

Nothing. She placed the bag in her lap for further inspection. Still no card. Finally, she dumped the contents of her purse onto the passenger seat. Even with the window cracked, her shirt was beginning to cling to her chest and her fingers were moist against the steering wheel. Maybe she *should* have eaten at the mall. Maybe she should cut back on her private sessions in the bathroom. Purging had zapped her strength.

She must have left her card at the jewelry store or maybe that shopper had picked her pocket when she bumped into him. She made a U-turn and headed back to the mall. That's when she heard a police siren and a cop pulled her over. She turned off the engine as the cop approached her. He was a tall, burly-looking man with a red handlebar moustache. She memorized his name. Officer McNair asked for her license and registration before returning to his patrol car. A few minutes later he returned them to her. She asked him why she had been pulled over. He told her that she was driving erratically, swerving from side to side. A Breathalyzer test revealed that there was no alcohol in Heather's system.

"I left my credit card at the mall, and I guess I panicked. That's where I was headed when you stopped me."

He peered into her eyes. "Your eyes look a bit glazed. Are you on anything?"

She just stared at him.

"Miss Grey, are you taking any prescription drugs or illegal medication?"

"No, Officer. I'm just coming down with the flu."

"Do you think you can make it home all right?"

Heather nodded. "I just want to go pick up my card, and I'll head straight home."

The officer took out his pad. "Look, I'll issue you a warning this time, but next time . . ."

"There won't be a next time. I assure you, Officer Mc-Nair."

"Good." He walked to his patrol car and drove off.

Heather headed back to the jewelry store. She had indeed left her card. From there, she went straight home and crashed. She didn't give the earrings a second thought.

Ava called later that night to invite her to a lingerie party.

"No, not tonight," Heather told her. "Can I take a rain check?"

"Have you ever been to one?" Ava asked.

"No, I haven't."

"I'll be modeling, chickylicky. I guarantee you'll have a good time. It'll be fun," Ava tried to convince her.

"Maybe next time."

"Let me know if you ever want to host one."

"You'll be the first to know."

15

Charisma

In keeping with tradition, Charisma, Heather, and Tangie got together on Christmas eve to exchange gifts. That year, Tangie played hostess. Charisma and Heather picked up a dozen hot and spicy Jamaican beef patties from Wilson's and headed over to Tangie's. They kicked back, opened gifts, and sipped champagne. It was well after midnight when they left.

Charisma spent Christmas with her parents. As she drove to their home, she was grateful that the weatherman was wrong about expecting three inches of snow that morning. She parked in the driveway, unloaded the gifts from her car's trunk and walked up the steps to the house. Charisma let herself in. Her brother Eric was just pulling up in his car.

Jena whipped up breakfast for her husband and children and they sat down to eat. Afterward, they headed to the living room to open presents. Underneath the live seven-foot-high Christmas tree were presents galore. Charisma got her mother a gold Greek key bracelet that she had been eyeing for months. Her father was so easy to please. He loved his royal blue silk pajamas, and her brother told her that for once she had bought him a fragrance set he could live with. She jabbed him affectionately in the arm. Hours later, Charisma left with her gifts. She made out like a fat rat heading home with tri-colored gold earrings, a perfume gift set, champagne flutes, a jogging suit, and a leather jacket.

Heather and Tangie spent New Year's eve over Charisma's for their annual pajama party.

"You know what I need right now?" Charisma asked without waiting for an answer. "I need Ed Gordon to wrap those juicy lips around me and keep me warm tonight."

"They're even juicier in person," Heather recalled.

"You always did like those Clark Kent types, Charisma," Tangie told her.

"Hey, two men for the price of one." Charisma shrugged. "What's wrong with that? So who's your switch flipper, Heather?"

"Terrence Howard," Heather sighed. "Those sexy, green eyes and smooth baby skin, what I wouldn't do to him."

"You're a nut," Tangie told Heather, laughing. "But I wouldn't mind making it an LL Cool J night." She refilled her flute with champagne. "Look at us. What's wrong with this picture? We are three thirtilicious women sitting home on New Year's eve fantasizing about men we will never have, let alone meet. Let's vow in the New Year to be all we can be and make things happen. And remember, ladies, behind every successful woman is herself."

After the holidays Chase waltzed into Freeman LTD without a care in the world. Her layered blond locks curled gently before grazing the middle of her back. When she removed her mink coat, it was obvious that she was dripping in diamonds. Apparently, Santa had been good to her. Charisma took one look at her and decided she needed more caffeine.

Ellis Dearborn called his daughter late one Friday evening. He hadn't seen her since Christmas and was anxious to spend some time with his firstborn especially since he had run into her boss a few days earlier at the bank. Ellis had spoken frankly with Nate and told him he wanted to see him step up to the plate with his daughter.

"Don't think I haven't tried, Ellis, but we both know how stubborn Charisma can be."

"She's just like her mother," he had agreed. "I've never said this to another man before, but you have my blessings."

Ellis and Charisma agreed to have breakfast Saturday morning at IHOP. Ellis picked up his daughter and they headed over to the restaurant. After a ten-minute wait, they were seated at a table for two. They each ordered coffee, buttermilk pancakes, and sausages—Ellis with an omelet, Charisma without.

Ellis got straight to the point. "So, princess, how's life been treating you?"

"Well, Daddy, work is basically back to normal after that Chase Martini fiasco."

"And Nate?" he asked.

"He's still my boss, if that's what you mean," she said simply.

"I think it's time that you start planning for your future."

"What do you mean?"

"You know I love you and only want what's best for you. I hate seeing you waste the best years of your life with the wrong man," he said, referring to Dex.

"Oh, and Nate's the One?"

"I know we've only met Nate once, but your mother and I think that he's the one for you."

"Really?" she asked, matter-of-factly.

"Yes, really," he said in return. "We know we can't force you to do anything you don't want to do. You're a grown woman, but for our sake, will you at least think about it?" he asked as the waitress returned with their meals.

"Daddy, you're really putting me in an awkward position."

"How so?"

"I've never even dated a colleague, let alone my boss."

"Stop being such a prude, Charisma. Office romances happen everyday. Many of them lead to marriage. We can all see that he's attracted to you, and all it would take is a little encouragement on your part to seal the deal."

"And what if he's not who *I* want?" she asked.

"Then you haven't lost a thing. And another thing, who are you waiting for—Prince Charming? I hate to burst your bubble, but life isn't a fairy tale. I don't know if you realize it, but do you know what makes the best marriages?" he asked without waiting for an answer. "Men can be real dogs. The best marriages are when the man loves the woman a little more than she loves him. And that's the kind of marriage I think you'll have with Nate. Look, do your mother and I ask for much?" he asked, cutting into his omelet.

"No," she admitted.

"Then will you do us this one favor and give Nate a chance?"

"Yes, Daddy," she sighed, holding a forkful of pancakes and wondering why it was virtually impossible to say no to her daddy.

"Princess, if you remember nothing else in life, just know that I will love you forever and that you deserve joy."

* * *

True to his word, Nate wasted no time stepping up his game with Charisma. First thing he did was invite her out for coffee, to which she asked for a rain check. So the next day he asked her out to lunch, another offer she coyly refused. Then he got lucky. One night after work she had a flat tire. Since the office was nowhere near public transportation, she'd have to call a cab.

By the time Nate left the building, Charisma was sitting in the dark with her head down on the steering wheel. He walked over to her car and tapped on the driver's-side window, startling her.

She rolled down the window and explained to him that she had a flat.

"Do you have a spare?"

"I don't think so."

"Pop open your trunk for me. You probably have a doughnut."

She did as told. He had the tire changed in no time. She offered to pay him, but of course, he wouldn't hear of it.

He offered to follow her home just in case there were any more problems, but she wouldn't hear of it.

He pulled rank on her. "I insist," he said simply. "What kind of man would I be if I let you go home alone, knowing that you're having car trouble? Charisma, if nothing else, I'm a gentleman."

"Are you?" she teased him, smiling.

"Why don't you let me prove myself to you? Unless . . ."

"Unless what?" Charisma asked.

"Unless you're afraid of a *real* man. Some women can't handle one."

"I'm not one of those women," she said. "And to prove it, I really would appreciate it if you would follow me home."

"Lead the way, Miss Dearborn. I'm right behind you."

Charisma drove off with Nate behind her. She was home in no time. Like a perfect gentleman, he waited until she was safely inside. Just as he was about to pull off, he took one last glance at her house. She opened her door and quickly ran toward his car.

"I thought maybe you'd like to come in for a drink," she said.

"I thought you'd never ask. Let me park, and I'll be right in."

Nate ended up parking all the way down the block. Walking in the frigid air was a small price to pay to be in Charisma's company and off the clock at that. He hoped that her invitation was just the start of something interesting between them. He had told her father that he'd give it his best shot, and he was a man of his word. Charisma would have to meet him halfway. Maybe tonight she was finally ready to take that first step. He hadn't been to her house since he took her to see the Knicks that night. It was good to be back.

Nate rang her doorbell, and she welcomed him into the warmth of her living room, helping him off with his coat and scarf.

"Whew! It's cold out there." He rubbed his hands together.

"Tell me about it. Why don't you sit down and thaw out. I'll be right out." Charisma returned momentarily, totally relaxed in a white tank top and a pair of black leggings. Nate looked down at her pedicure and couldn't stop grinning. Apparently, he had a foot fetish, Charisma decided.

"Let me see if I remember," she said, heading for the bar. "A screwdriver with just a splash of cranberry juice."

"You're good." He smiled, loosening his tie and removing his jacket.

Charisma handed him his drink and poured herself a glass of white wine. She joined him on the sofa.

"So to what do I owe the pleasure of this invitation?" He rolled up his sleeves. "It's warm in here."

"Well, you came to my rescue tonight. I had to do something."

"Thank you would have been enough, but why don't we do dinner?"

She looked at him for a minute.

"I've heard it a thousand times. You don't do windows, and you don't do bosses. Surely you do dinner?"

"And where will that lead?" she asked.

"Wherever you do or don't want it to."

"You don't give up, do you?"

"That's why I'm the boss."

"Yeah, you're *my* boss," she reminded him.

"Let me ask you something. If I weren't your boss, would I stand a chance?"

"Maybe."

"Let me tell you something. If I weren't your boss, I would've had you by now."

"You're real sure of yourself, aren't you?"

"Just keeping it real."

"How so?"

"Your biggest defense from day one has been that you don't do your bosses. Not that I'm not your type or we're not attracted to each other or we're not compatible. Am I right? It's always been our working relationship that's prevented me from going further. So all I'm saying is that if our nine-to-five relationship wasn't the issue, we wouldn't even be having this conversation. In fact, we'd probably be in your bedroom right now, wearing each other out."

"You're something else. I don't know how much more I can take of this."

"Stop fighting it. We both want the same thing. What is it about me that you fear most?" Nate asked.

Charisma took another sip of wine and thought for a moment. "I guess I'm afraid of losing control."

"That's not always a bad thing."

"Well, I'd certainly be sacrificing my principles."

"Gee, thanks a lot."

"No, I didn't mean it like that. I just meant that I'd be doing something totally against my character."

"Sometimes people need to get outside their comfort zone." He took the wine glass from her hand and placed it on the coffee table. They turned to face one another. He cupped her face in his hands. She covered his hands, still cold, with her own.

"Relax, baby," he whispered in her ear.

She closed her eyes and kissed him, their tongues easing into the warmth.

"You're beautiful. Do you know that?" he whispered.

"And you're delicious," she told him, ready for another kiss.

"I knew you'd taste like cinnamon toast," he joked. "You play hard to get for months, and now you're giving me a hard-on."

"What can I say, you wore me down."

He slid his hand underneath her tank top and unhooked her bra. "All I want to do is please you, Charisma." He kissed her tenderly.

She smiled up at him and began to unbutton his shirt. Then she unzipped his fly. Nate kissed her hungrily. She moaned as she eased down onto the sofa.

Suddenly, Charisma's phone rang. She reached behind her head to answer it. Nate grabbed her hand. "Not this time," he said. They wrestled playfully until her machine picked up.

It was her mother in tears. Nate hopped up, and Charisma quickly picked up the receiver.

"Mother, what's wrong?" Charisma asked. "Oh my God. Uh-huh. Which hospital? Okay, I'll meet you there." Charisma looked at Nate with fear in her eyes. "I have to go. My father's in North Shore's emergency room."

Nate stood, zipped up, and put his jacket back on. "I'll drive you. You don't need to get stranded on the road somewhere," he said.

"Are you sure?" she asked.

"It's the least I can do," he said.

"Thanks, Nate. I owe you one."

16

Tangie

"Would you believe Tony still hasn't called?" Tangie exclaimed to Heather and Charisma over breakfast at IHOP.

"It hasn't been that long," Charisma insisted, sliding a bacon strip in her mouth.

"It's been long enough," Tangie decided.

"What's he like, anyway?" Heather asked.

"Let's just say he's got a thick . . . neck," Tangie said. "But seriously, he definitely seemed interested," she recalled.

"Did he give you his number?" Heather asked.

Tangie shook her head.

"Maybe he's married," Heather said.

"I don't think so." Tangie poured more syrup onto her buttermilk pancakes. "Maybe he's on a special assignment."

"It's possible," Charisma agreed.

"I don't know if I can handle getting involved with an FBI agent," Tangie admitted.

Tangie kept herself busy so that she wouldn't think about Tony not calling. Even though she didn't know him that well, she had hoped that he'd be the *one*. Apparently, she was wrong. Again. She threw herself into work at the gym, practically doubling her paycheck with overtime. It was a shame that she needed a man or lack thereof to help get her finances straight.

Tangie was looking forward to spending a nice, quite evening at home when Heather and Charisma called her to go ice-skating at Rockefeller Center. "You guys go ahead without me. I'm running on fumes," she told them.

"It'll be fun," Charisma said.

"All I want is sleep." Tangie's bed felt like heaven. "Are we still on for tomorrow morning?" she yawned.

"Uh-huh. Are you sure you don't wanna join us?" Heather asked.

"Positive. Have fun," Tangie insisted before hanging up.

Never mind counting sheep. Tangie always drifted off to sleep doing her Kegels. Nothing beat a tight coochie. By seven-thirty, Tangie was already in la-la land. Somewhere around nine her phone rang again, and she blindly reached for it.

"Hello," she said groggily.

"Sounds like I called at a bad time."

Tangie instantly perked up upon hearing the familiar male voice on the other end. It was Tony. She sat up in bed and turned on the lamp on her nightstand, secretly smiling.

"Not at all. I must've dozed off. I'm awake now."

"Are you sure?"

"Positive," she told him.

"Feel like getting a bite to eat?"

"I'd love to. Where'd you have in mind?"

"What do you say we take a ride into Manhattan and have a nice dinner?" he suggested.

"Sounds like a plan," she said softly.

"May I pick you up?"

"You certainly may." Tangie began to give him her address.

"You don't think I'd get your phone number without getting your address?" He laughed and Tangie joined in. "What time shall I pick you up?"

Tangie checked the clock on her nightstand. "How about in an hour?"

"See you then," he agreed.

Tangie hung up, giggling as she hugged her knees to her chest. It was amazing how the right call could revive her from the snatches of exhaustion. She was wide awake.

She jumped into the shower, pampering her skin with a fragrant body wash before wrapping herself in a thick, thirsty towel. Tangie then slathered on her favorite moisturizer and body lotion before heading back to her bedroom. Next, came the hard part, deciding on something to wear. Tangie had three outfits laid out across her bed, black denim jeans, black cords, and black suede pants. Okay, she tossed the jeans. Finally, she decided on the suede bootcuts, paired with her favorite lime green sweater, and black patent leather shoeties. The green of the sweater made her golden brown skin pop. She spritzed on perfume and returned to the bathroom where she proceeded to apply her makeup. Finally, she unwrapped her layered locks, pleased with the way they fell below her shoulders.

She checked her watch. Tony was due in less than ten minutes if traffic wasn't too heavy. Tangie suddenly became anxious. She practiced deep-breathing exercises to calm herself—in through the nose, out through the mouth. She closed her eyes for a moment, and when she opened them, the doorbell ran. It was Tony.

"Hi," she said simply. "Come on in."

Tony walked through the door looking better than she had remembered. "Wow, you look great." He kissed her gently on the cheek.

"Did you have any trouble finding me?" she asked.

"None at all."

"Give me a second, and I'll be all set," Tangie said, heading toward her bedroom. Finally she returned, grabbed her coat and purse from the sofa, and out the door they went.

Tangie laughed as Tony helped her into his silver CLK 350 Benz.

"What's so funny?" he asked her once he was in the driver's seat.

"Oh, nothing. It's just that this is my dream car." She smiled.

"Is that right?"

She nodded.

"Well, maybe you'd like to drive." He handed her the car keys.

"Are you serious?" she asked.

"Why not? I wanna be the man who makes your dreams come true. All of them."

Tangie and Tony got out of the car, switched seats, and sped off. Tangie was loving it. The Benz rode nothing like her Nissan. Driving was pure pleasure, and they floated into the city like they were on a magic carpet. Tony instructed Tangie to park in a nearby garage, and she willingly obliged. Then they walked a few short blocks to the restaurant. Tony wrapped his arm protectively around her shoulder, and she loved it along with the smell of his aftershave. It was a frigid night, but she had refused to wear a hat and ruin her long, flowing mane.

Like most New York hot spots that night, Finger Lickin' was jam-packed. Even with reservations they had to wait, but Tangie didn't mind. The twenty minutes flew by and before long they were seated at a cozy little booth near the fireplace.

Tangie loved soul food. As she looked over the menu, each dish sounded better than the last. "So what do you suggest?" she finally asked Tony when she couldn't make up her mind.

"I'll tell you what," he began. "The portions here are so huge that we can order two separate dishes, split them, and still walk out stuffed. And I promise not to hold it against you if you don't eat like a bird."

"Eat like a bird? Don't let this size-six body fool you."

"So now that I know your size, what's your favorite color?"

"Lime green," she said simply.

"You wear it well." He winked.

Tangie blushed ever so slightly at the compliment. The waiter came around to take their orders—smothered chicken with cabbage and macaroni and cheese and roast beef, mashed potatoes and gravy, and string beans. Tangie said her grace and they dove right in. The food was so well seasoned that Tangie flashed back to her grandmother's kitchen on any given Sunday. Wanting to make a good impression on their first real date, she tried to eat like the perfect lady, but it wasn't easy.

When they had both finished, Tony picked up her napkin. "Hold still," he said as he gently wiped the corner of her mouth. "So was it good for you too?"

"You have no idea." She smiled.

"Trust me. It gets better," he said, tossing her the car keys.

The next morning Tangie called Heather and Charisma. "Mmm, I slept like a baby last night," Tangie purred.

"Yeah, you were knocked out. We had a ball at Rockefeller Center," Heather said. "You should've been there."

"I had other plans. I hung out with Tony," Tangie said, gloating.

"What?" Charisma asked. "I know you did not diss the sisterhood for a man."

"Can I help it if I'm still a little boy crazy?" Tangie asked.

"A little?" Heather and Charisma said.

"Yeah, a little," Tangie insisted.

"So how did it go?" Charisma asked.

"It was wonderful," Tangie began. "He called me about an hour and a half after you guys and invited me out to dinner. We went to this new soul food place in the city. Oh my goodness, I ate like a pig."

"Is he a good kisser?" Heather asked.

"Don't know," Tangie said. "Yet."

"Losing your touch?" Charisma teased.

"Don't think he didn't try," Tangie told them. "I made sure it landed just a smidgen to the right of my lips. He walked me to my door, and I shook his hand. Playing a little hard to get never hurts any relationship. You know what they say, make a man chase it, before you let him taste it."

"I hear ya," Charisma agreed.

"What time is it?" Heather changed the subject." We better get started if we're getting our hair and eyebrows done."

"Be ready in an hour?" Tangie asked them. "I'll pick you both up." Tangie said.

"Okay, see you in a little while," Charisma said.

Tangie, Heather, and Charisma arrived at Daisy's somewhere around ten-thirty. It had been a struggle getting out of her nice, warm, inviting bed, but Tangie had promised to pick up her girls so she got up. Reluctantly, but she made it.

"*Hola, chicas,*" Daisy said as they entered her beauty shop. One of the things they liked about the Dominican salons is that they were in and out in no time. It was never an all-day affair.

Two hours later they were on their way to When We Were Queens to have Cinderella do their brows. Naturally, Cinderella had a shop full of women waiting to be waxed and tweezed, but she paused to greet them, kissing the girls on both cheeks. Cinderella fluttered around her customers, giving each the attention they deserved, applying lipsticks, foundation, and the like.

Amazingly, the shop emptied out and Cinderella was left with just Tangie, Charisma, and Heather. "So what's going on, my queens?" she asked them.

"I met someone," Tangie said.

"You mean Blade's history?" Cinderella asked. "Thank God. Call the cops! Well, how'd you two meet, my queen?" she asked as she put wax on Tangie's brows.

"At a job fair," Tangie admitted.

"I can tell you like him already. Just take it slow and get to know each other," Cinderella advised.

Tangie nodded as Cinderella removed the wax from her eyebrows. She finished up with Charisma and Heather, and the girls left the shop with fresh brows and bags of cosmetics and skin-care products.

"Without God and you we truly cannot survive," Cinderella reminded them as she hugged them good-bye.

Later that evening Tony called Tangie. She so wanted to accept his invitation for drinks but opted out. She had already mapped out her strategy, and there was no room for being too available. So she took a nice, hot bubble bath, had a nice big mug of hot chocolate, and called it a night.

Somewhere around eight o'clock her phone rang again. She had just drifted off.

"Tangie?" It was Blade.

"What do you want?" she asked, punching her pillow.

"I'm in the hospital. I have two cracked ribs and a dislocated shoulder. I messed with the wrong people and got my ass kicked," he whispered. "It's a long story."

"Payback's a bitch."

"Tell me about it."

"So why are you calling me?"

"I'll be here a few days. I thought maybe you could stop by and visit. . . ."

"Listen, Blade. I'm sorry about your situation, but I don't have time for this."

"Hold up, Tangie. Don't hang up."

"Good-bye, Blade." She clicked the phone in his ear and turned right over. She slept like a baby that night.

The next morning she received a very special delivery—a dozen lime green roses.

17
Charisma

"When are you going to let me take you out to dinner?"
Nico Antonelli asked Charisma as they bumped into
each other shopping at Roosevelt Field one Saturday. Nico
and Charisma barely knew each other in high school. From
time to time they would run into each other, and his first
question was always the same. He had done quite well for
himself. Today he was the corporate attorney for Chase's
grandfather, Stone Canyon.

"Nico, how are you?"

"Better now. Even in jeans and sneakers you're gorgeous.
You know that?"

Charisma smiled. "You're such a flatterer."

"Hey, I just call 'em as I see 'em. Now back to dinner. I'll
keep asking until you say yes. What are you doing tonight?"

"Tonight?"

"Yes, tonight," Nico repeated, displaying perfect pearly
whites. "And I won't take no for an answer."

Charisma thought for a moment. "Tonight it is then."

"Beautiful."

"Where would you like to meet?"

"Meet? I'm a gentleman. I'll pick you up."

"That'll be okay." She gave him her address, and they exchanged phone numbers.

"I'm looking forward to seeing you tonight," Nico said.

"Me too," she agreed as she walked away.

Charisma finished up her shopping and headed over to Daisy's for her weekly shampoo. She was in and out in about an hour. She returned home and took a hot bath. She wondered if she could really go through with dinner because she didn't normally date white men. According to Tangie, the word around Canyon's Club was that Chase was his for the taking. His response was basically thanks, but no thanks. Chase would flip, knowing that Nico was practically begging to give it to her. And if Charisma were to conveniently let it slip that Nate was interested in her too . . . Chase would go into conniptions. Revenge could be awfully sweet. Charisma couldn't help but smile. Yes, her association with Nico might prove interesting if she played her cards right.

She wore black velvet jeans and a gray cashmere sweater. Because it was an unseasonably warm night, she was able to get away with wearing a leather jacket.

Nico arrived promptly at seven. They dined at a little Italian restaurant in Manhattan called Sotto Voce. The veal parmigiana practically melted in her mouth. Afterward, they went to Serendipity for the frozen hot chocolate.

"This has been really nice," she said to Nico over dessert.

"I hope this is just the first of many, Charisma." He looked deeply into her eyes until she looked away.

"Time will tell," she said simply.

"Absolutely," he agreed.

Nate read the promotion list at Monday morning's staff meeting. Unfortunately, Charisma was not on that list, but Chase was. A fresh dose of bile spewed up in Charisma's stomach. She headed straight for the ladies' room. A few minutes later, Lauren came in to check on her.

"Hey, Charisma," Lauren said. "I know it's hard, but there'll be other promotions."

"I know. I'm just tired of losing out to her," Charisma said.

"I know, girl, but just remember what my grandmother used to say."

"What's that?" Charisma asked.

"The higher up you go, the more expensive the toilet paper."

Charisma called Nate right before lunch to request a few minutes of his time. She wanted to discuss the promotion list.

"I've been expecting you, Charisma," he told her as she sat down in his office.

"All I want to know is why *her*?"

"Let's look at the facts, Charisma. Chase's performance has been superior. She always takes on extra assignments." He paused for a moment. "And don't forget, she saved all of our hides on the Madison account."

"Which she sabotaged to begin with, I might add."

"Do you have any proof, Charisma?"

"No. Just my intuition."

"I'm sorry, Charisma. I can't run this company on intuition. Female or otherwise. Just because you had your tongue down the boss's throat doesn't give you dibs on the next promotion."

"Fine. I think you've covered all the bases." Charisma got up to leave. It would be a cold day in hell before she locked lips with him again.

Chase and her coworkers left work that night and headed for their cars. There was a bitterness in the air, and everyone seemed to be in a hurry to get home. She spotted Nico across the street, checking out Charisma.

"Hello, handsome." Chase got to him first. "Did Grand-daddy tell you about my promotion?"

"Hello, Chase," Nico said.

"Why don't I let you take me out to dinner to celebrate?" She tossed her hair behind her back and placed her hand on his shoulder. Then Chase slid her other hand up behind his neck. Nico slid his hand up to meet hers and then pulled her hand back down to her side. Neither seemed to notice Charisma walking toward them.

"Nico," Charisma said gently, letting his name roll of her tongue. Chase spun around at the sound of another woman calling his name, and her eyes narrowed.

"Hey, gorgeous." Nico smiled.

"Well, hello yourself," Charisma said, sounding throaty as ever.

"I was hoping we could go out for drinks," he told her.

"How can I say no to an offer like that?" Charisma asked Chase, laughing. Chase seemed to bite her tongue in anger. Charisma grabbed Nico's arm, and they headed for his car just as Nate drove by. Apparently, Charisma had killed two birds with one stone.

Charisma had her girls over for breakfast. They practi-cally spent the whole day together.

"Can we help with anything?" Heather asked as they walked in.

"No, everything's ready. Come on. Let's eat," Charisma said. They sat down at her beautifully set table, complete with fresh flowers. Charisma put the dishes of food on the table. There were scrambled eggs with cheese, home fries, and bacon.

Just as she was about to sit, she jumped up. "Oops, I al-most forgot." Charisma brought over a dish of salmon cakes and a basket of piping-hot homemade cinnamon raisin biscuits and fresh-brewed coffee.

Tangie said a super-abbreviated grace and dug right in. "Let me tell you the latest. Blade got his ass kicked and had the nerve to call me from the hospital."

"No, he didn't. What happened?" Heather asked.

"I don't know all the details but the word around the gym is that Chase's grandfather had him jacked up. They probably warned him to back off, but Blade always thinks he's so slick."

"Aren't you glad that's all behind you?" Heather asked, sipping her coffee.

"Please, that's an understatement," Tangie admitted, turning to Charisma. "You told us all about Chase's promotion, but how are things with you and big Willy?"

Charisma shook her head. "Sometimes, I just want to scratch his eyes out. Then he'll stop by my office and look at me in a certain way and I wanna wet my pants. He's driving me nuts. But after siding with Chase over me he'll never, ever taste this again."

"What about your revenge?" Heather asked her.

"Oh, I've already started my revenge." Charisma smiled while taking a bite of her salmon cake. "She'll get everything that's coming to her."

"What did you have in mind?" Tangie asked between bites of bacon.

"Nico Antonelli," Charisma said, gloating.

"Got it," Tangie laughed.

"Who?" Heather asked.

"Nico is her family's attorney. Their very attractive, very single attorney who I just happened to go to school with. Miss Crappuccino has the hots for him." She paused. "But he has the hots for me. Do you see where I'm going?"

"But you're not into white men. Tell me he looks like Matt Lauer," Heather said.

"No, he doesn't, but in this case I may have to make an exception." Charisma swallowed her home fries.

"Why, because he's all that or because of the Chase factor?" Tangie asked.

Charisma thought for a moment. "Does it matter?"

"Yes, it does," Heather admitted. "You're compromising your principles just to get back at Chase. You can barely stand the sight of biracial couples, and now you're ready to become one?"

"I never said I couldn't stand the sight of biracial couples," Charisma said.

"Charisma, you mean to tell me that if you were to see my parents walking down the street, you wouldn't thumb your nose up at them?" Heather asked.

"No, I wouldn't. Just because *I* don't practice interracial dating doesn't mean no one else can. To each his own. Everybody deserves to be happy."

"Well, if you don't practice interracial dating, why start now?" Heather shot back.

"Drastic times call for drastic measures." Charisma shrugged.

"You'd just be using him," Heather said.

"Not exactly. Our association would be mutually beneficial," Charisma decided.

"How?" Heather asked.

"Well, he'd be doing me a favor as far as Chase is concerned in exchange for the pleasure of my company. Lots of white men have a thing for black women. He wants some of this stuff real bad, and sometimes you have to use what you got to get what you want." Charisma laughed.

"So you're willing to sell yourself," Heather told her.

"I'm not selling myself," Charisma insisted.

"Then what would you call it?" Heather asked.

"A business transaction." Charisma sipped her coffee.

"But he doesn't know that," Heather reminded her.

"Ignorance is bliss," Charisma said.

* * *

Charisma and Chase collided in Freeman LTD's ladies' lounge Tuesday morning. Charisma knew it was just a matter of time before they had it out—again.

"So Nico's slumming," Chase said. "Unbelievable. How do you two know each other anyway?"

"Girl, you are wearing that green; brings out the blue in your eyes. It's very becoming. I love it."

"Me, jealous? Of you? Don't flatter yourself. I can have any man I want, including Nico."

"Too bad he doesn't want you."

"Charisma, you should know by now that whatever Chase wants, Chase gets. Haven't you learned that yet? What are you, dyslexic?"

"That's what I love about you, Chase. You're so . . . What's the word? Optimistic," she said patronizingly as she put the finishing touches on her makeup and zipped up her bag of tricks. "Keep hope alive."

"You're nothing but a cheap bitch," Chase said, staring at the minute diamond earrings in Charisma's ears. "And I see you have the jewelry to match."

"Chase, I'm just a woman who doesn't need a million bucks to look like it. You, on the other hand, do. Money can buy fashion, but take a good look in the mirror. Evidently, it can't buy style. Maybe if you had some, Nico would be chasing *you* instead of *me*." Charisma left Chase to pick her face up off the floor.

Just before lunch, Nate called Charisma into his office. She wondered what was up this time.

"You wanted to see me, Nate?"

"Sit down, Charisma. Let me get straight to the point. You did an impressive job on the Smyth account. In fact, Bob Smyth told me to personally thank you. And off the record, Charisma, are you dating that guy I saw you with the other day?"

She grinned as he stood and walked toward her. "Off the record, does it matter?"

"Off the record," he repeated, his face just inches from hers. "I think you could do a lot better."

"Let's see. Who could you possible have in mind?" She didn't move an inch. "How about a hint. I'm clueless."

"Tell you what. You think about it awhile and get back to me." He slid his hands in his pockets.

Charisma headed toward the door. She turned just in time to see him gazing at her assets. "I'll do that," she agreed. *But you'll never get this.*

Charisma returned to her office. Her phone began to ring just as she sat at her desk. It was her mother.

"You sound like you're in a good mood," Jena told her. "Your father and I just wanted to invite you over for breakfast Sunday morning."

"What time?"

"Tenish," Jena said.

"I'll be there."

"Great, hold on. Your father wants to talk to you."

"Hey, princess." She could hear the love in his voice.

"Hey, Daddy. What are you doing home so early?"

"Oh, your mother wanted me to take her grocery shopping. You know how she hates going alone. Anyway, are you coming for breakfast?"

"Of course," she told him.

"I was thinking. Why don't you bring Nate by?"

"Huh?" Charisma asked.

"Your boss. Why don't you invite him over if he doesn't have plans?"

"Daddy?"

"Your mother and I have been discussing him. We think he's just what you need in your life. I thought you agreed to give it a chance."

"You sound like the president of his fan club, and you've only met him one time," Charisma reminded him.

"Your mother and I went together for three months before I proposed. Three months. And we're still together thirty-five years later," he reminded her.

"I know, Daddy, but this is different."

"How?"

"Ooh, Daddy, I gotta go." Charisma pretended she had an urgent matter to attend to.

"Think about what I said, Charisma."

"Okay, Daddy. Buh-bye." She hung up and sat back in her chair. Her phone rang again.

"Hey gorgeous." It was Nico.

"Hi, Nico. What's going on?"

"Lunch, I hope. I'm in the neighborhood. I just finished up with a client, and I thought you might want to get a bite to eat."

"Sure, why not?"

"I'll be there in about five minutes," he told her.

"See you then," she said simply. Charisma had just enough time to touch up her makeup. She headed for the lounge, hoping to run into Chase. Unfortunately, Chase was nowhere to be found.

Nico was ready and waiting in the front of the building. He picked her up and whisked her off to a diner down Sunrise Highway famous for their cheeseburgers. After just one bite, Charisma had to agree that they were definitely in her top five.

"Top five?" Nico asked. "These cheeseburgers have got to be in the top two at least." He wiped his mouth.

"Top two? Why stop there?"

"Because there's only one other place that has these burgers beat."

"And where might that be?" she asked, already knowing the answer.

"What are you doing Friday night?"

"I have a date—with the best burger in New York."

"Great, I'll see you at my place around seven."

"I should have seen that coming." She feigned surprise. "I'll just have to stay on my toes."

"You'd look good in a tutu." He took another sip of his coffee and smiled.

Charisma looked across the table at him and smiled back, not quite sure what she was getting herself into. He seemed like a nice man, but could she go through with her plans? And was Heather right? Was she merely selling herself to get back at Chase? On one hand, she *was* attracted to Nico. After all, he was handsome and successful with just the right amount of confidence. What available woman wouldn't want an eligible bachelor vying for her attention? On the other hand, he was still a white man, and that was a line she had never crossed in thirty-four years. She adored brothers too much to have it any other way. So why was she agreeing to dinner at his place knowing full well that she was encouraging him to go a little bit further? To get back at Chase. Simple as that.

When Charisma arrived home from work she took a nice, long shower and tossed up a garden salad to go with her broiled steak. Normally, she tried to stay away from red meat, but every now and then she craved a good steak.

She was just sitting down to dinner when her phone rang. It was Tangie.

"What's up, girl?" Charisma asked.

"You're not going to believe this. Blade came by, begging me to take him back. Said his life hasn't been the same without me, and he's finally ready to introduce me to his family."

"What?"

"It gets better. He pulls out a jewelry box from his pants pocket, drops to one knee, and proposes."

"Get outta here." Charisma put her fork down.

"I could've caught a swarm of bees with my mouth. He apologized for every single mistake he ever made, every single one, and you know how good my memory is. Oh well, it was just too much, too little, too late. His run is done. Ya know?"

"I know, girl. I know, but what did the ring look like?"

"Oh, it was beautiful. It was a pear-shaped solitare with little stones on the side."

"I almost forgot to tell you. Nico's cooking for me Friday night."

"So the plot thickens."

"Yep. I'll talk to you later. I got another call." Charisma clicked over. It was Nico.

"Hey, gorgeous. I'm at the market shopping for Friday's dinner and it suddenly occurred to me. Are you allergic to seafood?"

"I love it," she said.

"Great, that's all I needed to know. I'll talk to you later, okay?"

"Okay," she said simply. What happened to the burgers? That Nico was slick, inviting her over under false pretenses.

If it hadn't been for her BlackBerry, Charisma would have missed her gynecologist appointment. She was on her way to work when she realized that she had a nine o'clock appointment with Dr. Vale. She called Nate to tell him she'd be late.

Dr. Vale's office was in Elmont, but since she had the first scheduled appointment of the day, she was seen on time. Dr. Vale was a friendly fortyish woman with warm brown eyes and auburn, shoulder-length hair. She examined Charisma, taking an annual Pap smear and giving her a routine breast exam. After the exam, Charisma got dressed and met with Dr. Vale in her office.

"Charisma, how have your periods been lately?" she asked.

"You know something?" she answered. "They're actually heavier than usual. I thought they were supposed to lighten with age, but lately I'm flowing heavier."

"What about cramping?" Dr. Vale asked, removing her glasses.

"No more than normal."

"You're still young, but it's time you start thinking about children if you plan on having them. You're clock is ticking loud and clear."

"I know, Dr. Vale. I know, but I think I'll wait a little longer."

"Do you need another prescription for the Pill?"

"Yes."

"Okay," Dr. Vale said as she wrote out the prescription. "See you in six month."

"Thanks, Dr. Vale."

When Charisma finally got to work that morning, there was a beautiful bouquet of fuchsia roses in her office. She assumed they were from Dex. He always sent fuchsia roses. She opened up the card. *Looking forward to Friday night, Nico.*

Nate dropped off some paperwork. "Nice flowers," he said, admiring the roses. "I bet you have lots of admirers. You must have a hot date."

"What can I tell you?" She shrugged her shoulders.

"Apparently, you're doing something right."

"Somebody thinks so." She grinned.

"Do me a favor. If there's any question in your mind after tonight about who's the better man, give me a call."

Moments later he was gone and the secretary popped

her head in the doorway. "They're beautiful, but Chase and Lacey have been snooping around trying to read the card all morning long."

"Thanks, Dee," Charisma said, smiling, the card still in her hand.

Chase fluttered around Charisma like an annoying gnat, searching for clues. Finally, she cornered Charisma in her office.

"Are those from Nico?"

Charisma rolled her eyes. "What do you care? I thought you liked coffee in your milk, at least *this* week anyway."

"Don't worry about how I like it," Chase told her.

"Hmph, you better wake up and smell the crappuccino."

"You gutter girls are so ignorant. It's cappuccino," Chase gloated. "C-A-P—"

"No, in your case it's *crappuccino* cause you're full of shit. Now get the hell out of my office."

Friday came sooner than Charisma expected. Once again, Nico sent a dozen roses to Charisma's office. Later that day, Charisma and Nate were engrossed in conversation around the printer. Everyone else had gone to lunch, leaving them both behind.

Nate grabbed her left hand. "What, no engagement ring?"

"No."

"The way he's been wining and dining you with roses and Lord only knows what else, I thought for sure you'd be off the market by now." He dropped her hand.

"No," she repeated.

"I'm sure he's fine with vanilla, but I bet he wouldn't even know how to handle chocolate thunder. Does he do it for you?"

Charisma didn't answer.

"You want a white boy over me?"

"You don't understand."

"Then make me." His eyes searched hers. When she didn't answer, he spoke for her. "Yeah, that's what I thought," he said, walking away.

Charisma locked herself away in her office for the rest of the day. She didn't want to see or hear from her boss. She was too ashamed to admit that she wasn't feeling Nico at all. He was just a pawn in her scheme to get back at Chase. It was all an act. If Nate found out the truth, he'd probably lose all respect for her as a woman and a human being. That would devastate her.

She worked a full day, came home, showered, and got ready for dinner with Nico. She drove to his condo in Baldwin, dealing with heavy traffic the whole time. She found a parking spot not too far from his building and sat in her car for a few minutes, collecting her thoughts. She looked over her hair and makeup one last time. Satisfied, she got out of her car and walked the block-and-a-half distance to his building. It was a bitter cold night, and by the time she reached his building, she wished she had worn a hat. When he buzzed her inside, the warmth was a welcome relief.

She took the elevator up to the fourth floor. When the elevator door opened, Nico was right there waiting for her. He ushered her inside, helped her off with his coat, took her into his arms, and planted a nice, warm kiss on her lips.

"It's good to see you, gorgeous," Nico told her.

"Likewise," she said, looking around at his black leather and cherrywood living room. "Nice place."

"Glad you approve."

"Oh, I didn't mean it like that."

"I know. I was just joking. Can I get you some wine?" he asked her.

"I'd love some. By the way, the roses were beautiful."

"My pleasure. Have a seat and make yourself comfortable." He walked over to the bar and poured her a glass of white wine.

"Thanks," she said, taking a sip of wine. "I bet you're some cook."

"Well, I do all right," he said modestly.

"I bet you do more than all right," she said, grinning.

"You can be the judge of that. Let me check on dinner, and I'll be right back."

"Can I help with anything?" she asked.

"No, just sit back and relax. Everything's under control. I hope you're hungry."

About twenty minutes later dinner was served—Caesar salad, lobster Alfredo, asparagus, and Italian bread. The aroma alone could have led Charisma to the dining area.

"Oh, this is why you asked if I was allergic to seafood," she said, twirling her pasta.

"I didn't want to have to make a run to the emergency room." He laughed.

"It's delicious." She gazed into his hazel eyes.

"So you work with Chase Martini."

"I guess somebody has to." She shook her head.

"I know the feeling. She's been sweating me for years." Nico grabbed a piece of Italian bread. "But she has a good heart, Charisma. She really does."

"Oh, yeah? Maybe one of these days, I'll see it." She wiped her mouth with a napkin.

"I hope you saved room for dessert—apple pie à la mode."

"I couldn't eat another bite," she admitted.

"Maybe later," he said as they made their way back to the sofa. They both sat and he pulled her legs up onto his lap, removing her shoes and massaging her feet. She eased back onto the sofa, closing her eyes. Nico removed her knee-highs, and she smiled to herself, enjoying his touch on her bare feet. Before she realized it, he had made his way up to her end of the sofa and had begun massaging her neck and shoulders. His technique felt so marvelous that she didn't want him to stop. When their lips met, she didn't stop him. His tongue darted into her mouth, and his hands slid down to her breasts, milking her nipples through her silk blouse until they stood erect. Finally, he began to unbutton her blouse very slowly, revealing a lacy, black bra underneath. Though their lips never left each other's, they managed to stand and remove her blouse and his sweatshirt. They stopped kissing just long enough to remove their pants and return to the couch. Charisma stretched out on her back, and Nico slid on top. He reached behind her back and unhooked her bra, letting it fall to the floor. He gasped at her beauty. Charisma smiled to herself, enjoying the sensations she felt as he pleasured her breasts with his mouth. Before long his hand slid from her shoulder down to her panties. His slender finger found its way inside to her swollen lips. She spread her legs ever so slightly, allowing him easier access to her privates.

Slowly, he stood and removed his briefs. Charisma stole a quick glance at his dick before he sat down on the leather sofa. It was all pink and wrinkled. He pulled her up next to him so they sat side by side. Then, he reached for her hand and covered his dick with it. She squeezed him gently and a tiny drop of semen oozed out. All she could think about was raw chicken. She began to gag. Charisma looked at him apologetically. This was not going to work.

18
Tangie

"We'll have two martini pops," Tony told the bartender over the weekend crowd.

"A martini pop? That's a new one," Tangie said. "What's in it?"

"Vodka, strawberry and banana puree, and a splash of pomegranate juice."

"Well, I'm game," she said as the bartender returned with their drinks.

"Cheers," Tony said simply as he took a sip. He waited for Tangie to do the same. "What'd'ya think?"

"Mmm, it's good," she admitted.

"Stick with me and we'll go places," he told her, smiling.

"I may have to take you up on that," she said.

"So tell me, Tangela, we've been on what, six, seven dates now and each time I see you, you're wearing a ring on your left ring finger. What's up with that?"

Tangie smiled slightly and took a sip of her martini pop before speaking from the heart. "I wear a ring on my left ring finger as a bandage. Every time I look down on my bare finger, I'm reminded of all the men in my life that I've given myself to who have rejected me. I'm reminded of the takers. So this ring hides my pain from the world. If I were bald, I'd wear a weave. If I wanted green eyes, I'd buy contacts. If I wanted to cover gray, I'd dye my hair. It's a defense mechanism. People do what they have to do to survive."

Tony was silent for a moment, choosing his words carefully. He raised his glass in a toast. "No more scars."

"From your lips to God's ears." Tangie changed the subject. "Where in the world did you ever find lime roses?"

"Did you like them?"

"Like them? I *loved* them. I never even knew lime roses existed. Where'd you find them?" she repeated.

"A special lady deserves special roses. I had them flown in just for you."

"Oh, you got it like that, huh?" she joked.

"Well, you know I have my connections."

"I bet you do," she agreed.

Tony looked around, his eyes fixated on a guy across the room. "Let's get outta here," he said, draining his glass.

A few days later Tony surprised Tangie by meeting her for lunch. It was an instant day-brightener.

"Nice," she said simply as they ate at the food court. "No work today?"

"I'm always working in one way or another," Tony replied, looking fresh as new money in a black turtleneck and trousers. "But no more job fairs, thank God. So, you'll never know where I'll show up."

Tangie sipped a smoothie while Tony enjoyed a brisket of beef on rye. She was too excited to eat even though she did her best to appear laid-back about their lunch date. Inside, though, she was like a little wiggly worm.

"So what are you doing tonight?" he asked her.

"I'm just going to take it easy."

"What about you?"

"I have to go out of town tonight—on business."

"Oh," Tangie said simply.

"But I'd love to see you tomorrow night if you're free."

"I think that can be arranged." She laughed.

"Good. Pencil me in."

"I already have." Tangie checked her watch. "Oops, I'm late."

"Let's get you back to work." Tony stood and helped her with her coat. They hurried across the street just as raindrops began to fall. Right before she went inside, Tony leaned forward to kiss her. This time Tangie allowed his lips to gently cover hers. As Tony left and Tangie returned to work, the grin on her face remained for the rest of the day.

When Tangie woke up Saturday morning, her first thought was of the night to come. She rolled over onto her side and hugged her pillow, feeling calm, excited, nervous, anxious—in other words, all of the above.

The phone rang and she rolled over onto her other side to answer it. It was Blade.

"You trying to make me look bad?" he asked.

"What?"

"You heard me. I saw you and your little friend yesterday outside the gym. Don't be throwing your little boy toy up in my face cause two can play that game."

"Go crack another rib," she told him before hanging up.

Blade called her right back. She let her answering machine pick up.

"Tangie? Pick up the damn phone."

She picked up and immediately slammed the phone down into the receiver. Apparently, he got the message because there was no third call. Tangie was seeing Tony that night. She wasn't about to let Blade spoil her mood.

She spent the day cleaning her house from top to bottom and running errands. She went to the grocery store, the drugstore, and the dry cleaner's. By the time she got home, she had three messages on her answering machine. The first was from Charisma. Her father hadn't had a heart attack after all. His heart was fine. He'd had an anxiety attack. He was out of the hospital and home recuperating. Thank God for that. She erased the second message the moment she heard Blade's hostile voice.

The third message was from Tony. She instantly perked up.

"Hey, babe, it's Tony," he began. "Listen, I'm going to have to cancel on you tonight. Something came up, and I can't get out of it. I'll give you a call as soon as I get back in town." Sure, she was disappointed, but Tangie didn't stress or get upset. Smiling, she recalled a quote from Diane Ackerman in an old issue of *O* magazine: "Give a man enough rope and he'll wrap himself around your little finger."

"So how's that mystery man of yours?" Charisma asked Tangie over Heather's one night.

"You probably know as much as I do," Tangie replied, sitting on the couch. "I mean, I can't even get him on the freakin' phone half the time. I might as well be dating a ghost."

"At least you know there's not another woman," Heather said.

"Are you kidding me? A woman I can compete with. A job is a whole different story," Tangie admitted.

"How long was he gone?" Charisma asked.

"Too long." Tangie shook her head. "But he did bring me Cold Stone ice cream."

"That was sweet," Heather said.

"Yeah, that he is. I gotta give the man his props."

"What else did you give him?" Charisma asked slyly.

"You are *so* bad," Tangie told Charisma.

"I was joking," Charisma said.

"No, you weren't," Tangie insisted.

"So what's new with Blade these days?" Heather changed the subject.

"Nada. He's still a first-class ass," Tangie said. "The other night he was waiting for me when I got home from work. When I didn't let him in, he called me from his cell phone every fifteen minutes until I finally had to take the phone off the hook. Why can't he just let me go?"

"Now, if you were chasing him, he wouldn't give you the time of day," Heather said.

"You know a man can't handle the thought of another man savoring his ex's flavor," Charisma told her.

"Rubber or not, if he even thought he was gonna stir his dick in Miss Crappuccino's cup and then put it back in me . . ." Tangie shuddered at the thought.

"Just be glad you found out when you did," Charisma told her. "It may have been a blessing in disguise."

Eventually, the conversation made its way to Charisma and Nico. Apparently, Charisma had surprised herself.

"I thought I'd do just about anything to get back at Chase, but the bottom line is, I'm too much into the brothers. Life is too short to waste on the wrong guy. I tried, but I just couldn't." Charisma shook her head.

"In other words, you dissed him," Tangie said.

Charisma thought for a moment. "Uh . . . yeah."

"What exactly turned you off?" Heather asked.

"Hey, if you weren't feeling it, you weren't feeling it," Tangie decided.

"Do you think you could sleep with a white man?" Charisma asked them.

"Don't get me wrong." Tangie laughed. "Brothers can put you through hell, but I love 'em too much to even think about going anywhere else. On the other hand, when a white man is into sisters, he's really into sisters. Don't get me wrong, I've had offers, but none that I couldn't refuse. I guess it comes down to what price are you willing to pay?"

"I had a white boyfriend in college," Heather admitted.

"Where were we?" Charisma asked.

"Oh, you guys had already graduated," Heather said.

"How was he?" Tangie asked.

"Different," Heather admitted. "Not unpleasant, just different."

"Would you do it again?" Charisma asked.

"I don't know." Heather thought for a moment. "So getting back to Nico. I still can't figure out why you even thought you could go through with it."

"I don't know what I was thinking. He's a nice guy, but it never should have happened." Charisma slid down into the love seat, relaxing to the sounds of Alicia Keys. .

"What happened?" Tangie and Heather said in unison.

"I told you we went out on a few dates, right? No problem. I didn't mind the stares we got on the street from the brothas." Charisma paused for a moment to rub the back of her neck. "And you know I couldn't care less about the stares from the little blond chicks."

"So what was the problem?" Tangie asked.

"He cooked dinner for me one night, and afterward we relaxed on the sofa. One thing led to another, but I couldn't go through with it. I was so embarrassed. All I could do was put my clothes on and leave. He's tried calling me a few times since, but when I saw his number on my caller ID, I just let it go to voice mail. Eventually, he got the hint and stopped calling."

"You should never have gone out with him in the first place," Heather said. "I know you just wanted to get back at Chase, but happiness is the best revenge."

"That's what they say," Charisma sighed.

"It really is. She'll get hers one day," Tangie reminded her. "Trust me."

"I know. I'm just tired of waiting," Charisma said.

"We know," Heather agreed.

Tangie woke up Tuesday morning feeling like a worn-out dishrag. She had nausea, diarrhea, and a fever. Achey and damp, she promptly called in sick and made herself a cup of tea. Tangie barely had enough time to make it to the bathroom before the bile rose up in her throat. She crawled back into bed and drifted off to sleep. Somewhere around eleven her phone rang, jarring her awake.

"Hello?" she answered, her voice raw and irritated.

"Tangela? Are you okay?" It was Tony.

"Oh hi, Tony. I think I'm coming down with the flu."

"Poor baby. I just got back last night. Can I bring you anything?"

"All I want is sleep."

"Have you eaten?"

She looked over at the cold cup of tea on her nightstand. "I don't think I can keep anything down."

"I'll be right over."

"No, I'm a mess."

"I don't care. I'm on my way."

Tangie tried to brush her teeth without gagging, took a super-quick shower, and changed into fresh pajamas. She lay down for a few minutes, mustering enough energy to get the door for Tony when the bell rang.

"Hey," she greeted him simply.

"You look terrible." Tony walked in carrying a big bag of groceries, which he proceeded to take into the kitchen.

"You didn't have to bring me anything." Tangie ran her hand through her hair and followed him into the kitchen.

"So sue me," he said, emptying the contents of the bag onto the table. There was chicken soup, orange juice, oranges, herbal tea, a box of tissue, and throat lozenges. Tony took off his coat and washed his hands. "Why don't you get back into bed, and I'll whip you up something?"

"The pots are . . ."

"I'll figure things out," Tony reassured her.

"Ooh, I feel a little light-headed."

"Go get some rest."

Tangie did as she was told. She got back into bed and turned on the television. Naturally, nothing much was on except daytime soaps. Thank goodness for the remote. She channel-surfed from one station to the next until finally Tony appeared with lunch.

"Hungry?" he asked, placing the tray on her lap.

"Starving," she admitted.

"Good. I have a bowl of nice, hot chicken soup and crackers for you and a big, greasy burger for me," he said, sitting in a nearby chair.

"You have some nerve eating that big, fat hamburger in front of me. Is it topped with red onions?" she asked.

He nodded.

"What I wouldn't do for a bite of that." Tangie blew on a spoonful of soup before tasting it. The chicken soup was good, but she knew it couldn't compare with Tony's lunch—flu or no flu. She slurped it down, even though the smell of the burger was beginning to make her nauseous. Unfortunately, she didn't make it to the bathroom in time and ended up throwing up all over her sheets. Embarrassed didn't begin to describe how she felt.

"Stop apologizing, Tangela. Where's your linen closet?"

"Down the hall, second door on the left."

Tony got up from the chair. "Can you make it to the bathroom okay?"

She nodded, not trusting herself to talk. When she returned to the bedroom after cleaning herself up, he had already stripped the bed.

"Here, sit in the chair while I clean the bed and the mattress pad."

"I'm so sorry, Tony." She shook her head. "I mean, you don't even know me that well."

"I'm here for you, Tangela, for as long as you need me, okay? And all those fly-by-night guys in your past are making it real easy for me because I'm not going anywhere."

Tangie threw her head back and laughed. "You are too much."

"And something tells me you can handle every bit of it."

She laughed even harder and Tony joined in. He ended up spending the night with Tangie, watching over her from the recliner.

"You had the flu? You should have called us," Heather told Tangie after breakfast at Charisma's one morning.

"Tony took such good care of me I didn't have time," Tangie admitted. "The man has the best bedside manner I've ever seen. I mean, he cooked for me, washed dishes, even cleaned up my bed when I puked all over my sheets. It was incredible. I keep asking myself, what did I do to deserve him?"

"Are you kidding me? You deserve the best." Heather smiled.

"He's wonderful and he hasn't even tried to get into my bra, let alone my panties. If he doesn't hurry I'll take them off for him," Tangie joked.

"Sounds like a keeper," Heather said.

"It gets even better," Tangie admitted.

"There's more?" Charisma asked.

"Yep, he invited me to his church tomorrow," Tangie said.

"Get outta here!" Heather exclaimed.

"This man means business." Charisma laughed.

"And I'll be glad when it turns into pleasure." Tangie grinned.

* * *

As usual, Tony was right on time Sunday morning, and as usual Tangie was running just a little behind schedule. Tony checked his watch as he sat in her living room.

"Tangela, we're going to be late," he said.

"Okay," she said simply. "I'll be out in a minute."

Tony stood, unbuttoning his coat. It didn't take long for beads of perspiration to glisten on his freshly shaved head. He checked his watch. "Tangela?"

"I'm coming," she said, picking up her coat from the sofa. Tony followed her out the door and helped her into his car.

Half an hour later they were seated in the pews of the Great Deliverance AME Church. The large congregation appeared friendly, and several members nodded to Tony in acknowledgement. The pastor preached on God's divine order from the changing of the seasons to the direction of our lives.

When the service was over, a couple approached and invited them out to breakfast. The man, an old friend of Tony's, shook her hand vigorously, and Tangie heard his wife whisper in Tony's ear that Tangie was beautiful. Tangela was pleasantly surprised that he introduced her as his girlfriend. Tony declined their offer, but agreed to a rain check.

After they said their good-byes, Tony grabbed Tangela's hand and guided her through the crowd.

"Hungry?' he asked her when they reached the car.

"Feed me."

"I'm going to take you to this secluded little spot where they have the best breakfast in Queens."

"I bet it's packed."

"Not a problem. I know the owner personally."

"I can hardly wait."

Twenty minutes later Tony and Tangela pulled into the parking garage of his co-op. Tangie smiled to herself as they took the elevator to the eighth floor. Tony unlocked the door and ushered her in.

"Let me take your coat," he said, helping her out of hers before removing his. "You smell good." He took her in his arms and buried his face in her hair. "I could just sniff you all day. You know that?"

Tangie laughed, enjoying the moment. "But then I wouldn't get the chance to sample your world-class break-fast."

"Okay, Tangela, but remind me to pick up where I left off."

"Oh, you don't have to tell me twice." Tangie kissed his full lips.

"Let me put some music on for you," he said, program-ming the CD player. "Make yourself comfortable while I start breakfast."

"Can I help with anything?" Tangie asked.

"No, you just relax and let me wait on you."

"Okay," she said simply, easing into the jazz and the sofa's plushness.

Before long the aroma of breakfast reached her nostrils, and she knew she was in for a treat. Tony had whipped up cheese eggs, bacon cooked just the way she liked it, butter-milk biscuits, and the best home fries she'd had in years. She enjoyed every morsel.

"I see why this spot is so highly recommended," she joked. "I hope I'm invited back."

"Being invited back implies that you have to leave first. Why don't you spend the night with me?"

She looked at him closely. "You're serious, aren't you?"

"No question."

Tangie thought for a moment. "You know I'm high main-tenance, and I don't have a thing here."

"So take my car, go home, throw a few things in an overnighter, and come back."

"You amaze me," she said.

"You mesmerize me. Now here, take my keys and get busy," he said, tossing her his car keys, which she caught in midair.

"Are you sure about this?" she asked one last time.

"Positive." He playfully slapped her on the butt. "Now hurry back."

Tangie didn't have to be told twice. She took the elevator down to the garage and within a few minutes was behind the wheel of her dream car. She smiled to herself, relishing the moment as she turned the ignition. Maneuvering down Queens Boulevard—aka, the boulevard of death, she was reminded of just how cautious drivers had to be with pedestrians trying to cross against the light.

From the Van Wyck Expressway she eased into the Belt Parkway and before long she was back in Springfield Gardens. She peeled off her suit and changed into a coral jogging suit with white piping. Next, she threw a pair of jeans and the essentials into a bag, choosing her jewelry and makeup carefully. Within the hour, she was on the road again and back in Tony's building. He welcomed her with open arms. They spent the rest of the day talking about their favorite authors and movies. They both had eclectic taste in music, loving R & B, gospel, jazz, pop, hip-hop, and Frank Sinatra.

That night, he drew her a hot bubble bath and massaged scented body lotion into her skin afterward. Tony and Tangela shared childhood memories as well as their hopes and dreams for the future. They drifted off in each other's arms, sleeping more peacefully and deeply than either had in quite some time. Monday morning they each took a mental health day and went shopping at Queens Center Mall. Tony insisted on buying something for Tangie. She declined his offer, but he insisted. Finally, she allowed him to buy her a beautiful silk scarf. They had lunch in the food court, and he drove her home later that afternoon. It was the perfect day.

"I think I'm falling in love," Tangie exclaimed to Charisma and Heather over dessert one night. "I know. It's mad crazy, but I think he's the *one*. And do you know what the beauty of it is?" she asked without waiting for an answer. "We haven't even fooled around yet."

"How do you know he's not gay?" Charisma asked.

Tangela sighed. "Trust me. He's not. And guess what he's doing tonight?"

"Apparently not you." Charisma laughed.

"Oh, you got jokes," Tangie said.

"So what he's doing tonight?" Charisma asked.

"No, forget it." Tangie shook her head.

"Don't be like that," Heather insisted.

"No, it's not important," Tangie said. "But I think I've found the man of my dreams. One day you guys will too. Where the heck is that waiter?"

Tangie looked around. As if on cue, the waiter returned with their dessert. They raised their glasses in a toast.

"Behind every successful woman is herself," Tangie said, smiling.

Tangie received her Valentine's Day bouquet early that morning. The moment she saw the lime green roses floating on the delivery guy's arm, she knew who they were from. The card read *Can't wait until the stars appear in the sky, and you are by my side.* She smiled to herself as she tucked the card away. A swarm of coworkers invaded the front desk, admiring the roses' vibrant color. None had ever seen lime roses before. From the oohs and aahs Tangie assumed they were impressed. She heard a few mumble under their breath that Tangie had probably sent them to herself. She shook her head. There was always at least one in the bunch. It never ceased to amaze her. Females were a trip.

That night Tony took Tangie out to dinner at a new spot in the city called the Posh Café. Tangie looked around.

"This place is . . ." she searched for the right word. "Indescribable." She felt as though she was seated in a wedding reception hall. The candles, the floral arrangements, the table linen, and the stemware were exquisite. "How do you find these places?" she asked him.

"It comes with the job. It's just one of the perks."

"Well, I for one love it."

"And this is just the beginning. Trust me."

They had a four-course dinner that night and ended up at Tony's afterward. Once inside, Tony led Tangie to the sofa, where he pulled her onto his lap.

"I've been thinking about you all day," he said huskily before kissing her.

She closed her eyes and smiled as his kisses became intoxicating. She opened her mouth wider, allowing his tongue access to hers. Tony cradled her head with one arm and slid his hand up her back. She rubbed his head as he unloosened her bra, eager to feel his hands on her flesh. What she felt instead was his mouth gently sucking on her nipples until they were hard and her body tingled with anticipation. Her body ached for him in other places, but it was the wrong time of the month for the kind of pleasure she sought. So she pulled his mouth back up to hers, rehooked her bra, and said good night.

Tony made another date with Tangie the following night. Tangie wasn't surprised. She knew he wanted some real bad, and if it hadn't been for the onset of her period, she probably would have given in. She had to admit she liked being in control. It was fun.

They went out for drinks, and she purposely wore a skirt—a very short skirt at that. He walked her to her door and she invited him in. Tangie sat on the sofa and crossed her legs, revealing her toned upper thigh. She ran her hand through her hair seductively.

As if on cue, Tony sat next to her, ready to play her game. She leaned over, placed her hand on his shoulder, and kissed him on the earlobe first and then his lips. Tony kissed her back, sliding his hand up her thigh and tugging on her pantyhose. Tangie tried to pull his hands away, but he was too strong.

"What's a matter, baby?" he asked between kisses. "I know you want me too."

"You know I do," she said. "But I have my period."

"Oh," he chuckled, sounding relieved. "I was starting to get a complex. I thought maybe I should change deodorant or something. You sure are calm, though. Some women are real bitches around that time of the month."

"Trust me. I know. In my book *P-M-S* stands for 'pass me swiftly'. Unfortunately, sometimes it does, and sometimes it doesn't. Be patient with me?"

"There's no rush. I'm not letting you get away." He rose to his feet and pulled Tangie up too. "Get some rest, baby, and I'll call you tomorrow. Okay?" He kissed her on the forehead.

She nodded, thinking to herself that maybe her luck with men really had changed.

"Okay, I'm in love," Tangie told Heather and Charisma via threeway.

"We know. You told us already," Charisma reminded her.

"No, I said I was *falling* in love. Now it's official. I'm in love. I've reached my destination."

"Did he wear you out last night?" Heather asked.

"Honey, we didn't even go there," Tangie said.

"You fall in love faster than anyone I know," Charisma said.

"I guess I'm just meant to be part of a couple," Tangie confessed.

"And who said, and I quote, 'When you give away your heart, you give away your power'?" Charisma reminded her.

"What I meant was that when you give away your heart to the wrong person, you give away your power," Tangie clarified as another call came in. She checked her caller ID. "Let me get that. I'll talk to you guys later," she said before switching over.

"Question," Tony began. "What are you doing this weekend?"

"So far, nothing."

"Good. Keep it open for me. I want you to meet my parents if you're up to it."

"Really," she said simply.

"Really," he repeated.

"Are they here in Queens?"

"No, they live in Bayshore. I told them about you, and they want to meet you."

"Oh." She smiled.

"So how about it?"

"I'd like that," she said slowly.

"Great. I'll tell Mom and Pop to expect us."

"You do that," she said before hanging up, amazed at just one more way Tony was different from Blade. They were like night and day. She and Blade had gone together for two years, and he hadn't even introduced her to his dog. And here Tony wanted to introduce her to his folks after a few months. Some things couldn't be explained without driving oneself nuts.

A single lime rose was delivered to Tangie on the day she was to meet Tony's parents. It came with a simple message. *I know they'll find you as irresistible as I do.*

Tangie smiled to herself and got dressed. Tony picked

her up around three and they headed out to Bayshore. Normally, she had no problems making a good impression on parents, but this time her hands were moist with perspiration, betraying her lack of confidence. As if reading her thoughts, Tony reached for and gently squeezed her hand as he sped down the Southern State. They drove in silence for a moment. Finally, Tony spoke.

"Relax. My parents will love you. You'll see."

Before long, they were pulling up to a ranch-style brick house surrounded by two huge bar oak trees. As usual, Tony walked over to the passenger side to help Tangie out. Together, they walked up to the door, and Tony rang the bell.

His mother, clad in a floral apron, answered the door. The excitement was evident on her face as she quickly flung her arms around her son in an embrace.

"This must be Tangela," she said warmly, ushering them in and closing the door.

"It's so nice to meet you," Tangie replied, extending her hand.

Gloria Banks flung Tangie's hand away and gave her a hug. Tangie immediately felt welcomed.

"Honey, Anthony's here," she told her husband.

Herb Banks rose from his chair in the living room to greet Tony and his guest. They embraced as well before Tony introduced him to Tangie. Mr. Banks was pleased to meet her, eagerly shaking her hand with both of his own.

"Let me take your coats," Mrs. Banks said as they joined Tony's dad in the living room. He folded up the newspaper and gave them his full attention.

"Something smells good, Ma," Tony said. "What 'cha make?"

"Your favorite," Tony's mother replied. "I hope you're good and hungry."

"Nobody makes roast chicken, garlic mashed potatoes,

and fresh string beans like my mother. Nobody. Trust me," he told Tangie.

"Well, it sure smells delicious," Tangie said.

"Thank you," Mrs. Banks said, rising to her feet to check on dinner.

"Can I help with anything?" Tangie asked her.

"As a matter of fact, would you mind helping me put the biscuits in the oven? I don't see as well as I used to, and I'm always burning myself," Mrs. Banks said.

"Oh, I'd be happy to," Tangie said, following Mrs. Banks into the kitchen and leaving the men to talk about the upcoming basketball game.

The kitchen was just as warm as Mrs. Banks with its floral curtains and tablecloth. It was a huge kitchen with a wooden island in the middle. Tangie took the pan of homemade biscuits from the counter and slid it in the oven, closing the oven door carefully. Mrs. Banks stood over the table with the electric mixer in hand, making the mashed potatoes. She motioned for Tangie to have a seat.

"So tell me how you and my son met," she said.

Tangie proceeded to tell Mrs. Banks about the job fair that brought them together and how long they'd been dating. Just repeating the story brought a smile to Tangie's face.

"Anthony doesn't bring many girls home to meet us, so the fact that you're here means a lot. He thinks highly of you," she said matter-of-factly.

Tangie listened, nodding slowly.

"How do you feel about my son?" Mrs. Banks asked.

"He's wonderful. You and Mr. Banks must be very proud of him."

"Yes, we are." She smiled. "Tangela, would you check on the biscuits for me? They should be about done."

"Sure," Tangie said, rising to her feet. She peered through the oven window. The biscuits were a pretty golden brown, and their aroma tickled her nostrils in the most delightful way as she opened the oven door and placed the biscuits on the counter.

They ate in the dining room, which was just off the kitchen. Mr. Banks said grace. Mrs. Banks fixed her husband's plate, and they all dug in.

"When Anthony was a little boy," Mr. Banks began, "every time he won a Little League game, he wanted roast chicken and mashed potatoes. And when he was in junior high and high school, he wanted it every time he won a basketball game. So when he called and asked his mother to fix it today, we knew you must be a gem." He grinned at his son cutting his chicken.

Tangie discovered that Tony was absolutely right. If his mother didn't make the best roast chicken, Tangie didn't know who did. With each mouthful, Tangie tried to decipher the recipe. When she could stand it no more, she hinted about how she'd love to have the recipe. Smiling, Mrs. Banks mentioned that it was a family secret. Dessert was just as delicious—homemade lemon coconut layer cake and ice cream. Tangie couldn't wait to drop the thank-you card in the mail. Two weeks later, she received a reply—Mrs. Banks's roasted chicken recipe.

19

Charisma

Charisma finally forgave herself for the way she treated Nico. Every morning as she walked into work, she laughed to herself. Let the cat-and-mouse games begin. She was getting bolder with her boss with each passing day. One afternoon she sat at her computer, drumming her fingers. She e-mailed Nate that she needed some good music, and did he have any. He e-mailed her back that all his music was in his car, but that maybe they could make some of their own. Your desktop or mine, was her first reaction, but she decided against transmitting it. Unfortunately, she hit the wrong key, and two minutes later, Nate was standing in her doorway with a mischievous grin on his face.

He walked over to where she was sitting. "You are bad," he told her.

"Sometimes my fingers have a mind of their own."

"Keep it up, and you'll end up on your back."

"I'll remember that," she said as he walked away, his hands in his pockets.

* * *

When Charisma arrived at work the next morning, a beautiful bouquet of orange roses was waiting for her. The secretary said they had arrived a few minutes before Charisma did. Charisma opened up the card and smiled. It was signed, *Your desktop lover.* Blushing, she tucked the card safely away in her pocket.

Later, when Nate stopped in to drop off a report, he noticed the roses on her desk. "Wow, somebody must think you're really special," he said.

"It looks that way," she said coyly.

"Well, whatever you're doing, you must be doing it right." He winked as he returned to his office.

For the rest of the day, they flirted with each other when they thought no one was looking. Finally, at around five o'clock Nate called Charisma into his office.

"Close the door," he told her. "I have a proposition for you."

"Really?" she asked.

"You know Presidents' Day is coming up, and I thought maybe you and I could go away for the long weekend."

She smiled. "Where did you have in mind?"

"Mexico. Cabo San Lucas."

"Really?" she repeated.

"I mean, you, me, a few days in the sun. What could be better? Tell you what. Take a few days to think it over and get back to me."

"I'll do that."

The next night Charisma met Heather and Tangie after work at Red Lobster. Surprisingly, they all arrived at the same time. They had made reservations so they didn't have to wait long for a table. They ordered drinks and dinner. Right away, Tangie and Heather noticed Charisma's glow.

"What are you talking about?" Charisma asked.

"Girl, you must be getting some good juice," Tangie said.

"You are sick," Charisma answered.

"Then what's up? Something's going on?" Heather hinted.

"Well, my boss sent me roses. . . ." Charisma began.

"And seeing that it's not Secretary's Day, and you're not his secretary, I think he's moving in for the kill," Tangie surmised.

"I was just as shocked as you are," Charisma admitted.

"Yeah, right. Tell me anything. I'm half black," Heather said. "Like my mother always says, when your body is trying to tell you something, listen to it. You didn't have that glow with Nico, and Dex definitely didn't give it to you."

"No, Dex was giving it to her, all right." Tangie laughed. "But I think he's about to get his walking papers."

"There's more," Charisma said as their drinks arrived. "He wants to take me to Cabo San Lucas."

"Get outta here!" Heather exclaimed.

"I know you said yes," Tangie insisted.

"I told him I'd think about it." Charisma sipped her piña colada.

"What's there to think about?" Tangie asked.

Heather looked at Tangie. "Just the fact that she didn't flat-out say *no* means that she's going."

"I didn't say that," Charisma said, shaking her head.

"You didn't have to." Heather grinned.

"Have a ball," Tangie said to Charisma, raising her glass. "To Cabo," she toasted, waiting for Charisma to join in.

"I must be a fool. To Cabo," Charisma finally said, shaking her head.

Charisma got in that night and drew herself a hot bath. The scented heat felt delicious on her skin. She needed time to herself, time to think, and she always did her best thinking in the tub. Should she or shouldn't she go away with Nate? Sure, her father would be thrilled, but what did

Charisma want? She couldn't deny that she and Nate had chemistry. Just looking at him made her juices flow. On the other hand, he was divorced. God only knows what kind of emotional baggage he was lugging around. And most leaders were control freaks. Then again, he was only asking her to go on a trip to Cabo with him, not a trip down the altar. What did she have to lose?

She picked up the cordless phone and dialed his number. He picked up on the second ring.

"Nate, it's Charisma. Did I catch you at a bad time?"

"Not at all, Charisma."

"I've been thinking about your proposition, and I've decided to take you up on it."

"Really," he said, the smile evident in his voice. "Wow, that's great. I think we'll have a lot of fun together."

"I'd like to invite you over for breakfast Saturday morning if you're not busy."

"Sounds like a plan. What time shall I come by?"

"How about around ten?"

"Shall I bring anything?"

"Just yourself."

"Okay, see you tomorrow, Charisma," he said before hanging up.

Charisma had her nails done Thursday and her hair done Friday after work. Daisy's was practically empty and she was in and out. Charisma always said nothing made her feel more like a million bucks than a fresh do. A woman could be dressed to kill, but if her hair was whacked, she'd look like crap. On the other hand, if she had on a pair of worn-out jeans but her hair and makeup were flawless, she could still stop traffic. Charisma loved the power of stopping traffic.

Charisma headed over to Cinderella's to have her eyebrows done. Naturally, it was busy, and Cinderella was a so-

cial butterfly. So, Charisma had a bit of a wait on her hand.
Cinderella's assistant worked on one customer's brow
while Cinderella rang up a couple of sales and finished another pair of brows.

Finally, she motioned for Charisma to have a seat in her
chair. She didn't have to be told twice and hopped in the
chair as two more women entered the shop. Cinderella
stopped momentarily to greet the new customers and introduced everyone. She cleaned Charisma's brows and applied wax.

"So how's everything?" Cinderella asked Charisma softly
as she began working on her brow.

"Everything's good," Charisma whispered.

"You know you're glowing? Is there something you want
to tell me?"

"No, Cinderella. I'm having breakfast with my boss tomorrow morning."

"He took you to the Knicks game awhile back, right?"

"You remember that?"

"Of course, my darling. I remember how you lit up when
you talked about him." Cinderella finished waxing and
picked up the tweezers. "I've tasted your breakfasts, I hope
you're cooking."

"I am," Charisma admitted.

Cinderella concentrated on her brows for a few moments
in silence. Finally, she finishing up and handed her the mirror.

"Now I can face the world again," she said, admiring Cinderella's handiwork. Charisma paid her and fished around
her purse for her car keys.

"Power to the people. You know without God and you
we truly cannot survive," Cinderella said before kissing her
on both cheeks. "Enjoy yourself tomorrow, my queen, okay?
I love you. Everybody say good-bye to Queen Charisma."

Charisma left amidst a chorus of good-byes. Once home,

she cleaned her house from top to bottom. By the time she got into bed that night she was exhausted.

Charisma awakened at about eight o'clock Saturday morning, changed the linen on her bed, and watered all of her plants. She then took a shower and slipped into a pair of jeans and a black T-shirt. By the time she headed for the kitchen, it was a little after nine. Breakfast wasn't until ten.

She busied herself chopping onions and green peppers and shredded sharp cheddar for the omelets. Then, she began cooking bacon in the oven. It was a trick she learned from her mother that saved her the pain and annoyance of hot grease burns. She whipped up half-a-dozen buttermilk biscuits, putting them aside until just before Nate arrived. Next, she made her famous cinnamon raisin pancakes, making certain they were kept warm. She put on a pot of fresh coffee and heated a bottle of syrup for the pancakes. At the last minute she decided to make some salmon cakes but decided against home fries. She didn't want to overdo it.

When Nate called, everything was under control. He was five minutes away so she popped the biscuits in the oven and made certain the kitchen table was set just so. Nate arrived moments later with fresh flowers, kissing her on the cheek as he walked in.

"Twice in one week? I'm impressed." She smiled, taking the flowers into the kitchen. She returned with a bottle of water and put the flowers in a vase on her coffee table.

He took off his coat and laid it along a chair. "Wow, something smells good."

"Just a little something I whipped up. Do you like omelets?" Charisma asked.

"That's fine."

"Well, why don't you have a seat, and breakfast will be ready in a few." She returned to the kitchen to make the eggs. The salmon cakes and biscuits were done, and before long, the omelets were ready too. She placed everything on the table.

"Hope you're hungry," she told him as he sat at the kitchen table. "Would you like juice with your coffee?"

"Thank you."

She got up to get the orange juice.

"No, you sit. I'll get it. You've done enough this morning." He headed to the refrigerator for the half gallon of juice, poured them both a glass, and sat back down. "This looks delicious," he told her.

"I just wanted our first breakfast together to be special."

"Well, mission accomplished. I don't know where to start," he said, tasting the omelet. "You are something else. Do you know that?"

Charisma laughed, chewing on some bacon. "I'm glad you're enjoying it."

"I see you know the way to a man's heart, but then I think you already have it."

They ate in silence for a few moments. Charisma smiled to herself. Who would have thought that she and Mr. Camry would be breaking bread together?

"I don't think I've ever had pancakes like these. They almost taste like oatmeal raisin cookies. And you even heated the syrup? You're some cook."

When they finished breakfast, Nate insisted on doing the dishes.

"Uh-uh," Charisma said. "I'll do them later."

They returned to the living room and cuddled on the sofa. They were both stuffed.

"Now about Cabo," he said, rubbing her shoulder. "What's the word?"

She turned and looked him in the eye. "I'm game if you are. When do you wanna leave?"

"How about if we leave Friday and return Sunday. That way we'll have Monday to recuperate."

"Sounds good to me." She smiled at him.

"Do you have a travel agent?" Nate asked.

"Yeah, she finds the best deals."

"Why don't you give her a call, so we can go see her," Nate advised.

"How about Tuesday?" Charisma asked him.

"Tuesday's fine. You know, I still can't believe you're agreeing to this."

"Believe it, Nate."

He kissed her on the neck. "No, I'll believe it when we're airborne.

Charisma and Nate saw the travel agent Tuesday after work. Late that night after she got in, Charisma called Tangie and Heather.

"It's official. We're going to Cabo San Lucas."

"We need details," Heather insisted.

Charisma brought them up to date. "I still can't believe it."

"I prayed for you," Heather admitted. "And you know what they say. Prayer changes things."

"How much you wanna bet you two don't wait until the weekend to get your groove on? And I would love to be a fly on the wall when you finally do." Tangie laughed.

"And if that mattress could talk . . ." Heather began.

"You need a man," Charisma told Heather.

"Why? Honey, my vibrator does just fine," Heather responded.

"Yeah, until you wear out those doggone batteries." Tangie laughed.

"Hey, nothing's perfect," Heather reminded them before they all hung up.

* * *

All day Friday Charisma and Nate played it cool. Since Charisma was closer to Kennedy Airport, Nate wanted to take a cab, stop off at her place and pick her up, and then proceed to JFK. Charisma, on the other hand, wanted to meet him at the gate. She won. Their American Airlines flight would depart at eight-thirty so they agreed to meet at the airport around six-thirty. All they had to do was rush home and get their bags. Since they'd only be gone a couple of days, they agreed to bring carry-on luggage only.

Nate got to the gate first and relaxed. It had been a hectic day, but now he was ready to enjoy some fun in the sun with Miss Dearborn. He expected her momentarily. He glanced at his watch. It was seven o'clock. Her taxi was probably tied up in traffic. Fifteen more minutes went by, and he decided to call her cell. Damn, it wasn't on. He left a message. Where the hell was she? Five minutes later he called again.

Nate was beginning to get concerned. Did she get cold feet at the last minute? She seemed just as excited as he was about the trip. So what was going on? He checked his cell for messages. There were none. He got up and grabbed his two bags and began walking around the airport, hoping to find her. By 7:45 it was time to start boarding. Damn, where the hell was she? He waited and waited. Was he actually being stood up? He may have wasted one plane ticket, but he'd be damned if he wasted two. Nate took one last glance behind him, gave the agent his boarding pass and ID to check, and boarded the airplane alone.

It was a long flight. The woman next to Nate tried to make small talk, but he completely ignored her, nipping it in the bud. He was in no mood to be polite. He'd been played for a fool. And she'd been so smooth about it.

The flight attendants came by, taking orders for cocktails. Nate ended up having three. By the time the plane landed, he had a slight buzz. By the time he settled in to his hotel room, he was downright drunk.

He slept hard that night, getting up twice to pee. By morning he was famished. He ordered room service, then called back to cancel. Hell, it was a beautiful day, and he was on a beautiful island. He might as well enjoy himself. He showered, dressed, and had breakfast at one of the hotel restaurants. It wasn't as good as Charisma's, but he'd survive.

Life was funny. Just yesterday—was it only yesterday? He had been offered a position in the Manhattan office. He had turned it down because he wasn't quite ready for another career move. He wondered if the position had been filled. Maybe it *was* time for a change. So much for Ellis Dearborn's blessings . . .

Charisma got to work Tuesday, not knowing how she was going to make it through the day. She hadn't returned Nate's calls from the airport Friday night, and she hadn't tried calling him at home once he returned from the trip.

It was a real mess. She just couldn't go through with it. Yet, she didn't have the heart to tell him. So she took the cowardly way out and failed to show up. She didn't even answer her cell phone. She knew he'd be devastated, but she only thought of herself.

They steered clear of each other all morning. That afternoon Nate called a staff meeting. It was her first time seeing him that day. Everyone sat down around the conference table, and Nate got straight to the point.

"I've been offered a manager's position in the Manhattan office," he began. "And after much thought I've decided to accept it. This Friday will be my last day here."

Shocked, Charisma looked at him closely, but he avoided her gaze altogether.

"I know I've only been here a short time, long enough to

get on some of your nerves," he joked. "But each of you has taught me something valuable about the world and about myself. It's truly been a privilege working with you, and I wish you all the best in your careers."

Wow, he's leaving. Charisma was stunned.

After the meeting, they had a moment alone.

"Nate, I'm sorry . . ." Charisma began.

"Hey, no apology necessary." He shrugged his shoulders, his hands in his trousers pockets.

"I hope I had nothing to do with your decision to leave." She searched his eyes.

"Don't flatter yourself," he said coolly before walking away.

Charisma began to wonder if she was her own worst enemy. What was wrong with her? Maybe she didn't feel that she deserved to be happy. Nate was a man who had obviously been interested in her, and yet basically she hadn't given him the time of day. She couldn't lie and say that she hadn't been feeling him because the chemistry was obviously there. So why did she stand him up at JFK? It was mean. No, it was more than mean. It was cruel. And now he was gone, out of her life. She couldn't forget the iciness in his eyes at the staff meeting that afternoon when she approached him. Now it was her turn to feel rejected. Life at Freeman LTD went on without Nate Arquette, but Charisma felt the loss. That month she went on a shopping spree, charging over five hundred dollars on her American Express. When her bill arrived she was literally sick to her stomach. She called her mother and cried on her shoulder.

"I don't understand you, Charisma. How many handbags do you need? How many shoes can you wear?" Jena asked her.

"Mother, I didn't call for your approval," she snapped.

"When you were my age, you had a marriage, a mortgage,

and me. All I have is me. If I wanna treat myself sometimes, I will."

"Okay, Charisma, you have *all* the answers. Good-bye."

Chase Martini also felt the emptiness of Nate's absence. Now, who would she flirt with? Certainly, none of the remaining cast of characters. She didn't have time to waste on them. What could they do for her?

March definitely came in like a lion. The first week was filled with seven days of cold, bitter rain. She dreaded getting out of her warm, king-sized bed to brave the windy, frigid temperatures, but if she didn't work, how would she get ample wear out of her business suits and attire? And if it weren't for the new sports car her granddaddy had just bought her, how would she find the energy to make it to work on those freezing mornings?

Interesting enough, her disposition brightened when she was asked to represent the office at a marketing conference in Vegas. Sure, she'd have to attend meetings during the day, but Vegas's nightlife was awesome. A few fun-filled days in the sun would do her disposition good. Everybody in the office was jealous, but hey, what else was new?

She arrived in Vegas on Wednesday in plenty of time for the conference's meet-and-greet night, which took place in the Luxor Hotel. It was wonderfully warm that night—about eighty-five degrees—and she hobnobbed with lots of people she had only known via phone calls and e-mails. So, it was nice to finally put faces to voices and names.

On her last night there she made plans to hook up with an old friend from college. Unfortunately, their plans fell through and she ended up drinking alone at the bar.

"Chase?" she heard a familiar voice say.

She turned around in her chair. It was Nate.

"Nate?" she asked. "How are you?"

"I'm good. Mind if I join you?"

"I wish you would. There's plenty of drinks to go around."
She already had a buzz.

He sat next to her. "I didn't expect to see you here," he
admitted.

"Disappointed?" she asked, smiling wickedly.

"Not at all."

"Good. Let me buy you a drink," she said, swiveling a bit
in her chair.

"Trying to get me drunk?"

"Oh, I've been trying to get you drunk for a long time."
She laughed.

"Well, maybe tonight you'll get lucky."

"I sure as hell hope so." She tossed her blond hair.

Charisma couldn't recall the exact moment when she
sensed that something was terribly wrong. Her menstrual
periods had been getting longer and heavier and sometimes the cramping was unbearable. So much so that she
began missing days at work or leaving early. Double sanitary pads had become the norm. When she could stand it
no more, she made an appointment with Dr. Vale for the
following week. Hopefully, her period would be over by
then and the gynecologist would be able to see her.

Dr. Vale examined her and immediately ordered a
sonogram. The results indicated that Charisma had uter-
ine fibroids—one of which sat directly on her right ovary.
Charisma was devastated by the news. She didn't want to
believe her ears. There had to be some mistake. Fibroids?
Impossible.

The doctor tried to assure her that the fibroids were usually benign and were quite common in African American
women. Charisma's fears were not quieted. She got second
and third opinions from other gynecologists, but the diag-
nosis was the same. If she ever hoped to have children, they
had to be removed.

Charisma went home to her mother's and sobbed.

Jena held her daughter in her arms and rocked her gently. She began to cry too. "We'll get through this together, sweetheart. You'll see. And when you get out of the hospital, I'll come stay with you for as long as you need me to. Or you can stay here and sleep in your old room. Whatever you want to do, but everything will be fine. You'll see."

Charisma met with the surgeon and the procedure was scheduled for next month. Her insurance would practically cover everything, and she'd be hospitalized for about two days. If there were no complications, she could return to work in about three weeks.

Charisma met Tangie and Heather at IHOP one Saturday morning to fill them in. She had never so much as had her tonsils out, so she was petrified at the thought of going under the knife.

"What if they give me too much anesthesia, and I don't wake up?" Charisma exclaimed.

"You'll be fine." Heather grabbed her hand. "I pray for you guys every night. Are you kidding me? We're Howard's Angels. Did you forget?"

"And we'll be right there when it's over." Tangie grabbed her other hand.

"Promise?" Charisma asked.

"Promise," Heather and Tangie said together.

20

Heather

"Don't tell me that's Jamal again," Charisma said to Heather as her cell phone rang for the third time that night. They were all hanging out over Tangie's.

Heather glanced at the display. "Who else but?" She shook her head. "Ever since that night at his apartment, he has been blowing up my phones big time. Half the time I don't even answer. Here, listen to some of his messages," she told Charisma and Tangie, passing them the phone.

"That man is whipped," Tangie said, getting up for some more cheese doodles.

"Whipped? On what? My breath?" Heather exclaimed and Charisma burst out laughing.

"You're driving him nuts."

"I know," Heather admitted. "I bet he'll think twice the next time he flips a light switch."

"Look at you. The pounds are melting off," Charisma said as Tangie returned from the kitchen.

Heather was amazed herself. "Thirty pounds."

"Wow, that's amazing. And without setting one foot in the

gym. I can't get over your progress," Tangie said, shaking her head.

"Have you contacted that modeling agent lately?" Charisma asked.

"Well, as a matter of fact, I have. He wants me to come to the studio and take some photos." Heather smiled.

"Girrrl," Charisma said.

"So when do you go?" Tangie asked.

"This weekend," Heather exclaimed, unable to contain her excitement.

"Nice," Charisma said.

"Wanna come with me?" Heather asked them.

"Are you kidding me? We'd be ticked off if we couldn't," Tangie said, smiling. Then she turned serious. "I know I give you a hard way to go sometime, but I'm really proud of you."

"Thanks." Heather took another sip of her mudslide and laughed. "This alcohol is going straight to my coochie." She reached for her purse, fishing inside for her cell phone. She dialed Jamal's number. "Hey, Jamal, it's Heather. I know. I just found my phone. I had dropped it under my car seat. Uh-huh. Yeah, listen, when are we going to get together? I miss you." Heather paused for a moment, filling her mouth with mud slide. "Tonight sounds like a plan. Let's meet at my house. Uh-huh. Okay. I'll see you in an hour." Smiling, Heather flipped her phone shut and stood. "Well, I gotta go," she told Tangie and Charisma. "I'll talk to you guys tomorrow."

Tangie walked her to the door. "Have fun," she told Heather.

"Fun?" Heather laughed. "Well, you've got the first two letters right."

"What happened to our prim and proper librarian?

Heather, you're a hot mess." Charisma gave her a kiss on the cheek. "Get home safely."

"Ciao." Heather jumped in her car and sped down Springfield Boulevard. Within minutes she was back in Laurelton.

Her mom was working a double shift at the hospital. Once home, Heather took a quick shower with her favorite scented body wash. She had barely hopped out of the tub when her doorbell rang. Still wet, she wrapped a bath sheet around her ample body and answered the door, leaving a trail of wet footprints behind her.

Jamal's smile said it all. He stepped inside and into her arms in one easy motion. Heather planted a quick kiss on his lips. It was freezing outside, and he gladly shut the door. Jamal slid his tongue into her mouth as she tightly held on to the towel with her right hand. Gently, he tried to pry the towel from her hand. They played tug-of-war for a few moments until Jamal gave up. With knees slightly bent, he leaned back against the door and welcomed her into his personal space.

"Uh-uh-uh." She rolled her forefinger at him as she clung to the bath sheet with her left fist. "Let me catch my breath before you completely devour me at the door." She took him by the hand and led him downstairs to her apartment. "Have a seat," she told him, taking his coat.

"Don't get dressed on my account." He smiled from the couch. "I'm enjoying the view."

Shaking her head, Heather returned to the bathroom. She quickly lotioned up and returned to the living room wearing a robe.

"So what's going on?" he said.

"Hungry?" she asked, sitting next to him.

"I'm good."

"I bet you are." She grinned.

He leaned over and kissed her softly on the neck. "You smell like a dream. I bet you taste like one too."

She laughed softly.

"What are you thinking about?"

"I'm thinking about how I would absolutely love a nice, long body massage."

"This is your lucky night. I have two big, strong hands that are just aching to pleasure you."

"Best offer I've had all day. Follow me." Heather and Jamal eased into her bedroom, where she hit the dimmer switch and removed her robe. She wore a cute little baby doll with black lace and red piping. Heather dove onto her queen-size sleigh bed with its white down comforter and turned her cheek to one side. She paddled her legs ever so slightly in anticipation of his touch. Smiling, she closed her eyes.

Jamal did a quick search of her bedroom until he found exactly what he was looking for—a bottle of baby lotion. He squeezed out a quarter-sized amount, warming it in the palms of his hand. Then, he began to massage her back and shoulders in deliberate, circular strokes.

Heather let out a sigh as his hands wandered down her shoulders to her arms and then inwardly to her sides. He kneaded the flesh of her back so intensely that she couldn't decide if she felt pain or pleasure. When his hands trailed down to the backs of her inner thighs, she knew precisely what the deal was. Instinctively, she spread her legs ever so slightly, turning her cheek to the other side.

Taking this as a green light, Jamal paused momentarily, resting on his feet. Heather opened her eyes in response as he quickly pulled his hoodie over his head and removed his sneakers and socks. He unbuckled his belt and dropped his jeans to the floor before stepping out of them. Only his briefs remained, and the vision of that damn six-pack before she closed her eyes once again.

Jamal leaned over and kissed her from the nape of her neck and beyond. He gently kissed one shoulder blade and then the other before caressing the small of her back with his tongue. He grabbed her generous behind with both hands, squeezing her amber-colored flesh. Then, he gently rolled her over and slid on top of her.

Heather's body was wide awake. He supported both sides of her neck with his hands and kissed her deeply. There was nothing gentle about it. Her telephone began to ring, but she barely gave it a second thought. How could she with Jamal unbuttoning her nightie, his mouth finding her breasts like a newborn reuniting with his mother. In no time her nipples were as hard as the tender nipple between her thighs. She reached for his hand and led it down below, where it found warmth and wetness.

Jamal reached inside the opening of his brief and pulled out his dick. She squeezed it, feeling it rise and spit in her hands. Jamal got up from the bed once again to put on a condom. Heather smiled to herself as she watched him roll the rubber up what had to be his pride and joy. He joined her on the bed momentarily, lightly brushing his nose against hers. Tickled, she laughed softly before his lips returned to hers.

Jamal reached down and rubbed the single nipple between her thighs until it practically cried for joy, showering his fingers with its tears. He brought his fingers up to his lips and tasted her, then sunk his tongue deep into her mouth. She kissed him back just as hard.

Heather grabbed his manhood and slid it inside her. It felt so good as they gyrated together under the comforter. Heather was almost embarrassed by the primal sounds escaping her lips. Almost. Thank goodness they had the whole house to themselves. Jamal's sweat joined hers as they both noisily climaxed together.

"You're incredible," Jamal said, trying to catch his breath. Panting, he rolled off of her and onto his back.

Heather heard her mother's front door shut just as Jamal got up to use the bathroom. Timing was indeed everything.

Heather, Tangie, and Charisma rode the Long Island Railroad into New York's Penn Station. From there they walked three blocks up Seventh Avenue to the A+ Size Modeling Agency.

The bright March sunshine had coaxed city dwellers outside, and though the thermometer barely touched forty degrees, it didn't stop some from walking around with their coats and jackets unbuttoned. The office took up the entire top two floors of the glass-structured building. Don's office was on the ninth floor. The mirrored elevator opened to a reception area and a receptionist politely welcomed Heather to the agency. Charisma and Tangie sat while the receptionist took Heather's coat and ushered her into Don's office.

Though Don was on a phone call, he looked up and smiled at Heather, acknowledging her presence while he worked on his laptop. Heather sat down on the ivory sofa by the window. She tried not to eavesdrop but couldn't help but hear his side of the conversation.

"I don't give a flip if her German shepherd had kittens. If she's one minute late for that shoot, she's history." Don slammed down the phone and grabbed the large bottle of water on his desk, taking a few chugs. "Divas," he said in disgust. "Look like 'em but never act like 'em. I'm sorry. I'll be right with you." Don returned to his laptop, pounding out his frustrations before giving Heather his full attention. "Long time no see, Heather. So how have you been?"

"I'm good," she said.

"And you sure do look it." He smiled. "Why don't we take

some photos of you just as you are now. Then you'll meet with a makeup artist, and we'll take a few more. How's that?"

"Sounds great."

"Good." He picked up the phone and called in his assistant. Brittany was a tall, slim white girl with a thick red-bobbed hairdo. She escorted Heather to the studio where she was introduced to the photographer, Chip.

Chip instantly put Heather at ease. The brother wore a pair of designer jeans and a crisp white shirt. He immediately snapped a few shots of Heather, then put his camera down. He had Heather sit on a stool against a white background. Chip took a few more shots of her before turning on the fan. Heather had just shampooed and blow-dried her natural curls out earlier that morning so her long, bone-straight hair was now blowing down her back.

"Beautiful," Chip commented as he snapped away. At that point, Heather dropped her eyes and blushed. "Coy, are we?" he asked. "I love it." He laughed.

Heather looked up and tossed her hair back. Chip took a few more pictures before Brittany returned. She took Heather to the makeup artist. Sherry was a short, plump brown-skinned woman with jet-black curls. She wore a white V-neck and black jeans underneath a black overcoat.

Sherry smiled, revealing two rows of even pearly whites. "Nice to meet you, Heather. Have a seat."

Heather sat as told and Sherry immediately went to work. She turned Heather away from the mirror.

"You have lovely skin, by the way." She began by lightly tweezing Heather's eyebrows. "Your brows have a beautiful arch. I just want to get rid of a few spares." She gently plucked them away. Cinderella would be pleased. Next, Sherry applied a light foundation. She applied a touch of under eye concealer, eye shadow, eyeliner, and mascara before adding blush and lipstick. She finished up with a top coat of lip gloss. "Perfect," she told Heather as she turned her around in the swivel chair so that she faced the mirror again. "You have amazing features. All you need is a little makeup to bring them out."

Heather looked at her image in the mirror. She was impressed. Not one to normally wear much makeup, she felt like a supermodel—at least from the neck up.

Don peeked his head in the doorway. "You look amazing. Let's do this." He escorted Heather down the hall to the studio for the second shoot.

Chip was reloading his camera. "Damn," he said as he set eyes on Heather. "Let's get this party started. Now I want you to show me some attitude."

Heather was center stage. This time there was no stool, no props. She was completely on her own. Don eyed her intently. She posed. She laughed. She danced. Heather was having the time of her life. Then it was over. She thanked them all and Brittany returned to escort her back to the reception area. Charisma and Tangie were flipping through fashion magazines. They both stood on her arrival.

"Wow," Tangie said.

"Girl, I am scared of you." Charisma said, laughing and handing Heather her coat.

"All done?" Tangie asked.

"Uh-huh. Don said he'll call me once the proofs are developed. Until then, I'll just have to sit tight." Heather buttoned up her coat.

"Alrighty," Tangie said as they walked toward the elevator.

"We should celebrate tonight," Heather said.

"Where do you want to go?" Tangie asked.

"I don't know," Heather said. "But I know one thing. I'm not washing off this face."

Ten hours later Heather, Charisma, and Tangie were being seated at a table for four at Cabana's Forest Hills location. They began the evening with a large pitcher of san-gria.

Heather raised her glass in their traditional toast. "Be-hind every successful woman is herself."

"You know it," Tangie agreed. "What a day, huh?"

"Like a dream." Heather smiled, digging into one of two plates of appetizers. "I don't remember the last time I had so much fun. I mean, it was incredible, you know?"

"I can only imagine," Tangie said, letting Heather bask in the moment. "So what did your mom and Jamal say?"

"Jamal is thrilled and to hear my mother talk, you'd think I was on the cover of *Vogue* or something." Heather laughed.

Charisma was unusually quiet. Heather turned to her and asked, "Any word on Nate?"

"Not a word," Charisma said, shaking her head.

"If you had a second chance, would you do things differently?" Tangie asked.

Charisma sighed. "Does it even matter? I mean, hindsight is twenty-twenty, right?"

"Every time," Heather agreed.

Heather returned to work Monday morning still floating on air. Though the makeup was long gone, the aftereffects remained. Nothing could ruin her day, not the snotty high school senior who needed help with her term paper or even her coworker, who relieved her half an hour late for lunch.

She and Jamal were supposed to meet for an extended lunch. Heather called him to reschedule. To her surprise, he was patiently waiting in his car out front. He rolled his window down.

"You're still here?" she asked him. "I'm flattered."

"You know you're worth it," he insisted.

Heather walked around the car and got in on the driver's side.

"Where to?" he asked.

"Feel like the food court?"

"Here on the avenue?"

"Not exactly."

"Where then? Talk to me, woman."

"Green Acres. They have the best Philly cheesesteaks and—"

"Okay, I'm sold. Green Acres it is," he said, starting the ignition. Jamal took Merrick Boulevard to Springfield Boulevard before making a left onto the Conduit and heading down Sunrise Highway to the mall.

Jamal quickly found a parking space and in no time they were upstairs in the food court. Heather had a grilled chicken salad and a diet soda. Jamal, on the other hand, had a Philly cheesesteak.

"You're really making me look bad," he told her. "I thought you were getting one too."

"Well, you know it's a woman's prerogative to change her mind."

"Then exercise your right, baby."

"I forgot, you like your women thick."

"Exactly. If some is good, more is better." He checked his watch.

"I know, time to go. Do you think we have time to stop by Macy's for a second?"

"What's at Macy's?"

"Shoes. There's this pair I wanted, but Roosevelt Field and Queens Center didn't have my size."

"And Green Acres does?"

"Yeah, I called last night, and they'll hold them for twenty-four hours."

"You are so conniving." He grinned and picked up their

trays. "Let's go, Imelda Marcos," he said, referring to the Phillipine shoe maven. "Let's go back to the car, and I'll drive you around to Macy's."

"Okay, but I'm not conniving. I'd prefer to call it resourcefulness."

"Whatever." He shook his head. "Either way you get your shoes."

"Exactly."

Jamal drove the short distance to Macy's and parked the car. He checked his watch again."

"Do you wanna wait in the car?" she asked.

"No, I wanna see what all the fuss is about with these shoes." They both got out the car, walked into Macy's, and up the escalator to the second-floor shoe department. Jamal was surprised that the department was so busy for a Monday afternoon. He said as much to Heather.

"Are you kidding me? There's never an off time for shoe shopping," she told him. Heather went up to the register and a few moments later, the sales associate returned with her shoes. She sat down and eagerly tried them on. Heather eyed her reflection in the full-length mirror. The shoes were a royal blue high-heeled patent leather peep toe pump. "Perfect," she breathed deeply, the sight of the shoes on her feet giving her a rush.

Jamal walked over to the display, checked out the price of her shoe fix, and let out a whistle.

"And they're worth every penny," she told him.

"But Heather, they're just shoes."

"Just shoes? Just shoes?" she repeated. "Don't you know that in the right shoes a woman can run the world? You better be glad you're a man cause you'd never make it as a woman."

"Well, after all that moaning you did the other night, you better be glad too."

21

Tangie

Tangie and Tony had just come in from the movies. They were over Tony's relaxing to the sounds of the Isley Brothers and sipping on a little wine.

"Spend the night with me," Tony whispered in her ear.

"I can't," she began.

"Why not?"

Tangie thought for a moment.

"Exactly. Looks like you're mine tonight. All night." He grinned. Tony stood to dim the lights and then returned to the sofa. He removed his shirt and unbuckled his belt before taking off his sneakers and socks. "Your turn," he told Tangie as he unzipped her sweater and removed her jeans.

She didn't object and was down to her bra and panties in no time. Tangie was glad she had worn her racy, lacy lingerie. Apparently, so was Tony, who climbed on top of her. He kissed her lips ever so slowly, ever so softly. He was in no rush. They had all night.

Tangie relaxed under his touch. Here was a man who had nursed her when she was sick, even cleaned up her vomit. He was spiritual and took her to church. He had taken her to meet his parents, another plus. He got to know her before trying to get inside her jeans. And how could she forget those beautiful lime roses? It didn't take Tangie long to do the math. She had found the perfect man.

Tangie gave into her feelings, smiling to herself as he removed her bra and panties. Then, he took those beautiful, full lips of his that she loved so much and kissed her breasts, gently sucking on her nipples. He kissed her stomach, her thighs, everywhere he thought would possibly bring her pleasure.

When she could stand his hot kisses no more, she reached for him to enter her. He scooped her up in one easy gesture and whisked her off to his bedroom. He laid her on the bed and proceeded to remove his undershorts before joining her. Tony eased himself into Tangie. Tangie couldn't believe this was finally happening. It was like a dream. A soft moan escaped from her lips and then another. She loved his rhythm, the way he rocked her.

He rolled her over until she was on top, holding her by the waist with both hands. Tony tweaked her nipples until she came loud and hard. Then he rolled her over onto her back, cumming too moments later.

They lay in silence for a minute, catching their breath. Finally, Tony spoke. "I've wanted to make love to you from the day we met," he said.

"I know."

"You didn't know." He laughed.

"I did," she exclaimed. "The shoe compliment was a dead giveaway."

He took her in his arms gently, rubbing her shoulders. "Are you hungry?"

"Famished."

He got up to get them robes. "Let's raid the kitchen." Tony ended up making hamburgers and peanut butter milkshakes. The burger joints couldn't touch it if they tried.

"You are so beautiful," Tony told her from across the kitchen table.

"What I am is stuffed." She held her stomach with one hand for emphasis.

"Let's go in the living room."

"Let me clean up the kitchen."

"The dishes can wait." He stood, and she followed him into the living room.

Their clothes were in a heap on the floor just as they had left them. Tony popped a Whispers CD into the stereo.

"Let's dance," he said simply, helping her to her feet. He untied her robe and slid his arms around her bare body. After about three slow jams, Tony stopped dancing and looked her straight in the eye.

"Tangela Winterhope, will you marry me?"

Shocked, she took her arms from around his neck but her eyes were glued to his. "You're serious," she said slowly.

"I am. Tangela, will you marry me?" he repeated.

"Oh my God. Yes!"

And just like that, Tony and Tangie were on their way to the altar.

"I'm engaged!" Tangie exclaimed over Heather's the next night.

"Oh, my goodness," Charisma and Heather said.

Tangie told them all about the proposal. "I still can't believe it," Tangie admitted. "It's incredible. I wasted two years with Blade. Tony pops the question in a matter of months."

"Just goes to show you he's a man who knows what he wants and not afraid to go after it," Charisma said.

Tangie laughed. "That's my kind of man."

"That's what I'm talking about," Heather agreed.

"When's the wedding?" Charisma asked.

"Not soon enough." Tangie sipped her coffee. "I mean, we could elope as far as I'm concerned."

"Are you serious?" Heather asked her.

"Most def," Tangie admitted. "Tony's almost too good to be true. Sometimes you just gotta strike while the iron's hot."

"Sounds good to me," Charisma said. "No use tempting fate."

"Wow, this calls for a cookie break," Heather said, getting up from the kitchen table and heading over to the cupboard for her assorted stash. "So what's your favorite cookies these days, Tangie? Let me rephrase that. What's Tony's favorite cookie?" It was a private joke amongst the three of them that whatever her latest preferred was Tangie's cookie du jour. The same could be said for how she ate her eggs.

"We both like Nutter Butters," Tangie said with a straight face.

"Well, isn't that a coincidence." Heather shook her head.

"We can't help it if we're in sync. Don't hate," Tangie told them.

"Yeah, yeah, yeah. Tell it to the Marines," Heather said, searching for the requested cookie. She was the only person Tangie and Charisma knew who organized her sweets alphabetically. It had to be the librarian in her, they had decided. "Here we go," Heather said upon locating Tangie's cookies. "Charisma, what about you?"

"Just call me Lorna. Lorna Doone," Charisma added.

"Coming right up," Heather said. "I see we're going with the mellow cookies tonight. Let me get my pecan sandies and we'll be straight."

"Wait a minute." Tangie got three glasses and a half gallon of ice-cold milk from Heather's fridge. "Now we can get this party started."

"Tangie, we haven't met Tony yet, but I already like his style." Charisma raised her glass in a toast.

"And anybody who keeps you smiling is all right in my book. To Tangie and Tony." Heather said, raising her glass.

"To Tangie and Tony," Charisma agreed.

"So when are we going to meet Prince Charming?" Heather asked.

"I'll check his schedule. Maybe we can all get together for breakfast this weekend," Tangie said.

"It's about time," Charisma said simply.

Tangie floated through the rest of the week. Work was a breeze. Cooking, cleaning, laundry, everything was a breeze. Luckily, Tony and Tangie were both free Saturday morning and they met the girls at IHOP. Heather and Charisma arrived first. They slid into a booth and waited for the happy couple. The waitress brought them coffee and menus, returning several moments later to take their orders. Charisma explained to her that they were expecting two more.

Heather reached in her purse for a tiny plastic bottle of hazelnut creamer. She poured some into her coffee and stirred. Then she took a nice, long sip. She looked up and whispered to Charisma, "Here they come now."

Tony removed Tangie's down jacket before removing his own. A glowing Tangie introduced Tony, and they slid into the booth to join Charisma and Heather. The waitress returned to take the couple's order, and then once again to bring their coffee.

"So you're the man who has our girl walking on air," Heather said.

Tony grinned. "Don't think I'm trying not to." He put his arm around Tangie and gently squeezed her shoulder.

"Well, you're doing one helluva job." Charisma laughed.

"That's the plan," Tony said. "Tangie deserves to be happy. I'm just doing my job."

"As long as she stays that way, you won't have a problem with us," Heather told him.

The waitress returned with their orders. Tony blessed the food, and they all dug in. Tangie couldn't wait to suck down those world-famous beautiful brown pancakes. It had been so long. Too long.

Charisma took another mouthful of her omelet before speaking. "Tony, if you ever, ever hurt Tangie, you'll wish you were dead." Smiling, she popped a piece of bacon in her mouth. "And that's a promise."

Tony chewed his steak and swallowed before speaking. "Well, I'm glad I know where I stand," he said. "I can see how much you love Tangela. I do too."

"Good." Charisma smiled. "I'm glad we're all on the same page. Let's relax and enjoy breakfast."

Tony shook his head. "I gotta hand it to you. You ladies are tough." He took out his handkerchief and wiped away imaginary beads of sweat from his brow.

"Do you want your Oscar now or later?" Heather asked good-naturedly as she took another bite of her toast.

"I studied theater in college," he said. "I guess it's finally paid off."

"Don't quit your day job," Charisma said and they all laughed.

Tangie smiled to herself. She was out eating her favorite meal with her three favorite people. What more could a woman ask for?

"Ma, you're not going to believe this," Tangie began. "I'm getting married."

"What?" Della Winterhope exclaimed over the phone.

"Tony and I are getting married."

"Are you happy?"

"Yes, Ma. I'm happy."

"Then, I'm happy for you.

"Is he still with the FBI?"

"Uh-huh."

"I don't know, Tangie. That could be really dangerous."

"Ma, he's not a spy, if that's what you mean."

"Have you spoken to your father about him?"

"No, everything happened so fast. I haven't had a chance yet. Besides, you know every time I call his house his wife hangs up on me. She's such a witch. I don't know what he sees in her."

"You and me both," Della said under her breath about the heifer who broke up her marriage. "But that's no excuse. Call him at work or try his cell."

"I want you and Daddy to meet Tony. I know you'll both love him. Maybe the four of us can meet over my house. I'll make dinner."

"Okay, baby. Just keep me posted. And congratulations. Wow, we have a wedding to plan."

Next, Tangie tried calling her father at home. Naturally, his wife hung up on her the instant she heard Tangie's voice. Tangie had to count to ten to stop herself from jumping in her car, driving over there, and slapping her upside her head. But it didn't work. She had her car keys in her hand and was out the door before she made it to seven. Tangie sped off. She was on her way to her father's house.

She took the highway. Luckily, traffic was light. By the time she pulled up to the house, her heart was racing. She sat in the car for a few minutes to calm herself before hopping out and ringing the doorbell.

Naturally, "she" answered the door. She was so paranoid that someone would steal the husband she stole, that she watched him like a hawk. Tangie pushed the door open before a startled Blanche had a chance to slam it in her face.

"Where's my father?" Tangie asked.

"He's not here."

"Liar," Tangie said. "His car's in the driveway."

"He took a walk to the store."

"Daddy?" Tangie yelled. "Daddy?"

Ted Winterhope came to the door. "What's going on here?" Ted asked his wife and daughter.

"As usual, she won't let me see you," Tangie answered.

"Come on in." He motioned, ignoring his wife. He lead Tangie into the living room, where they both took a seat on the sofa.

"You really need to do something about her," Tangie said.

Blanche stood in the foyer, pretending to be busy.

"I need to speak to my father alone," Tangie told her firmly.

Blanche let out an exaggerated sigh and sauntered off into the kitchen.

"Now," Ted turned to face his daughter. "What did you want to discuss?"

"Well, Daddy. I'm engaged."

"My little girl's getting married? Who is he?"

Tangie told her father all about the new man in her life, from how they met to the dinner she was planning to introduce him to her parents. "But Daddy, I'm telling you now. Blanche is *not* welcome in my house."

"Tangie, don't be bitter."

"I mean it, Daddy. I do not want that witch in my house." She stood to leave. Ted walked his daughter to the door. "You're an adult. I guess I'll have to respect your wishes. Can't wait to meet my future son-in-law."

"Thanks, Daddy." She kissed him on the cheek. "It'll probably be next week sometime. I'll call you and let you know when."

"Okay, baby. Drive carefully, and I'll see you soon."

The next week Tony cleared his schedule for his bride-to-be. Every day after Tangie got off of work, she and Tony hit all the local jewelry stores in search of the perfect engagement ring. When their Queens and Long Island search turned up empty, they headed to Manhattan's diamond district. Walking along Forty-seventh Street, Tangie noticed that Tony seemed a little distracted. She followed his gaze to a young thug in baggy jeans that sat ultralow on his hips. His gray eyes seemed to lock with Nate's for a split second, and then he disappeared in the crowd without a trace.

Entering the stores, Tangie realized that she had never seen so many diamonds before in her life. Finally, on the third day of shopping, Tangie found a ring that she was so smitten with that it practically took her breath away. It was a marquise-cut solitaire with baguettes on either side set in platinum. Her eyes popped when the jeweler read the price tag. Unfortunately, Tony could not afford it. He asked to see other rings that were more reasonably priced. Finally, they settled on another ring, and he had the jeweler measure Tangie's finger. Tony told the jeweler that he'd be back to pickup the ring in a couple of days.

"Before sundown," the jeweler reminded Tony.

"Yes, before sundown," Tony agreed.

Saturday night Tangie made dinner for Tony and her parents. It was a very relaxed evening, and Ted Winterhope took an instant liking to Tony. Della helped her daughter in the kitchen while Tony and Mr. Winterhope watched a basketball game in the living room. Tangie peeked her head out the kitchen to hear what the men were talking about.

"I love your daughter very much, Mr. Winterhope. There's nothing I wouldn't do for her," Tony was saying.

"Tangie tells me you work for the FBI," Ted said.

"That's correct."

"And you don't think her safety would ever be an issue? I have to protect my daughter."

"I understand, but I promise you that I would never take an assignment that would jeopardize her safety. I give you my word, man-to-man," Tony promised.

Tangie's mother pulled her back into the kitchen. "Let

the men be," she told her daughter. "You invited us over for dinner, and it's not even ready. My child, my child." She smiled and shook her head.

Tangie spent the next half hour or so concentrating on dinner. However, she did manage to pop her head out one last time to hear the men wrap up their conversation.

Ted looked his prospective son-in-law in the eye. For a moment neither spoke. Finally, he extended his arm and they both stood and shook hands.

"Then, you have my blessings," Ted said simply.

Smiling, Tangie breathed a sigh of relief as she finished cooking. After dinner, they all watched the second half of the doubleheader. During a commercial break, Tony reached into his pocket and pulled out a little red box.

"Since I have your parents' blessing, I think it's time we made this official." Tony got down on one knee. "Tangela Winterhope, will you marry me?"

Tangie whispered, "Yes."

Tony revealed the contents of the box. It was the platinum marquise.

"Oh my God," was all Tangie could say. "Oh my God."

"I have a surprise for you," Tangie said as she met the girls for pizza one night.

"What's that?" Heather asked.

"Tah-dah," Tangie said, displaying her ring finger.

"Oh my goodness. It's beautiful," Charisma exclaimed.

"I love it," Tangie agreed.

"Wow." Heather's eyes popped.

"Looks like it's official," Charisma added.

"You know it," Tangie said. "I still can't believe it. I guess when you least expect it, expect it. I wish we could all be happy at the same time. Charisma, I still can't believe you stood Nate up at the airport. What's wrong with you? He was all that, and you just go and blow him off. What exactly are you looking for in a man, anyway?"

"I know I messed up big-time, girl. And now it's too late. He relocated to the Manhattan office. So I don't even see him anymore. If I had to do it over again, I'd do things differently. I really would," Charisma confessed.

"That shoulda-woulda-coulda stuff will eat you alive," Heather added.

"Don't I know it." Charisma rubbed the hair down on the back of her neck.

"Well, hopefully your guardian angel is working things out for you as we speak," Tangie said.

"From your lips to God's ears," Charisma prayed.

22

Charisma

Jena Dearborn couldn't sleep. Something wasn't right. She couldn't put her finger on it. She couldn't explain it, but her gut was telling her that something was terribly wrong. She looked over at her husband, who was sleeping peacefully.

Not wanting to disturb him, she got out of bed and headed for the kitchen to make herself some herbal tea. She glanced at the clock above the oven. It was six AM. Ellis would be up in about half an hour.

She sat and sipped the tea nervously, running her fingers through her hair. Then the strangest thing happened. In her heart she began reciting the Lord's Prayer, but this time it was different. It was as though someone was actually walking through the valley of the shadow of death to get to the other side. It was eerie and surreal, and she shuddered at the thought. A chill went through her entire body.

Jena washed out the cup, saucer, and teaspoon and headed back to bed. She snuggled up to her husband. He was terribly still. Too still. She shook him gently.

"Ellis, sweetheart?" She shook him harder. Ellis didn't move a muscle.

"Oh my God," Jena screamed. "Oh my God."

Just like that, he was gone. He had passed away in his sleep.

April first started out like any other normal weekday for Charisma. After her alarm went off, she lay in bed for a few moments to collect her thoughts and thank God for another day. Then, it was off to the bathroom to brush her teeth. She had just gotten out of the shower when the phone rang. It was her mother, sobbing.

"Mother, what's wrong?" Charisma asked.

"It's your father," she cried. "He's.—" Jena was hyperventilating.

"Ma, is Daddy okay? What happened?"

"He's dead, Charisma."

"What?" she yelled.

"Your father's gone."

Charisma's legs gave out. She collapsed on her bed, the tears welling up in her eyes. Her father was gone. How could that be? It was too soon. She wasn't ready to say good-bye. She tried to be strong for her mother's sake.

"Have you called Eric?" Charisma asked.

"No, I haven't told your brother yet. You're the first person I called. I haven't even called 9-1-1."

"I'll break it to him, Mother. We'll be right over, okay?"

"All right, honey."

"Do you need me to bring you anything?"

"No. Just come as soon as you can." Jena was tearing up again.

"We're on our way."

Chase Martini had rehearsed it a thousand times in her mind, but as she sat at the dining room table along with her parents and grandparents, her mind drew a complete blank. How was she going to tell them? Dress rehearsals were a breeze compared to the real thing. She took a sip of her orange juice, cleared her throat, and took a deep breath.

It was true-confession time, but did she have the strength to tell all? She cleared her throat again, and this time Stone and Lola looked up at their granddaughter. Her parents were in deep conversation about something or other. Chase was oblivious to exactly what. She took another sip before speaking.

"There's something I need to tell you," Chase said, barely audible.

Roberto and Sloane looked up at their daughter. "What is it, Chase?" Sloane said, sensing an urgency and giving her her full attention. "We're all listening."

Five minutes later Stone clutched his throat as his chest tightened in a viselike grip. He couldn't speak or breathe.

"Oh my God, Daddy, are you all right?" Sloane asked.

Lola jumped up and walked over to her husband at the other end of the table. "Sloane, call 9-1-1."

Sloane was frozen with shock.

"Now," Lola barked, unbuttoning her husband's collar.

Within minutes the ambulance had arrived. Roberto escorted the emergency medical technicians into the dining room.

"Mr. Canyon, can you tell us what happened?"

Stone couldn't utter a word.

"Mr. Canyon, you're having a heart attack. We're going to get you to the hospital. Mrs. Canyon, is your husband allergic to any medication?" the EMT asked.

"Not that we know of," Lola said.

Glued to her seat, Chase watched in horror, stunned by the effects of her news on her grandfather. She sobbed softly as chaos loomed all around him. *Oh God, if anything happens to Granddaddy, I'll be to blame.*

Charisma and Eric arrived over their mother's around the same time. They were both in shock.

"How did Mom sound?" Eric asked, falling into step with his sister.

"She's taking it real hard. We have to be strong for her, Eric."

"I know," he said, squeezing her shoulder. He unlocked the front door with his key. They walked inside.

"Mother?" Charisma said.

"In here," Jena answered from the kitchen. She was sitting at the table, sipping coffee and looking dazed. They walked over and embraced, hot tears spilling down all three of their faces. Finally, Jena got up to get a tissue. She wiped her eyes and blew her nose before sitting back down.

"Mom, can we take one last look at Dad?" Eric asked.

"Of course, honey," Jena said.

Eric and Charisma's eyes met as they tried to prepare themselves for one last look at their father as the coroner pulled up at the house. They climbed the stairs together—first Charisma and then Eric.

The covers were still wrapped around Ellis as though he was trying to stay warm. Charisma's eyes moistened at the sight of her father in the pajamas she had bought him for Christmas. The lump in her throat made it virtually impossible to swallow. She began to sob, deep gut-wrenching sobs that tore at her heart. How would she survive without her daddy? Soon Eric was crying too—big, salty tears that chased each other down his cheeks.

Charisma threw her arms around her brother and they cried together. Then, while holding on to her brother with one hand, she gently touched her father's shoulder with the other.

"Daddy," she prayed. "I just want you to know how much we love you and how much you'll be missed. What are we going to do without you?" Her voice cracked.

Eric gently rubbed her back. "Until we meet again, Dad."

They dried their eyes and went down to the kitchen just as the coroner and the medical examiner were finishing up with Jena. They asked her if she wanted to donate his vital organs. Jena told them that Ellis was already a registered donor. They offered their condolences and quickly removed his body.

They took a few moments for themselves before beginning the difficult task of contacting family, friends, and coworkers. There was so much to do.

By now it was after eight o'clock. Charisma called Freeman to give them the news. Her boss was saddened to hear of Ellis's passing, and asked if Charisma wanted an e-mail announcement sent out. Charisma had no objection. She agreed to keep her posted with the final arrangements as they became available.

After Eric called his boss, he offered to make them all breakfast. Jena wouldn't hear of it. She called the boutique and then tried to fix breakfast for her family. She had no way of knowing that the dinner she had prepared last night for her husband would be the last she'd ever make for him. She began to cry all over again.

"It's okay, Mother," Charisma said. "Let it out."

"I'm going back to bed," Jena said.

"I'll fix breakfast and bring you up a plate," Charisma told her.

Jena simply nodded and went back upstairs.

For Charisma, Ellis's funeral, which was held three days later, was all so surreal. She and her brother sat on the front pew on either side of their mother, comforting her as best they could. The service immediately followed the wake. Then came a long processional of friends and family—hugging, kissing, trying to console. Charisma's makeup was smeared all over her face. She stared down as tears found their way onto her lap.

Someone standing in front of her bent down and handed her a handkerchief. She looked up. It was Nate. She stood and they embraced for a long moment without speaking.

"I was so sorry to hear about your father," Nate said.

"Thank you for coming," she whispered in his ear before letting go.

"If there's anything you need . . ." He searched her eyes. "Call me."

"I will." She smiled through her tears.

Nate took her hands in his, brought them up to his lips, and kissed them gently. "I'm here for you, sweetheart. I mean it."

After the funeral and the trip to the cemetery, everyone went back to Jena's. Charisma was happy to see Tangie and Heather. They never let her down. Her girls were always there for her. Both had been very fond of Ellis. Tangie had known him since kindergarten and Heather since college. With all the holidays, barbecues, and parties they had shared with the Dearborns, they were like family, helping out in the kitchen without being asked.

Charisma's family was scattered all over the country. Unfortunately, it wasn't often that they were all together. She was happy to see her relatives—most of them, anyway.

Her cousin Dora cornered her in the kitchen. "So, are you married yet?" she asked, examining the two-karat wedding band on her left hand as though it were an unidentified sparkling object.

"Am I supposed to be?" Charisma answered, leaving Dora to pick her chin up off the floor.

Charisma returned to the living room. Grandma and Grandpa Dearborn were sitting quietly on the sofa. Charisma squeezed in between them. They say that burying a child is the hardest loss to bear. The sadness in their eyes said it all.

She put her arms around them. "Can I get you anything, Grandma, Grandpa?" Charisma asked gently. "I know it's hard. How are you two doing?" She rubbed their arms and shoulders gently.

"Well . . ." Marie Dearborn began to tear up. "Not so well. I mean, if we can't get through the first week, how do we get through a lifetime?"

"I know, Grandma. I've been asking myself the same thing." She grabbed their hands, trying to console them. Grandpa was still. He never said much, just kept it all in. She looked at her grandpa and saw a tear slide quietly down his cheek. She kissed him gently on the cheek before making a mad dash to her old bedroom. She prayed for the strength to make it through the night.

Charisma took two weeks off to try and get her life back in order. For the first few days she stayed in bed, sleeping on and off. She did manage to call and check on her mother and brother, and she postponed her fibroid surgery. One night she watched *Meet Joe Black*. She and her father had made a point of watching it every Father's Day. It was their favorite father-daughter movie. She cried like a baby at the ending, but only this time it truly hit home.

Toward the end of the first week she was able to get up, take a hot bath, and put on some clothes. She even started returning phone calls. Heather and Tangie had called several times, but she hadn't the energy to talk. She called Tangie and then threewayed Heather in. She assured her girls that she was fine, just taking it one day at a time. They made her promise that she would call if there was anything she needed.

Little by little her appetite returned. Mourning had caused her to drop a few pounds so she could afford to splurge. She made herself a grilled cheese and bacon sandwich. It was the perfect complement to a hot, comforting bowl of tomato soup.

She glanced up at the clock on the kitchen wall. It was only twelve-thirty. She had been in for days. Houseatosis was setting in. She decided to go out for some fresh air. Maybe take a drive to the supermarket. The cold air felt refreshing against her skin. She wore no makeup, only a hint of lip gloss.

Charisma walked up and down the near empty aisles. Early-afternoon grocery shopping was a pleasure, especially during the week. Halfway down the bread aisle, she flipped open her cell phone and called her mother. Jena gave her a small list of items to pick up. Charisma breezed through the checkout line and headed over to her mother's.

It was amazing how a little fresh air and sunshine could lift her spirits. She pulled up to the driveway and sat in the car for a minute. Then she gathered up the groceries, got out of the car, and let herself inside the house.

Jena was in the kitchen fixing dinner. She gave her mother a big hug and kiss and put the bag of groceries away. Jena tried to pay her daughter, but Charisma wouldn't hear of it.

"Mother, how's Eric doing? I've only heard from him once since the funeral."

"Your brother's like your grandfather. He doesn't say much, but still waters run deep. As a matter of fact, he called this morning. He wanted to know if it was all right with me if he kept your father's gold cuff links—the ones he wore to the funeral. Of course I told him it was fine."

She took lamb chops out of the fridge. "Hungry?" she asked Charisma.

Charisma knew her mother had to be lonely. "Sure. Need some help?"

"No, honey, you just relax while I throw these chops under the broiler. And I made mashed potatoes and green beans."

"Mmm, sounds good." She began setting the table. It felt strange not setting a place for her father. A tear ran down her check. Charisma wiped it away with her sleeve before her mother could see it. Charisma wasn't really hungry, but she didn't want her mother to eat alone. It must he hard getting used to an empty house.

They ate dinner and sat and talked for awhile. Charisma cleaned up the kitchen before she left. When she returned home, she took another bath—with bubbles this time—and slipped into her favorite silky pajamas. She loaded up her stereo with her favorite CDs and lit a scented candle in her father's memory. She had done that every night since he passed. Then she curled up on the sofa with a mug of hot chocolate.

She must have dozed off because she woke to the persistent ringing of her doorbell. Charisma jumped up. She looked through her peephole. It was Nate. She quickly ran her fingers through her hair before opening the door.

"Did I come at a bad time?" he asked.

"Not at all. Come on in."

Nate removed his leather bomber and placed it in the chair. He joined her on the sofa.

"I was surprised to see you at my father's funeral," Charisma began. "Nicely surprised," she added.

"I wanted to pay my respects. Your father was a good man."

"That he was," Charisma agreed.

They were silent for a moment.

She rubbed the back of her neck. "There's something I've wanted to say to you since Presidents' weekend. I chickened out at the last minute, and not a day goes by that I don't regret what I did to you. I'm sorry I stood you up. I really felt bad about it, and I still do. I was afraid of you, of us."

"And now?"

"And now . . . now I want a second chance," she said softly.

"Are you sure?" He searched her eyes.

She nodded.

"I was very bitter for awhile. I even did things against my better judgment."

"Like what?" she asked softly.

"You don't want to know, but I will say that I promised myself that given the chance I'd do whatever it took to get you back. So here I am."

"We're finally on the same page," she agreed, suddenly shy.

"Charisma, you're going through a lot right now. I don't want our relationship to put any pressure on you. We can take it slow. I'm not going anywhere."

Charisma looked at Nate and began to cry. "I don't want to be alone tonight," she said slowly.

"You shouldn't have to be."

She relaxed as he rubbed her back.

"You must be tired," Nate said.

"Exhausted," she agreed, yawning. "I'm ready to turn in."

"Why don't I take a shower, and I'll come join you." He rose to his feet. "By the way, where's your bathroom?"

"Down the hall to the left, and the linen closet's across from the bathroom."

"Thanks." He kissed her on the lips and headed for the shower while she headed for the bedroom.

Charisma pulled back the duvet and slid between the

cool sheets. Her lids were heavy. A few minutes later, Nate joined her, a towel wrapped around his middle. They lay hugged up for the entire night, almost as though they couldn't hold each other close enough. Charisma drifted off to sleep, her lips curled up in a smile.

Nate returned home early the next morning to shower and change before going to work. Charisma decided that she had postponed her fibroid surgery long enough. She called Dr. Vale's office and left a message with her nurse. Dr. Vale made arrangements with the surgeon and called Charisma later that afternoon. The operation was scheduled for early next month.

Just as she hung up with Dr. Vale, her phone rang again. It was Nate.

"Hey, baby, how are you feeling today?"

"Okay."

"I have an idea. Are you up to going out to dinner tonight?"

"I'd like that," she decided.

"I'll pick you up around seven?" he asked.

"I'm looking forward to it." Charisma hung up smiling. She was looking forward to a nice weekend. She was overdue. She decided to get her hair done. Daisy's shouldn't be too crowded this time of day. She gassed up her car and drove to the salon.

"*Cómo está,* Charisma?" Daisy greeted her as she entered the shop.

"So-so," Charisma answered.

"My dad passed away last week."

"*Tu papa murió?* I'm so sorry, Charisma."

"Thank you, Daisy."

"*Cómo está tu madre?*"

"As well as can be expected. She's hanging in there. We all are."

"If there's anything I can do, let me know."

"Thank you, Daisy."

"Wash and blow?"

"Sí,"

An hour later, Charisma walked out of the salon feeling like a new person. She wasn't over her father's death by any means, but she knew that life had to go on. She stopped by her mother's before heading back home.

Jena was at the kitchen table, pages of documents spread out before her. Charisma sat down opposite her mother.

"How's it going?" she asked.

"Oh, I'm getting some papers together for Chuck." Chuck Garner was the family attorney. He had taken over his father's practice after he retired several years earlier. "Thank God your father kept good records. It's just a matter of sifting through everything."

"Need some help?" Charisma asked.

"No honey, I'm fine. Your hair looks nice. Just coming from Daisy's?"

"Uh-huh."

"Funny how a good hair day always makes a woman feel good."

"I know, and I have a date tonight."

"Good for you, honey."

"With Nate," Charisma added.

Jena smiled and removed her glasses. "I must be out of the loop."

"Ma, do you ever get tired of the fight? I've been doing a lot of thinking since Dad passed. Why am I fighting so hard to resist a man that deep down inside I really want? Life is so short."

"You can wake up one morning and realize that half your life has gone by if you're not careful. Charisma, I'm going to tell you what your grandmother told me when I met your father. She said that life takes courage, to trust my gut. And I know that's what your father would've wanted to leave with you—the courage to trust your gut."

Charisma reached across the table and squeezed her mother's hand. "You wanna hear something funny? Last night I dreamed about Daddy. I can't remember what happened. It was really hazy, but I felt his presence. Something about a poem. It was so beautiful." She shook her head. "Oh Mother, I can't remember it."

"Don't worry. It'll come to you, honey. Have fun tonight."

Three hours later Charisma and Nate were having a cozy dinner for two at Ruth's Chris Steak House in Garden City. It was all so elegant. They dined on petite filet and shrimp and sipped champagne until the wee hours of the morning.

Nate got straight to the point. "So, Miss Dearborn, when are we really going away together?" He sipped his champagne slowly.

"You are just determined to get me out of the country. Aren't you?"

"I just want to take you someplace where you've never been before. Ever been to . . . the Virgin Islands?"

"Yep."

"How about Bermuda?"

"Uh-huh."

"Paradise Island?"

"Ooh, I'd love to go to Paradise Island."

"So it's settled. When can you get away?"

She shook her head. "I have so much on my plate. I haven't had the chance to tell you, but I have to have surgery."

He put his fork down. "What's wrong?"

"Fibroids. I'm scheduled for surgery next month. And I'm scared, Nate," she said softly. "What if I can't have children?"

He reached for her hand. "Listen to me. You and I will get through this together. And after it's all over, and they wheel you into recovery, I'll be right there waiting for you."

"I'm going to hold you to it."

"You do that," he said, intertwining his fingers with hers. "Ready to order dessert?"

"Only if it's not on the menu." She smiled mischievously.

"Your place or mine?" he asked.

"Yours is closer, but can we stop at my place for a second?"

"Sure." Nate drove her home and closed the door behind them. They removed their coats. Then he took her in his arms and slid his tongue into her mouth. She kissed him back hungrily, traces of champagne still on his breath. His right hand gently squeezed her breast, causing her to ache with desire.

"I'll be right back," she said, tearing herself apart from his warmth and heading for the bedroom. Nate sat down and grabbed the remote control, turning on the television. He flipped a few channels and waited for Charisma. And waited, and waited, and waited. He reached for his leather jacket as he heard his cell phone ringing.

"Mr. Arquette, how long would it take you to walk from the living room into my bedroom?" she asked from underneath the sheets. Next thing Charisma knew he was standing in the doorway of her dimly-lit bedroom, the jasmine-scented candles flickering in the background. Her breathing deepened ever so slightly as he made his way to the bed. Nate quickly removed his pants and sweater. Soon he was only wearing briefs and a gold chain around his neck.

Charisma's eyes nearly popped, scoping her nearly naked ex-boss. She couldn't believe that this was actually happening. When he slid under the covers with her and took her in his arms, she knew it wasn't a dream.

Nate made love to Charisma slowly that night, learning

her body as she learned his. He was especially tender with her, holding back until she was completely satisfied. They both lay back exhausted and fulfilled. Charisma looked over at Nate as he drifted off to sleep. Thank goodness she had finally found the courage to trust her gut.

Three weeks later Charisma prepared for surgery. On the morning of the procedure, Jena stayed by her daughter's side until she was wheeled into pre op. The operation took approximately two hours and a groggy Charisma was wheeled into recovery.

Dr. Walton, the surgeon, spoke with Jena privately. He was able to remove all of the fibroids. Unfortunately, three of the fibroids were lodged on the top of her ovaries and a portion of both ovaries had to be removed.

Jena was horrified. "Will my daughter be able to have children?"

"Mrs. Dearborn," Dr. Walton began. "The chances are slim to nil that Charisma will ever be able to bear children. I'm terribly, terribly sorry." He shook his head.

"Wait a minute, Doctor. Isn't there anything else you could have done?"

"The fibroids had to be removed. If we allowed them to just sit there, they may have ruptured, resulting in an emergency hysterectomy or worse. Would you like to break the news to Charisma or shall I?"

"I'll tell her," Jena said.

"Barring no complications, she should be discharged tomorrow morning."

"Okay, Doctor."

Jena went to see about her baby girl. Just as she was about to reenter the recovery area, a nurse stopped her.

"Oh, no, you can't go in now," the nurse said. "Her husband's here."

Puzzled, Jena looked ahead. Nate was approaching Charisma's bedside. His suit and tie must have made him look like husband material, and only one visitor was allowed in at a time. Jena smiled at the nurse and found a seat in the waiting area.

Nate stayed long enough to reassure himself that Charisma was okay. He promised Jena that he would check on Charisma tomorrow.

"I'm going to try and get her to stay with me for a few days, but you know how hardheaded Charisma can be," Jena said.

"Tell me about it," Nate agreed. "But she said she's in a lot of pain. She just may take you up on your offer, or at least have you stay with her."

"Okay, Nate, let me get back inside. Thanks for coming."

"Let me know if you need anything, Mrs. Dearborn."

"It's Jena."

"Jena," he repeated. "Do you need a ride home?"

"No, I drove, thank you anyway. The doctor said Charisma should be discharged tomorrow if things go well tonight. I'll keep you posted."

"I'd appreciate that, Jena."

Jena checked on Charisma. "How are you feeling, honey?"

"I hurt," she said simply. "And I'm starving." Charisma hadn't eaten anything since midnight. "Can you ask the nurse to bring me something?"

"Sure, honey," Jena left and returned shortly with a nurse carrying a small container of gelatin and a plastic spoon.

"Do you think you can keep this down?" the nurse asked Charisma.

Charisma nodded, and the nurse removed the plastic wrap from the gelatin and the spoon and began to feed her. It wasn't much, but it was better than nothing, Charisma decided. Two minutes later she threw it all up.

"It's the anesthesia," the nurse said. "It'll be hard to keep anything down until it wears off. You should be fine in time for dinner."

Half an hour after Charisma was settled in her room, there was a knock at her door. She had drifted off to sleep, but when she opened her eyes, Tangie and Heather were smiling down at her. She smiled back despite the pain.

"How are you feeling, sweetie?" Heather asked.

Charisma grabbed her stomach in response.

"You gotta hear this one," Tangie began. "Heather dragged me out to a club over the weekend, and this guy had been scoping me all night. So finally he comes over talking about he's packing something big-time just for me. So I said, 'Yeah, I know, a sock.' "

Heather and Charisma fell out. "Oh God, it hurts. Please don't make me laugh," Charisma cried. The pain was excruciating. "I'll pop my stitches."

"More like a funky sock if you ask me," Heather added, rolling her eyes.

"Stop it," Charisma laughed, tears streaming down her face. "You're torturing me. I'm gonna have to put you both out."

"Can I just tell you one more thing?" Tangie asked.

"No," Charisma yelled.

After a restful night Charisma was released the next morning. Her mother picked her up and brought her home. Jena was only too happy to spend a week over Charisma's. Jena did the cooking, cleaning, and laundry. Charisma could tell that her mother loved feeling needed. Heather and Tangie called often. In the evenings, Nate would stop by, and Jena would use that time to go grocery shopping and run errands.

One evening after Nate had gone, Jena decided that it

was time that she and Charisma talked. They were sitting around the kitchen table eating ice cream.

"I bought you some sanitary pads, but your periods will probably be a lot lighter now that you've had the surgery," Jena said.

"Thank goodness. I think my stomach has even shrunk."

"I'm not surprised." She looked at her daughter gently before continuing. "Honey, Dr. Walton had to remove a portion of both your ovaries to get all the fibroids. And . . ." She sighed.

"And."

Jena took a deep breath. "And he feels that you may never be able to conceive."

"Oh my God. Oh my God," she repeated. "There must be some mistake."

"Honey, he's only a doctor. He's not God. My mother used to say that man's extremities are God's opportunities. Remember that, honey. I promise you. One day we'll have our Joy," she said. Joy was the name Charisma had chosen for her firstborn daughter.

Charisma looked at Jena with big fat tears welling up in her eyes and racing down her chin. "Well, I guess there's no need to get back on the Pill."

"It's okay to cry." Jena went over to her daughter and held her in her arms. "Let it out, honey."

23

Tangie

Tony had been working undercover a lot lately in Manhattan, and he was careful to keep that part of his life separate from his personal life. He took serious measures to ensure that his cover would not be blown. Now that Tangie was in his life, he had to be even that much more cautious. So if he had to lie to her about his whereabouts, so be it. It was for her own good.

That morning Tony woke up feeling uneasy. In his gut he knew that something just wasn't right. He showered and shaved, made himself a bacon-and-eggs breakfast, and got dressed. Tony made certain the wire he wore was hidden securely under his black shirt before grabbing a pair of designer frames and a baseball cap and heading into the city. He carried a change of clothing in a duffel bag for after work. He was doing surveillance on the Estrada case. Jorge Estrada was a member of one of the biggest drug cartels operating on the East Coast. Tony was working as a bouncer in a midtown strip club Estrada frequented.

He got to the club before eleven, keeping his eyes and ears open. It was a slow day. Somewhere around two PM,

Estrada and his street urchins entered the club. Tony had orders to escort them to Dave's office in the back. Once inside the office, Estrada took out a big, fat Cuban cigar. He lit it and took several puffs before telling Tony to get lost.

"He stays," Dave said. "He's cool."

"Search him," Estrada told two of his flunkies. Once satisfied, they all sat. No one said a word except Dave and Estrada.

"So when's the next shipment of coke due in?" Dave asked Estrada.

"Don't worry about it," Estrada said.

"I want in. I have a contact at Homeland Security who'll whisk you in like you're the Queen of England."

"We don't need your damn contact. We have our own." Estrada grinned.

"I know. As we speak he's singing like an American Idol. You're being set up. And with all the evidence the Feds now have against you, they'll put your ass away for a long time."

"Bullshit."

"Go ahead. Call your boys. You'll see." Estrada picked up his cell phone and pressed speed dial. He spoke a few words in Spanish, his body tense as he hung up.

"Now," Dave said before lighting up a Cuban and blowing out smoke for emphasis. "How much is my contact worth to you?"

Tony parked down the block from of Canyon's Club later that evening and waited for Tangie. He was picking her up since her car was in the shop. She was already ten minutes late, and he was getting fidgety. It had been a long day. Hopefully, the Feds had enough evidence on Estrada to nail him.

Tony decided to get out and stretch his legs, leaning on the passenger's side of his Benz for support. He had an uneasy feeling in the pit of his stomach all day. He gently wiped the sweat from his dome in one easy motion and reached for his cell phone to call Tangie just as she exited the building. Smiling, she spotted him instantly. He watched her walk the half block to his car. Just as she was about to give him a hug, two men in deep conversation accidentally bumped into her.

"I'm so sorry," one of them apologized.

"Be careful," he warned. "A woman as beautiful as you can get hurt."

"I'm fine," Tangie said.

"You certainly are," the other agreed, winking at Tony.

Tony recognized them instantly. It was Estrada's flunkies. Tony rushed her into the car, closed the door, and got in next to her. He sped off without saying a word.

"Babe, you're sweating. What's wrong?" Tangie asked.

"Nothing, baby. Just tired is all."

"You know I love it when your head glows. Why don't we go back to my place and really make it shine?" She laughed.

"How about a rain check? I'm exhausted."

"I'll let you off the hook this time," she said.

They drove the rest of the way in silence. Tangie sensed that Tony needed some space. Apparently, she was right. He didn't call her for several days.

Tony had a lot on his mind. He vividly remembered the conversation he'd had with Tangie's father and his promise to never compromise her safety. Now he was in a situation he never imagined he'd be in. As much as he wanted otherwise, it wasn't going to work. He'd have to let her go. Life was a bitch.

Tony picked up his phone and dialed her number. She wasn't home, so he left a message on her cell to call him. Tangie returned his call about nine o'clock that night.

"What's up, babe?" she asked him.

"I need to see you," he said simply.

"Wow, sounds serious." She laughed. "Is everything okay?"

Tony was silent.

"Babe, what's wrong? Tell me what's going on. You're beginning to worry me."

"Are you early or late tomorrow?"

"Late. I'm not due in to work until eleven."

"Why don't I come by for a little while. I just want to see you, baby."

"Okay," she said softly. "See you in a few."

Tony took his own sweet time getting to Tangie's that night. Besides, it was a foggy night and visibility was poor. When he finally arrived at Tangie's, she was wearing the lime green silk teddy he'd bought her, making it difficult for him to stay focused. He took both of her hands in his, kissing them gently before sitting on the sofa next to her. They sat in silence for a moment.

Finally he spoke. "When I met you, I fell hard and I fell fast. The more time I spent with you, the more I wanted to be with you. I had no doubt in my mind that you were the woman I wanted to spend the rest of my life with. None whatsoever. Lately, I've been having second thoughts. I don't think I'm ready for marriage. Have you seen *A Bronx Tale* with Robert De Niro?"

"No." She shook her head slowly. "I haven't."

"Well, the main character idolizes this mobster, and the mobster tells him that when it comes to women, you only get three great ones. Tangela, you're number two." He tried to make light of the situation.

"So in other words, you want out."

"I'm just not ready for a commitment, Tangela. I thought I was, but I'm not."

"Just like that you're not ready." Tears started to flow down her cheeks.

"Baby, it's not you. It's me."

She began to cry. "Famous last words. I don't believe you. All of a sudden, out of the blue you're not ready?" She wiped her nose with the back of her hand. "Is there someone else?"

"Tangela, trust me. There's nobody else. I just can't marry you."

Tony stood. "I have to get going, Tangela. I have an early morning tomorrow." He held her one last time, and she nearly collapsed in his arms. Then he kissed her once on the forehead before leaving.

He hadn't even driven away before the first gut-wrenching sobs escaped from Tangie's throat. Somehow she couldn't believe that just like that her engagement was off. Was she having an out-of-body experience? She couldn't believe this was really happening to her. She was numb. What was she going to do? How was she going to face the world? She felt like her life was over. Tangie went through the motions of removing her makeup and brushing her teeth before getting into bed. Curled up in the fetal position, she cried on and off all night. Finally, somewhere around dawn, she dragged herself out of bed, put on her pj's, and climbed back into bed.

She slept until the phone woke her up somewhere around noon. It was her boss.

"Where the hell are you? You were supposed to be here an hour ago," he said.

"I know. I'm having a family emergency."

"And you couldn't call in?"

"I'm sorry," she said. "It's just been crazy."

"Will you be in later?"

"No, I'll probably need to use a few personal days."

"Okay, Tangie. It just would have been nice if you had had the common courtesy to call. I'll see you later in the week, and let me know if we can do anything."

"Thanks, Brooke," she said before hanging up.

Tangie hadn't eaten in over eighteen hours, and yet the thought of food didn't appeal to her. She finally got up, took a shower, put on a fresh pair of pajamas, and brushed her hair back into a ponytail. Anything more than that was too much of an effort.

She went back to bed, gazing aimlessly out her bedroom window as a fresh batch of tears ran down her cheeks. The sun was shining and all around her were signs of spring, but she felt as though her life was over. She checked the clock radio on the nightstand. It was just after one o'clock. Charisma was probably out to lunch. She decided to give her a call on her cell.

"Charisma?" Tangie began.

"What's wrong, Tangie?"

"It's over."

"What's over?" Charisma asked.

"Tony called the wedding off." Tangie started crying all over again.

"What happened?"

"He just said he's not ready." She was in a daze.

"Did you have a fight?"

"No. He said he was having second thoughts, and then he brought up some Robert De Niro movie where the guy says you only get three great loves."

"*A Bronx Tale?*"

"Yeah, can you believe it? I can't. I'm still in my pajamas. Can you and Heather come over after work?"

"Sure. We'll be over. Can we bring you anything?"

"No."

"Have you eaten today?"

"No, I'm not hungry. Why can't I ever have who I want? I can't deal with this, Charisma." She wiped her nose with her pajama sleeve.

"Of course you can. Everything's going to be all right. You'll see. I'll call Heather, and we'll be over later. Okay?"

"Okay. And Charisma, thanks."

"Hey, that's what best friends are for. See you soon."

Tangie grabbed the remote and turned on the TV. Daytime television was a trip. Practically every channel she flipped to showed a scantily-clad couple bed-hopping or in the throes of passion. It was all just another reminder of her loss.

She switched the TV off and got back under the covers. Tangie drifted off to sleep and was awakened by the sound of her doorbell. She got up instantly, thinking it was Tony. Then she remembered that he was no longer a part of her life.

It was Charisma and Heather. They both gave her a big hug, rubbing her back for comfort.

"We stopped by Pizza Hut and brought dinner," Charisma said. "You have to eat something."

They all headed into the kitchen. Tangie sat listlessly while Heather and Charisma got dishes and napkins for the table. They sat and poured soda.

Heather lifted her glass in a toast. "Behind every successful woman is?"

Tangie sighed heavily before answering. "I'm not in the mood."

They all dug into the pizza, still hot from Five Towns. Tangie had to admit the stuffed crust pizza hit the spot, especially since it was her first meal of the day. She was almost ready for her second slice when Charisma said, "Tell us exactly what happened."

Tangie tried to make sense of it the best she could. When she finished, Heather and Charisma were just as confused as she was.

Heather chose her words carefully. "Do you think there's another woman?"

"At this point I don't know what to think. Everything seemed fine a week and a half ago. And then all of a sudden things changed. I've gone over it a million times in my head. If he were cheating on me, you'd think my being with Blade would have made me an expert on spotting it. I don't know what to think anymore. I just don't know."

"Well, men come and go, but the three of us are forever," Charisma assured her.

Tangie took two more days off and then returned to work. She merely went through the motions, never realizing how hard it all was. Tangie was just trying to live. Simple as that. She didn't give a monkey's behind what her coworkers thought, but by the end of the week, she still hadn't told her parents that the wedding was off.

Ted and Della Winterhope cried alongside their daughter when they heard the news. Tangie knew her mother felt her pain as only another woman could. As Ted and Della left Tangie's that night, they speculated on what may have happened to cause the breakup. Ted recalled the man-to-man chat he'd had with his prospective son-in-law. Tony had declared his love for Tangie and promised that if they ever broke it would be his way of protecting her. He said as much to Tangie's mother.

"You think that's what happened?" Della asked him.

"More than likely. I mean, they hadn't been engaged a hot minute when he breaks it off. I think he was on the up-and-up. I really do. I don't think there was another woman."

"Too bad *you* couldn't say that," Della shot back. "Hey, I couldn't resist."

Ted shook his head and continued. "As I was saying, I don't think he was unfaithful. I think he really does care about Tangie."

"I'm just tired of my baby getting her heart broken over and over again," Della sighed. "When will it end?"

* * *

Tony soon realized that it was easy to cut Tangela out of his life, but it was hard cutting her out of his heart. Like most men, he was determined to make the cut as quick as possible. He rid his home of all the little mementos that reminded him of her—photos, receipts for the lime roses he sent her on a regular basis, even her favorite cookies. Out they all went. He couldn't allow himself the luxury of living in the past, of hanging on. Sure, he spent many nights hanging out at local bars drowning his sorrows, but that was to be expected.

A month went by and just as Tony regained control of his emotions, Tangie called.

"Hi," she said.

"What's going on?" He was caught off guard.

"I just needed to hear your voice."

"How are you feeling?"

"Okay. And you?" she asked.

"I'm good."

"Maybe we can get together sometime."

"Umm. I don't think that's a good idea. I met someone, and I've been really busy lately," he lied.

"Oh, I see," she said. "Well, can I at least stop by and pick up my things? I left a couple of things over your house."

"You know what? I'm on my way out, but I'll mail 'em to you, okay?"

"All right."

"I'll talk to you later." He disconnected the phone, holding it to his chest momentarily before putting it back on the cradle.

"He's seeing somebody else," Tangie exclaimed to Charisma and Heather over Tangie's one night.

"How do you know for sure?" Heather asked.

"Because he told me," Tangie said, pouting.

"Oh," Heather said. "Well, you can meet someone too."

"It's not that simple," Tangie admitted.

"Why not?" Charisma said. "Maybe it's time to move on. Apparently, he has."

"You don't understand. We were supposed to be married till death do us part. I can't just turn it on and off like that," Tangie insisted.

"We just hate seeing you depressed," Heather told her.

"Excuse me, but it hasn't even been two months yet. Don't rush me," Tangie said.

"We're not rushing you, Tangie, but look at yourself. Have you checked your mirror lately? When's the last time you stepped foot in Daisy's?" Charisma asked. "I've had enough of your ponytail. Not to mention your bushy eyebrows."

"I know. I've been busy," Tangie said.

"Too busy to take care of yourself? Is this coming from the woman who was crowned Miss Hot Fudge Sundae in college?"

"Yeah, yeah, yeah with a cherry on top," Tangie said sarcastically.

"We know that when you're down you let yourself go," Charisma told her.

"We just wanna help," Heather added. "Let's go to Cinderella's Saturday and hit Daisy's Sunday."

"We'll see," Tangie said.

"Okay. That's a start," Charisma said, standing.

"Thanks for the pizza." Tangie walked them to the door and gave them a hug.

"Hang in there," Heather said.

"What else can I do?" Tangie tried to laugh.

A few days later Tangie received the package from Tony. She opened it up, hoping for a card, a note, something from him. She removed her nighties and toiletries. There was nothing else in the box. It was empty.

Against her better judgment, Tangie picked up the phone and dialed Tony's number. When his answering machine picked up, she quickly debated leaving a message or hanging up. At the beep she sang her response in her best Stephanie Mills impersonation of "If I Were Your Woman."

Tony picked up the phone. "Tangela, you are bugging."

"But I still love you, Tony," she began to cry. "I still love you."

"Let me call you back. Will you be home tonight?"

"Of course, Tony."

"Okay. Talk to you later."

Tangie stayed home that night. In fact, she stayed home for the next seven nights, waiting by the phone. She even took the phone into the bathroom with her when she bathed. Tony never called. Reaching a new low, she felt completely humiliated.

The next morning she made a phone call of her own. She called Charisma and Heather.

"Another man, another scar," Tangie sighed. "But don't count me out yet."

"It ain't over until the fat lady sings, and I haven't said a word," Heather said.

24

Heather

Heather finally did it. After years of ignoring Tangie's advice, she joined Canyon's Club. It was rough fitting exercise into her schedule, but her weight had reached a plateau. Her metabolism was slowing down. The library left her drained enough, but forty-five minutes at the gym on top of that left her totally exhausted. Her goal was to start slow. She'd limit herself to a steady half-hour walk on the treadmill and some exercises on the Nautilus machines twice a week. Tangie came over and showed her how to use the equipment since she had never used them before.

"You expect me to walk for *how* long?" she asked Tangie as she punched in sixty minutes. "What ever happened to starting slow?"

"You *are* starting slow," Tangie told her. "I'm starting you at a level three. You can probably do that in your sleep. An hour will fly by."

"How about half an hour?" Heather negotiated.

"Forty-five minutes," Tangie insisted.

"Okay already," Heather sighed as the treadmill started. She kept her towel over the time display and tried concentrating on the overhead TV. Oprah's guest, her fitness coach, Bob Greene, was saying how it was impossible to maintain permanent weight loss without exercise. Just what Heather wanted to hear. She snuck a peek at the timer. One minute and fifty-eight seconds had gone by. She rolled her eyes at the clock as though it actually gave a damn. It was going to be a long forty-three minutes.

"I'm whipped," Heather told Charisma and Tangie one night after her workout.

"How long have you been working out?" Charisma asked.

"Twice a week for three weeks," Heather said.

"Have you been watching your diet and not eating past eight o'clock at night?" Charisma asked.

Heather nodded.

"Then I guarantee you, you'll see results in a couple more weeks, but we need to step up your workout. Those elliptical machines burn more calories than the treadmill, and they're easy on your joints. And don't be afraid to try the other equipment," Tangie advised.

Three times a week Heather began taking aerobics. She waddled out of the class pooped, but sure enough, Heather began seeing results. Within the next couple of weeks, Heather's clothes began to fit her less snugly. Encouraged, she finally stepped on her bathroom scale. She was five pounds lighter. Pleased with that—along with lost inches—Heather practically kissed the reflection of her nose in the mirror. On top of that, Don from the modeling agency called. They had developed her photos and liked what they saw. She photographed well. Heather hugged herself as she hung up. Yes, she'd definitely keep up the good work.

The next few weeks Heather's determination to lose more weight reached a new high. She stepped up her game, working out at the gym four times a week and taking long walks for lunch. Even with her secret ritual, the pounds would not budge.

One evening after work as she climbed on the elliptical machine, someone gently called her name. She looked to her left and locked eyes with a somewhat familiar face. She gazed at her for a moment, but she couldn't quite place her.

"Heather Grey," the woman said, smiling. "We went to Bayside High School together. Don't tell me you don't remember me."

Heather thought for a second. "Oh my goodness, Paula, is that you? I almost didn't recognize you. You lost so much weight."

"It's me," Paula laughed. In high school Paula wore nothing but skirts and dresses after her jeans split wide open in her sophomore year when she bent down to pick up her books. She quickly covered herself by tying a cardigan around her waist. The news spread faster than a New York minute. By the end of the day, the entire school was abuzz and Paula parted crowds of students like Moses parted the Red Sea.

As a fellow full-figured female, Heather felt compassion for Paula as snickers followed her in the weeks to come. That's when Heather befriended her by offering her a tampon during gym when the locker-room dispenser was empty. Paula thanked Heather for her unsolicited kindness and a week later invited her home to study for the upcoming biology exams.

Despite being one to study alone, Heather decided to take Paula up on her offer. She met her one Saturday morning and within minutes they took over the kitchen table with textbooks, notebooks, highlighters, and pens. Paula's mother checked in on them around noon, fixing them tuna-salad sandwiches on giant kaiser rolls. They stopped, had lunch, and picked up studying where they had left off.

Somewhere around three, they called it a day. They hung out for awhile in Paula's room listening to music as they stretched out on her bed with a plate of chocolate chip cookies between them. Paula leaned over and gently brushed Heather's lips with her own. Heather wiped her mouth, got up, and never spoke to her again.

"So how've you been, Heather?" she asked, increasing the intensity of her workout.

"Pretty good," Heather said simply. "You look great."

"Thanks. I've lost eighty-six pounds since graduation." She wore a cropped T-shirt with skintight leggings. Her shoulder-length auburn dreads were pulled up and away from her face into a loose bun.

"How'd you do it?"

"Just good old-fashioned exercise and portion control. There's no magic potion, just a hell of a lot of hard work." She took a few swigs from her water bottle and with a towel dabbed at the sweat forming on her brow. "You don't look so bad yourself."

"Please." Heather shook her head. "I'm trying to get to where *you* are. Are you married, any children?"

"Divorced, no crumb-crushers, thank heavens. What about you?"

"No to both."

"So how often do you work out?"

"About three to four times a week," Heather said.

"That's the way to do it. Hey, I have an idea. Why don't we get together one of these days. Maybe I can give you some pointers on losing weight."

"I'd like that," Heather told her, determined to meet on neutral ground. Fool me once . . .

Heather and Jamal met later that night at his place. After a full day at work and an hour and a half in the gym, she was exhausted.

"I ran into an old high school classmate at the gym, and I couldn't believe it," Heather told him. "She's like eighty pounds lighter. Eighty pounds. She looks amazing."

"You look amazing," Jamal said.

"But I still have a ways to go."

"You'll get there. You're already on your way."

"Anyway, we're meeting next week so she can give me some tips."

"Sounds good, but don't lose too much.'

"Why not? Afraid someone might snatch me away from you?" Heather smiled.

"It's happened before."

"Well, I know who I want. I'm looking at him."

"That's what you say now."

The following week Heather and Paula got together after work at Yum's. Heather arrived at the Austin Street restaurant first and grabbed a table near the bar. She ordered a mudslide while she waited for Paula. By the time Paula arrived, she was on her second drink.

"Sorry I'm late," Paula apologized as she sat across from Heather. "Traffic was murder on the Van Wyck. Some knucklehead got pulled over for talking on his cell phone and tried to flee from the cops. They chased him from Jamaica Avenue. all the way to Queens Boulevard. What a mess." She shook her head. "What are you drinking?"

"A mudslide."

"This is where the tips begin. Do you know how many calories are in that thing?"

"No, but I'm sure you're gonna tell me."

"Put it like this. If you had half a glass, you'd still be in a whole lotta trouble. Cut out alcohol and all the white stuff and the pounds will run for dear life."

"That's how you did it?"

"Uh-huh," Paula admitted. "You're already on the right

track as far as exercising is concerned. Just tighten up your mouth."

"It's not like I don't try," Heather said. "My kitchen is packed with low-fat, fat-free, sugar-free, but I'm plateauing."

"Just be careful. Sometimes that can work against you."

"Tell me about it. If something has half the calories, I eat twice as much."

"I know, girl. Who you telling?" Paula motioned for the waiter, who came right over. "I'll have a diet Seven-UP."

"That's all well and good," Heather said. "But every now and then I like to treat myself." She took another sip of her mudslide.

"And you should. Actually, what I do is eat the straight and narrow during the week and splurge on the weekends. Come Monday morning, I get back on track. And another thing, have a meal plan. Know what I mean? Don't ever wonder about what you'll have for dinner when you get home. That's a surefire way to screw up."

"I know. The road to hell is paved with good intentions."

"Uh-huh, and calories galore. Oh, and try to eat small meals and snacks every few hours to raise your metabolism and control your hunger pangs."

"Just a lot of common sense," Heather summed it up.

"Exactly."

"And that's how you lost eighty pounds?"

"Don't forget the other six," Paula warned. "They were as hard as all the rest. But yes, that's how I did it."

"Just like that?" Heather asked.

"Just like that."

Heather made it home just in time to rush down the stairs and answer the ringing phone. It was Don from the modeling agency.

"How are you, Heather?" he asked.

"I'm fine."

"Good. Let me get straight to the point," he began. "I know you haven't reached your goal weight yet, but we want to sign you on as a client."

"Oh my goodness," she exclaimed. "Thank you so much."

"You're more than welcome. By the way, do you have a fax machine?"

"No, I don't, Don."

"No problem. We'll mail you a contract. Look it over. Call me if you have any questions."

"I don't believe it. You'll have to pinch me." Heather laughed.

"I'll FedEx that contract out to you first thing tomorrow morning. Oh, and check in with us once a week for possible modeling assignments, okay? Sweet dreams, Heather."

"Thanks again, Don. Take care."

"Let's celebrate tonight," Heather told Tangie and Charisma the next morning over the phone.

"What exactly are we celebrating?" Charisma asked.

"I just signed on with the A-+ Size Modeling Agency."

"Get outta here!" Tangie shrieked. "That's wonderful."

"Where do you want to go?" Charisma asked.

"Let's go to Cabana," Heather said.

"Nah, I was there last week. Let's go to Pssst," Tangie suggested.

"Okay," Heather agreed.

"Parking'll be tight. Why don't I pick you guys up, say, around eight?" Charisma asked.

"Okay," Tangie said.

"See you then," Heather agreed before hanging up.

She spent the rest of the day running errands, stocking up on groceries at Pathmark, and picking up her dry cleaning. Once her laundry was done, she took a few moments to exhale on her sofa. The phone rang, breaking the mood.

It was Paula. "Hey, Heather, what's going on?"

"Nothing much. What's new with you?"

"I'm out trying to get my brows done, and the shop is all boarded up. So, I'm really in a bind. My brows look a mess. Where do you get yours done?"

"When We Were Queens. Cinderella does them."

"Where's that?"

"In Springfield Gardens across from Pathmark on Merrick Boulevard."

"Oh, I know where that is. Is she good?"

"The best."

"I'll give her a try. Talk to you later."

Heather had barely hung up the phone when it rang again. It was Jamal.

"Hey, babe. I want to see you tonight. Let's get together."

"You should've called me sooner. I already made plans. Can I take a rain check?"

"Oh, okay," he said, his voice tainted with just a touch of disappointment. "How about we do brunch in the morning?"

"That'll work. See you tomorrow." Heather napped for a couple of hours before getting ready for a night out with the girls. A long hot shower mellowed her out. A pair of bootcut indigo blue jeans and a black T-shirt totally relaxed her. She combed her damp hair into a ponytail and before long golden curls trailed down her back. She applied copper eye shadow to her lids, mascara, blush, and lipstick, smiling at her reflection in the mirror—until her eyes latched on to her nose. She still thought about plastic surgery. Unfortunately, she didn't have the time to dwell on that tonight.

An hour later the trio were seated in Pssst, sipping blackberry-tinis and bouncing to Jennifer Hudson.

"Heard anything from Tony?" Heather asked.

"Nope. It's over, but you know what hurts the most? I

really, truly thought that he was the One. You know? I mean, he was my soul mate." Tangie sighed.

"I used to believe in soul mates. Many moons ago," Heather added.

"What changed you?" Tangie asked.

"Life," Heather said. "Remember Omar? I thought he was all that, but when he pulled that stunt on my birthday, I was devastated. I hit rock bottom. After that I vowed to never let a man get too close. Now, it's hurt or be hurt, and I don't intend to be hurt anymore."

Heather and Omar had been going together for four years. Her birthday was drawing near, and Omar was hinting about proposing. Unfortunately, two days before her birthday, he had to run out of town unexpectedly on business.

Heather's heart sunk to her knees when she stopped at the grocery store the morning of her birthday and found his car parked in the lot. Stunned, she sat glued to her car seat, devastated. A few moments later, he waltzed out of the store, groceries in hand, without a care in the world.

Heather felt a flood of emotions—anger, pain, sadness, shock, disappointment. She backed out of her parking space, nearly hitting a shopping cart as she quickly sped away. Hyperventilating, she made it home before her bowels broke. Maybe he wanted to surprise her, she reasoned as the hours ticked by. He didn't even call.

Upon his "return" days later, when she asked him how was his "trip," his only response was that it went well except that he had forgotten his cell phone. Heather never got over it, and she never looked at men quite the same ever again. She was forever changed, reaching deep within herself for some vestige of strength and surprising herself that she had found it.

"I wish I had your strength," Tangie told Heather.

"You will have it when you need it most," Heather reassured her.

                              *   *   *

"Baby, I'm starving. I thought we had a brunch date."
When Jamal's message on Heather's answering machine
reached her ears, she rolled over and grabbed a pillow to
cover her head. She had hung out late with Tangie and
Charisma the night before, and the bed definitely had a
hold on her.

Luckily for Jamal, she was completely awake by his third
call. Apparently, he was hungry.

"Feel like IHOP?" he asked.

"Nah, I don't want to set foot out of this house today."

"Want me to come over and cook?"

"Would you?" she asked.

"If that's what you want."

"I want," she said simply.

"Then I'll be over shortly."

Heather dragged herself out of bed, brushed her teeth,
and took a quick shower. She slipped on a nightshirt just as
Jamal arrived with a bag of groceries in hand. He gave her a
kiss on the lips and made himself at home in her kitchen,
pulling out pots and pans, dishes, and utensils. She offered
to help, but he only shooed her out of the kitchen.

She didn't have to be told twice. Instead, she went into
the living room, kicked her feet up, grabbed the remote,
and turned on the TV. Nothing grabbed her interest. Nothing at all, but the aroma permeating from the kitchen
grabbed her nose, forcing Heather to her feet.

"Wow, something smells good," she said. "What'cha cooking?"

"Codfish and onions, eggs, and toasted bagels," Jamal
said, standing over the stove. "Ready to eat?"

"Honey, I was past ready when you walked through the
door."

"Then let's eat," he said simply.

Heather reached in the cabinet for plates and glasses.

She took utensils and napkins from a nearby drawer while Jamal placed the dishes of food on the table.

"Orange juice?" she asked him, getting up.

"No, you relax. I'll get it." He returned to the table with an ice-cold gallon of OJ. He filled their glasses and they began eating.

"Boy, this is good," Heather said.

"Glad you like it."

"Hold that thought," she said as her phone rang. She hurried into the bedroom where she left the cordless, and returned a second later. "That was my old classmate from Bayside. Remember I told you she lost eighty pounds? Well, she wants me to meet her at the gym for a workout."

"What d'ya tell her?"

"Not today. I just want to chill, but after all this I should probably tell Paula I'm ready to run three miles on the treadmill." She piled a bit more eggs and codfish onto her plate.

"My ex-wife's name is Paula. She went to Bayside too." He took a sip of juice.

"Really? What's her maiden name?" Heather asked him.

"Little. Paula Little."

"Shit. Small world," Heather said. "I didn't even know you were divorced. Why'd ya break up?"

"She's a lesbian," Jamal said simply.

Heather's mind immediately flashed back to that day in Paula's bedroom when she tried to kiss her. "How long were you married?"

"Two years."

"Wow. Did you love her?"

"Yeah, I really did."

"I'm sorry."

"Hey, it's not *your* fault, but do me a big favor, Heather."

"What's that?" she asked

"Just be careful. She can be a conniving bitch. Don't let that soft voice of hers fool you."

25

Tangie

Tangie and Charisma were in Daisy's for their weekly shampoo. Tangie was also getting fresh highlights, so as usual she had to wait for Daisy.

"Okay, what's he like?" Tangie said, referring to the guy Charisma wanted to fix her up with.

"His name is Jordan Newport, and I've known him for years. He's a CPA. His father's done my family's taxes for as long as I can remember."

"What's he look like?"

"Nice." Charisma smiled. "He's about five-seven and—"

"You know I prefer tall men," Tangie protested.

"Please, they say what a man lacks in height, he makes up for in length."

"How do you come up with this stuff?" Tangie shook her head. "That's like saying what a woman lacks in boobs, she makes up for in behind."

"Hey, whatever works."

"So why weren't you interested?"

"He was married. Now he's divorced."

"Any children?"

"No. Anyway, when I saw him earlier this year, he said he's finally ready to start dating again. I instantly thought of you, but you were seeing Tony. Now you're both available. So why don't we all get together for dinner and a movie, and you two can meet?"

Tangie just looked at her.

"Come on, Tangie. You said you were ready to get back in the game. I'm holding you to it." Charisma stood as Maria called her for her shampoo.

"All right. You talked me into it. Set it up," Tangie said before she lost her nerve. Then she headed over to Daisy's chair for caramel highlights.

The next few days Tangie debated canceling her date with Jordan. Luckily, Charisma was going too so there would be no blind-date pressure. She picked up Tangie and the two headed over to the Midway Theater on Queens Boulevard for a movie.

It was a balmy, early June evening. As they waited in front of the theater to see Sanaa Lathan's latest romantic comedy, Charisma made small talk.

"I know you get highlights every summer, but these are awesome. You are one hot mama."

"Thanks," Tangie told her. "Nice try. I know you're trying to distract me, but if he's not here in five minutes, I'm out." Just as Tangie looked up, Jordan appeared, and Charisma made the introductions.

"Tangie," he said slowly. "And that's short for . . ."

"Tangela," she replied.

"I like that," he admitted. "May I call you Tangela?"

"Tangie is fine," she insisted, vowing that no other man would be allowed to call her by her full name ever again.

"Hey, no problem," he said simply.

Tangie couldn't help but mentally compare Jordan to Tony—his height, his build, his features, the way he dressed. She could go on and on. The two stood shoulder to shoulder, and that was with Tangie's modest two-inch sandals. Instead, she smiled and shook his hand. Jordan seemed pleased to meet her. He held her hand just a moment longer than necessary, gazing intently into her eyes. Uncomfortable, Tangie was the first to look away.

Jordan insisted on paying for the movie, despite protests from Tangie and Charisma. He also bought a huge tub of buttered popcorn and three sodas. They found seats just as the trailers began. Tangie sat in the middle. Charisma and Tangie exchanged glances throughout the movie. Jordan seemed oblivious, caught up in Sanaa's beauty.

Afterward, they walked the short distance to Friday's on Austin Street for a bite to eat. Tangie was friendly, but not overly so toward Jordan. As Tangie sipped her second mudslide, she checked out the scene around her. Having not had a decent meal that day, she was getting a buzz from the alcohol. She bit into a buffalo wing to calm her stomach. She looked up and both Charisma and Jordan were staring at her as if waiting for an answer.

Charisma quickly caught Tangie up. "Jordan has tickets to the Alicia Keys concert at the Garden on Sunday. Interested?"

As much as Tangie loved Alicia Keys, deciding was like a mental tennis match. Should she or shouldn't she? "I'd love to," she said finally. Her mama didn't raise no fool, and she had tried for weeks to get tickets. By popular demand a third show had been added for Sunday afternoon, and Jordan was lucky enough to get tickets before they sold out.

"Alicia's the bomb. Her shows are awesome. You two'll have a great time," Charisma said.

Aw shit. Tangie had assumed Charisma was going too. What had she gotten herself into?

Tangie found out soon enough. Jordan picked her up in a late-model Maxima badly in need of a paint job. It was a

far cry from the sleek silver dream machine Tony had chauf-
feured her around town in and occasionally let her drive.
She knew better than to judge a man by his ride, but once
you get used to a Benz, anything else just didn't cut it. She
thanked God for small miracles. At least the car wasn't
smoking.

They took the Midtown Tunnel into Manhattan. Traffic
was moderately light for an early Sunday afternoon except
for a brief rubbernecking incident by LaGuardia Airport.
Luckily, they got to Madison Square Garden with plenty of
time to spare. The line for the performance was all the way
around the block.

Tangie and Jordan were seated, and the air-conditioning
came as a welcome relief. Jordin Sparks was the opening
act, and Alicia strutted onstage to a standing ovation. For
two and a half hours she wowed the audience with their
old favorites as well as a few cuts from her soon-to-be-
released CD. She was definitely a class act. Tangie was
floored by her talent and style as was the sold-out crowd.

Jordan said as much to Tangie as they left the Garden.
"Whew, she is something else! Feel like a bite to eat?"

"Okay. Where to?"

"How about Junior's? If we're lucky, we can eat alfresco."

"You want to go to *Brooklyn*?" she asked, surprised.

"No, there's one in Times Square."

"Lead the way," she said simply, looking forward to a slice
of the world-famous cheesecake.

It was a gorgeous day, perfect for a stroll up Seventh Avenue. Before long they were inside the theater district
eatery. Jordan gave his name to the host and immediately
requested a table outside. It was such a lovely afternoon
that they had to wait, but it was well worth it.

They ordered drinks and split a huge brisket of beef
sandwich. Tangie had to admit that the date turned out better than she expected. A lot better.

* * *

"So how was your date with Jordan?" Charisma asked Tangie Monday night over the phone.

"Not bad. We're going out again this weekend."

"Oh yeah, where to?"

"Out to Westbury to see Stephanie Mills and Brian McKnight."

"Nice."

"Yeah, and you know who loves Stephanie Mills," Tangie said, matter-of-factly.

"Uh-huh, I remember. Tony's her number-one fan." Charisma changed the subject. "You know what I love about the early stages of dating? There are no expectations. Just two people getting to know one another and enjoying each other's company. So go and have a good time."

"That's the plan," Tangie said.

"And it beats sitting home watching *Martin* reruns."

"I don't know, Charisma. Some of those episodes are hilarious."

"You know what I mean."

"Point taken. Have you talked to Heather lately?"

"She called me yesterday. She wants to make sure we're still on for breakfast Saturday at her house. She said you two have been playing phone tag."

"Tell her breakfast on Saturday is fine if you talk to her before I do."

"See you Saturday."

Tangie hung up, feeling hopeful. Jordan wasn't Tony, not by a long shot. He didn't have that wow factor, but he seemed like a nice man.

She said as much to Heather and Charisma over breakfast Saturday morning. Heather's spread included scrambled eggs with cheese, bacon, home fries, bran muffins, coffee, and orange juice.

"I just have one question for you," Heather said. "Do you

still read Tony's horoscope?" Heather believed that if you still read your ex's horoscope you weren't over him yet.

Tangie hesitated only slightly as she helped herself to more home fries. "Sometimes."

"Well, you're almost there, girl." Heather smiled.

Charisma smelled something burning. "Is the stove still on?" she asked.

"Oh my gosh. I almost forgot about the baked apples." Heather jumped up and ran to the stove to turn it off. They were burnt to a crisp. "Oh well, sorry," she apologized, scraping out the pot and filling it with water from the sink.

"It's okay," Tangie said as Heather returned to the table.

"Don't worry about it," Charisma added. "There's enough here for a feast. As it is, I've popped a couple of buttons."

Charisma and Tangie were stuffed to the gills by the time they got up from the table. They waddled back to the living room, where the collapsed.

Heather had eaten lightly." What time is the concert? Eight o'clock?" she asked.

"Yeah, Jordan's picking me up at seven," Tangie said.

"So are you just taking it easy till then?" Charisma asked her.

"Uh-huh. I don't know what to wear, though," Tangie admitted. "Maybe my white linen pantsuit."

"Good choice," Heather said. "If I had your figure, girrrl. Thank goodness I only have breakfasts like this once a month. "

"I know the feeling," Charisma said.

"Well, whatever you wear, look good. You never know what the night has in store for you," Heather told her.

Tangie took a nice, long bath to relax her mind and wash away the stress of the day. Then, she polished her skin with her favorite perfume and scented lotion. She tried on three different outfits before she decided on a little black dress with white piping and a peekaboo keyhole. Her fresh caramel highlights popped against her sun-kissed skin. As she checked herself out in her bedroom's full-length mirror, she had to admit that she looked pretty good.

Jordan called to say he was running a little late but that he was on his way. He picked her up about twenty minutes later, and his eyes lit up when she answered the door. Yep, she had dotted every *I* and crossed her *T*s.

The concert was sold out. Some chick in the slow-moving entrance line turned around and rolled her eyes at Tangie. Tangie, in turn, gave her a don't-hate-me-because-I'm-beautiful look. The girl turned back around and tossed her hair.

A comedian opened the show and though Tangie and Jordan missed the beginning of his act, the parts they saw had them in tears, crying for mercy. By the time he walked off the stage, it took Brian McKnight only a few moments to appear. How many times had she and Tony made love listening to "What's My Name?" The memories hurt her heart. He sang for an hour before relinquishing the stage to Stephanie Mills. The second she stepped onstage, the crowd went wild.

"Hello, New York," she said in response before her petite, energetic frame belted out hit after hit after hit. Brian joined her briefly for "Feel the Fire," the hit she made famous with Teddy Pendergrass. Then she sang two more hits before a standing ovation and chants of *Stephanie* carried her off the stage.

Jordan grabbed Tangie's hand, and they made a mad dash for the exit, anxious to leave the building. After a slow migration they reached the parking lot and got inside Jordan's Maxima.

What Tangie saw next out of the corner of her eye made her do a double take, taking her breath away. It was Tony. He was helping some woman into his car before walking around to the driver's side. Just as he was about to get in, he turned his head ever so slightly to the left, and that's when he spotted Tangie.

Their eyes locked. They were so close that with the window rolled down, Tangie could smell his aftershave.

Tony spoke first. 'Tangela, how are you?"

"I'm good," she said, just a little too cheerful. "This is Jordan. Jordan, this is Tony, an old friend of mine." Tangie hoped the spark in her eyes wasn't too obvious.

"Nice to meet you," Tony said. "This is Olivia."

Olivia leaned forward in the passenger's seat. "Hello," she said simply.

Tangie smiled. "Great concert, huh?"

"You know Stephanie's my girl," Tony agreed. "She never disappoints."

"That's for sure," Jordan added.

"You take care," Tony said, easing into his Benz and starting the engine. He trailed Jordan briefly before driving off on his own.

Tangie calmed herself as best she could, but her mind, not to mention her heart, was racing like a thoroughbred. She knew she was bound to bump into Tony sooner or later, but yet she wasn't prepared for it. And who the hell was Olivia? Was she his date for the evening or something more? Tangie hadn't gotten that good a look at her, but just the fact that she was with Tony was enough to upset her equilibrium. Big-time. Had Tony told his latest that they were once engaged? Did Olivia even give a damn? It was easy to be smug when you were a man's latest "it" girl, but how quickly things could change. Tangie learned that from experience. Life had a way of wiping that smirk right off your face.

"Seems like a nice guy," Jordan said.

Chewing her lip, Tangie said nothing.

* * *

"I need to see you," Tangie told Tony over the phone the next morning, her eyes bloodshot from a sleepless night, her hands moist with emotion.

"What's wrong?" he asked her.

"What's your schedule look like today?"

"I'm working today, Tangela. Is this an emergency?"

"Yes."

"How about if we meet after work?"

"Your place or mine?" she asked.

"I'm working in Jamaica today. Let's meet on neutral ground. Say Montebello Park?"

"That'll work. What time?"

"Is five-thirty good for you?"

"That's fine, Tony. See you then." Tangie hung up, silently thanking God for another chance at happiness. Though it was only 7:10 on a Sunday morning, she got up, unable to squeeze another ounce of sleep out of her now wide-awake eyes. She sat on the edge of the bed, swinging her legs back and forth.

First, she got up and cleaned the house, mopping the kitchen floor, vacuuming, and dusting the living room and dining room. Then, she did the bathroom tile, the tub, toilet, and the face bowl. Finally, she mopped the bathroom floor and took a break. It was only ten-thirty. Three hours down, seven more to go.

Next, Tangie decided to draw herself a bath and soak. She added a generous amount of bath gel to the running water, and soon the room's scent brought a smile to her face. She removed her pajamas, threw them in the hamper, and stepped into liquid perfection. She laid there for a moment, her eyes shut, just enjoying the warmth. It didn't get much better than this. She gently washed her body like the treasured possession it was. It had given her much joy and pleasure over the years, and standing in the bathroom mirror afterward, she inspected herself with pride. Tangie lotioned her body until it glistened like silk. She put on a pair of denim shorts and a white *I Love New York* T-shirt, before piling her hair up on her head and going into the kitchen. She whipped up some homemade blueberry muffins and a peanut butter banana smoothie. After Heather's breakfast yesterday, she had to watch her calories. Another hour down.

Suddenly, it occurred to her that Tony may want to come back for dinner. She checked her cupboards and fridge and made a quick list. She stuffed her wristlet with her driver's license and registration, keys, and a few bills and headed for the grocery store. She bought the fixings for pepper steak, summer squash, and that pasta dish Tony loved so much. Then, she stopped next door at the liquor store and got all the ingredients for a martini pop.

When Tangie got home, she put the groceries away, popped some CDs in the stereo, and poured herself a glass of wine. She sat up on her couch and imagined all that the evening with Tony could hold. Her mind raced with possibilities, starting with *if onlys* and ending in *buts*. Before she knew it, Tony was calling her to say her was just getting off work, and that he'd see her in half an hour.

Tangie went to her jewelry box, put on a pair of tricolor hoops, ran her fingers through her hair, and applied lip gloss. She took one final look at herself in the mirror before meeting Tony in Montebello Park.

She drove down Springfield Boulevard with the windows down, smiling to herself at the sounds of children's laughter, motorcycles, and other sounds of summer. Shortly after she parked and got out of her car, Tony pulled up behind her. He must have just gotten his ride washed because it was buffed to a high sheen, reminding Tangie of the hooptie she had ridden in last night. Tony was humming a cut from Stephanie Mills's latest CD, and as he leaned over to hug Tangie, she could detect his favorite aftershave. Just the hint of it on his collar made her weak in the knees, forcing her to practically collapse like a deck of cards. He steadied her in his arms, and for a split second it felt like old times.

They walked to the table area and sat across from one another. Her second favorite man, Mister Softee, had pulled up and a group of children and their mothers had gathered around the ice cream truck. Tangie watched them intensely, biding time and trying to decide where to begin.

Finally, she spoke. "Didn't take long to replace me, huh?"

He shook his head. "Don't do this, Tangela." He kept looking around as if he was a security guard doing surveillance.

"No, I mean, it's been—what, a few months—and already you've moved on?"

"I could say the same for you," he said.

"Jordan's just a friend."

"So is Olivia."

"How do I know that?" she asked. "Tell me anything. I'm black." They both burst out laughing, easing the tension.

"Tell me about her," she said.

"What's to tell?" he began. "We've been seeing each other for about a month, nothing serious. We're just taking things one day at a time."

"So how'd you meet her?"

"We met at the supermarket."

"Which one?" she asked.

"Why? Does it matter? She's a nice lady and—"

"You used to think I was nice too, once upon a time."

"I still think you're nice," he admitted, eyeing a black car suspiciously.

"Then why?"

"Tell me about Jordan." He changed the subject.

"I met Jordan through Charisma. He's a CPA. He's very attentive and kind."

"How long have you been seeing him?"

"We've only dated a few times. He's divorced."

"Any kids?"

"No, from what Charisma says, he's really interested in me."

"That's exactly what you need. So what's the problem?"

"You still don't get it." She rolled her eyes.

Tony looked down at her hand. "I see you're still wearing the engagement ring."

"Sometimes," she admitted. "It's so beautiful. How can I just put it away in a box? Jewelry's to be worn and enjoyed."

"But on your left ring finger?" he asked.

"It fits that finger best."

"Whatever makes you happy, Tangela. But don't you know that the man of your dreams may see that ring on your finger and be afraid to step to you?"

"No, the man of my dreams wouldn't let a ring stop him from making his interest known. Would it have stopped you?"

"No, but every man's not like me."

"Well, thank God for that," she said, her voice dripping with sarcasm.

"I'm sorry, Tangela," he said, looking deeply into her eyes.

"And what exactly are you sorry for?"

"For hurting you so deeply. For not being able to deliver. For reneging on our future together. For having to let you go. Not a day goes by that I don't feel your pain." Tony reached across the table for her hand and squeezed it gently. Right there in the park, amid the sounds of Mister Softee and laughing children, Tangie wept.

Tangie needed some time off from work, but she was determined not to make the same mistake twice. The first thing she did was call her boss to request time off. Her boss made a deal with her. If she came in that day and tomorrow, she could have the rest of the week off. Deal. Tangie miraculously made it through Monday and Tuesday and had the rest of the week free.

She was back to square one concerning Tony. He had seeped back into her system like water spilled on a silk blouse. She found herself daydreaming about him, night dreaming about him, and everything in between. Tangie had smuggled one of his pillowcases off his bed and right out of his house one night. Whenever she needed a hit, she'd take it out of her bottom drawer, bring it up to her nose, and inhale deeply like an addict in need of a fix. She was smiling in no time at all. Like most addicts, she now had a heightened sense of confidence. She picked up the phone and dialed his number. There was no answer, but it was early yet. She hung up the phone, went into the kitchen, and poured herself a glass of wine. It may have been early in the day, but it wasn't that early.

By three PM she decided that she had waited long enough and called him on his cell phone. He picked up on the fifth ring.

"Hey," she said simply.

"How are you feeling?" he asked gently.

"Lonely."

"With all the friends you have?"

"I'm not that kind of lonely."

"I see. So what do you plan on doing about it?"

"You tell me," she said.

"Why don't I come by tonight?"

"I'll make dinner."

He thought for what seemed like a mini-eternity. "I'd like that. I miss your meals," he admitted.

"I miss your other things." She laughed.

"Tangela, what am I going to do with you?"

"We'll think of something." Tangie hung up the phone.

She could hardly wait. Smiling, she jumped up and headed for the stereo, filling her home with its songs, a mix of old and new school. Next, she took some pepper steak out of the freezer to thaw on her kitchen counter. Tangie changed the linen on her bed, humming as she plumped up the pillows in midair, and put the dirty sheets and pillowcases in the hamper.

The pepper steak was still frozen solid so she nuked it in the microwave. Once it was defrosted, she washed, seasoned, and put the meat on to cook along with peppers and onions. It wasn't long before the spicy, pungent aroma filled the air. Tangie took a relaxing bath and resumed kitchen duties. She made the shrimp and pasta dish Tony loved and steamed some broccoli. She quickly set the table, deciding against candlelight. He would be there any minute.

The familiar chime of Tangie's doorbell brought a smile to her lips. She counted to ten before walking through the living room and opening the front door. She could tell by the way his head shone that he had just come from the barber's. She clinched her fists behind her back to avoid caressing his dome as she ushered him inside. Tony took a seat on the sofa.

"Can I get you a drink? A martini pop, maybe?" Tangie asked him.

"Wow, I haven't had one of those in a while. Sounds good."

"Coming right up." She went into the kitchen and returned with two glasses and a martini-filled shaker on a tray. She placed the tray on the coffee table opposite the sofa and sat down next to him.

Tony poured Tangie a drink and then one for himself.

"What shall we drink to?" she asked.

"To old friends."

"To old friends," she agreed. Tangie sipped the drink slowly, enjoying the moment.

"This is nice," Tony said simply.

"What do you mean?"

"I mean, the music, the drinks, the delicious meal I can't help but smell from the kitchen, not to mention you."

"Did you bring your appetite?"

He nodded.

"Good, let's eat." They left their drinks in the living room and headed for the kitchen.

"Can I help with anything?" he asked.

"No, everything's under control." Tangie had set a beautiful table with white and gold china and gold lace placemats. A bouquet of assorted colored roses graced the table's center.

"You are going to make some lucky man one helluva wife."

Tangie said nothing as he sat down opposite her.

"You've been busy," he said.

"Uh-huh."

Tony and Tangie bowed their heads as he said grace. She opened her eyes and looked up a second before he finished. He was still a beautiful man, and the fact that he was a God-fearing one only made him more attractive.

Tangie waited as Tony dug in and fixed his plate before she fixed her own.

"This steak is so tender," he said between bites.

She wasn't that hungry after having cooked all afternoon, but it pleased her to see him enjoy his meal. In fact, he had seconds of everything before he was finished.

"You haven't lost your touch, Tangela." He wiped his mouth with the napkin.

"That's good to know." She laughed.

"No, I mean it."

"Thank you." She stood and began clearing the table.

"Let me help you with the dishes."

"That's okay."

"No, I mean it," he said. "You relax, and I'll clean up the kitchen. Go enjoy Luther."

"All right." She left him alone.

As Tony took care of the dishes, Tangie headed for the bedroom to slip into something more comfortable. She opened the top drawer and chose a short, purple satin nightie. She quickly removed her clothes and slid into the garment. Tangie turned back the bedspread and slipped between the sheets, loving the coolness on her skin.

She lay there for a moment, straining her ears to hear if Tony was still washing dishes. He was. She hopped out of bed and lit several jasmine candles before turning off the lights and returning to bed. If she played her cards right, he'd be making breakfast for her tomorrow morning.

Tony walked in and sat down on the bed. "Tired?" he asked.

"A little."

He leaned over and began rubbing her neck and shoulders, where she carried most of her stress. She rolled over on her stomach, and he massaged her body from head to toe, concentrating on her nape and back.

Then, he pulled his T-shirt over his head, unbuckled his pants, and removed his socks. Wearing only his boxers, he climbed up on the bed and nestled his body next to Tangie's.

"Baby?" she said softly.

"Sshh," he whispered in her ear, holding her even closer.

She smiled, imagining the night's pleasures. Unfortunately, she couldn't weaken Tony's resolve.

26

Charisma

When Charisma got back from lunch Wednesday afternoon, she found that Nate had left two messages on her voice mail. She immediately returned his calls.

"Hey, Mr. Arquette," she said, smiling.

"Hey, baby. All packed for Paradise Island?"

"You know it. Do you want me to meet you at JFK tomorrow morning?"

He laughed. "Hell to the no. I'm not letting you stand me up twice."

"I wouldn't do that to you twice. Once maybe, but not twice."

"Oh, you got jokes. I will stay at your place tonight, and we'll leave together in the morning."

"See you tonight. Don't forget I'm hanging out with Tangie and Heather after work so I'll be home late."

"Enjoy yourself," he said before hanging up.

Tangie, Heather, and Charisma met for dinner at Applebee's. Surprisingly, Heather was the first to arrive, followed by Tangie and then Charisma.

"Girl, you are looking tight," Charisma told Heather. "How much weight have you dropped?"

"Can you believe ten pounds and counting? But you're the one glowing like a June bride. Look at her, Tangie," Heather said. "Something's up."

Tangie gave Charisma a long look over before speaking. "I think she's getting some good juice."

"Well, there is a little something I forgot to tell you guys," Charisma admitted. "I'm leaving for Paradise Island in the morning."

"With whom?" Heather asked.

"A friend of mine," Charisma said. "You may have heard me mention him once or twice."

"His name, Charisma. What's his name?" Tangie asked.

"Nate Arquette."

"Get outta here!" Tangie exclaimed.

"When did all this happen?" Heather asked.

"After my dad's funeral things just started falling into place. It's the strangest thing. I can't explain it," Charisma told them.

"Well, honey, don't even try. Just accept it and enjoy it," Tangie said.

"Exactly. Please don't sabotage your happiness this time, Charisma," Heather begged her.

"Hey, we almost forgot," Tangie said, raising her glass. "Behind every successful woman is herself."

"I know that's right," Charisma agreed.

Twelve hours later Nate and Charisma's plane landed at Nassau International Airport. They gathered their luggage and were greeted by a tropical breeze as they boarded a shuttle bus for the hotel. From the moment they left New York, they were like a couple of honeymooners—snuggling, cuddling, holding hands.

They arrived at the hotel and settled into their suite. Unpacking was the first thing on the agenda. Charisma grabbed her Lysol wipes and disinfected every surface imaginable. She was truly her mother's daughter. Then, they each showered and donned the lush complimentary white bathrobes.

Charisma and Nate decided to order in and dine on the terrace underneath the stars. It was a beautiful night. They shared a champagne toast and savored a delicious lobster salad.

After dinner they returned to the bedroom, setting the mood with candles and baby-making music. Charisma headed into the bathroom where she changed into a sheer black teddy. When she reentered the room, Nate took her into his arms and they danced.

Charisma was in heaven, praying that the moment would never end. It amazed her how a short time ago she was grieving her father's passing, and today she was frolicking with the man of her dreams. Maybe Tangie was right. Maybe her father was on the other side working things out for her. She smiled to herself at the thought.

"What's so funny?" he whispered in her ear.

"Just enjoying the moment." She held him closer, loving his scent. That night they enjoyed many moments.

After sleeping like babies, Nate and Charisma woke up the next morning, showered, and had a nice, big breakfast in one of the restaurants. They were both famished. After breakfast they changed into swimming suits and found two empty lounge chairs by the huge, kidney-shaped pool. They lounged for hours, dozing for a while and then taking dips in the water to cool off. They swam to the swim-up bar and ordered drinks. There were vacationers from New York, Florida, Maryland, and Rhode Island. One New Yorker said that he had just lost at the casino, but he admitted that a bad day on vacation beat a good day at work. They all laughed in agreement. Charisma and Nate remained poolside through the early evening hours. Then they napped on the room's king-sized-bed for a couple of hours, enjoying the freedom that comes with not being on the clock.

That night they dressed for dinner and dined at an Italian hot spot before hitting the casino. She marveled at how the greedy slot machine ravished her coins on the DL and yet spit out every puny reward with bells and whistles for all to hear. It was a strategy designed to bring 'em all in with false hope. And it worked. Nate was pretty lucky that night, winning several hundred dollars at the blackjack table.

They left the casino around four in the morning, stopped to eat a light breakfast, and crashed. That afternoon they hit the beach. Nate swam in the ocean while Charisma listened to tunes on her iPod and read Tyne Travis' latest *New York Times* bestseller. Later, they had a couple's massage, complete with manicures and pedicures. Relaxed, they left the spa feeling like new money and took a nice, long nap.

After dinner Charisma and Nate took a midnight walk along the beach. She paused for a moment while Nate spread a blanket on the sand. They were alone with the ocean. He sat down first and beckoned for her to sit in his lap. She wore only a white tank top and a full tropical print skirt with nothing underneath. Obligingly, she sat in his lap and he covered then both with the second blanket.

With one swift motion, he slid his hand underneath her skirt. Smiling, he unzipped his fly. She repositioned herself in his lap until they were both satisfied. Kissing, they rocked gently to the sounds of the ocean. Yet at the same time they were oblivious to them. A chill went through Charisma as she suddenly realized what was happening. It was her dream.

Nate held her close and buried himself in her neck, loving the scent of her skin. He slid his arms underneath her top, massaging first her strong back and then her breasts, one at a time. He bent down and slid one breast into his mouth, loving its fullness and taste. Before long, she was panting and they were both rocking underneath the blanket. He stiffened as he came while her cries of pleasure rolled out to sea with the waves.

On their last night they hung out at a club, ordering drinks freely. By karaoke time, Charisma and Nate had a serious buzz. They watched the courageous sing their hearts out amid the cheering crowd. Maybe it was the drinks or maybe it was the thrill of their first vacation together, but Charisma decided to get up there and have some fun.

"I'm going up there next," she told Nate. "Yep." She drained her glass.

"Do your thang, baby."

Before Charisma lost her nerve she jumped up and headed for the stage. She chose Aretha Franklin's "Natural Woman." She practically knew the song by heart, relying on the prompter only occasionally. With the spotlight on her she could not see out into the audience. She was engulfed in darkness. She drew on the crowd's energy, having a ball.

Just as she was about to wrap up the song, a shadow crossed her field of vision. It was Nate, singing how she made him feel like a natural man. Melting into each other's arms, they kissed and began to laugh.

Then Nate did the unthinkable. He dropped down on one knee, took Charisma's hand in his, looked her straight in the eye, and proposed. Feeling like she dreaming, Charisma could not have imagined a more perfect proposal. The audience went absolutely wild.

"Yes. Yes," she whispered in his ear as he rose to his feet. Nate scooped her up in his arms and carried his fiancée back to their suite.

Once home, Charisma had the unpleasant task of breaking the news to Dex. Nate offered to be by her side when she told him, but she wouldn't hear of it. She was a big girl. As much as she appreciated the offer, it was something she needed to do alone.

They agreed to meet for drinks after work at Peaches. In spite of her car's air-conditioning, Charisma had a rough time gripping the steering wheel. Sweat was practically hemorrhaging from her palms. Was it guilt? As she stopped at the red light on Francis Lewis Boulevard, she reached inside her purse for a tissue to wipe her hands. A few minutes later she was sitting in the parking lot, and he pulled up right next to her.

They went inside and took a booth away from the big-screen TV. The sports bar was practically empty. Dex ordered a beer and she had a Sprite. They sat silently for a moment. Finally, she began, choosing her words carefully.

"I guess you're wondering what I wanted to talk to you about," she said.

"I have a feeling I already know." He took a sip of his beer and looked up at the TV, ignoring her gaze.

"I don't know an easy way to say this, so I'll just say it. I'm engaged." She rubbed the back of her neck.

"So that's why you dumped me. You were boning your boss all along."

"It wasn't like that, Dex." She lowered her voice.

"Then how was it, Charisma?"

"It just happened."

"It just happened," he repeated.

"Exactly." She took a sip of her Sprite.

"I've been trying to marry you for years, and he comes along and swoops you right up. Son of a bitch. I hope he makes you happy, Charisma. Lord knows *I* couldn't."

"I don't know what to say. It just happened."

"You said that already."

"Look, I'm really sorry. I hope there are no hard feelings," she added.

"No, Charisma," he sighed. "There are no hard feelings. And to prove it, I want to congratulate you." He stood and smiled. "Give me a hug."

"Good-bye, Dex." She stood and gave him a hug in return. He kissed her on the cheek. It never failed. The one who's moving on always lets go first.

No one was more excited about Nate and Charisma's engagement than Tangie and Heather—except, of course, for Jena. For the couple's engagement party, Jena reserved a room at the Shore's Inn. Nate's parents and sisters came from Los Angeles, and his son Sean came from San Diego.

Charisma was pleasantly surprised that Sean seemed to take an instant liking to her. Nate's parents and sisters made her feel like part of the family from the start. Tangie came with Jordan while Heather came alone. Charisma's coworker Lauren insisted that she knew something was brewing between them almost from the beginning. She said as much to Charisma and Nate.

"You didn't know," Charisma said, laughing.

"Are you kidding me?" Lauren asked. "I saw all those glances you two exchanged during those staff meetings, and in passing when you thought no one was watching."

"Can't put anything past you, huh, Lauren?" Nate grinned.

"But you know who's gone ballistic?" Lauren asked without waiting for an answer. "Chase."

"That's a shame," Charisma feigned concern.

"Baby, excuse me for a minute. I want to talk to my dad about something," Nate said. "Good seeing you, Lauren."

"Likewise, Nate." Lauren smiled. She returned her attention to Charisma. "Yeah, girl, the Martini is flipping out. You'll see when you get back to work next week."

"What's she saying?" Charisma asked.

"It's not what she's saying. It's what she's doing—slamming drawers and doors. Just your typical spoiled brat."

"Money can't buy everything."

"Nope." Lauren laughed. "And it certainly can't buy love."

Charisma smiled to herself. Happiness truly was the best revenge. Maybe Chase wasn't part of the privileged sect, and maybe Charisma had won after all.

Charisma stopped by Cinderella's after work one day to buy some skin-care products. She lucked up. The last customer had just left, and she had Cinderella all to herself. Cinderella just looked at her and smiled.

"Is there something you want to tell me?" she asked Charisma.

"Cinderella, I'm engaged."

"That's wonderful. Mommy called and invited me to the engagement party. I wanted to surprise you, but I couldn't make it. I don't care what comes up. I will be at your wedding. That's a promise. Do you remember what I told you the day you came in before your date with your boss?"

Charisma nodded. "Cinderella, you were right."

"When I looked at you that night, I knew. Something told me that your boss was the *one*. We may think we have all the answers, but God knows what's best for us. And don't forget your father's on the other side now."

"I miss him so much." She began to tear up. "When he passed, I felt like my heart had been ripped out of my chest."

"God gives us pairs for balance, my queen—two eyes, ears, arms, legs, even parents. When we lose one, our equilibrium is thrown off and we need time to regroup, to compensate, to heal. But God has a way of softening our pain. It's almost as though someone has to pass before another can come forth. Don't be surprised if your firstborn is a son. And when you look into his eyes, you'll see your father all over again."

Charisma smiled for a moment, and then burst into tears.

"I can't have children. When they removed my fibroids, they took out a good part of my ovaries too. The doctors say my chances of conceiving are practically zero."

"The doctor? What do they know? We know who's in charge. You have to put your trust in God. Not man. Just keep the faith, Charisma. Have you told Nate?"

"Not yet."

"Does he have any children?"

"He has a sixteen-year-old son."

"Does he want more?"

"With my luck, a houseful. What am I going to do, Cinderella?"

"You're going to tell him the truth. And if he's the man for you, he'll understand. Everything'll work itself out, my queen. You'll see."

Saturday night Charisma invited her fiancé over for a nice home cooked meal. She spent all afternoon preparing his favorites—shell steak, macaroni and cheese, candied yams, turnip and mustard greens, jalapeno and cheddar cornbread, and peach cobbler.

"I feel like I'm being fattened up for the kill," he said as they sat down to eat.

Actually, Charisma was trying to guarantee that he'd be in a good mood for the Talk. She didn't know how he'd react to the news of her not being able to bear children, but she knew that the way to a man's heart was still through his stomach.

After dinner they stretched out on the living room sofa and listened to the stereo. That is, until the NBA finals came on. Somewhere after midnight, Charisma ended up going to bed and leaving Nate watching the game. He finally came to bed around two, and even though she was now wide awake and ready to talk, he was out as soon as his head hit the pillow.

Sunday morning Nate wanted to take her out for breakfast, but Charisma wasn't in the mood. She fixed a light meal in the hopes that they'd have a chance to talk.

"Honey, there's something we need to discuss," she began.

"Okay."

"I don't know how to say this."

"Baby, I'm a big boy. Give it to me straight, no chaser."

"Okay, here goes." She took a deep breath. "My doctors don't think I'll ever be able to have children. I'm sorry. I want you to know what you're getting into before we tie the knot. I want you to be sure that I'm the woman you want to spend the rest of your life with."

Nate was silent, allowing the news to register. When Charisma could no longer stand the silence, she spoke.

"Nate? Say something."

Finally, he spoke. "I know this must be hard for you to deal with, Charisma, but it's not the end of the world. I love you, and I want to spend the rest of my life with you regardless of whether or not we can have children. If you want, we can always adopt. You don't have to deprive yourself of motherhood, okay?"

She nodded.

"Now, let's go pick out our wedding bands, baby." He kissed her on the forehead.

Charisma jumped up and flung her arms around his neck. Cinderella was right. Things truly did have a way of working themselves out.

Charisma met her girls for breakfast at IHOP. She couldn't wait to show off her engagement ring—a two-karat princess cut wide band ring. Heather and Tangie squealed with delight, feasting their eyes on it. Even the waitress did a double take as the multi-facets winked her into a spell while Charisma ordered.

"So how did Dex take the news?" Heather asked.

"Better than I expected," Charisma admitted.

"That's a relief," Tangie said.

"Tell me about it," Charisma said. "Got anything planned for this afternoon?"

"No," Heather and Tangie said in unison.

"Let's go to the city and start looking for gowns," Charisma suggested.

Their faces lit up.

"And you'll never guess where we're getting married."

"Where?" Heather and Tangie both asked.

"On a dinner yacht circling Manhattan," Charisma said.

"Oh my God," Tangie exclaimed, looking at Heather in disbelief.

"That's what you've always wanted," Heather said. "I'm gonna cry."

"Heather, I want you to be my bridesmaid. And Tangie, would you be my maid of honor?"

"Oh my goodness. Of course," Heather said.

"I haven't been your best friend since kindergarten for nothing." Tangie smiled as the waitress returned with their meals.

"And I promise to choose gowns that you can wear even after my wedding day," Charisma assured them.

"Every bride since the beginning of time has told that very same lie," Tangie said, enjoying every bit of her pancakes.

"But we know you mean well," Heather added. "Just don't have me looking like a stuffed frog." She put a little salt and pepper on her egg white omelet.

"As svelte as you're getting? Please," Charisma said, digging into her French toast.

Heather blew her a kiss. "You're sweet."

"So," Tangie said. "Did you decide on your wedding colors?"

"We've narrowed it down to iced periwinkle or gray. Nate's leaving it up to me."

"What a man," Tangie said, smiling.

"Does he have a twin?" Heather joked.

"Not hardly. I must be the luckiest woman on the planet," Charisma admitted.

"Yeah, but too bad you don't do your bosses," Tangie reminded her.

"Okay, I had that coming," Charisma agreed. "But since he wasn't my boss when we got together, technically I didn't compromise my standards."

"Whatever you say, boss lady," Tangie said.

They finished the rest of their breakfast. "We better get a move on if we wanna beat the traffic into Manhattan."

Murphy's Law struck again. Charisma was due in Manhattan for her final fitting in an hour. When she and Jena got to the Long Island Railroad's Jamaica Station to transfer to the train to Penn Station, all service was suspended in both directions. They waited and waited for a taxicab, but apparently none were available. They decided to take the subway. They would never make their appointment, but what else could they do? They called the bridal shop, and then hopped on the E train. The ride was four times as slow as the LIRR, and as the subway crept along, Charisma couldn't help but being ticked-off.

"I don't believe this," she told her mother, disgusted.

"I know, sweetie, but there's really nothing we can do."

"Why does everything always happen to me?" She shook her head. "If they can't fit me in, then what?"

"Honey, it'll be okay. Really. You worry too much." Jena put her arm around her daughter.

Charisma laid her head on Jena's shoulder. "It has to be."

They traveled in silence for awhile as they watched the cast of subway characters come and go. There was the musician who played "The Star-Spangled Banner" on his saxophone as riders tossed loose change and bills in his cap, and the young goth guys, with their black nails, lipstick, and spiked hair. They wore black leather jackets despite the heat. Unfortunately, the scent of the homeless man who boarded the train at Roosevelt Avenue forced Charisma and Jena and several other passengers to move to another car. Charisma and Jena were forced to stand until someone exited and Charisma grabbed the seat for her mother.

By the time they entered the bridal shop, they were forty minutes late. Mimi assured Charisma not to worry, immediately putting the bride at ease. She and Jena had to wait thirty minutes to see the fitter, but the complimentary fresh melons, seltzer, wine, and cheese helped them pass the time.

Seeing Charisma in her gown nearly took Jena's breath away, and the fit was perfect. Charisma stared at her reflection in the mirror. The gown was everything she had imagined for herself. Now, if she could just wait until her wedding day to put it on again.

They schlepped back to the subway station, with wedding gown in tow. They made it through the turnstile and Jena headed for the downtown E train to get back to Queens.

"No, Mother, this way," Charisma said, pointing in the opposite direction. "Remember, we're uptown girls." Charisma always had a trick for remembering things.

Amused, Jena laughed all the way back home.

Charisma had never been big on male strippers, so the day before her wedding, in lieu of throwing her a bachelorette party, Tangie and Heather treated Charisma to a day of indulgence at Pure Harmony Day Spa. Upon arrival, they undressed, donned plush pale yellow terry-cloth robes, and were quickly whisked away to a scented candlelit room where they were each treated to a hot stone massage and deep-tissue muscle treatment. By the time Charisma had her scalp massage, she was so relaxed that she actually drifted off to sleep. Then they each showered and were escorted to another room for their manicures and pedicures. By the time they left Pure Harmony their skin was smooth and glowing like silk.

Nate called her the night before the wedding. "I know it's bad luck to see you the day before the wedding, but I figured I could sneak in a phone call now without tempting fate. Everything under control?"

She hesitated. "Uh-huh," she lied.

"What's wrong, baby? I can tell when something's not right."

"I'm trying to keep it together for my mother, but I can't. Nate, tomorrow we're getting married, and my dad won't be here."

"I know, baby. I know. But do you know that your father gave us his blessings before he passed?"

"Huh?" she asked in disbelief.

"Your father wanted us to be together. He made me promise him that I'd give it my best shot. So after Cabo didn't happen, and I relocated to Manhattan, I realized that I hadn't been true to my word."

"I've been such a fool. Thanks for not giving up on us."

"How could I? We were meant to be," he assured her. "Now get a good night's sleep, and I'll see you at the altar."

Charisma fell asleep with a smile on her face. She woke up feeling refreshed. All that was left for her to do that day was to visit the hair salon. Her biggest fear was being trapped there all day. Luckily, Daisy opened the shop early just for her, and she was able to whisk Charisma right through. Her mother picked her up afterward so she didn't even have to deal with the stress of traffic.

Charisma tried not to even think about Nate's bachelor

party, blocking all thoughts of it from her mind. She was convinced that what she didn't know couldn't hurt her. Rather, she spent the rest of the day at her mother's. She had specifically wanted an evening wedding so that she could be completely calm and relaxed for the nuptials.

She lit candles and prayed, wiping away tears at the thought of her father. Then something amazing happened. She started to remember bits and pieces of the poem she had dreamed about her father.

Excited, she rushed into the kitchen to tell her mother. "I don't remember all of it," she told her. "But I do remember the title. It was called 'Joy Cometh In the Mourning'. And *mourning* was spelled with a *u*."

Jena began to tear up. "That's beautiful, honey."

Charisma hugged her mother and they both began to cry. "He's still with us, Mother. He never really left."

"I know. I feel his presence all the time. We better stop crying or we'll both look a hot mess for your wedding." She grabbed two napkins from the holder and gave one to Charisma. "Now, dry your eyes and go put a cold washcloth over your face so you don't puff up."

Charisma headed for the bathroom to drench a washcloth in cold water before returning to her bedroom to lie down. It wasn't long before a fresh batch of tears made their way down her cheeks. The soft knocking at her door forced her to wipe the tears away. It was Tangie and Heather. They sat on the bed with Charisma.

"How's it going, kiddo?" Tangie asked.

"This is hard," Charisma told them, reaching for a tissue.

"It's allowed," Heather said, rubbing Charisma's arms.

Charisma blew her nose and smiled. "We've got an aisle to walk down."

Jena stuck her head in the doorway. "The photographer's here, honey."

"Okay, send him up," Charisma told her mother. "Time to get the show on the road." She laughed.

Nick, the photographer, came in. He took a few pictures of the girls before going back downstairs.

Then there was another knock at her door. This time it was Cinderella.

"You made it," Charisma exclaimed.

"Oh, darling, you know I wouldn't have missed this for the world." She smiled. They headed for the bathroom. Cinderella made up Heather and Tangie, choosing colors that complemented their iced periwinkle gowns. Then she moved on to Jena. Jena was a vision in peach. Cinderella spent the majority of her time on the bride. She had waited so long for that moment, and she was honored by the privilege. It was truly a labor of love. When she finished with Charisma, she was all set for the most special day of her life.

Jena walked back into the room, and her eyes lit up. "Your father would be so proud." She choked back tears.

"Mother, I just wish he were here to walk me down the aisle." Tears rolled down Charisma's cheeks.

"I know, honey. I know. But we know your daddy's up there rejoicing, and no one can take that away from you." Jena took a tissue and wiped Charisma's tears away. "My beautiful daughter, I love you so much." She hugged her tightly.

The photographer returned and took more pictures of the women and of her brother Eric, who arrived just in time for the limo ride to the pier in Manhattan. Right before they headed out, Jena suggested that they all have a moment of prayer. She prayed for the traveling grace of the wedding party and all the guests, but most of all she prayed for Charisma and Nate's future.

As the *Butterfly Princess* set sail, all the wedding guests were safely onboard. Though Saturday-evening traffic was heavy, everyone managed to arrive at the pier on time. After all, no one was about to miss the wedding.

Nate stood at the altar, beads of sweat forming just above his brow. Finally, Jena was seated and the ceremony began just as the sun began to set. He watched anxiously as his best friend escorted Heather down the aisle, and his brother, who was the best man, escorted Tangie.

The guests stood as Charisma and Eric made their grand entrance. Her strapless champagne-colored silk gown was a showstopper. All eyes were on the bride, and the sight of her took Nate's breath away. She was that beautiful. He was truly a blessed man.

As they said their vows, the lump in Nate's throat grew. After all she had been through these past few months, he wanted nothing more than to spend the rest of his life protecting her and making her happy. They exchanged rings. Charisma's hands shook ever so slightly as she placed the ring on his finger. He took her hands in his and brought them to her lips tenderly. The minister pronounced them man and wife, and he kissed his bride.

It was official. They were married. Everyone applauded as the happy couple left the ceremony.

"We did it," Charisma told her husband.

"Yes we did, Mrs. Arquettte. By the way, are you hyphenating or—?"

"Not," she said, barely giving him a chance to finish the sentence.

They walked down to the lower level of the yacht with barely enough time to catch their breath before the well-wishers were huddled all around them. The photographer took loads of pictures of the bridal party as the upper level was revamped for the reception.

Charisma could not believe her eyes when she and Nate walked into the reception area. The room was bathed in candlelight and white flowers. As Nate and Charisma took the floor for their first dance, the videographer busied himself capturing the moment. They chose Heatwave's "Always and Forever" for their first dance.

Later, Jena and the bride danced to the Stylistics "You Are Beautiful", a song that expressed how both she and Ellis Dearborn felt toward their daughter. After that dance, there wasn't a dry eye on the yacht.

Jena took the microphone. She wanted to present the newlyweds with their wedding gift. "When Charisma was a little girl," she began. "She walked around with a little suitcase and wanted to be called Traveling Barbie. My husband, Ellis, promised her that one day he would take her abroad, but life got in the way. We were never able to go. We first met Nate when my daughter invited him over for Thanksgiving dinner. Afterward, Ellis said that Nate was the One. So before he passed," she said, turning to Charisma and Nate, "we made arrangements to send you and my new son-in-law on a very special honeymoon—to Paris."

"Oh my goodness!" Charisma exclaimed, tears rolling down her cheeks. Nate kissed her tears away, and Jena hugged them both. As the yacht circled Manhattan, they danced the night away under the stars.

Three days later Nate and Charisma's plane landed at Charles de Gaulle International Airport. They were staying at the Hilton, just minutes away from the Eiffel Tower. It was a lovely room with a king-sized bed and a large bathroom with a bidet. There was even a large-screen TV, but they didn't intend on watching it much.

They would spend ten days in Paris. The weather was gorgeous. The first day they did absolutely nothing, but they had dinner at a nearby château recommended by the concierge. They ordered the duck and a wonderful bottle of champagne. Charisma and Nate strolled back to the hotel hand in hand. It was a beautiful night, and they made beautiful love.

One evening they had a local street artist sketch their portraits. Then they took a trip down the Seine River on the Rive Gauche, snapping pictures of Notre Dame and the St. Michael Bridge. By the tour's end it was nightfall, and the Eiffel Tower was all aglow.

An older Parisian couple asked if they were honeymooners. Nate and Charisma smiled at each other.

"*Oui.*" The Parisienne lady smiled.

"Why don't you let me take a photo of you and your bride and the Tower," the gentleman asked.

"*Merci, monsieur.*" Nate handed him the digital camera.

"You're French is very good. You are Americains, no?"

"*Oui,*" Nate and Charisma said as he snapped a couple of pictures.

"May you always be as happy as you are tonight," the Frenchman said, returning the camera.

"*Merci beaucoup,*" Nate said.

"Au revoir," the couple said.

The next morning Charisma and Nate rose early to start the day. They had a light breakfast in the hotel before heading out to see the world's most famous museum, the Louvre. No stranger to New York museums, they were totally unprepared for the Louvre's magnificence. They entered the glass pyramid and made their way down into the building that housed such famous masterpieces as the *Mona Lisa*. and the *Family Jewels*. There was even an entire wing dedicated to Egypt. It was easy to see how one could spend days in the Louvre without seeing it all. Charisma left the museum awestruck.

From there they did some light shopping along the Champs-Elysées. Very light, once they saw the price tags in some of those ritzy boutiques. Nate bought his wife some of her favorite French perfume, and she in turn bought him a pair of shades.

That night they went to the very risqué Moulin Rouge for dinner and a show. Charisma smiled to herself when she finally spotted a fat Frenchwoman. Who said they were nonexistent?

They hopped into a taxicab just as it was beginning to drizzle. Nate gave the driver the name of a chic jazz club recommended by the concierge. As they entered the hot spot Charisma was reminded once again of the Parisians love of cigarettes. She still wasn't used to all that concentrated smoking, but the jazz was too sweet to cut short. They left around three in the morning, and Charisma was relieved to reacquaint herself with the fresh night air. She held Nate close.

"Cold, baby?" he asked as they cuddled in the cab.

"Just enjoying my husband," she whispered in his ear, nibbling as she spoke. "His scent, his touch, his taste. I could go on and on."

Nate paid the driver. "Then let's take this party upstairs." He gently pulled her out of the cab.

"*Oui, oui monsieur,*" she said, grinning.

On their last full day in Paris, they slept until noon and ordered room service—omelets, fruit, fresh-baked croissants with jams, and the most delicious coffee.

"So what's on the agenda today, Mr. Arquette?"

"Well, I thought we might go see the Arc de Triomphe. I know how much you love Manhattan's version in Washington Square Park."

"That'll be fun," she said. "Let's get dressed."

Nate got up from the table and pulled Charisma toward him, then gently eased her back unto the bed. He moved on top of her, sliding his hand up her silk robe. She wore nothing underneath except a lace thong, which he tugged at with his forefinger and pulled completely off. She moaned in anticipation, untying her robe and completely opening it up.

Nate slid his tongue into her mouth, kissing her hard. She had to catch her breath as he gently tickled her clitoris with his fingertip. Then, he rolled her over until she was lying on top. He sat up. Charisma mounted him as he bent his knees and supported her back with the front of his thighs. She began rolling her hips as he bucked his. He grabbed her tits. Faster and faster she gyrated, throwing her head back. As he rubbed her nipples between his thumbs and forefingers, she churned his dick into her honey well, making sure it teased and lubricated just the right spot. Nate fucked her until she thought she'd lose her mind. When she could stand it no more, she broke out into a spasm so strong that all she could do was collapse back onto his thighs. A moment later, the dam seemed to break as he flooded her with his juices. They both laid there for a moment, glued together by their love. After a quick nap, they showered, dressed, and said au revoir to the City of Lights.

27

Heather

After another round of musical chairs, Heather was third in line for Cinderella's eyebrow seat. It was a Saturday morning and Heather's once ice-cold bottle of water was now tepid, condensation wetting her palm and fingers. Cinderella concentrated on doing brows while her assistant rang up sales of cosmetics and skin-care products. By the time it was Heather's turn to have her eyebrows done, the shop had emptied out.

Cinderella paused to answer the phone before giving Heather her full attention. "So how are you, my queen?" she asked Heather.

"I'm okay," Heather said. "Just trying to stay cool."

"Tell me something." Cinderella readjusted her lab coat. "Who is Paula?" she asked, lowering her voice as she applied warm wax to Heather's brows.

"An old classmate from high school. You know her?"

"Honey, Paula came in here a couple of weeks ago saying she wanted eyebrows just like yours. I looked at her as if to say 'are you for real?' "

"What did you tell her?"

"I told her that you are one of a kind and so are your eyebrows, but that based on her face shape I could give her brows that would flatter her most."

"She's *still* a trip." Heather shook her head.

"There was just something about her. I think she has a hidden agenda. Just watch your back, my sister. She's not your friend."

Heather and Tangie were seated in IHOP, awaiting breakfast. Heather glanced around at the other patrons. There was a man sitting a few tables away from them sipping coffee and watching Heather's every move. Their eyes met, and she quickly looked away.

Breakfast finally arrived. Tangie said grace and sunk her teeth into delicious melt-in-your-mouth pancakes, an omelet, and turkey sausages. Heather looked up from her mushroom omelet, and the coffee man was staring her down again.

"He's got it bad," Tangie whispered, referring to the middle-aged bespeckled man. "What do you *do* to these men?"

"I didn't do anything," Heather insisted. "I'm sitting here eating my breakfast like everyone else."

"In other words, you just got it like that." Tangie laughed. "And look, here it comes now."

"I couldn't help but notice you from across the room," he began. "You're beautiful. Are you mixed?" He waited for a response from Heather, which didn't come. "I'll make a deal with you," he continued. "I'll pick up the tab for you and your friend if you'll have dinner with me tonight."

This time Heather smiled. "Thanks, but no thanks."

"Are you sure?" he asked.

"Positive," Heather replied.

"Okay, then, you ladies enjoy your day." He waddled off.

"I am so sick of being asked if I'm mixed. Aren't we all?"

Heather rolled her eyes. "Apparently, someone failed American history."

"Wow, a free breakfast offer." Tangie smiled at Heather. "Having you for a friend definitely has its privileges."

The weekend ended and Monday morning rolled around sooner than Heather would have liked. Mondays meant one thing to her—gym day. She dreaded it more than almost anything, but hey, she had to admit, that the results spoke for themselves. She called A+ on her lunch break, but unfortunately, there were no assignments for her. Sighing, she hung up the phone. Another week and no shoots.

After work Heather drove her car the short distance from the library on Merrick to Canyon's Club's underground parking lot. It was relatively easy to find a spot since most people who worked in the area were leaving for the day. Heather secured the Club to the car's steering wheel, unsure if anyone wanted her hooptie or not.

Tired from a day at work, she slowly climbed the stairs, gym bag in hand. She exited the garage, reacquainting herself with the summer sun. It felt wonderfully warm against her skin, and the sounds of summer brought a smile to her cheeks. As she passed the Jamaica Multiplex on the corner, she couldn't help but think how she was looking forward to dropping a few more pounds in the coming weeks.

Heather opened the door to the gym and headed up the steps, remembering a time not too long ago when the elevator was her vehicle of choice. Slightly out of breath, she whipped out her Canyon card and made her way through the turnstile. Heather looked around. The gym was full. She was tempted to turn around and make a hasty exit, but something pushed her onward. She quickly changed in one of the changing rooms, locked up her personal items in a locker, and headed out onto the floor.

By that time, the gym had emptied out slightly, and she was able to grab an elliptical machine. She programmed it for thirty minutes and began her routine. After a few moments, Tangie walked by, giving her two thumbs up. Grinning, Heather shook her head and kept going. She watched *Girlfriends* on the overhead TV and before she knew it, the thirty minutes were up. From there she worked on her inner and outer thighs before heading over to the slant board for some ab work. By now her T-shirt and navy leggings were damp. She chugged down a few mouthfuls of water from her bottle, wiped the beads of sweat from her brow, and headed for an exercise mat. Totally exhausted, Heather closed her eyes for a minute or two. When she opened them, a smiling Paula was walking toward her.

"Finished your workout?" Paula asked her.

"You got that right," Heather said.

Paula extended her hand and helped her to her feet. "I know you're on your way out, but do you have a minute?"

"Sure, what's up?" Heather asked.

"Can we go someplace to talk?"

"How about Dunkin' Donuts?"

"Great. Let's get our things and grab a coffee," Paula said.

They both emptied out their lockers and headed over to the coffee shop. The tempting aroma of doughnuts slapped them in the face. The young Indian girl at the register took their order. Paula ordered a skim-milk iced latte, and Heather had a caramel coffee coolatta. Paula insisted on paying. They chose a seat away from the door.

Paula took a sip of her iced latte before speaking. "You really have your gym routine down pat."

"I'm just trying to get slim and trim like you," Heather said, savoring the flavor of her coolatta.

"I'm afraid I haven't been completely honest with you." She paused momentarily. "I told you I lost over eighty-six pounds by working out and counting calories."

"And you didn't?"

"Not exactly," Paula continued. "Sure, I did those thing, but that's not the whole story."

"So what is?"

She took a deep breath. "I take these special diet pills that work like magic. I lost the weight in seven months. The pounds melted off."

"So that's how you did it." Heather took another sip. "So what does that have to do with me?"

"Well, I have a proposition for you, if you're interested."

"I'm listening."

"I know how determined you are to slim down. I just got a fresh shipment of pills. I thought that maybe you'd like a free sample."

"What's the catch?"

"No catch," Paula insisted. "I just want to help a full-figured sister out. That's all."

"Are they over-the-counter pills or available by prescription only?"

"Actually," she hesitated, stirring her iced latte with the straw. "They're not FDA approved. Not yet. But I assure you they're safe. I haven't had any problems. I feel great. You'll see."

"There must be a reason why they're not FDA approved. That's scary."

"It's just a matter of time before they get approval. In the meantime, you won't have to wait. So if you want in, you'll have to keep it on the DL."

Heather thought for a moment. "This sounds too easy."

"I'm living proof, Heather. I don't know how much you want to lose, but in a few months you can be at your goal weight too. You'll lose weight like crazy."

"Just like that," Heather said.

"Just like that," Paula agreed.

* * *

By the weekend Heather had her first supply of Z3K diet pills. She took one tiny yellow pill every morning with a glass of grape juice on an empty stomach just as Paula suggested. She did feel a little queasy at first, but that soon passed. She ate lightly throughout the day and continued her workout routine after work. Paula was right. She was already losing weight. Three pounds melted off. She ditched her old diet pills.

Jamal was amazed at her weight loss. He had been out of town for a week and a half and upon his return a slimmer Heather removed her hot pink baby doll nightie and jumped his bones. She could tell by the look on his face under her bedroom's 100-watt bulbs that he was blown away by her little lap dance, especially since her lap was smaller than when he had left. Exercise made a big difference.

"So what have you been up to lately?" he asked her as they both lay back on the bed, catching their breath.

"Just working it out," Heather answered, deciding not to mention Paula's pills.

"Yeah, I can see that. Keep working it out, baby." He suddenly turned serious. "You know what I love about you, Heather?"

"What's that?"

"You know exactly what you want."

Heather was getting ticked-off. It had been awhile since she had signed with the modeling agency, and she had yet to be booked for her first shoot. She said as much to Don one afternoon on the phone

"Try not to get discouraged, Heather," he told her. "Success doesn't happen overnight. Have you lost any more weight?"

"I've lost another five pounds—thirty three since we met in the mall that day."

"Get outta here!" Don exclaimed. "You're really doing it."

"Damn straight."

"Tell you what. Call my assistant tomorrow to schedule another photo shoot.

Those extra pounds may make all the difference in the world with your head shots."

"Thanks, Don."

"No problem, doll."

Heather called the next morning and scheduled a photo shoot for that weekend. This time she went alone. Don and Sherry were both pleased to see her, giving her double air kisses. They whisked her through hair and makeup before planting her in front of Chip and his amazing camera.

"So good to see you again, Heather," he said, giving her a single air kiss. "You were hot before, but my goodness, look at you now." He held her hand and viewed her from all sides. "Now," he paused. "Let's accentuate that weight loss."

An hour later, Heather was on the railroad headed back to Queens. The photo shoot with Chip went well. Heather was hopeful that she would soon secure her first assignment.

As promised, Paula hand-delivered a week's supply to her every Saturday. Best of all, there were no side effects, and Heather felt fine. The Z3K pills were a godsend, melting away her past sins. What more could she ask for?

Heather found out the answer to that question the following week. Don called about her latest photos, which he had shown to a few prospects. They all said the same thing. Her face needed a bit more definition—say, another ten pounds to be competitive. She'd have to work even harder.

She called Paula about her next shipment, and that's when she got the devastating news. Paula was having trouble securing more pills from the pharmaceutical company.

They were cutting back on the manufacturing, to artificially drive up their profits once the pills were granted FDA approval.

"So many clients, so few Z3K's. You understand my predicament, Heather. Don't you?" Paula asked her.

"I really need those pills."

"I know, honey. I know. Maybe we can come up with a deal."

"What did you have in mind?" Heather asked.

"Something that's beneficial to both of us."

"Like what?"

"Well," she said slowly. "Ever since I kissed you that day on my bed, I haven't been able to get you out of my mind." Her voice turned husky. "I'm sure if we put our heads together we could come up with something."

Heather was silent. Paula was just proving another reason why she didn't trust most women. They always had something up their sleeve. Paula was still an opportunistic, conniving sneak. Heather had another call coming through. "Hold on, Paula."

"No, why don't I give you some time to think it over? I want to take you to the next level—in more ways than one. I'm sure we'll be in touch. I can feel it."

It wasn't often that Leola Grey had the pleasure of having dinner with her daughter. Between their busy work schedules and Heather's extracurricular activities, there wasn't much time left for mother-daughter talks. So an evening in with Heather was a nice change of pace.

Leola licked barbecue sauce from her fingers. "You are turning into some cook."

"Thanks," Heather said, slurping Crystal Light. They ate in silence for a moment, relishing the barbecue chicken, macaroni and cheese, and green beans.

"So what's going on, boobie?" Leola asked her daughter. "Besides getting all slim and trim?"

"Well, the modeling agency wants me to lose another ten pounds."

"Don't get carried away. It's not worth getting sick over. You've lost so much already."

"I know, but they think that with ten more pounds the assignments will start pouring in," Heather told her.

"And what do *you* think?"

"I'm willing to give it a shot."

"So what's the problem?" Leola sucked on the bone.

Heather put her fork down and took a deep breath. "Ma, what if you got the chance to make all your dreams come true. What price would you be willing to pay?"

"Only you can answer that, Heather. Only you know how much your dream is worth. I can't answer that for you."

Heather placed her chin in her hand and sighed. "I guess that's what makes life so hard."

That weekend Paula literally took Heather to the Next Level—Manhattan's trendiest gay bar. Heather was amazed at how many women were trying to catch her eye—moving in and invading her personal space ever so slightly as they said hello. There were blacks, whites, Latinas, Asians, all incredibly gorgeous, circling like piranhas in heat. Heather had to admit it gave her a rush. She squirmed in her seat slightly.

Paula leaned over and whispered in her ear. "I have to run to the naughty girls' room. Are you okay, hon?"

"Uh-huh."

"I'll be right back." She massaged Heather's bare shoulder with her perfectly manicured fingernails.

Heather sipped her peach martini as she watched Paula walk downstairs. A beautiful Latina zeroed in on Heather,

her eyes roving over her mocha tank top with its scripted *bling it on* in gold letters. Heather sensed that her tanned twins were what was drawing her attention. The confident Latina actually reached for Heather's nameplate necklace, marveling at the golden links. Her hand grazed Heather's breast as she returned the chain to her neck.

Then she whispered in Heather's ear. "Wanna dance?"

"No, that's okay."

"Oh come on. It'll be fun," she insisted, moving her hips seductively to the music and gently grabbing Heather's hand. The Latina ran her fingers through her long, thick mane, checking for split ends. "You don't know what you're missing, *mami*. Once you have a woman, you never go back. One hit of all this," she said, rubbing her hands over her hips, "and you're hooked."

They say the same thing about crack. Heather shook her head.

"If you change your mind . . ." She winked before leaving.

"I'll let you know," Heather promised, breathing heavier than usual. She was just beginning to sweat as Paula returned.

"Everything okay?" Paula asked her.

"Yeah," Heather agreed.

"Good. Let's get outta here."

28

Tangie

Tony left Tangela's house that morning and headed home. He knew what had to be done—for her sake. She deserved so much more than he could ever give her.

Last night he had come this close to jumping her bones. The moment he nestled up against her soft, warm flesh, he had to grab a pillow to wedge between his knees to camouflage his hard-on. Her scent still drove him nuts, reminding him of a time when she was his for the taking.

Tony closed the door to his eighth-floor co-op. As he walked from room to room, he opened up the blinds. Sunlight flooded his home. He headed for the kitchen and made himself a cup of coffee before returning to his home office.

It was time to find out who the hell this Jordan was. Tony had jotted down his license plate number the minute he got home from the Stephanie Mills concert that night. Like they say, the dullest pencil is better than the sharpest mind, and he definitely didn't want to leave something like Jordan's license plate to chance.

He tapped into several databases and before the morning

was over, he knew everything about Jordan Newport, from his first grade teacher's name to his shoe size. He knew all his favorite hangouts, as well as the magazines he subscribed to. Yep, working for the FBI definitely had its privileges.

"Gosh, you're glowing," Tangie said to Charisma, fresh from her honeymoon. The three met up at Applebee's for drinks.

Heather added, "You look like a million bucks. Are you happy?"

Charisma grinned.

"It shows. Marriage definitely agrees with you." Tangie nodded.

"So how was Paris?" Heather asked.

Charisma summed it up in one word. "Incredible. I'll e-mail you the pictures, and you wouldn't believe how hard it was to order toast in the morning. I think I put on five pounds, but it's good to be home. God bless America. I missed you guys. Catch me up. What's been going on?" She took a sip of her strawberry daiquiri.

"I have been hitting that gym like Muhammad Ali beating on George Foreman," Heather said.

"You look good, girl," Charisma told her.

"You should see her at the gym," Tangie said. "She's working out like nobody's business."

"I am on a serious mission." Heather laughed. "And if you don't know, you better ask somebody."

"That's what I'm talking about," Charisma agreed.

"Ready for some more news?" Tangie asked without waiting for an answer. "Tony and I are back together," she exclaimed.

"What?" Heather and Charisma said in unison.

"We spent the night together. I still love that man. I still love him," she said simply.

Heather spoke first. "We don't want to see you hurt again." She toyed with the straw of her diet soda.

"I'm a big girl," Tangie reassured them. "And you know I've never stopped loving him. Please be happy for me."

"We *are*, Tangie. You mean the world to us. You know that. You're our girl, but are you sure he's not going to hurt you again?" Charisma asked.

Tangie took a sip of her martini pop and scooted a bit in the booth. "No, of course not. Nothing in life is certain. Life is a gamble, and I'm willing to take that chance. Again."

"Well," Charisma said, raising her glass in a toast. "Behind every successful woman is herself." The three clinked glasses, silently saying a prayer for Tangie.

Tony leaned back in his chair, gazing out the window of his downtown Manhattan office. Now that he had gathered all of this information on Jordan, what was he going to do with it? Was Jordan Tangela-worthy? He didn't know. He picked up the phone and dialed Jordan's number. He swiveled back around and grabbed a pen, tapping it on the cherrywood desk. No answer. He checked his watch. It was only three-thirty. He'd try again later. It was time he and Jordan had a man-to-man. It was one thing reading a dossier. It was a totally different matter speaking with someone in the flesh.

That night Tony got his wish. He and Jordan met at a bar down Hillside Avenue. They had a couple of drinks at the bar before switching to a booth for privacy.

"So what's this all about?" Jordan asked.

"I'll give you two guesses."

"I bet I only need one: Tangie."

"Tangela it is." Tony winked, raising his beer.

"So you're the one anointed to call her Tangela. I guess you know her better than I ever will," Jordan admitted.

"Maybe not. If you play your cards right."

"Since you seem to know all the secrets, are you willing to help a brother out?" Jordan asked.

"Hey, it's every man for himself." Tony's eyes could have drilled a hole in him.

Jordan got up to leave.

"And it looks like you've lost before the game's even begun."

The two men stared at each other as though they were preparing for a game of chess. After they emitted enough testosterone between them to start a forest fire, something made Jordan sit back down.

"Another round?" Tony asked him, draining his glass.

Jordan nodded. "Why not?"

That was a week and a half ago. Tony believed that he'd done right by Tangela, but the lump in his throat begged to differ. No matter how much he loved her, he was first and foremost a realist. He was a company man. And no matter how many times he mulled it over in his head, the answer was still the same. He and Tangela could never be. It simply wouldn't work. The FBI was like a jealous wife. She allowed no room in his life for a demanding mistress, even a legal one. Hell hath no fury like a woman scorned. Tony picked up the phone and dialed Tangela's number anyway.

Tangie had just gotten back from lunch when she was paged to the club's front desk. Apparently, it was urgent. They paged her three times before she left the staff locker room, but she was in no mood to rush. Until, of course, she spotted a delivery boy carrying a bouquet of lime green roses. Smiling, she quickened her step. She was anxious to read the note, recognizing Tony's scroll instantly. *Let's make tonight unforgettable.* Tangie smiled at the thought.

She fumbled in her sweatpants pockets for a dollar. Then on second thought, she tipped him two. It was that kind of day.

Tony must have gotten the delivery confirmation because shortly after he sent her a text message.

Your place or mine?

Tangie was in the middle of a transaction when she got his message. She thought for a moment before responding. Mine, definitely mine.

He answered back immediately. Name the time and I'll be there.

Eight o'clock, she replied, before getting back to work, counting the hours until quitting time. She hadn't taken anything out for dinner. Everything was frozen. So she mentally scrambled to put together a menu as she drummed her fingers on the mousepad. What did she cook the last time they were together? She drew a complete blank, but as she clocked out, she knew there'd be no time to hit the supermarket. Hopefully, she had all the fixings to whip up something delicious.

Tangie got jammed in trying to maneuver her way though Jamaica Avenue traffic. The streets were packed with summertime shoppers. Didn't they know she had a hot date with her man that night? Evidently not. The light turned green, and she hit the accelerator, but pedestrians jumped out of nowhere, strolling across the walkway like she had all the time in the world. Not. New Yorkers were a mess. Of course, they had the right of way. By the time the walkway cleared, the light had turned red. Damn. It was already 6:15. Luckily, when the light turned green this time, she was able to make her turn and be on her way. She was home half an hour later.

Tangie took a quick shower and headed for her bedroom. She noticed that her answering machine light was blinking and quickly played the message. It was Tony. Don't cook, he told her. He'd pick up Pizza Hut.

Tangie breathed a sigh of relief. No need to worry about dinner. She slipped into a pair of denim shorts and a baby blue halter top, checked herself in the mirror and smiled. She didn't know exactly what the future held for her and Tony, but she was determined to enjoy the ride. Her phone rang again. It was Jordan. She let her machine pick up.

Tangie went to the kitchen to pour herself a tall glass of raspberry lemonade. She then programmed her CD player and turned on the stereo before relaxing on the sofa. Her eyes feasted on the luscious lime roses she had brought home from work, recalling the very first time Tony had surprised her with them. The sound of the doorbell brought her back to the present.

She answered the door. Tony walked in waiter-style, balancing the pizza box on one hand above his right shoulder. He headed for the kitchen, where Tangie got plates and napkins.

"Let's eat in the living room," she said as he cracked open the box, revealing a piping-hot cheese crust pizza with her favorite toppings—black olives, mushrooms, and extra cheese. It was pure, unadulterated cholesterol heaven, and they enjoyed every artery-clogging morsel.

"So how's it going?" Tangie asked him, taking a sip of her lemonade.

"Okay," he said, biting into another slice.

"Oh, let me get you something to drink."

"No, don't get up. I'll get it," he said, heading for the kitchen and returning momentarily with a beer.

Tangie picked an olive off her pizza and popped it into her mouth. "Ever think about us getting back together?"

"All the time," he said seriously.

"We're so right for each other. I know we can make it

work. Can't you see that?" She wanted to open up his head and pour some sense into him.

"Listen to me, Tangela," he said gently. "You and I will always be connected. And if you ever need me, I'm here for you. My love for you hasn't ended. It's just switched gears. One day, it will all make sense to you, and you'll thank me."

29

Charisma

Married life was sweeter than either Charisma or Nate could possibly imagine. They were six weeks into their nuptials, and the honeymoon was hotter than ever. They had already christened every room in Nate's town house with their lovemaking. Even the laundry room had been a tight, yet satisfying fit.

Every day Charisma would come home and start dinner. Nate never knew what she planned to cook, but by the time he arrived home, the most delicious aromas filled the air. Charisma loved cooking for her husband. She had almost perfected his favorite dishes, and he didn't mind telling her how he loved having a wife who satisfied his appetite in and out of the bedroom.

Charisma was all settled into her new home. They had already decided before the wedding that since his place was larger, she'd move in with him. Sure, she missed her condo; she had lived there for years. But she loved her husband even more. She appreciated the little changes that came with marriage, like no longer having to make what she called the single girl's call the minute the bank opened on payday to make certain the deposit was there. And a beautiful thing happened one Saturday morning when Nate was out playing tennis. She was watching her favorite home-shopping channels and decided to buy a pair of gold earrings. It had been so long since she'd placed an order, and of course her phone number and address had changed. The representative actually had to look her up. That's when she realized that she didn't need the earrings and canceled the order.

She told Nate about it later that evening. "No, you don't understand, babe. I was a serious shopaholic. Once upon a time I'd go barefoot before I'd wear a round toe shoe in a pointy toe season. I was a hot mess. Tangie and Heather were planning an intervention."

"So now you're a recovering shopaholic. Thank God," he said, laughing.

"You laugh, but our marriage could have been on the rocks right about now."

Nate's secretary held all her boss's calls while he sat in on a weekly morning conference call. By the time the call ended, he had two messages from Chase Martini marked urgent. He returned Chase's calls later that afternoon when he had a free moment. He quickly dialed her cell phone.

"Chase, it's Nate. What's up?"

"I need to see you. It's important."

"What's it about?"

"I can't go into it over the phone. I'm on Fiftieth between Fifth and Sixth. Can you meet me in Starbucks inside Rockefeller Center? I'll be here for another hour."

"See you at four-thirty?"

"Sure," he said before hanging up, wondering what she could possibly want to discuss. Nate called his bride to tell her he'd be home a bit late then finished up at work before leaving for the day.

Nate walked the short distance to Starbucks along Manhattan's crowded streets. Between the street vendors, the dog walkers, and the tourists taking pictures, he could barely maneuver through the congestion. When he reached Starbucks, Chase was already there sipping on an iced coffee.

"Thanks for coming," she said politely.

"What's this all about?" he asked, sitting down.

She hesitated for a moment. "I'm pregnant."

"You're what?" he asked in disbelief.

"I'm pregnant," she repeated.

"I don't believe this," he said, his voice tinged with disgust.

"Nate, I'm five months pregnant."

"Five months? You're not even showing. Is it mine?"

"Yes, it's yours," she said adamantly.

"Aren't I the lucky one." He spewed sarcasm.

They stared at each other in silence.

"So why didn't you just have an abortion?"

"Just have an abortion? I'm Catholic."

"So premarital sex is fine, as long as you don't have an abortion afterward? You're such a hypocrite. Your family would skin you alive for bringing home a black baby. So what does that leave? Adoption?"

Chase didn't answer at first. "You think I want to give my baby away?" she asked him bitterly, tears welling up in her eyes. "Huh?"

"I think you'd give away your ass if you thought it would save your lily-white name. On second thought, maybe if you had, we wouldn't be in this mess now."

"You don't understand, Nate. When I told my family, it nearly killed my grandfather. He's a very proud man."

"Yeah, I can just imagine. He's so proud that the thought of a black great-grandchild probably gave him a heart attack, right?"

"You're just as much to blame as I am. So don't you dare act like this is all my fault. You got that?"

Nate felt like he was living a nightmare. How the hell was he going to tell Charisma that not only did he have a one-night stand with a woman she despised, but that she was now carrying his child? Charisma put up a brave front, acting like being childless didn't bother her. But he could see the sadness in her eyes when she thought no one was watching, and he felt her pain. How could he expect to stay married behind all this drama? Charisma loved him, but she wasn't a saint. Damn, if he could only relive that night in Vegas. He'd regret it for the rest of his life. Somehow, he couldn't let her have the baby. Otherwise, he and Charisma would be history.

He tried another tactic. "What is it that you want, Chase?" he asked gently.

"I don't know what I want. I just want all this to be over. I want my life back."

"And you can have it back, if that's what you really want. You can make that happen. And I'll be there with you every step of the way. I promise."

"I am not supposed to be sitting here talking about having an abortion. This is not how my life is supposed to be. Abortions are for other women. Not women like me. I'm above that."

"Of course you are, Chase." He grabbed her hand. "We need to take care of this discreetly before any more time goes by. No one will ever know what really happened. And your honor will be restored. We can go away for the weekend, and you can tell your family you miscarried. There's got to be a doctor somewhere who can handle this."

"It's not going to be as easy as you make it sound."

"Who else knows you're pregnant besides your family?"

"Just my best friend, Loren."

"Can you trust her?"

"With my life."

"Well, if you rather she go with you, I'll understand. But if you need me, I'll be there too." He squeezed her hand, and she squeezed his in return.

"I can't believe I'm even considering this."

"Do you go to confession?"

"Twice a year."

"And do you think God forgives you for your sins?"

She nodded slowly.

"Then he'll forgive you for this one too."

Charisma had the dream again last night. She was alone in a restaurant full of strangers, blacks, whites, Asians, men, women. They were all dressed in black, a stern look planted on their faces. When any one of them glanced her way, a chill went through her. They all seemed to want to make eye contact with her, every last one of them. It was almost as if she was on display. Then one by one, they stood and passed by her table, looking her squarely in the eye before exiting. She woke up with a jolt, her heart pounding fast in her chest. She reached out for Nate, but he was not there.

Nate was downstairs pouring himself a drink at the bar. He hadn't had a good night's sleep since learning of Chase's pregnancy. If she refused to have the abortion, how the hell was he going to tell Charisma? He scratched his head nervously. Even though he had gotten Chase pregnant after Charisma stood him up at the airport and they weren't yet a couple, he knew that she would never forgive him. His hands were tied. Nate polished off one drink and poured himself another. His mind was racing, but the alcohol helped slow it down. He dozed off, the drink still in his hand. He was awakened by Charisma's touch as she shook him gently.

"Babe, come to bed," she said. "Come on."

Startled, Nate drained his glass as Charisma led him back to bed. "What time is it?" he asked.

"It's after two. You have an early meeting in the morning."

Nate was out the moment his head hit the pillow, but he had a restless sleep, tossing and turning all night. He woke up exhausted, barely making it to work on time.

Chase had had a restless night as well, but when she woke up, the answer to her problem was crystal clear. She would have the abortion. Her doctor made a few phone call and knew a doctor who specialized in high-risk, late-term abortions. Chase decided an abortion was best for all concerned—herself, her unborn child, and even Nate. Not that she was concerned about his welfare. Chase wasn't trying to make it easy for him. She just wanted control of her life back. Unfortunately, her baby would pay the price.

Later that day she called Nate to tell him the news. He was obviously relieved to hear of her decision, offering to be by her side for support. Chase declined his offer and hung up, promising herself that she would never speak to that bastard again.

Nate left work early, opting to enjoy the August sun. The past week had been torturous, waiting for Chase to decide. Now that she was having the abortion he could exhale, but he'd have to carry that secret to his grave.

As he boarded the railroad home, a smile of relief graced his face. Occasionally, he would glance out the window, marveling at what a difference a phone call could make. He decided to pick up Charisma from work, as he exited the train and found his parked car. Her car was at the mechanic's, and he didn't want her cabbing it. If he hurried, he could just about make it.

He parked across the street from Freeman LTD, his eyes glued to the revolving door, awaiting her exit. Finally, he saw her, his beautiful, loving wife. She had no idea that he had almost lost her. He had come *this* close to screwing it up for them, but thank God he was able to talk some sense into Chase.

Charisma spotted her husband and smiled. As she crossed the street, he leaned over and opened the door for her. She greeted him by planting a big, fat juicy kiss on his lips.

"What a nice surprise," she said.

"Just trying to be a good husband." He started the car, and they drove off.

"Honey, you missed the exit," Charisma reminded him.

"No, I thought maybe we'd go out to dinner. I want you nice and relaxed tonight. It's been a long week."

"Ooh, I like that. Where to?"

"Name the spot."

"How about Cabana?"

"You got it."

They drove to Forest Hills and parked a few blocks from the restaurant. It was a gorgeous August evening, and Nate couldn't help but check out his wife's figure as she walked beside him. Charisma wore a sleeveless form-fitting melon-colored dress and matching high-heeled sandals. She made summer look good. Apparently, mesmerized by her curves, several men stopped talking as she and Nate walked by.

As usual for a Friday night, Cabana was packed, and they waited over half an hour for a table. Once they tasted the meal, they knew the wait had been worth it. They ordered a pitcher of sangria and then dined on salmon and steak, eating off of each other's plate.

"Do you know how much I love you?" Nate asked his wife.

"I'm a lucky woman."

"No, I'm the lucky one." He grabbed her hand and kissed it. "Why don't we go home and both get lucky?"

"You read my mind. Let me run to the ladies' room, and I'll be good to go." After a few moments, Charisma returned to the table, smiling mischievously.

Nate paid the check and they left. Charisma snuggled against him in the car, eager to get home and get naked with her husband. He slid his hand under her dress and up her bare thighs, pleasantly surprised that she wore no panties underneath. Before long his fingers were covered with her wet stickiness. He brought his fingers up to his lips, licking them in anticipation. He stopped for a red light and pulled her toward him, spreading her lips with his own. Before the light turned green, she had unzipped and hiked up her dress, returning his kiss. She climbed off his lap as another car drove up behind them. Charisma grabbed her husband's bulging dick through his underwear. It grew in response to her touch.

"Damn it, baby. You're driving me crazy," he said, turning off onto a wooded, dead-end street.

"We're almost home." she told him.

"Uh-uh. I want you now." He led her to the backseat of the car. Like two hot, sweaty teenagers, they relieved themselves within the cramped confines of the Camry. It was a fast, hot fuck, and they lay back satisfied, yet exhausted.

Nate and Charisma laughed softly as they readjusted their clothes. Nate cracked the window.

"I see I'm gonna have to dust you for fingerprints when you come home in the evening," he warned.

"Why?"

"You go to work without panties, and you ask why?"

Charisma laughed as she reached for her purse and retrieved her panties. She quickly put them back on, explaining to him that she removed them in Cabana's restroom.

"Oh, you're good," he said. "You planned this whole thing and made me think it was my idea."

She laughed wickedly as they returned to the front seats. Nate started the car just as a cop car drove by. They were home in no time and fell asleep in each other's arms.

Before Nate's secretary even arrived his phone was ringing off the hook. It was Chase.

"What's going on?" he said drily.

"I can't do it, Nate."

"Are you crazy? I thought this was settled." He sat down at his desk.

"I know, but I changed my mind."

"Look, you're just scared. That's all. I'll meet you after work and we'll discuss this rationally."

"There's nothing to discuss. I'm not doing it. I'm having this baby."

After a pause, Nate spoke. "Do whatever the hell you want." He slammed the phone down just as he heard his secretary walk in.

"Good morning, Nate," she said.

"Good morning, Pam. Hold all my calls," he told her, slamming his office door shut.

For a moment he sat at his desk in utter disbelief, convinced that he was living the worst day of his life. He wondered if he could convince her to have the abortion. Then again, she sounded like her mind was completely made up. *Think, Nate. What are you going to do?* It was only a little after eight, but already he needed a damn drink. Surprisingly, he made it through lunch and then through the rest of the day. He spent a good part of the day at his desk mulling over in his head how to break the news to Charisma. One thing for sure, he was running out of time. True, Chase was barely showing, but that would change shortly. He'd just have to confess even though there was no painless way of doing so. And not being much of a procrastinator, Nate decided to tell Charisma that night.

By the time he arrived home, Charisma was busy in the kitchen preparing dinner.

He kissed her quickly on the cheek and decided to take a quick shower.

"Dinner'll be ready in a few, baby," she told him as he removed his tie and headed upstairs for the bathroom.

He stripped and stepped into the master bedroom's bath, allowing the cool stream to massage the knot of tension in his back and shoulders. He stood there for a moment before reversing his position so that the water beat mercilessly against his chest. Nate soaped up, rinsed, and was through in a matter of minutes. He lotioned down and put on a T-shirt and a pair of sweats before heading back downstairs.

He paused for a moment and took a deep breath before entering the kitchen. The table was set, and Charisma was removing garlic bread from the oven. They were having chicken parmigiana. *Great, another Italian dish, as if Chase hadn't been enough.* He sat and Charisma joined him. He blessed the food, and they dug in.

Charisma proceeded to tell him about her day. Nate listened with only half an ear. Sensing his preoccupation, she asked if something was wrong.

"We need to talk, Charisma." He put his fork down.

"You sound so serious." She grinned. "What's wrong?"

Nate wiped his mouth with the dinner napkin and clasped his hands together, resting his elbows on the table. "I am truly sorry. There's no easy way to say this."

Charisma put her fork down too. She gave her husband her full attention.

"Chase Martini is pregnant. It's mine." He exhaled.

Charisma took a few seconds to digest the news. She looked at Nate with disgust, her voice low and angry. "With all the women you could possibly pick, you choose the bitch I hate the most to have an affair with? You fucking bastard." She jumped up from the table, trashed her barely eaten dinner, and stormed out of the kitchen.

He was right on her heels, grabbing her arm from behind and spinning her around. "We need to talk, Charisma."

"Get off me!" She wiggled free. "I don't have a thing to say to you. I can't even have a baby, for God's sake, and you're out making babies? And now you have the audacity to want to *talk* about it? Give me a fucking break."

"I know you're upset. You have every right to be, but it's not what you think."

"Oh, no? My husband gets another woman pregnant, and it's not what I think? Last time I checked there was only one way to make a baby. So, don't insult my intelligence, okay?"

Charisma ran up the stairs, heading for the spare bedroom. Nate climbed the stairs two at a time to keep up. She took an overnighter out of the closet and headed for the bedroom. Once there, she began packing, throwing a pair of jeans, a couple of T-shirts, and underclothes into the bag.

"Would you just stop and listen to me for a minute?" he pleaded.

"Give me one good reason why I should. You just *had* to have her. We haven't even been married a year, and already you're out gallivanting."

"It wasn't like that. I swear to you, Charisma. I've never cheated on you. Do you remember when I transferred to Manhattan after you stood me up at the airport on Presidents' weekend?" He continued without waiting for a response. "Well, about a month later I ran into Chase at the marketing conference in Vegas. I was still trying to get you out of my system. We had both been drinking pretty heavily, and one thing led to another. You have no idea how sorry I am. I swear to you, it only happened once."

"Well, lucky for you it fell on fertile ground," she spat the words out, adding more clothes to the bag.

"Haven't you heard a word I said? I didn't cheat on you."

"Lucky me." She looked him dead in the eye as she dragged the overnighter off the bed.

"Where are you going?" he asked.

"The hell away from you!" With her purse in one hand and the overnighter in tow, Charisma headed for the closest hotel.

30
Heather

Heather ran into her old high school classmate, Ava, at Patty World during lunchtime.

"Hey, chicklylicky, what's new?" Ava asked.

"Not much. You must live here," she joked.

"No, but I love me some chicken. Come join me." She moved her bag out the way, and Heather took a seat across from her in the Caribbean eatery. "Didn't I see you and Paula at the club the other night?" Ava asked.

"Girrrl . . ."

"Wouldn't have to do with a pill deal, would it?"

Heather was embarrassed. She took another bite of her brown stewed chicken, had a forkful of rice, and stopped. "Paula's a trip."

"Trust me. I know all about it." She took a bite of her spicy Jamaican beef patty, washing it down with a sip of ginger beer. "She uses drugs as a ploy to lure women in. You're just her latest victim."

"How do you know?"

"I was in your shoes once."

"How'd you do?"

"I lost thirty pounds, and then I kicked her to the curb. She can't stand my guts."

"Her loss," Heather said, and they both laughed.

"Paula usually brings her latest victim to the Next Level before she goes in for the kill. I have an idea. Why don't we beat Paula at her own game?" Ava asked.

"What do you have in mind?"

"You look fantastic, by the way, but you really want those pills, right?"

"Uh-huh. I signed up with a modeling agency, and they want me to drop a few more pounds."

"So get them. They sell everything on the Internet. Everything," she stressed.

"Why didn't I think of that?" Heather asked.

"I don't know, Miss Librarian. Why didn't you?" She grinned. "But you need to get with the program."

"What would I do without you?" Heather exclaimed.

"Be her love slave," Ava said. "Now maybe you'll be mine."

Heather's eyes widened.

"Relax, Heather. I'm joking. Put those flying fingers of yours to work on the Internet, and go get your diet pills, girl."

By the end of the week, Heather had received her first shipment of Z3K. It was easy. Almost too easy.

"Look at you," Charisma told Heather. "You were something before, but you're a hot mama now." She slid a coconut shrimp in her mouth as they shared a Red Lobster girls' night out.

"How much weight have you lost?" Tangie asked.

"Thirty-seven and counting," Heather said, sipping her raspberry lemonade.

Tangie bowed her head and said grace. "I told you. Once you add exercise to the mix, you're home free."

Heather smiled. "I have good news. I'm going on my first photo shoot. They had wanted me to lose another five to ten pounds, but apparently somebody's interested."

"Finally," Charisma said.

"Look out, world. Here comes the next Tyra Banks," Tangie said, raising her banana daiquiri in a toast. "Behind every successful woman is herself."

"I'll drink to that." Heather raised her lemonade, and they clinked glasses. She had another forkful of crab Alfredo, relishing its creamy flavor. "I probably should have ordered the grilled chicken Caesar salad," Heather admitted.

"Hey, you gotta celebrate sometime. You've earned it," Tangie told her.

"Well, I'm enjoying every bite." She reached for another biscuit, savoring one of her all-time favorite comfort foods one bite at a time. Heather looked at Charisma, who was seated across from her. "Charisma, is everything okay? You don't look so hot."

"I'm okay," Charisma said.

Tangie took a second look at Charisma and thought for a moment. "No, you're not. What's going on?"

"Chase is pregnant with Nate's baby." Charisma held her head in her hand.

"What?" Heather and Tangie said.

"Remember when he asked me to go away with him, and I stood him up at the airport?" Charisma asked.

They both nodded.

"Well, after he relocated to the city, Chase went away for a business trip, and they ran into each other. Unfortunately, the rest is history," Charisma summed it up.

"Oh, Charisma, we're so sorry," Heather said.

"Wow, that's rough," Tangie added.

"Yeah, tell me about it," Charisma agreed. "I'm sick. I can't even give my husband a baby, and this heifer is having one. She's won." Charisma began to cry. Heather reached in her purse and passed Charisma some tissue. Charisma blew her nose.

"She hasn't won," Tangie insisted. "I bet she would love to be in your shoes. Trust me. How do you deal with seeing her at work every day?"

"She took a leave of absence, thank God," Charisma said. "But I just don't know what to do," she admitted through her tears.

"We'll get through this like we have everything else. You'll see," Tangie said.

Heather had her very first shoot in Midtown Manhattan for Flow Cosmetics. Although Charisma declined, Tangie came to lend moral support. Freshly shampooed and without a lick of makeup, Heather drove to Tangie's. They took the railroad and were in the city in no time.

She went from hair and makeup to wardrobe. By the time she was ready for the shoot, she was perspiring slightly, so the makeup artist had to touch up her face. The entire shoot lasted less than thirty minutes.

An hour later, she and Tangie were in Macy's. The fall collections had arrived, and they were both looking for new shoes to add to their arsenal. The crowded elevator opened to the fifth floor, showcasing shoes as far as the naked eye could see. No matter what the hour or day of the week, the fifth floor was packed. There never seemed to be enough associates on the selling floor, and that day was no different. After trying on three pairs of shoes, Heather settled on a pair of peep-toe animal print pumps while Tangie walked out with a pair of red patent leather slingpumps. It was a good day.

Heather was on pins and needles awaiting word from the modeling agency. Each day she rushed home to check her messages. Nothing. By the fourth day, she was welcomed home by the flashing red message light. Smiling, she listened to her one message. It was Paula. She had gotten the long-awaited fresh shipment of Z3K's, and she wanted to give Heather first dibs. Heather wasn't interested and did not even bother returning Paula's call.

Instead, she called the modeling agency and left a message for Don. He called her later that evening. Yes, Flow Cosmetics had sent over the proofs from the photo shoot. He needed her to come into the office and have a look at them.

Heather took a day of from work and schlepped back to Manhattan. She caught the 10:32 train at the Jamaica Long Island Railroad station and arrived at Penn Station before eleven. She was right on time for her eleven-thirty appointment with Don. She walked the three blocks and was seated in the busy reception area in no time.

Heather passed the time flipping through the latest issue of *Vogue* as she waited. The elevator doors opened and a beautiful brown-skinned woman stepped out. Her hair and makeup were flawless. She must have been a model. She saw the receptionist, apologized for being late, and took a seat next to Heather.

"Are you interviewing for the personal assistant?" she asked Heather.

"No, I'm a model," Heather replied, smiling to herself as the words sank in.

"Oh, okay." She smiled, looking obviously relieved that she was not sitting next to her competition.

The receptionist had one phone call after another. A multitasker, she transmitted several faxes and prepared packages for FedEx pickups without battling an eyelash. Finally, she stood and informed Heather that Don was ready to see her, then escorted Heather back to his office.

Heather gathered that Don was on a call with their Los

Angeles office. They were in the process of scheduling a fashion show on the West Coast and needed models for the catwalk. Don looked up and motioned for Heather to have a seat. She sat opposite his chrome-and-glass-top desk and tried to appear relaxed. Inside, she was anything but.

The conversation ended and Don apologized for the delay. He got straight to the point. "Heather, we have your proofs from the mascara shoot. Those extra pounds you lost have made all the difference. You photograph beautifully, by the way." He spread the head shots on his desk. "Come have a look."

Heather came around the desk and checked out the photos. He was right. The extra pounds had paid off. Her face had a definition she hadn't seen in years. "So did I get the job?" she asked.

"They like your photos, Heather. They really do, but there's one problem."

"What's that?"

"Let me just say that they were very impressed with you." He paused. "But you have a slightly deviated septum, and this is a mascara ad. They felt that if they magnified your photo, they'd have to do too much airbrushing to reduce the bump on your nose. So they've decided to pass. Sorry, love."

Heather let out a deep sigh. Just when she thought things were working in her favor, up went another roadblock. She couldn't win. "I see," she said.

"You might want to consider plastic surgery. I can give you the number of an excellent surgeon who does great work." His eyes searched hers gently. He checked the address book on his cell phone before jotting down the number on a business card.

Heather accepted the number and stood to leave. "I'll be in touch," she sighed.

"You do that, Heather. Keep your chin up."

* * *

"You know something, Heather. I'm not feeling the love," Jamal told her one night over the phone. "How long has it been since we've spent any time together?"

"I know," she agreed emphatically. "I've been so busy working out and running back and forth to Manhattan that I've been neglecting you. I'm sorry."

"What's your schedule look like? Think you can carve out some time for me tomorrow?"

"I think that can be arranged."

"Good."

"How about my place?" she asked.

"That'll work."

"Seven-thirty?"

"Seven-thirty it is."

"Cool, see you tomorrow." Just as Heather hung up, her phone rang again. She picked up again, assuming that Jamal had forgotten something. "Yes, Jamal?"

"Heather?"

"Yeah?"

"Who's Jamal?"

"A friend. What's up?"

"Didn't you get my message? I have more pills. I've been trying to hold on to them just for you, but the demand is hot. Know what I mean?"

"Of course," Heather said simply.

"Have you thought any more about my proposition? I mean, I can't hold on to them forever."

"I know, Paula. As a matter of fact, I was about to call you."

"You've decided?"

"Uh-huh. I appreciate the offer, but I think I'll pass," Heather told her.

"You'll pass? Do you know how hard it is to lose weight and then keep it off?"

"I'm willing to try, Paula."

"You'll be sorry, you little pussy teaser. I guarantee you."

"Don't hold your breath, but you must be really desper-ate to use pills to hook women. You're pathetic." She hung up, seething, not knowing whom she was more mad at—Paula for making such a ridiculous offer or herself for al-most agreeing to it.

She ran herself a bath, fascinated as the bath gel Jamal had given her succumbed to the assertive stream of water, producing offspring bubbles. She soaked until her skin began to shrivel. Having lost her appetite, she turned in early. Punching her pillow as she tried to find the right spot, she realized just how tense her body was. Tomorrow, she'd see Jamal. He'd work out those kinks.

Eight-thirty and Jamal was nowhere to be found. Heather had left messages on his cell and his home phones. Noth-ing. Curled up on her couch, she wondered what in the world was keeping him. He wasn't always punctual, but then again, he wasn't normally this late either. She sighed and sipped her wine, grabbing the remote from a nearby end table. Those damn *American Idol* contestants seemed extra-pitiful this season. Had they no shame? Apparently not, but as she headed for her bedroom in search of some batteries, neither did she.

Evidently, Heather had dozed off, awakening to the sound of the telephone sometime after midnight. It was Jamal.

"What's going on?" she asked, checking the clock on her nightstand.

"Well, you tell me. You think you know somebody pretty well, and then you realize you don't know jack."

"Life's funny like that," she said, not knowing where the conversation was headed.

"You should know."

"Whad'dya mean?" she asked.

"I got a really interesting call tonight on my way over to see you."

"Oh yeah?"

"Yep, stopped me dead in my tracks."

"Really. From whom?"

"My ex. You remember Paula?"

"Of course. What did she have to say?"

"Plenty. I got a real earful."

"Is that right?" She yawned.

"I guess I know why you haven't had time for me lately. You were too busy sleeping with her."

"What?" She was wide-awake now. "You're buggin'."

"She filled me in on all the details."

"Oh please, she's lying. She's mad because she couldn't buy me with her little pill-deal scheme. So she's telling you we're lovers to get back at me. Don't believe the hype," she warned.

"What pill deal?" he asked.

"Her brother's a pharmacist, and he's been getting these special diet pills for me on the black market."

"Jay? Please, he's as straight as they come. You gotta be joking."

"Jamal, she's lying to you."

"Good-bye, Heather."

She called him right back, but he refused to answer. His machine picked up. Heather hung up, vowing that Paula would pay for her lies. If Paula wanted to play dirty, then let the games begin.

Sinking her heels into its plush, ivory carpet, Heather sat in the reception area of Dr. Speller's Upper East Side office awaiting her consultation. She had completed the questionnaire as requested. She looked at the women with their perfect profiles sitting in the room along with her, tossing their perfect hair with their perfectly manicured fingers. Their diamond rings alone could choke a bull, not to mention their stud earrings.

Even with an appointment, Heather waited over half an hour for her consultation. When she finally did see Dr. Speller, he immediately made her uneasy. There was just something about him she couldn't put her finger on. He was a tall, well-tanned man with cold blue eyes. He shook her hand and motioned for her to have a seat. He briefly reviewed her answers to the questionnaire before giving her his full attention.

"So tell me about yourself, Miss Grey."

Heather gave him the generic story of her life, ending with her recent thirty-eight pound weight loss.

Dr. Speller listened intensely. "I see," he said, making notes as she spoke. He paused momentarily before continuing. "How do you think rhinoplasty will change your life?"

Now it was Heather's turn to pause. "Well," she began. "I have always been self-conscious about my nose. I know the bump isn't huge, but when I look at myself in the mirror, it's the first thing I see. I've recently started modeling, and my nose appears to be a hindrance. I think it's time that it's dealt with."

He donned pair of latex gloves and walked over to Heather to examine her nose more closely. Dr. Speller gently held her face in his hands, viewing her nose from different angles before returning to his seat.

"Well, Miss Grey, you're a beautiful woman. Giving you a more flattering nose should not be a problem. It would be my pleasure. Of course, there are routine medical tests you need to undergo first, but barring any complications, I think you would be an excellent candidate."

"Thank you, Doctor. I know this is an expensive operation."

"Unfortunately, since this is a cosmetic procedure, it's

not covered by insurance. However, we do have affordable payment plans."

"How much are we talking?" she asked.

"Ten thousand," he said with his fingers intertwined and both forefingers touching his chin. "But it's well worth it. Believe me."

"Wow, that's a lot of money," she sighed deeply. "Why don't I think it over, and I'll get back to you."

"That'll be fine, Miss Grey."

Heather stood to leave. She wouldn't be back.

As Heather sat in the reception area of Dr. Taylor's office in Jamaica Hospital, she thought about how having nurse for a mother had its privileges. Her mother was able to get her an appointment with the heavily booked plastic surgeon just by pulling a few strings. Thank goodness for small miracles. Heather had already done her homework, reviewing Dr. Taylor's credentials and making certain that she was board certified. She had a private practice in Manhasset, and was also affiliated with Mount Sinai.

Finally, the nurse came and escorted her into Dr. Taylor's office. Dr. Taylor stood and greeted her prospective patient, immediately putting her at ease. The first thing that struck Heather about the doctor was her looks. She was drop-dead gorgeous with flawless brown skin, hazel eyes, and a thick mane of brown hair. She couldn't have been over forty. She reminded Heather of a Barbie doll with her perfect proportions and long, lean limbs. Noting her smile—a genuine smile—Heather instantly relaxed.

"Heather, if I could be your very own fairy godmother, what would you have me do for you?"

Heather put it bluntly. "I need a new nose."

"And you think a different nose will . . . what?" Dr. Taylor asked.

"It'll make me feel better about myself."

"In what way?" she delved.

"For one thing, I'd be able to look back at myself in the mirror."

"And you're unable to do that now?" she asked, making notes.

"I would feel more attractive and have more confidence without this deviated septum."

"I see." She made more notes. "I've always wanted to be a plastic surgeon. I thought that if I could make people happy with their appearance, they'd accept themselves and begin to love themselves. Sometimes, it's not that simple. Do you love yourself, Heather?"

"Of course."

"And do you like yourself?"

"Most of the time. I just lost thirty-eight pounds so it's a lot easier these days," Heather admitted.

"Thirty-eight pounds? That's quite an accomplishment. How'd you do it?"

"Diet and exercise, mostly."

"That's wonderful. You'll have to have a complete physical before I can determine if you're a good candidate for the surgery. Are you on any medication?"

Heather hesitated. "No, not really."

"Is that a yes or a no, Heather?" Dr. Taylor asked. "Everything shows up in the lab work."

"I . . . I've been taking diet pills—Z3Ks."

"Z3Ks? They're not even FDA approved. How are you getting them?"

"Originally from a pharmacist but now off the Internet," she admitted.

"You're jeopardizing your health, Heather. Do you realize that?"

"I haven't had any side effects."

"That you know of," Dr. Taylor reminded her. "You don't know what those pills are doing to your body. Why do you think they're not FDA approved? As a physician, it's my responsibility to report this pharmacist. What's his name?"

"I never should have told you."

"You could be saving someone's life. Maybe even your own. Do you realize that?"

Heather thought for a moment. Paula never ever mentioned his name, but Jamal did once or twice. "His last name is Little. Jay Little? Jack Little? No, I'm pretty sure it's Jay. Jay Little. If this gets out, I'm toast."

"Don't worry, Heather. This conversation is strictly confidential. You have my word. In the meantime, I want you to begin taking this supplement to prep your body for surgery." She picked up her pad and began to write. "You can find it in any health food store. Set up another appointement with my nurse. You'll need to take the physical after you've finished your thirty-day supply of the supplement. Your deviated septum is very slight. It shouldn't be a problem to correct." She tore off the sheet from the pad and handed it to Heather.

A few days later Heather stopped by the health food store after work for the prescribed supplement. The salesperson said he had never heard of it. She made him double-check. He did. There was no such drug listed in the computer. Heather was stumped.

31

Charisma

"Mother?"

"Charisma, what's wrong?" Jena could hear the tears in her daughter's voice.

"Mother, I left Nate."

"What happened? Where are you?"

"I'm on my way over. I'll see you in a few." She wiped her face with the back of one hand while driving with the other.

Twenty minutes later, Charisma was in her mother's kitchen, snotting like there was no tomorrow. Jena managed to put the story together between the near hysterics.

"Charisma, I can only imagine the pain you must feel with another woman carrying your husband's child. You have every right to feel angry and bitter and enraged. But when all is said and done, if Nate got her pregnant before you two got together and it was a one-night stand . . ."

"Are you taking his side?"

"No, but you're a married woman, and you need to start thinking like one. Marriage is a grown woman's game. Life is hard sometimes, honey. Lord knows it's not easy being a woman. But you can't leave your husband every time he does something wrong, especially if it was before he married you. Your father and I were married nearly thirty-five years, Charisma. If I left him every time he did something stupid, we wouldn't have lasted a month. Do you understand? What do you want? Do you want to be right or do you want to be married? The choice is yours. What price are you willing to pay?"

Charisma was so angry. She barely had time to wipe away one batch of tears before a fresh batch replaced them. She almost hated to admit it, but she wanted to save her marriage. The phone rang and she jumped.

"Hello?" Jena answered, pausing ever so slightly. "Hi, Nate, how are you?" She looked at Charisma.

Charisma shook her head vehemently.

"No, Nate, she's not here. I certainly will. Okay then. Bye."

"Whew," Charisma exhaled. "Thank you, Mother."

"Charisma, you can stay here for a couple of days. After that I want you to go home and see about your marriage."

Nate was miserable without his wife. He went to bed alone and he woke up alone. Days were long. Nights were even longer. He blew up Charisma's cell phone, leaving a bunch of messages, but he knew she needed her space right now. He was tempted to call her at work just to hear her voice, but thought better of it.

By the end of the week, when he couldn't stand it anymore, he and the fellas went drinking after work at a Manhattan sports bar. They watched a couple of baseball games and talked smack. There was no rush to go home to an empty house and a cold bed. Around midnight his married buddies started packing it in. They had to get home to their wives. Nate stayed another hour then headed to Penn Station to catch his train. He got to Lynbrook, picked up his car, and drove home.

Nate unlocked the front door with his key, letting himself in to the dark, quiet foyer. He missed Charisma so much that he could almost smell her perfume. He flipped on the light switch and nearly jumped out of his skin. Charisma was sitting on the sofa in the dark. For a moment, neither spoke.

"Hi," he said simply.

"Hi."

"How long have you been here?"

"A couple of hours, I guess," she told him.

"In the dark?"

"I think better in the dark."

"I see," he said. Exhausted, Nate sat on the couch next to Charisma. "I missed you so much," he said simply.

"I missed you too, babe. I couldn't bear staying away from you another day. That's why I came back, but we still have a lot to work through, Nate."

"I know."

"It won't be fixed overnight, but I'm willing to do what it takes to save our marriage."

He planted a kiss on her forehead, then on her right cheek, and then on her lips. She kissed him back hard. He loved the scent and the warmth of her skin. He had missed his wife. It was good to have her home again. He swooped her up in his arms and carried her into the bedroom.

They made love tenderly that night, and this time she was the first to doze off. He watched her sleep, nestled in his arms. Whatever it took. He'd make it up to her.

Charisma needed a big favor from Tangie. She needed to know where Chase's grandfather, Stone Canyon, would be lunching that afternoon or maybe Tangie knew someone who knew someone who knew. Charisma called her on her cell.

"Hey, girl, what's up?" Tangie asked.

"I need a favor."

"What's that?"

"I need you to find out where Stone Canyon'll be lunching tomorrow."

"He doesn't always touch bases with the staff here, but I overheard the manager say that he usually lunches at O'Neil's, but let me put out a few feelers, and I'll get back to you."

"Cool."

Two hours later Tangie called Charisma on her cell. "Today and tomorrow he has a one o'clock reservation at O'Neil's and Friday he'll be at Fox's."

"I knew you'd come through for me."

"Are you sure you wanna do this?"

"Positive," Charisma said. "Payback's a bitch."

"Then, handle your business, girl." Tangie said simply. "Handle your business."

Thursday afternoon Charisma walked into O'Neil's. Luckily, the maître d' seated her in the center of the room, and she had a panoramic view of her surroundings. The clinking of the silverware only made her more nervous. A waiter came by, filled her water glass, and left a menu.

Stone walked in alone promptly at one PM. His freshly coiffed white hair made his blue eyes pop, and his blue tie only complemented them.

The maître d' seated him at a table not far from Charisma's. Charisma took a deep breath, a sip of water, and walked over to Stone's table. He was examining the menu, but looked up, sensing her intrusion.

"Stone Canyon? I'm Charisma Arquette."

"Have we met?"

"Not exactly."

"Mrs. Arquette, I don't have time for guessing games. My time is very important."

She refused to be intimidated. "This won't take long." She sat without waiting to be asked. "I'll make this short and sweet."

"I don't know what you're offering, Mrs. Arquette," he said, looking her over. "But trust me, I'm not interested."

Charisma ignored the remark. "Let me get straight to the point. Your granddaughter, Chase, is carrying my husband's child."

"You have my condolences."

"And you must feel as betrayed as I do."

"I have nothing against you people personally. I'd just rather avoid complications. You understand."

"Absolutely, but unfortunately, Mr. Canyon, it's not that simple."

"What are you talking about?"

"You thought that by forcing Chase to get rid of the baby, your lily-white family would be left intact, but guess what? You were wrong."

"I think your husband's infidelity has gone to your brain, and that's understandable. You have my sympathy, but my attorney is due any minute. We're through here."

"All that blackness you've tried to dodge has found its way back to you. Life's funny like that." She leaned in closer to Canyon, speaking barely above a whisper. "Did you know Ellis Dearborn?"

"The loan officer? My loan didn't get approved because of his ass."

"Well, he was my father. I did my homework, Mr. Canyon. You received your new heart on the same day my father passed away. You do the math. There's a chance that the heart ticking in your chest belonged to him. It's a scary thought, isn't it?"

The look of horror on Canyon's colorless face told Charisma that he would rather have been dead.

"So the next time you take a breath, maybe you should thank a black man.

"Let me leave you with this tidbit, Mr. Canyon, seeing that you're so thrilled to be alive. Most transplants last ten years, but who knows. Maybe you'll get lucky." She walked out of the restaurant and smack-dab into Nico Antonelli. "I think you should check on your client."

Nate noticed a slight change in his wife's disposition. It was a subtle change, but it was a change nonetheless. She was softening toward him, becoming more gracious. About a week later she stopped wearing her granny gowns to bed. It was a sure sign that she was allowing him back in their bed.

That night Charisma lay wide-awake as Nate slept evenly beside her. She thought about the predicament, the triangle, that she, Nate, and Chase were in. Too bad life's problems couldn't be resolved with the wave of a magic wand. It was as if they were bound to Chase against their will. Maybe there was a way to make it work for all of them. So there'd be no losers. Charisma stayed awake until the wee hours of the morning, looking at the situation from every possible angle. Somewhere around five AM, she came up with an idea.

Charisma, Tangie, and Heather enjoyed a much-needed girls' night out. Once again, Heather's car was on the blink. Tangie picked her up en route to Applebee's. They ordered drinks at the bar as they waited for a table. It was a Thursday night and luckily the wait was not too long.

As they settled into their booth, Tangie asked Charisma, "So, how did your power lunch go with Stone Canyon?"

"It went as planned."

"So what was his reaction?" Heather took a sip of her mudslide.

"You should have been a fly on the wall. The color completely left his face, and he looked like he'd seen a ghost. I waltzed out feeling like Daddy had gotten the last laugh. I was in seventh heaven until I ran smack-dab into Nico."

"Get outta here! When's the last time you saw him?" Heather asked.

"That night in his apartment. And I dodged him for about a week after that until eventually he got the message and stopped calling. If it wasn't for the fact that I was afraid Mr. Canyon might be having another heart attack, we may have actually talked. It's funny. The minute I bumped into Nico, it's like reality slapped me in the face. I suddenly realized that my father wasn't getting the last laugh, and he would not be proud of my behavior. I wasn't raised like that. I was ashamed. Looks like your girl has some growing to do."

Tangie thought for a moment. "If you ask me, it's already begun."

After appetizers, another round of drinks, and the main course, they switched gears.

"So how's Miss Upper-Middle Ass?" Tangie asked, referring to Chase.

"She's having the baby. It's final." Charisma stared straight ahead without blinking.

"Ouch." Heather shook her head.

"I thought the first year of marriage was supposed to be full of bliss. I've been gypped," Charisma sighed.

Nate came home one evening with two tickets to the Dominican Republic. "I think a little R and R would do us some good, baby."

Charisma was thrilled. "Ooh, I can hardly wait," she squealed with delight. "Why don't I finish cooking, and we'll have dinner out on the patio."

They ate underneath the stars that night, the early autumn breeze tickling their cheeks. They chatted easily as though they hadn't a care in the world. Nate poured Charisma another glass of white wine. Before they knew it, the bottle was empty. They cleared the table and loaded up the dishwasher before heading upstairs to their bedroom.

Charisma put on a sexy red satin baby doll nightie while Nate took a quick shower. She lit candles and the room was bathed in a soft glow of light. Nate gasped as he came back into the room and saw her stretched out on the bed, her curves teasing him through the satin, her nipples winking at him through the sheerness of her nightie.

He walked over to her and she gently tugged at the towel around his waist until it fell to the floor. She laughed softly and rolled over onto her back, pulling her knees up and opening her legs.

They made love that night, and it was so slow and so good that tears rolled down Charisma's face as she and Nate came. They lay together for a moment, enjoying the silence.

Finally, Charisma spoke. "I've been doing a lot of thinking, babe, about us and Chase and the baby. I was wondering if maybe, just maybe, you and I could—I mean—if I could adopt the baby and—"

Nate sat up in bed. "Baby, are you serious?"

"Yes, I've given it a lot of thought. I mean, I can't have children, but this is *your* child, and we can give it a good life."

"I know Chase is not your favorite person in the world. Are you sure you want to raise her child?"

"I want to raise *your* child, Nate," she said. "How can I love you and not love your flesh and blood?"

Nate looked at his wife in awe. "You wanna know something, Mrs. Arquette? You are truly amazing, and I am truly blessed."

* * *

A week later Nate and Charisma were on a flight bound for the Dominican Republic. They spent five fun-filled days and four glorious nights Jet Skiing, horseback riding, and playing in the pool. On their last night on the island they went dancing at an intimate little nightclub where they played only slow jams. Then, arm in arm, they went back to their room and did what they did best—twice.

Charisma and Nate got up the next morning, had a nice leisurely breakfast, and headed for the airport. Once home, Nate called Chase. Without going into too much detail, he told her that they needed to sit down and talk. She agreed to stop by their house the following day.

Charisma was on pins and needles that night, anxious about their meeting with Chase in the morning. Nate tried reassuring her that things would be all right, but she tossed and turned all night and woke up exhausted Sunday morning.

They agreed that Nate would do most of the talking. Chase arrived on time. She waddled through the door, and they all sat in the living room. Charisma offered Chase decaf, which she politely refused. For a moment, no one spoke.

"Chase, I swear you've gotten huge since I saw you last," Nate said, taking a sip of coffee. "How's the baby doing?"

"The baby's just fine. I brought the latest sonogram." Chase reached inside her purse for the picture. "But I still don't wanna know the sex. There are so few surprises in life." She leaned forward and handed Nate the sonogram.

"I know what you mean," he agreed, looking at the photo of the baby before handing it to Charisma, who sat next to him on the sofa. Charisma looked at the sonogram, nodded, and handed it back to Chase.

"So you're still set on adoption?" he asked Chase.

"Yes," she said.

"That's why we called you over. Charisma and I have a proposition for you. We'd like to adopt the baby," he told her.

Chase chose her words carefully. "Charisma, let's be honest, okay? There is no love lost between us. None. And now you want to adopt my baby? Why?"

"Chase, you're absolutely right. We've had our moments—lots of them. And when I first found out you were pregnant, I could have killed you. But that baby you're carrying is also my husband's. Rather than having it raised by complete strangers, we would rather keep the baby in the family. True, you and I have had our differences, but let's not make an innocent child suffer because of it. Especially when there's a better solution."

"I think I'll take that decaf now," Chase said, rubbing her belly.

"No problem. Are you hungry?" Charisma asked her.

"I stay hungry. Pregnancy is unbelievable. No wonder I'm big as a house." Chase shook her head. "And I'm not due until December."

"You sit here and relax, and I'll whip us up some breakfast." Charisma stood.

"Is there anything I can help you with?" Chase asked.

"No, I'm good. You relax," Charisma said.

Charisma prepared fresh fruit, omelets, salmon cakes, English muffins, juice, and coffee. They ate in the dining room. Chase ate generous portions of everything.

Neither Nate nor Charisma pressured her in any way. They just let the conversation flow naturally, discussing work issues, the latest movies, and current events.

"Charisma, that was delicious. I can barely boil water, but you are some cook." Chase smiled.

"Glad you enjoyed it," Charisma said, sipping her juice.

Chase glanced at her Movado watch. "I hate to eat and

run, but I don't want to be late for an appointment. I'm learning that the world doesn't revolve around Chase Martini." She chuckled lightly. "And I'll think seriously about your proposition. Honestly." She got up from the table and checked her watch again.

Nate and Charisma escorted Chase to the front door.

"I'll get back to you both as soon as I can," Chase promised.

"We appreciate that," Nate said.

"Thanks." Charisma smiled. She closed the door behind her and breathed a sigh of relief.

"Well, we've done our part," Nate assured her.

"All we can do now is hope and pray," Charisma added.

Two weeks passed and no word from Chase. Charisma was a bundle of nerves. What if Chase said no? Then again, maybe no news was good news. Charisma had only mentioned their desire to adopt the baby to her mother, not wanting to jinx anything.

Jena had a heart-to-heart with her daughter. "I know you want a baby, sweetheart, but can you deal with raising a child of Nate's with another woman?"

"I think I can. As a matter of fact, I know I can."

"Then you have my blessing, and I look forward to my first grand."

Nate and Charisma ran out to When We Were Queens. Cinderella had developed an award-winning men's line that kept Nate's face baby smooth and free from razor bumps. He didn't mind dropping by the shop to replenish his supply, and he didn't mind investing the time, effort, and money required to maintain his appearance.

They had just returned home and were sitting down to dinner in the kitchen when they got the call.

"Hi, Nate, it's Chase."

"Just a second, Chase." He put the phone next to Charisma's ear so that she could hear too.

"I hope I didn't catch you two at a bad time," Chase began.

"Not at all," Nate and Charisma said.

"First of all, I owe you both an apology for taking the Madison account from you, Charisma, and making your life miserable," Chase admitted.

"Apology accepted, Chase," Charisma said.

"Thank you." Chase paused. "I guess I'll keep this short and sweet. I've decided that you can adopt the baby. At least I'll know that she's loved."

"She?" Charisma asked.

"Yeah, it's a girl."

"Oh my God. Thank you so much, Chase. How can I ever repay you?" Charisma asked.

"I feel that you'll be a good mother to my child, but Charisma, every time you look into my child's eyes, I want you to remember that all white women aren't bitches."

Chase was right. Charisma would never again refer to her as Miss Crappuccino or Upper-Middle ass. She began to cry tears of joy.

Nate spoke for them both. "Thank you, Chase. Thank you. Our attorneys will be in touch."

"I think it's best if we handle this as soon as possible. I'll see you both soon," Chase said before they all hung up.

The following week they all sat down with their attorneys to sign the legal adoption papers pending the paternity-test results. Charisma was only slightly surprised to see Nico representing Chase. Shaking both Nate and Charisma's hands, he conducted himself like the professional he was. She was grateful for that.

After the papers were signed, Nate went to bring the car around. Charisma and Nico had a moment alone.

"Listen, Nico. I'm sorry things didn't work out for us," she said.

"Don't worry about it," Nico said with his hands in his pocket. "I'm a big boy. I wish you and your husband all the best."

"Thank you, Nico."

32

Heather

Heather's scale had reached a new low when she stepped on it that morning. She was pleasantly surprised to have lost another four pounds. That brought her grand total to forty-two pounds. She was amazed. She jumped off, showered, and headed to work.

She parked her car on Hillside Avenue. By the time she walked into the library, she was huffing and puffing, trying to catch her breath. Although her breathing finally returned to normal, the pain in her chest remained. Heather tried to dismiss it, blaming it on her busy schedule and working out four days a week. By early afternoon, she was not doing any better. She told her boss she was exhausted and drove herself home. Heather went straight to bed, and slept all the way through the next morning. She didn't even hear her mother come in the night before. She was out for the count. When she did finally wake up, it was well past ten. There was no way she could make it in to work, so she called in. She dragged herself out of bed, barely able to lift her lead-like legs off the floor. What the hell was going on? Heather made herself a light breakfast—toast and coffee—and threw it right up. She was starving, but she couldn't keep anything down. She wanted to take some ibuprofen for her splitting headache, but couldn't on an empty stomach. So she prepared a cool washcloth from the bathroom for her forehead and went back to bed.

By the time her mother returned home that evening, Heather had a low-grade fever. Leola insisted that she come upstairs and get in her old bed. Leaning on her mother for support, she climbed the basement stairs. Settled in her old bedroom, Heather managed to keep a half bowl of chicken soup down—for a minute, anyway. She had just enough time to make it to the bathroom, but unfortunately, she couldn't get the toilet seat up fast enough. She vomited all over the toilet. Leola insisted that she get right back in bed, that she'd handle the cleanup herself. Too exhausted to argue, Heather gladly went back to her room and drifted off to sleep.

This time she awoke to the delicious aroma of her mother's baked chicken, mashed potatoes, and string beans. She was famished, having not had a real meal in two days. Her mother brought her a small plate of dinner on a tray, and she tried to eat as best she could. Moments later she was once again headed for the bathroom, but luckily this time it was a false alarm. Relieved, she headed back to bed.

Her mother came to check on her with a thermometer in hand. Heather's temperature had gone up another degree. Leola sponged her daughter down with alcohol, trying to make her as comfortable as possible. When she returned half an hour later, Heather's fever had jumped to 102 degrees, and her pulse was racing. It was time to go to the emergency room. She went down to Heather's apartment, grabbed some underclothes, a pair of yoga pants, a top and sneakers, and quickly helped her dress.

She drove Heather to Jamaica Hospital's emergency room. Having worked in the emergency room several years ago,

Leola was familiar with the staff. After waiting a few minutes, she was relieved for the prompt attention Heather received. Shortly after, a bed was found for her. Heather changed into a hospital gown, and a nurse took her blood pressure. The attending physician, Dr. Voltra, came by to prepare her chart. He spoke with Leola and she filled him in on Heather's condition. Then, he turned his attention to Heather. Did she have any known drug allergies? Was she pregnant? What medication, if any, was she currently on?

Heather hated to admit in her mother's presence that she was taking Z3K without being under a doctor's supervision, but her health was obviously being compromised. She sighed and grabbed the railing for support, her damp hair matted along her forehead. She couldn't bear to look in her mother's eyes, preferring to watch Dr. Voltra instead.

"I've been purging and taking Z3K for a couple of months. It's a diet pill that—"

"I know all about Z3K," Dr. Voltra assured her, making notes.

"Well, I don't," Leola said. "What the hell is Z three K?"

"It's the latest miracle diet pill on the black market. It's not FDA approved and for good reason. Based on preliminary testing, it carries a high risk of heart failure, diabetes, and stroke," Dr. Voltra told her. "And bingeing and purging also carry serious health risks."

"Heather, what the hell were you thinking?" Leola asked her daughter. "Are you crazy?"

"I just wanted to lose some weight," Heather insisted. "I was so tired of being fat."

"Then you cut calories, exercise, see a nutritionist. You don't try to kill yourself with pills, for goodness sake. You could've been killed. What's wrong with you?" Leola shook her head. "And purging?"

"I'm sorry." Heather began to cry. "I'm sorry."

"Okay," Dr. Voltra said. "Hindsight is twenty-twenty. Let's

bring that fever down and get you well. Heather, we'll be doing some blood work, we'll start you on an IV, and admit you as soon as a bed is available. Hang in there. Leola, can I see you for a moment?" he asked.

Leola joined the doctor a few yards away. Heather tried to make out what they were saying. It was hard, especially when another doctor was being paged over the PA system. Leola and the doctor spoke for several minutes before Leola returned to her daughter's side.

Three hours later Heather was admitted to five east. Once settled into her room, she insisted that her mother go home and get some rest. Her fever had broken and she was resting comfortably. Heather was hooked up to a heart monitor and every few hours a nurse would come in to check on her.

Early the next morning Heather got up and headed for the bathroom. Like all women forced to wash in a basin, she washed as high as possible, as low as possible, and then she just washed possible. It was bad enough washing with an IV attached. She thanked God that she wasn't on her period. That would have been a real mess. Heather was scheduled for a battery of tests. Wearing the same yucky green hospital gown that covered her body the night before in emergency, Heather made her way to the stress-test clinic with the assistance of an orderly named Felipe. The orderly safely secured her in a wheelchair before wheeling her into the elevator for the second floor. Still connected to an IV, Heather was starving, since she hadn't eaten anything since a bland chicken and mixed vegetable dinner six hours earlier. Her stomach churned as Felipe helped her out of the wheelchair and into a wooden seat outside the clinic.

After about fifteen minutes, Heather was called inside. The nurse helped her with her IV bag and led her into the room, which consisted of four treadmills. The nurse hooked up several monitors to Heather's chest and back before the testing began. She explained exactly what the test would consist of as she helped Heather climb up on the treadmill. The entire exam was over before Heather knew it. In fact, she waited longer for Felipe to return with the wheelchair than she did for the entire test to end. She watched an old rerun of *The Jeffersons* on the wide screen television in the waiting area with the other patients. A couple of nurses were chowing down on pancakes and sausages at the front desk. They smacked, swallowed, and slurped coffee, apparently oblivious to Heather's famished state.

Finally, Felipe arrived along with her ride. He quickly checked her identification bracelet, grabbed her chart from the nurse's station, helped her into the wheelchair, and together they headed back to five east. To say that Heather was relieved that breakfast was being served was an understatement. When she returned to her room, the bed had already been made and two fresh hospital gowns lay on the pillow. The bed next to hers was still vacant. She had the room to herself. Just as she was about to sit on the side of the bed, there was a light tap at the door.

Heather was never so happy to see her mother in her life. Carrying a large tote bag and dressed in her nurse's uniform, a smiling Leola walked in. She placed the bag in a nearby chair and gave Heather a big hug. Heather gave her mom a big, fat kiss before releasing her.

She grabbed the tote from the chair, rummaging through its contents. She was anxious to discard the hospital's best and change into her own pajamas. She quickly closed the curtain surrounding her bed for privacy. With Leola's help, it only took a few moments to slip into her pajama bottom and top and rearrange the IV bag. She was thankful that Leola had brought her personal toiletries and her comb and brush, which she immediately put to use. Her mother had even thrown in a couple of issues of *Ebony* and *Essence* magazines and a container of disinfectant wipes.

Heather placed the tote in her lower nightstand drawer, but not before Leola grabbed the disinfectant wipes and wiped down the nightstand and the bed. She then headed for the bathroom to sanitize the toilet, the face bowl and all the fixtures, as well as the doorknobs and light switches.

"I called your boss and told her you were in the hospital," Leola said.

"Did she give you the third degree?"

"No, I just told her that I rushed you to emergency, and that you were admitted."

"Oh, what time is it?" Heather asked.

"Ooh, I almost forgot." Leola reached inside her pants pocket and gave Heather her watch.

"Thanks."

It was a little past eight. Heather fastened the watch onto her right wrist as breakfast arrived. "I am so hungry," she admitted to the server, who grinned in return.

"That's a good sign," Leola told her daughter. "Here, get back in bed." She helped Heather adjust the table to a comfortable height and removed the cover from the plate.

Heather was given a low-sodium, low-fat meal. She frowned at the sight of the lukewarm oatmeal, a soft-boiled egg, and a slice of wheat bread. There was a pat of butter, a container of orange juice, and a carton of skim milk on the side.

"After all the weight I've lost, you'd think they wouldn't mind giving me something that would stick to my ribs." Heather sucked her teeth.

"I'm sure they're waiting for the test results before they decide on your dietary needs."

Heather tried to enjoy the meal as best she could, but it wasn't easy. "What time does the TV and phone man come?"

"Probably around ten. I'll leave you some money and tell them at the desk that you want your phone and TV connected." She handed Heather a twenty.

"Thanks, Ma."

"Well, I better get to work. Have one of the nurses call me when your doctor comes in. I want to hear what he has to say."

"Okay, Ma."

"Love you, gotta run. Now make sure you eat." She gave Heather a quick hug before opening the blinds to let the sun in.

"See you later," Heather said as she swallowed a spoonful of bland oatmeal. Barely touching her eggs, she took a few sips of the warm orange juice and called it a done deal. She laid back in bed, trying to rest her mind. She had never been hospitalized before and besides being completely bored, she was worried about her health. She wasn't in any real pain, but she felt a deep sense of pressure with every breath she took. Sure, she now looked better in her jeans, but at what cost?

Heather closed her eyes and tried to relax, blocking out the noise coming from the nearby nurses' station. Apparently, she had dozed off, awakening to the sound of a male voice. It was the phone-TV man. He was a short, middle-aged man dressed in a dark blue uniform.

"You want to be connected?" he asked.

"Yes," Heather answered. "How much is it?"

"Twenty dollars a day to hook up both."

"All right," she said simply, giving him the twenty-dollar bill her mother had given her. "How long will it take?"

"Give me about fifteen minutes." He reached in his left chest pocket for a pen and receipt book and handed her a receipt. On his way out, he nearly collided with the food server, who had returned to pick up Heather's breakfast tray. Evidently, they knew each other, stopping for a few moments to say hello.

"You hardly ate your breakfast," the twentysomething girl

said to Heather. She was from the islands. Heather couldn't tell which one.

"I guess I wasn't hungry."

"Nothing like home cooking, eh?" she said and they both laughed. "I know it's hard, but eat, get your strength back, and you'll be outta here in no time. Okay?"

Heather nodded. "From your lips to God's ears."

"Take care, now." She smiled on her way out.

Heather reached down, opened the nightstand drawer, and pulled out the disinfectant wipes. She proceeded to wipe down the telephone and the remote. She was truly her mother's daughter. Thank goodness the TV was on. She watched a few cooking shows before getting bored. Unfortunately, daytime TV didn't boast the most intriguing shows. She began flipping channels again before settling on one of the soaps. Funny, she hadn't seen that particular show in years, but she was able to catch up on a couple of the story lines.

One of the nurses came in to change the IV solution, advising her that the doctor was making rounds and would be in to see her shortly. Evidently, by hospital standards, *shortly* meant over an hour. She called her mother, who arranged to have someone cover for her and was there in no time. Heather had lunch, more bland food. This time it was fish and stewed tomatoes. Heather was not amused. How was she supposed to keep her strength up on this stuff when she could barely keep it down?

Heather got up to use the bathroom, fussing with each step she took. When she returned, she was relieved to see that the doctor had arrived. Dr. Goldberg was a slim white man of medium build. With a white lab coat over his suit and a stethoscope around his neck, he could have just returned from vacation in the sun.

"This must be our patient," he said as Heather got back

in bed. "I'm Dr. Goldberg, and you are a very lucky young lady."

"She certainly is," Leola said. "I'm her mother, Leola Grey. I work in neonatal."

"Nice to meet you, Mrs. Grey. Can I be blunt with you?"

"Please do," she said simply.

"As someone in the medical profession, I'm sure you know just how potientally dangerous your daughter's condition can be." He turned to Heather. "We found large traces of Z3K in your bloodstream. Now we've run a battery of tests, particularly on your major organs—your heart, kidneys, liver, and we're astounded." He paused momentarily. "There has been no damage to your organs. You are very, very fortunate. The bulimia caused a slight irregularity in your heart rate, but we expect that to return to normal."

Heather and Leola breathed a collective sigh of relief.

"I would like to keep you for another day or so just to make certain I can give you a clean bill of health. By the way, how did you even get the Z3K?" he asked her.

"Over the Internet," she said, ashamed.

"No one can force you to take care of yourself, Miss Grey, but if you continue abusing your body with this drug, there is no guarantee that you'll be as fortunate with the outcome next time."

"Understood, Dr. Goldberg," Heather said.

"What a relief," Leola said to Heather as he left. She walked over to her daughter's bedside and grabbed both her hands. "Let's pray," she said simply. With eyes closed they bowed their heads. "Father God, we thank you for this day and the blessings of this day. We thank you for the good news we've just received, and we know it's just by your grace and mercy that it is so. Lord, I ask that you give Heather a spirit of gratitude. Let her learn to be satisfied and happy with herself, to love herself, to stop tearing herself down and picking herself apart. She's beautiful just as she is. Others see that. Let her see that as well. Bless us Lord, and keep your loving arms of protection around us. In Jesus' name we ask all these blessings. Thank God. Amen."

Heather began to cry as her mother gave her a big hug.

"Before I leave, I have something for you." Leola reached into her purse and handed Heather a white business-sized envelope marked with her name in her mother's handwriting.

"What's this?" Heather asked.

"Something that I think you could really use right about now. It was in your diaper bag when I brought you home. I love you, Heather. Call me later."

"Okay," Heather said as she watched Leola leave and opened the envelope. Inside was a smaller, white envelope apparently yellowed with age. The word *BABY* was printed in large block letters on the envelope. Heather stared at the unfamiliar handwriting, somewhat puzzled as she opened the envelope's contents, a neatly folded two-page letter written on plain, white stationery.

Heather began to read the letter.

To my dear daughter, if you are reading this letter, I am assuming that you are all grown up. How I wish I could be with you today to share your joys as well as your sorrows. Unfortunately, that was not meant to be, and it hurts like hell. I wish things had been different, but what will be will be.

I met your father when I was a junior in high school. I had just turned sixteen, and he was a senior. I took one look at him and fell madly in love. Being that we lived in a small, racist town, we kept our dates a secret. After a year, he decided to join the

Marines. I was devastated. Our last night together I gave myself to him totally. That's when you were conceived. When my parents found out I was pregnant, they threatened to disown me. Your grandparents are good people, but they're old-fashioned. The thought of their underage daughter having a black baby was too much for them. When your father came home on a pass thirty days later, I gave him the news. He was elated, promising to marry me and make me a military wife. As much as I loved your father, I could not abandon my family. I let my parents talk me into giving you up for adoption.

Please forgive me. Maybe one day I can forgive myself, but not today. Maybe tomorrow or next month or next year, but not today. Today holds too much pain. Maybe tomorrow will be different. Pray for me.

Heather turned to the last page of the letter. It was blank, but an old photo fell out onto her lap. She turned the photo over. Nothing. She flipped it over again. It was an outdated photo of a biracial couple, her biological parents. The white girl and black guy were obviously very much in love. His arms were possessively wrapped around her middle. They were both laughing. Heather examined their faces. She was a combination of them both—her father's eyes and eyebrows and, oh my goodness, her mother's nose. She was shocked. The nose she had thought so often about going under the knife for. The nose that had brought her dismay each time she looked in the mirror was her only link to her birth mother. She had come *this* close to getting rid of it, cutting her mother out of her life forever.

Heather sobbed openly. She reached for a tissue from the nightstand, crying even harder at the irony of it all. Thank

God, Dr. Speller's prices were too expensive and Dr. Taylor wasn't scalpel-happy. She was spared from making one of the biggest mistakes of her life.

Heather gently refolded the letter and tucked it into the *BABY* envelope along with the photo of her birth parents. She slid the envelope inside the pillowcase, protecting it with her body as she lowered her head onto the pillow. Curled up in the fetal position, she cried herself to sleep, awakening an hour later by the sound of her ringing telephone.

It was Charisma. "Your mother called me. Are you okay?" she asked Heather.

"I'm going to be all right, thank goodness."

"What happened?"

"It'a a long story."

"Well, give me the abbreviated version."

"I was bingeing and purging and taking these illegal diet pills."

"Heather, no."

"Yeah, I got them off the Internet."

"What possessed you to try diet pills over the Internet?"

"An old high school classmate of mine took them and lost over eighty pounds. So I figured, why not? Her brother's a pharmacist, and he got them for me at first."

"So that's how you shrunk," Charisma figured it out.

"Exactly. And I'd make myself throw up."

"Wait a minute. Is that why we found a toothbrush and toothpaste in your beach bag?"

"Yeah."

So if your classmate's brother's a pharmacist, why did you have to buy them over the Internet?"

"She tried to blackmail me into sleeping with her for more pills, so I cut out the middleman and ordered them myself," Heather told her.

"Wow, I had no idea. You could write a book. How'd you end up in the hospital?"

"I came down with a high fever, and my heart wouldn't stop racing. My mother rushed me to emergency. Thank God there's been no damage to my internal organs. I'll probably be released tomorrow."

"You're blessed," Charisma said.

"You got that right," Heather agreed.

"Well, I'm glad you're all right. I hope you learned your lesson."

"Trust me. I have."

"Good. I'll fill Tangie in. We were worried sick when your mother called us. Are you up to visitors later?"

"I'm actually tired, and you two have been working all day. I'm okay. Why don't you come see me after I'm discharged?"

"Okay. Call me if you need anything," Charisma said.

"Thanks," Heather said before hanging up.

There was a knock on her door. It was Dr. Taylor, the plastic surgeon. She was as beautiful as ever. "Can I come in?" she asked Heather.

"Of course," Heather told her, sitting up in bed.

"So how's our patient doing today?" she asked, taking a seat opposite her bed.

"Much better. How'd you know I was here?"

"I didn't. When you missed your second appointment, my nurse got an e-mail that you had been admitted. I came to check on you."

"Thank you," Heather said sincerely.

"I'm not surprised to see you here. You could have been killed."

"I know." Heather nodded slowly. "Thank God all my tests came back negative."

"Yes," Dr. Taylor said simply. "Thank God. How are you feeling?"

"Like I need a long vacation." She laughed.

"That sounds like an excellent idea. Can you take some time off from work?"

"Yeah, I have plenty of vacation time."

"Then I think you should make that happen. It'll do you a world of good. And do me a favor, and keep in touch. Okay?"

"Okay, Dr. Taylor," she promised.

"Take care of yourself." Dr. Taylor stood to leave. "Oh, and Heather, as far as that pharmacist is concerned, that's all been taking care of," she assured her. "Get some rest."

Heather leaned back in bed and closed her eyes. The last sound she remembered hearing was the clicking of Dr. Taylor's heels as she walked down the hall. Heather slept for several hours, oblivious to the delivery of her lunch.

Awakened by the sounds of moaning and groaning, she learned that she was no longer alone. She had a roommate. She was a young woman in her early twenties. She was suffering with kidney stones. In between moans, she ate lunch. Heather looked across at her, giving her a sympathetic smile. She returned Heather's smile and introduced herself as Tammy. Tammy was a petite, white woman with a long ponytail.

"I feel for you," she told Tammy.

"Thanks," Tammy said, breaking out into a coughing spell before taking a sip of water. "How long have you been here?"

"Since last night," Heather said, removing the cover from her lunch. "I'm supposed to be discharged tomorrow."

"Good for you," Tammy said. She took a forkful of spinach and rolled her eyes. *Bon appetit.*

"Tell me it's not that bad," Heather begged.

"It's worse," Tammy said, and they both laughed.

Heather sampled the meat loaf, the spinach, and the mashed potatoes. Tammy was right. Thank goodness there wasn't too much they could do to fruit cocktail. That went down easily.

Tammy was a talker. Heather welcomed her conversation, but eventually succumbed to sleep. The nurse came in to remove Heather's IV bag. It was a relief being IV-free. Using the bathroom was once again a breeze.

Heather checked her watch. Her mother would be stopping by any minute on her way home from work. As if on cue, Leola walked through the door. She greeted Tammy on the way to Heather's side of the room, and immediately noticed that the IV was gone.

"That's a good sign," she told Heather. "I guess you're going home tomorrow, kiddo."

"I can't wait," Heather admitted. "You must be tired. Why don't you go on home, and I'll see you tomorrow?"

"Are you sure?" Leola asked.

"Absolutely. I'm fine, Ma."

"Okay. Call me if you need me." She stood to leave.

Heather slept like a baby that night, waking up only when the nurse came to take her blood pressure.

"How was it?" Heather asked.

"Normal," the nurse responded.

"Good," Heather said, getting reacquainted with the sheets.

"Dr. Goldberg has scheduled some more tests for you. The technician will take you down to the second floor tomorrow morning around seven."

"Okay," Heather sighed. "Do you know if I'll be discharged tomorrow?"

"It's up to your doctor. If all your tests come back normal, probably so."

The next morning Heather brushed her teeth, washed up, combed her hair, and put on a fresh pair of pajamas.

She was ready before the technician came to get her. She was only gone for about an hour.

When she returned, her bed was made. She smiled to herself. It was nice to be going home. Her tests must have come back negative. It was probably not premature to start packing her bags. She smiled as she threw items into the tote bag, humming to herself until she realized something was gravely wrong.

The photo of her parents that she placed inside her pillowcase along with the letter from her mother was gone. Tammy was awake. She asked her how long it had been since the housekeeper left the room. She estimated about fifteen minutes, but she admitted that between naps it was difficult to tell.

Panicking, Heather could have kicked herself for being so careless. Her picture was gone, damn it. She ran to the front desk in hopes of catching housekeeping. Too late. She dialed housekeeping and was told in no uncertain terms that there was no way to reclaim individual pillowcases. Hysterical, she called her mother, but unfortunately there was nothing Leola could do. Heather was devastated.

33

Tangie

The bed had a serious grip on Tangie. She lay in bed that morning fighting the sun's rays, but they were determined to filter through her blinds and win. She had hung out with Charisma and Heather the night before, inviting them to her pity party because she wasn't celebrating Tony's birthday party with him. She had called him several times to wish him a happy birthday, but he hadn't returned any of her calls.

"Think of it as one day out of three hundred and sixty-five." Heather had said.

"And tomorrow it'll be all over," Charisma had added.

Tangie opened her eyes, thankful that it was, indeed, all behind her. Now, she could go on with her life. She grabbed the remote from the nightstand and turned on the news, wiping the sleep from her eyes. She stifled a yawn. Today's weather called for rain, as did everyday that week. Great.

She turned up the volume as breaking news and a familiar face flashed on the screen. *"Thirty-year-old Olivia Wells is in a coma clinging to life after being shot by a bullet police say was intended for her companion at Spot in Mid-*

town last night. Onlookers saw the two were celebrating at the posh Manhattan nightclub when a fight broke out. Details are still sketchy, but cops say no arrests have been made. Her companion was unharmed. Channel Seven will bring you updates as more details become available."

Tangie couldn't recall where she knew her from, but she looked so familiar. Think, Tangie, think. Just as her feet hit the floor, it came to her. She was Tony's friend. That was the woman he introduced her to in the parking lot after the Stephanie Mills concert.

"Oh my God," she said, her hand shaking as she raised it to her mouth. "Oh my God," she repeated, plopping back down on the bed to steady herself. Tangie took quick, short breaths as she processed the information.

She picked up the phone to dial Tony, but then replaced the receiver just as quickly. She had to start thinking with her head, not her heart. She picked up the phone a second time, but dialed her mother's number instead.

"Hello?" Della Winterhope said.

"Ma, it's me," she began to cry.

"Tangie, what's wrong?"

"Can I come over? It's an emergency."

"Honey, what's wrong? Are you okay?"

"I'll be right over. I'm on my way." Tangie hung up. She quickly brushed her teeth, washed up, and grabbed a Yankee baseball cap to put over her wrapped hair. She snatched her purse, a raincoat to put over her pajamas, and an umbrella before heading out the door.

Wiping away tears all the way to her mother's, she ran two red lights before parking in front of the familiar brick home. She let herself in and collapsed in her mother's arms. Tangie sobbed openly as Della Winterhope took her umbrella and helped her out of her coat.

"Let it out," Della said, guiding Tangie to the sectional. They both sat as Della rocked her daughter in her arms.

"Tony's girlfriend," Tangie said between sobs. "Shot . . . coma."

"What?" Della got up and returned with a box of tissue.

Tangie took a tissue and blew her nose. She then took a deep breath and spoke. "Remember I told you I met Tony's new girlfriend at a concert a while back? Well, this morning I turned on the news and there's a story about her. She and a friend were out clubbing and she was accidentally shot. It had to be Tony. There was a cake in the background, and yesterday was his birthday. I know it was him. She's in a coma, Ma, a coma. If he and I were still together, that could have been me." The tears began to flow again.

"Are you sure it was him?"

Tangie nodded, unable to speak.

Just then the doorbell rang and Della got up to answer the door. It was Tangie's father. He put his dripping wet umbrella in the stand by the door and sat on the sofa next to his daughter.

"You were so upset that after I hung up with you, I called your father," Della explained.

Tangie began to cry all over again. "Tony and his girlfriend were out celebrating last night, and she was shot. Now she's clinging to life. That could've been me, Daddy. That could've been me." She grabbed another tissue.

"Wait a minute. I think that story's in this morning's paper. They were in the city, right?" Ted Winterhope asked.

"Uh-huh. At the Spot nightclub," Tangie told him.

"Yeah, it's in the *Daily News*. The bullet was meant for him. They didn't identify who the man was. That was Tony?" he asked.

"Yeah," Tangie said.

Ted took his daughter in her arms, resting her head on his shoulders. "Sweetheart, I never told you this before. I hate to say this, but I knew something like this would happen."

Tangie sat up straight, meeting her father's gaze. "What do you mean?"

"When you and Tony got engaged, he and I had a man-to-man talk. I made him promise me that if your safety was ever an issue, he would break it off with you. He sat down in my house, looked my dead in the eye, and agreed to never compromise your safety. I know you love him, but he's in a dirty, dangerous, cutthroat business, sweetheart. He's not the one for you," he told his daughter.

"So when he broke the engagement and said he wasn't ready for marriage, he wasn't telling me the truth." It was all beginning to make sense to Tangie.

"Tangie, we love you. We're just thankful that Tony is a man of his word. Tony loved you enough to let you go." He kissed her on the cheek, got up, and went into the other room.

"I know it hurts, Tangie," Della told her daughter. "Loving someone you can't have. It feels like a sick joke, but in time, the pain will fade. One day you'll meet someone who'll bring you joy. You'll look back on all of this and all the good memories you have of Tony will warm your heart. Remember how happy you were when you and Charisma got accepted to Howard University?"

Tangie smiled at the recollection and nodded.

"And what did I tell you, sweetheart, when you didn't get those football tickets to the first home game, and you cried for a week?"

"You told me to save my tears for more important things," Tangie recalled.

"That's right, honey. Tangie?" She hugged her tightly. "You can cry now."

With her mother by her side, Tangie let it all out—deep, gut-wrenching sobs that reverberated from her core. As much as she loved her father, she was grateful that he had given her time alone with her mother.

After half an hour or so, he called them into the kitchen. The table was adorned with Tangie's favorites—Western omelets, home fries, buttermilk pancakes with warm cinnamon syrup, and beef bacon.

"Wow, Daddy, you've been busy," Tangie brightened.

"Hungry?" he asked them both.

"Uh-huh," they said in unison as they sat.

"Good, there's coffee too." Ted brought the pot to the table and said grace. "Precious Lord, in the name of Jesus, we thank you for this day, for our life and health. Look down on Tangie, Lord. Give her the strength to get through this. Make her see that in spite of all the pain she's dealing with, it's still a beautiful world. Bless her from the crown of her head to the soles of her feet. And God, we ask a special blessing for Tony and his companion. He was selfless enough to let her go, and for that we are eternally grateful. Keep your loving arms of protection around him. We ask all these blessings in your precious name. Thank God. Amen."

As good as it was, Tangie could barely finish what was on her plate. After a few bites she put her fork down. She had no appetite.

"Don't force yourself, honey," Della said, gazing into her daughter's eyes.

"It's delicious, Dad. Really," Tangie insisted.

"It's okay, honey. You're old man has a thick skin." Ted laughed it off. He looked across the table at Della. "Should we tell her?" he asked.

"Tell me what?" Tangie asked, looking from one to another.

Della finally spoke. "Your father and I are back together."

Tangie's jaw dropped. "What? When did all this happen?"

"Last month," Della said.

"What about Blanche?" Tangie asked, referring to the stepmother from hell.

"I've filed for divorce. I thought you'd be happy," Ted said.

"I am." Tangie laughed. "I just don't believe it. You guys really caught me off guard. So you're getting married again?"

"Maybe. We're living together for now," Ted admitted, grinning.

"Here?" Tangie glanced at her mother.

Della nodded.

Tangie jumped up and hugged both her parents before sitting back down. "Wow, you two are full of surprises. I'm starving. Let's eat."

"You two are not going to believe this," Tangie told Heather and Charisma as they lounged around Heather's living room. "The woman who was shot the other night in the club in Manhattan is Tony's friend."

"What?" Heather said.

"And they were aiming for Tony."

"Oh my God," Charisma exclaimed.

"They never mentioned the man's name. Not even in the papers. Are you sure it's him?" Heather asked.

"But they splattered *her* picture all over the news. Remember I told you Tony introduced us after the concert?" Tangie reminded them.

"Oh, that's right," Charisma said.

"They were out celebrating and you know his birthday was the other day," Tangie said.

Heather didn't want to believe it. "Not necessarily. Maybe—"

"No, Heather, no maybe, nothing. It's him. Trust me. The only reason they haven't identified him is because they don't want to blow his cover." Tangie had tears in her eyes. "And do you know the *real* reason why he broke it off?" she continued. "After he proposed he and my father made an agreement that he would break off the engagement before he let any harm come my way. So apparently when things got too close for comfort, he had to let me go." Tangie wiped away a fresh batch of tears.

"Whew, that's deep," Charisma said.

"I've never been loved like that," Heather admitted.

"Maybe not by a man, but what about your birth mother? She loved you enough to let you go," Charisma reminded her.

"Maybe," Heather said, not entirely convinced.

"Well, I'll tell you one thing. It hurts like hell." Tangie wiped her nose with the back of her hand.

"But consider the alternative, sweetie." Charisma gently stroked her hair. "We need you around. It's too soon to break up Howard's Angels."

Tangie tried to smile, recalling their college nicknames. She brightened suddenly. "But I have some good news too. You're not going to believe this. My parents are back together."

"Say what?" Heather asked, caught off guard.

"You heard me," Tangie said.

"Guess it was a hot summer in more ways than one," Heather said, grinning.

"Apparently so," Tangie admitted.

"I'm glad somebody's having a happy ending. Something tells me I may never see Tony again. Life's funny. I remember him telling me that one day I'd understand completely why we weren't meant to be. And now that I do, I may never get the chance to thank him," Tangie sighed.

"He know's your grateful, Tangie. He knows," Heather reassured her.

Tangie was at home crying her eyes out and listening to Chaka Khan's "The End of a Love Affair." She was still in love with Tony. It hadn't gotten any easier. They say old lovers make the best friends, but she didn't know if she'd ever see him again.

Olivia was gone. It could just have easily been Tangie lying cold in the ground, but God was merciful. Ironically, the breakup saved her life. She finally got it. Rejection is protection against anything that was not for her highest good, and the surest way to lose something is to crave it too intensely. She wiped more tears away.

The doorbell rang. She smoothed her ponytail and answered the door, not expecting anyone. It was Tony.

"Hi," he said simply.

"Hi," she said, pausing. "Come on in. Can I get you anything?"

"No, I'm fine."

They sat in silence for a moment on the sofa. "You've been crying." He took her hands in his. "I'll be away on assignment indefinintely. I came to say good-bye."

"I see."

"The past two weeks have been crazy."

"Yes."

"But I had to see you. I came by to tell you that you are a quality person, and I'll always have a special place in my heart for you, Tangela."

"But not in your bed, right?"

"Tangela, don't be like that," he said softly. "Don't you know that I will *always* love you. *Always.* I will do anything to protect you, even if that means letting you go. But I will find a way to let you know that I am always with you."

He got up and headed for her CDs. He thumbed through them until he found what he was looking for: Tony Bennett and Juanes's duet of "The Shadow of Your Smile."

"Dance with me, Tangela." He pulled her to her feet.

"I'm a mess," she said.

"You're beautiful." He freed her ponytail.

She eased into his arms and closed her eyes as the tears

welled up again. It was such a beautiful song. They danced in silence, and she tried to capture and hold that moment in her heart—the feel of his body against hers, his scent, the warmth of his touch. She took it all in, wishing it would last forever. They continued dancing even after the song ended.

Finally Tony kissed Tangie on the cheek, but with a slight turn of her neck, his lips found hers. They kissed slowly. He slid his tongue into her mouth, holding her so tightly that for a moment he nearly took her breath away.

She felt like a flame leading him into her bedroom. They undressed quietly in the dark, both realizing that they were making love for the last time.

"Let's make tonight special," he said.

She lay back on the bed. He moved on top of her, kissing her neck and breasts. She closed her eyes as orgasms washed over her body in waves of ecstasy before he even entered her. She grabbed him and gently pulled his head back up to hers. She loved the feel of his fresh-shaved head in her hands and on her lips. The tears began to flow as she wished they could have a lifetime together.

"No more tears." He kissed them away, only to see them return.

"I love you," she cried.

"I know. I love you too." He cupped her jaws in his hands. "You will never perish from my thoughts," he whispered softly.

He entered her gently, and they spent the rest of the night pleasing one another. Tangie prayed that the sun would never come up. Finally, they drifted off to sleep in each other's arms.

As the first rays of dawn chased away the night, Tangie awoke to life's harsh realities. She was back in the real world. She looked over her shoulder at Tony, burning his image in her psyche. He was beautiful. Perhaps, sensing her preoccupation, he stirred and opened his eyes.

Tony stood and threw on his jeans and sweatshirt, momentarily fumbling for his sneakers and socks in the dark. "I guess this is it, Tangela." He pulled her out of bed, and they walked to the door.

"Let me fix breakfast before you leave," she suggested.

"I'm late already." He rubbed her arms and shoulders.

"This is the day I say thank-you. And not just for all those beautiful lime roses. Thank you for my life." She choked back tears.

"It was all my pleasure. All of it. Come here." He took her in his arms. "What am I going to do with you?"

"Love me."

"Always." He kissed her on the forehead.

34
Heather

Heather arrived home and checked her messages. All five of them. There were two from Tangie, one from Charisma, and two from Jamal. What did he want? She couldn't imagine. The last time he spoke, he all but called her a bald-faced liar for incriminating Paula and her brother in the pill deal. Now what did he want? She listened to his messages. He wanted her to call him ASAP. Well, he could just wait, she decided as she plopped down on the sofa.

Heather was still angry with herself for losing her parents' picture and the letter. Now she'd just have to use her semi-photographic memory to make them last an entire lifetime. She wiped away a tear, thinking how she'd come so close, but was now so far. It wasn't fair. Life rarely was.

Her phone rang again. She wasn't in the mood for Jamal.

It was her mother. "I made lasagna," she told Heather. "How does that sound?"

"It sounds great."

"Good. I'll heat some up for you in the microwave and bring it right down to you."

"I'm famished. Why don't you join me?" Heather asked.

"I'd love to. Why don't you take a shower and relax. Dinner'll be ready before you know it."

Heather got up, took a nice, hot shower, changed into a nightshirt, and headed for the kitchen. Her mother had set the table and brought down a pan of lasagna, salad, and garlic bread. Heather ate everything on her plate, loving every bit of it.

"Are you finished already?" Leola asked.

"I guess my stomach really has shrunk," she told her mother.

"After forty pounds, I guess so. Heather, promise me you're through with those pills."

"I promise. It wasn't worth it."

"Thank you."

"I keep thinking about the letter and the picture of my birth parents. I know it's not your fault, but why couldn't you wait until after I had gotten home to give them to me?"

"I was just trying to cheer you up, Heather. Don't blame me for that."

"I know it's not your fault. I'm not saying it's your fault. I just wish you had waited, Ma. That's all," she snapped.

"Well, forgive me for trying to put a smile on your face." She pushed her chair back from the table and threw her napkin onto the plate. "I'm going upstairs. Good night. Mothers get blamed for everything."

Heather ran the water for the dishes, slamming them in the sink. In the process, she cut her finger on a broken glass, drawing blood.

"Damn," she said as she sucked on her injured finger pad. Things had gone from bad to worse. She fought back tears as she covered the pan of lasagna with aluminum foil and put it in the fridge.

She owed her mother an apology. Sometimes it was hard for her to say she was sorry. It never came easy for her. Forgiving others was difficult. Forgiving herself was nearly impossible.

Her phone began to ring as she finished up in the kitchen. It was Jamal.

"Hey, Heather. How's it going?" he asked.

"I'm okay now, but I was in the hospital for a couple of days."

"What happened?"

"I was run-down. I was losing too much weight too soon, and it took its toll on me."

"Sorry to hear that, Heather. That's kinda why I'm calling. I owe you an apology."

She listened.

"I should have believed you when you told me about Paula and her brother."

"What made you change your mind?" she asked.

"Well," he laughed sheepishly. "I saw a little snippet in the *Daily News* the other day about him being busted and out on bail for selling illegal drugs."

"You're kidding?"

"And I felt so bad for the things I said to you."

"Jamal, I accept your apology."

"Thank you, Heather. I feel much better now. I'll let you get some rest. Talk to you later. Okay, Heather?"

"Okay, Jamal."

Heather took two additional days off before returning to the library. Her boss and coworkers were pleased to see her back. Unfortunately, after a couple of hours, she felt like she had never left.

For lunch she stopped by Patty World for the brown stewed chicken special. All the tables were occupied so she ordered take-out.

"Heather, over here," a familiar voice said. It was Ava.

Heather picked up her order and sat down. "So how's it going?" Heather asked her.

"I'm good. You look tired."

"Girl, I have been through the ringer."

"What's going on?"

"I just got out of the hospital last week."

"No," she exclaimed. "What happened?" She bit into a plantain.

"Those damn Z3Ks. I see why they're illegal. My mother had to rush me to the emergency room."

"Are you serious?"

"Serious as a root canal."

"Wow, I feel for you. I hope you stopped taking them."

"I flushed them bad boys right down the toilet," Heather admitted.

"So you're back to work?"

"Uh-huh. Today's my first day back," she said as she slid a forkful of chicken into her mouth.

"So how's it going?"

"So-so. I'm still a little tired."

"You should come by my house for dinner. My back rubs are legendary." Ava looked deeply into Heather's eyes so there would be no misunderstanding.

After a long pause, Heather finally spoke. "Maybe one of these days I'll take you up on that."

Heather knew what had to be done. She hadn't spoken to her mother in close to a week. That wasn't like either of them. When she came home from work that evening, Leola was in the living room, watering plants. She barely acknowledged Heather when she entered the house.

Heather cleared her throat and spoke. "Ma, we need to talk."

Leola continued with the watering.

"Can we talk for a second?" Heather asked.

Leola stopped what she was doing. "I'm listening."

"Let's sit down," Heather said on her way to the love seat. Her mother sat on the sofa.

"Okay."

"Ma, I'm sorry for snapping at you the other day. I apologize. I know there's no excuse, but all my life I could only imagine what my birth parents looked like, and what their story was. You came along with all the missing pieces to the puzzle for me. It was like a dream come true. Then I let it slip through my fingers, carelessly. I was angry at myself, and I took it out on you. I'm sorry, boobie."

Leola stood without saying one word. She went into her bedroom and returned moments later with a plastic sandwich bag. This time she joined her daughter on the love seat.

"This is yours." She handed Heather the bag.

Puzzled, Heather took the bag, examining its contents through the plastic. She reached in and removed the small brown paper bag inside. Inside that bag was a familiar two-page letter neatly folded on plain white stationery. The photo was there too.

Heather's eyes filled with tears. She grabbed her mother with both arms as the tears flowed down both their cheeks.

"But how?"

"Boobie, there's an old saying. God's favor ain't fair. It just is."

Heather realized that there was no sense in tempting fate a second time. She stopped by the Staples on the Van Wyck Expressway to make laminated copies of her mother's letter and of her parents' picture.

Heather practically begged the sales associate to be careful. He looked at the photo closely.

"Is this your mother? You look like her, especially your nose." He was young.

"Yeah, they're my birth parents." Heather surprised herself.

"You're mixed," he said simply.

"Mixed with love," she added, smiling.

"Me too," he said, smiling at her.

Heather checked her watch. She had an appointment next door with Dr. Taylor at Jamaica Hospital. The doctor was very busy and Heather appreciated her clearing a few moments from her tight schedule to see her. She rode the elevator up to the seventh floor, thankful that she was no longer a patient. She sat in the waiting area for a few moments before Dr. Taylor's nurse whisked her inside.

Dr. Taylor looked like she should be doing a spread for a fashion magazine. She motioned for Heather to have a seat in her office.

"Thanks for stopping by and catching me up on your progress. How are you?" she asked Heather.

"Much better." Heather smiled.

"I can tell. It's like night and day since the last time I saw you. I take it you're off the Z3K?"

"Definitely."

"Good. It's been in the news a lot lately."

"Whew, I couldn't believe all the malpractice suits and wrongful-death suits pending," Heather admitted.

"It's truly a blessing that yours wasn't one of them."

Heather's face registered the impact of her statement.

"So have you learned anything about life?"

"I've learned a priceless lesson. Favor ain't fair. It just is."

"I couldn't have said it more perfectly myself. Let me ask you another question. How do you feel about therapy? I think you'd be an excellent candidate. Would you consider it?"

"Absolutely. If it's good enough for Tony Soprano, it's good enough for me." They both laughed.

"Do you still want that deviated septum corrected?"

"Not on your life." Heather grinned.

"Wow, that's a switch."

"Why the switch?" Dr. Taylor asked.

"That's a long story." Heather shook her head.

"Well, in any event, I'm glad you've learned to accept yourself. By the way, did you ever get that supplement?"

"I almost forgot. I'm glad you brought that up. I tried a couple of stores, but they said there's no such drug."

"No such drug? There most certainly is," she insisted. "But from the looks of things, I think your body is beginning to manufacture it on its own."

"Really, how can you tell?" Heather asked her.

"Do you still have it with you?"

"I'm not sure I brought it with me." Heather rummaged through her bag, "Here it is," she said, pulling it out.

"Read it to me."

Heather attempted to pronounce the unfamiliar drug. "Evolfles?" she said.

"Here, let me help you." Dr. Taylor reached into her top desk drawer and pulled out a tiny compact mirror. She held it up to the prescription. "Try it again, Heather," she insisted.

Heather looked into the mirror and this time it was perfectly clear. "Self-love," she said, smiling.

"You got it," Dr. Taylor laughed, and Heather joined in.

Heather relaxed by treating herself to a nice, long bubble bath, filling her bathroom with scented candles and music. She was completely mellowed out by the time the last bubble trickled down the drain, and she towel-dried her soft curves. She layered lotion and body oil all over her skin until it glowed. The sound of her ringing phone brought a smile to her lips.

It was Jamal. "Hey, babe, I have an idea. Why don't we go out to dinner? Your choice."

"That's sweet, honey, but I can't."

"Why not? I thought you said you forgave me," he reminded her.

"I did."

"Then let's hang out."

"I can't," she repeated.

"Why not?"

"I'm exhausted," she lied.

"How about tomorrow then?"

She hesitated only slightly. "Okay, sounds good. I'll call you," she said before hanging up.

Heather slid into a pair of size-twelve blue jeans, loving the sleekness of her body as she viewed it from all angles in the bedroom mirror. Though she was no longer taking Z3K, she refused to make it easy for the weight to creep back on. She had gone back to working out at the gym with a vengeance. She topped off her jeans with a long-sleeve white cotton T-shirt and tiny diamond earrings. Heather pulled her hair into a curly bun on top of her hair before applying a touch of copper eye shadow and spicy bronze lipstick.

Once again the phone interrupted her thoughts, but this time it was the call she'd been waiting for. She blew her nose a kiss before snatching her keys from the coffee table and heading out the door. She floated all the way the way to Hillside Avenue.

She rang the bell to the Jamaica Estates co-op, warm with anticipation. Was she really ready for this? The door opened and Ava appeared, welcoming Heather into her home.

Heather looked around at the living room, the Asian influence evident in Ava's choice of artwork and furniture. There was even a little gold Buddha sitting next to a water fountain.

"Your home is lovely," Heather said simply. "You have great taste."

"Thanks, chickylicky," Ava replied. She took a step closer

to Heather and gave her a warm hug. She rubbed Heather's back and shoulders lightly. "You smell wonderful."

Being embraced by a woman in that way was a new experience for Heather. Ava wore a spaghetti strap tank top and a short denim skirt. Ava was so soft. The difference between being touched by a man compared to being touched by a woman was amazing.

"I've never done this before," Heather admitted.

Ava planted a kiss on Heather's cheek, just a fraction of an inch away from her lips. Unable to resist her, Heather moved a touch to the right and their lips finally met. She opened her mouth and allowed Ava's tongue in. They kissed nice and slow. Never in a million years did Heather imagine that another woman could turn her out. Ava reached down and gently squeezed Heather's breast before sliding her hand underneath Heather's top. Heather kissed her harder in response. Just as Ava's fingers were about to find Heather's swollen nipples, she stopped.

"Remind me where we left off," Ava said, giving her a quick kiss. "Let's eat." She took Heather by the hand and led her into the kitchen.

The table for four was set for the two to sit side by side.

"Make yourself comfortable," Ava said as Heather sat. "I hope you like eggplant parmigiana."

"I love it." Heather smiled as Ava placed salad and covered dishes on the table before sitting.

As Ava removed the lids, Heather noticed that the food was piping hot. The sight and aroma of the cheddar biscuits brought an instant smile to Heather's face.

"Dig in," Ava said simply.

Heather bit in to a biscuit, and her mouth practically had an orgasm. She chewed ever so slowly, enjoying the buttery, salty flakiness. Finally, she opened her eyes. "You are something else."

"Oops, I almost forgot. I made strawberry martinis."

"They make martinis out of everything," Heather said.

"You'll love it. I guarantee we'll be drinking 'em all night."

Heather had a few spoonfuls of the eggplant parmigiana and took a sip of the martini. "Mmm, I like this," she told Ava.

"I thought you would," she said, sipping her drink.

They finished dinner and had another martini. Ava looked at Heather, her head cocked to the side. She leaned over and kissed Heather lightly on the mouth. "You are so sweet. You know that?"

Heather took another sip of her drink. "Whatever you're selling tonight, I'm already sold."

"Then why don't we take our glasses and go into the living room," Ava said.

Heather followed Ava back into the living room, where they made themselves comfortable on the sofa.

"I think I'll have another drink," Heather said, draining her glass.

Ava brought the pitcher into the living room and refilled Heather's glass. "This is nice," Ava said.

"Uh-huh," Heather agreed.

"But you know what would be even nicer?"

"What's that?"

"This," Ava said, taking Heather's drink from her and placing it on the coffee table. She leaned over to kiss her. Heather kissed her back, all traces of inhibition disintegrating. Ava removed Heather's top, and gently eased her down onto the sofa. Next, she undid her bra, freeing Heather's breasts. Her mouth quickly found her nipples, sucking until they were erect. Heather reached up and removed Ava's tank top, excited by her bare breasts. Then Heather fondled Ava's full breasts until Ava raised up and popped a breast in Heather's mouth. Heather circled Ava's nipple with her tongue, sliding it in and out of her mouth before latching onto it and sucking oh-so-slowly.

Ava let out a moan. "Are you sure you haven't done this before?" Ava asked her.

"I guess I'm a fast learner," she whispered before getting back to work.

"Looks like I lucked up." Ava closed her eyes, enjoying Heather's mouth. Then she stood.

"What's wrong?" Heather asked.

"Why don't you take off your jeans and get more comfortable?"

Smiling, Heather did as suggested as Ava removed her skirt. Wearing nothing but panties, they got back on the couch, lying side by side.

"You wanna know something?" Heather asked without waiting for an answer. "I can already tell. You're dangerous."

"Dangerous? No. Addictive? You decide." She slid two fingers inside Heather's panties and Heather nearly lost her mind.

Heather dropped Jamal like a bell-bottom hem in a straight-leg season. He had left her several messages. Eventually, he tired of not having his calls returns. He stopped calling altogether.

Heather joined Tangie and Charisma at Cabana one night. They met for drinks and a movie. Heather was the first to arrive. She felt like a newlywed and apparently it showed.

"Well, look at you," Charisma said to Heather as she took a seat next to her. "We're gonna have to start calling you Bubbles."

"I don't know," Tangie began. "For someone who just got out of the hospital, something's got you glowing. Is it your doctor?"

"No, it isn't my doctor. Can't a woman just be happy to be alive and to hang out with her two best friends?" Heather asked.

"Yeah, right." Tangie nodded. "Tell me anything. I'm a woman. We've been best friends since college, but you just started rocking this new look."

"What's going on?" Charisma agreed.

"Nada," Heather insisted. "Not a thing." Heather's cell phone went off, making a liar out of her. "Okay, see you in a few," Heather told the caller. She stood. "Sorry guys, I gotta go."

"Let me guess. That was Nada," Tangie insisted.

"You got it," Heather said, and they all laughed.

Heather ran three red lights on her way up Queens Boulevard, praying all the while that a ticket wouldn't find its way into her mailbox. There was no way of dodging those damn cameras.

Ava met Heather at the door wearing a short, silky animal print robe, which Heather quickly untied. She put her hands inside and took Ava in her arms as their lips met. Ava wore nothing underneath. She broke free and climbed the stairs to her bedroom, which was bathed in scented candle-light. Heather was close behind. She stripped in record time and slid under the covers. Ava removed Heather's hair clip, freeing her naturally curly mane. Then she gave Heather a scalp massage that left her tingly and completely relaxed.

Suddenly she looked at Heather. "Are you sure?" Ava asked her softly.

Heather nodded.

"You're not just teasing me?"

"Not this time." Heather shook her head, smiling.

Ava climbed on top of Heather, her tongue deep inside Heather's mouth. They both rolled over until they were both on their sides facing each other. Her fingers kneaded

Heather's back and shoulders on their way to her breasts. Smiling, Ava sucked on her nipples until they were as big as grape tomatoes. Ava rolled over so that her back was facing Heather's front. Spooning, she spread her legs, allowing Heather easier access to her Brazilian domain. Heather's fingers found their way to Ava's pussy. Her fingertips searched for Ava's little honey nut. Ava's breathing told Heather that she had found it. She began gyrating on Heather's right hand until she came. She turned to face Heather, and drew Heather's fingertips into her mouth, relishing the flavor. Heather then kissed Ava on the mouth. Grinning, they both lay back on the bed.

Ava repositioned herself on top of Heather. She planted wet kisses on her neck, her tits, and her abs. Ava placed her hands between Heather's legs. She gently separated her dripping lips, exposing her beet-red pussy. Just the sight of Heather's clitoris peeking through practically made her cum. She slid down and kissed it ever so gently, creating a wet, slippery stream that ran down Heather's thigh. Ava slid her right hand between her own legs until her breathing came in short spurts. She plunged her double-jointed tongue all up in Heather's pussy until they both could stand no more. Heather's body went into spasms from head to toe as she covered Ava's lips with her cream. Catching their breath, they fell asleep in each other's arms.

They awoke the next morning and showered together. Ava insisted on making breakfast. They were both famished.

"We make some team. We should go on vacation together," Ava said. "We'd have a ball."

"I don't think I'm ready for all that."

"Suit yourself," Ava told her.

Epilogue

On the night before Tangie's birthday, she came home from work, filled her bathroom with scented candles, grabbed her iPod and speakers, and took a nice, long, relaxing bath. The water was as hot as she could stand it, and she felt as though she was at her own personal spa.

As the suds slid down the drain, Tangie was left feeling refreshed and pampered. She slipped on her favorite robe and decided to fix a light dinner. She was interrupted by the doorbell. She checked the clock above the kitchen sink, not expecting anyone.

It was the florist—with a single rose, a single lime rose. She found her purse, tipped the delivery boy, and closed the door. She already knew who it was from, smiling to herself as she read the attached card. *Can't wait until seven tomorrow evening, the first night of the rest of our lives together.* In anticipation, Tangie squealed with delight. Who would have thunk a couple of months ago that she and Tony would be spending her birthday together?

Suddenly, she was no longer hungry. She barely slept that night, feeling like a five-year-old on Christmas eve.

When she got to work the next morning, her coworkers at the gym surprised her with coffee and doughnuts. That afternoon a couple of the girls took her to lunch, which included a generous slice of birthday cake.

Tangie skipped her workout that afternoon and headed straight home to shower and get ready for her date. She didn't know what he had planned, so naturally she wasn't quite sure what to wear. She spritzed her skin with perfume and finally decided on a pair of skintight leather pants and a sleeveless form fitting top.

Tangie checked herself in the full-length mirror, viewing her reflection from every angle. Yeah, she still had it going on. Thank goodness she worked at a gym. So there was really no excuse for not keeping her body tight.

Next, she applied her makeup so well that it would bring a smile to even Cinderella's face. Tangie checked her watch. It was a 6:45. She poured herself a glass of white wine, sat down in her living room, and waited.

At two minutes past seven the doorbell rang. Tangie stood and smoothed down her clothes and hair. Smiling, an excited Tangie answered the door. The bouquet was so large that it hid his face. Finally, he lowered the lime roses. It was Jordan.

For a moment she was speechless. "How'd you know I liked lime roses?" she asked him, puzzled.

"Oh, a little birdie told me," said, winking. "I had them flown in just for you."

Remembering Tony's words, she threw back her head and laughed.

"May I come in?" he asked.

"Please do."

She took the roses from him and placed them in a vase on the dining room table, adding water. Jordan sat down on the sofa and Tangie joined him.

He turned to face her. "I will never hurt you," he vowed

as he removed the band from her left ring finger. "And you will never need to front behind this band."

She sensed Tony's presence all around. Oddly enough, knowing that she'd always have his love and protection gave her a newfound reservoir of strength.

She looked deeply into Jordan's eyes and smiled slowly. What made her think she had to skip mindlessly from one relationship to the next as though she was inadequate? She was enough. She was more than enough. She was whole. She was complete. All she had to do now was be open and receptive to the possibilities.

Charisma met Heather and Tangie in Macy's shoe department one Wednesday night after work. She had left work early and wasn't the least bit guilty about it. After all, what was leave for? It had been a while since they had all gotten together. They stopped by Red Lobster for a bite to eat.

They walked in and were seated immediately. The restaurant was relatively empty. The waiter returned momentarily with menus and their drinks, which they raised in a toast.

"Behind every successful woman is herself." Charisma smiled.

"Hear, hear," Heather and Tangie chimed in.

Charisma looked around. Where did all the people come from? Half of them were white. She had a strange sense of déjà vu. All of the other patrons looked strangely familiar to her. It was eerie. She glanced at each one of them. They each rhythmically made eye contact with her and nodded ever so slightly before resuming their conversation. It was perfectly choreographed. And then, one by one, as more customers arrived, they did the exact same thing. Tangie and Heather seemed oblivious to what was going on. It was as if it was for her eyes only. She couldn't have explained it if she tried. It was all so surreal. Then they stood. One by one, they smiled at her ever so slightly before leaving the restaurant. Suddenly, she realized that it was her dream. Only this time, peace had replaced her fear. Everything was in divine order. She smiled to herself.

Tangie was saying something.

"Huh?" Charisma asked her.

"So what's going on?" Tangie asked her.

"You're not going to believe this," Charisma began. "Nate and I will be raising Chase's baby. I'm adopting it." She took a sip of her chocolate martini, savoring the flavor.

"Are you serious? When did all this happen?" Heather asked her.

"Well, I got the idea a while ago, and I mentioned it to Nate. We discussed it with Chase, and she finally agreed."

"So you're gonna be a mother." Tangie smiled.

"Yep," Charisma laughed, raising her glass.

"I'm so happy for you. When's she due?" Heather asked.

"She's due right before Christmas," Charisma told them.

"What a blessing." Tangie shook her head.

"Pretty amazing, huh?" Charisma said.

"That it is," Heather agreed. "I have a confession of my own. I'm going on vacation next week."

"Where to?" Tangie asked.

"Aruba."

"Aruba is for lovers," Charisma said.

"And I am long overdue," Heather replied.

"You didn't tell us you and Jamal got back together." Tangie stirred her Miami Vice with a straw.

"We didn't. I'm not seeing him anymore. I'm going with an old friend from high school."

"No wonder you're still glowing. An old love, that's nice," Charisma said.

"No, more like a *new* one."

"I think this is where Nada comes in." Tangie nudged Charisma, joking.

"So you're ready to reveal his true identity?" Charisma smiled.

"Uh-huh," Heather admitted, taking a deep breath. "Only it's not a he, it's a she." She paused for a few moments to let it sink in.

Tangie and Charisma were silent for a moment.

"Heather, why didn't you tell us?" Charisma asked.

"We're your girls," Tangie said.

"I know," Heather said. "I guess I was afraid you'd judge me. This is all so new to me."

"Listen, Heather. We love you. We just want you to be happy," Charisma told her.

"Life is short, Heather. You've paid your stress dues. Just do you. Do you," Tangie told her.

"It takes a lot of courage to keep it real and live outside the box. I admire you," Charisma admitted.

"Thanks," Heather said, draining her glass. "You don't know how much you both mean to me." She stood, leaned over and hugged them both. "I gotta run. Love you."

"Love you too," Tangie and Charisma told her.

"Call us before you leave," Tangie insisted, watching her go.

"Our girl is something else," Charisma said.

"That she is," Tangie agreed.

"So how are things with you?"

"Incredible. You know something, Charisma?" she asked. "With every good-bye, you learn. Tony has taught me more about life than you will know."

"Kind of like a guardian angel, right?" Charisma smiled.

"Exactly." They both smiled.

Charisma checked her watch. It was 4:15. "I gotta get going."

"I thought we were gonna hang out," Tangie said.

"I know, but I have an appointment with Dr. Vale."

"Follow-up?" Tangie asked.

"Yeah, she wants to make sure everything's healing nicely."

"How do you feel?"

"Great," Charisma reassured her, taking one last sip of her martini and standing. "Maybe we can get together this weekend. I'll give you a call."

Charisma stopped at the light, the doctor's words still fresh in her mind. Could she make it home? For a moment she sat in disbelief, unsure if she could trust herself to even breath, afraid of breaking the spell. Slowly, she began taking small breaths, completely unaware of where one ended and the next began.

As the light turned green, the tears that had welled up in her eyes began chasing each other down her cheeks—big, fat, juicy tears. With the back of her hand, she wiped them away, but not before they splattered her jacket.

Charisma was expecting a baby! Through tears of joy she realized that life is about unity and connections—not separation and division. And that we are all more alike than different, needing love and acceptance.

A New Testament Bible verse came to mind—Matthew 5:9. As a child she had held it near. Somewhere along the way it had gotten away from her. *Blessed are the peacemakers for they shall be called the children of God.* Like an epiphany it was all revealed. Finally, she understood. Joyfully, she understood. Blacks are not the privileged sect. Whites are not the privileged sect. The children of God are the privileged sect.